W9-AAT-333

Red Rain

M I C H A E L   C R O W

RED RAIN

a Luther Ewing thriller

viking

VIKING
Published by the Penguin Group
Penguin Putnam Inc., 375 Hudson Street, New York, New York 10014, U.S.A.
Penguin Books Ltd, 80 Strand, London WC2R 0RL, England
Penguin Books Australia Ltd, 250 Camberwell Road, Camberwell,
Victoria 3124, Australia
Penguin Books Canada Ltd, 10 Alcorn Avenue, Toronto, Ontario, Canada M4V 3B2
Penguin Books India (P) Ltd, 11 Community Centre, Panchsheel Park,
New Delhi - 110 017, India
Penguin Books (N.Z.) Ltd, Cnr Rosedale and Airborne Roads, Albany,
Auckland, New Zealand
Penguin Books (South Africa) (Pty) Ltd, 24 Sturdee Avenue, Rosebank,
Johannesburg 2196, South Africa

Penguin Books Ltd, Registered Offices:
Harmondsworth, Middlesex, England

First published in 2002 by Viking Penguin,
a member of Penguin Putnam Inc.

10 9 8 7 6 5 4 3 2 1

Publisher's note
This is a work of fiction. Names, characters, places, and incidents either are the product of the author's imagination or used fictitiously, and any resemblance to actual persons, living or dead, business establishments, events, or locales is entirely coincidental.

LIBRARY OF CONGRESS CATALOGING-IN-PUBLICATION DATA

Crow, Michael, 1948–
Red rain / Michael Crow.
p. cm.
ISBN 0-670-03090-2
I. Title.

PS3563.O7714 R44 2002
813'.54—dc21 2001043516

This book is printed on acid-free paper. ♾

Printed in the United States of America
Set in Giovanni, with Crane display
Designed by Carla Bolte

for RBM

a soldier once, too young

acknowledgment:

thanks to Doug Grad

Red Rain

1

The wiper blades screech in protest through each jittery arc, trailing an oily smear on the windshield across my line of sight. Blurred, starry brake lights flash on in pairs, flash off, flash on, red glare richoceting off the rain-slick black asphalt. My eyes ache. It's a sour, clammy late August morning. Sullen smoke-gray clouds hang so low they're muffling the tops of office buildings and hotels. And we're trapped in a miles-long traffic crawl on York Road. Bad coffee from Teddy's Gyro Shop is already eating a hole in my stomach lining. The little cardboard pine tree Ice Box has hung from the rearview mirror is losing its fight against residual odors of pizza, KFC chicken, fries, Big Macs and all the rest of the nasty, hasty meals others who've cruised in this Crown Victoria have wolfed down on their shifts.

"I got two words for you, Ewing," Ice Box says, both hands white-knuckled on the wheel like an eighty-year-old with glaucoma who knows he shouldn't be driving on the clearest, sunniest day of the year, let alone in a downpour like this. "Just two words: Shut the fuck up!"

I stick my fingers in that lousy coffee and flick a few drops in his general direction.

"My best suit! Shit, man!" Ice Box squeals, taking both hands off the wheel to swipe at the wet spots, almost rear-ending a Ford Explorer.

"You call those Kmart overalls a suit? Anyway, doesn't your wife spray everything you own with Scotchgard, being familiar with your eating style?"

"I'm going to sit on your skinny bones one day and crack you open like a crab!" Ice Box is close to a giggle.

"Anything but that, IB, anything. I most sincerely regret all my impetuous gestures."

"How long, O Lord, how long?" Ice Box sighs. "What'd I ever do so wrong in life that got me stuck with this spook beside me, can you tell me that? Can anyone tell me that? I think about this a lot and I never get no answers."

Poor Ice Box. He's been stuck with me for almost two years now, ever since I came on as a detective with the Baltimore County Police Department. He didn't have a choice. Neither did I, really. It wasn't a job I much wanted or a place I specially picked, but my options, let's say, were few to none at the time.

But it's okay with me and Ice Box. Never like it was with my homies on the Alpha team in Iraq. Couldn't expect that sort of brotherhood anywhere out in the world. Only once, in a time, a place, a situation where if you aren't ultratight, somebody dies. Afterward, you have to settle for what you get. I got lucky. Ice Box made my cut. I made his too, though I still don't know what his exact parameters are. We trust each other on the job, we see each other off-duty as friends, he has me over to his house for holiday dinners and so forth. But we've yet to go up against anything truly hard together, and that's the only way you ever really find out what you need to know.

I'd just been asking him—idle teasing to get my mind off my stomach and my eyes and stir some life into a dead, dull day—if he's going to name the twins his wife is carrying something original like Cholesterol and Iodine instead of more traditional choices, like Tawana and Tasheba. "Just two words. . . ." IB's an unlikely tenor, almost always near the top of his range.

And that's a smile. The man's a white guy the approximate size and shape of a Sub-Zero. Not all pumped up, cut and buffed like the steroid freaks I see every day in the Department workout room. Just huge, solid as a sandbag. He looks like a fat man, but nothing ever jiggles or shakes when he moves, and he can move. Yes he can. You don't want to be in the way when the Ice Box moves.

I know exactly what to make of him, at certain levels. Joseph Cutrone, raised in "Bawlmer, Merlin," calls the ballteam the "Oreos," says we work for the "PO-leese." Runs out of the tough Highlandtown neighborhood where he'd spent his boyhood to the County just as soon as he's making enough money to do it. Like lots of white guys in his situation. The professionals, the dual-income couples, the young yuppies, they've already been out here for a generation or two. Their parents or grandparents fled the city to the first modest developments in the early '50s. The kids grow up, go away to college, come back and do better than their parents ever dreamed of, move farther out to grander houses on more land. The old folks die or retire to Florida, leaving behind places people like Ice Box can afford. Still safe, still easy, still good ground to raise kids. Total suburbia these days, the city a half-deserted war zone except for a few surrounded outposts, and showplaces like the Inner Harbor and Camden Yards, where all the money that could've gone to housing and schools got spent on a stadium and an aquarium. Only in the County's far north, near the Pennsylvania line, do the farms and neat, small towns survive. And it's just dumb, unimportant redneck crime out there: brawls in roadhouses, semitough family disputes, a few burglaries, cockfights and dogfights, once in a while an armed robbery. Only gunfire usually comes from hunters who down too much peach brandy against the cold, miss their deer, start blowing holes in traffic signs with their Savage and Winchester 30-06s. Working out their frustrations the way they do in rural areas.

I don't know anything about all this when I first come on. Learn as I go. Learn the place, learn the people. It's a skill. Ice Box, smart as he is, still doesn't know any more about me than I give him, and he knows more than anybody else in the Department, except Annie.

I like to think this is very deliberate on my part, something necessary, deliberately planned. Yet more and more lately I don't feel certain even I know the truth about myself. Seems I've had a couple of lives, each lived by a different person.

Poppa, or Gunny to everybody including me as a kid, was in the Crotch, a marine lifer, central casting's perfect choice for a scary spade top sergeant if they couldn't book James Earl Jones for the part. Two tours in the Nam, then moving around between Camp Lejeune, Quantico, Parris Island, embassy security in Hong Kong, Belgrade, Bonn. Some Fleet time, a little visit to Grenada too. Momma's Vietnamese. It pleases me to think she wasn't just another Saigon bargirl. It pleases her to claim she's part of an old Cochin China family, well bred and once well off, with illicit but far from scandalous aristocratic French connections. She drops French phrases into her conversations. It could be just a good act.

I never need an act. People's eyes go all puzzled when they check me out and try to classify me. I don't look like an African American. I don't look true Asiastic. My eyes are brown flecked with gold, my skin's sort of like copper left unpolished just a bit too long, I've got straight black hair, thick and glossy like Momma's. But my nose must have come from some rogue French gene in Momma's blood. It's narrow but big, high-bridged and long. Maybe her story's true. People generally make me for Native American. Or Mexican, Colombian, Nicaraguan, some sort of south-of-the border mestizo. But *they never feel sure.*

I get off on that. In the military I'm sly, get it going without actually saying so that I'm a full-blood Comanche. Oh man, the dudes dig that. They get *intensely* into the concept. They believe I have the powers—a man who moves and leaves no sign, a ghost rider who smells the presence of the enemy, a quick and silent throat slitter who fades to invisibilty after the kill.

It's easy not to disabuse them of these notions, since Gunny's idea of playing with little Luther never involved bats and balls, but some toned-down version of bootcamp and a lot of jungle stuff he'd learned in Nam. Training. Stalking squirrels in the Carolina boonies with a .22 rifle at eight, nailing rabbits with a .22 semi-auto pistol at ten, my first buck with a .243 Remington Model 7 at twelve. Full-auto action with an M16 at fourteen.

I go army at eighteen instead of the corps, which pisses Gunny off until he understands my motive. Too many Marines would know I was my father's son, maybe cut me some slack. He's proud when I make Special Forces, where they just dig the hell out of their Comanche. "You ever get into combat, Luther, make it real for 'em. Scalp your first KIA. You'll start a legend," Gunny says laughing, when I visit on leave after training and before assignment to my team. He's only half-joking.

I do worse. Little more than two years on, hair past my shoulders, warpaint instead of camo grease on my face and the teams getting high on it, I go insane in a crappy stucco house just outside Kuwait City and kill my military career. I want to be a lifer like Gunny, but I screw that right then, right there.

"I can't take it anymore!" Ice Box shouts, jolting me out of bad memory. He jumps the curb, guns around a mom waiting patiently at a red light in her Audi Quattro station wagon—silver, what else?—hangs a hard right and slams down over the curb onto Ridgely Road. I catch a glimpse of a tennis-tanned face, mouth open in a perfect O, and a dozing toddler well strapped into a safety seat behind her. Ice Box is up to almost 60 when he laughs, slows down to the 35 limit. We're passing through a '50s development, little tract houses all variations of the same Cape Cod theme on little quarter-acre lots where the fragile saplings and hedging the original residents planted so hopefully have burgeoned and prospered until they've almost overgrown the homes. We pass a Presbyterian church on a little knoll likewise sheltered, and Ridgely Junior High

School down a slope opposite. The three ball fields and the track below look like a swamp today. Then Ice Box goes left on Pots Spring Road, and we're flanked by custom homes, ranches and split-levels and colonial revivals from the '60s maybe, on two or three acres, a couple of vehicles in each curving asphalt driveway, Grand Cherokees and Land Cruisers for the soccer moms, fast little Acuras and Miatas and entry-level BMWs for their older kids. The shrubs are trimmed to scale, the lawns as manicured as golf greens.

"Their fuckin' kids never mowed a blade or clipped a hedge," Ice Box mutters.

"Professional job, you think?" I smile. "Good policework, IB."

"I got just two words to say to you, just two words. . . ."

"One. Turn," I say, and he does, heading us north on Dulaney Valley Road, newer and grander houses on much bigger properties on our left now, and to the right a great looming forest of rain-blackened pines planted in perfectly symmetrical rows in the 1930s to protect the watershed of Loch Raven Reservoir.

"They didn't think ahead," I say.

"Who?"

"The idiots who planted the pines."

"Say what?"

"They forgot trees grow," I say. The forest is now so damned dense, the trunks now two to three feet in diameter and the needle-carpeted alleys so narrowed you'd have to snake your way through on your belly. Can't see any water at all. I know it's down there, within half a mile or so, dark and deep, a long, sinuous lake that follows an old stream valley's twists and turns, only the streambed's now a hundred feet or more underwater.

As we move farther out, wipers still screeching, masssive waves of fog begin a slow tumble out from the woods and break over us, obscuring the road. Ice Box switches on the headlights. One's burned out, so he flicks to high beam. Fat drops of rain are smacking down harder and faster, sheeting on the unwaxed hood of the Crown Vic. The greasy streaks on the windshield worsen the glare bouncing back at us off the fog.

"Put the lights back on low," I say.

"Who, my man, is driving this ve-hicle? Is it the mighty Ice Box, or some squirrel they call Five-O?"

That's what I get for that Chlorophyll and Mercurochrome crack or whatever I'd said about his twins' names. He's punched my button. What can I do but laugh? Enough time's passed to laugh.

//

Just two weeks with the Department, under suspicion because I'd come in as a detective on orders from higher than anyone could see, on a nod-and-name basis with Ice Box and a colder version of that with the narc boss, Lieutenant Dugal, who likes to pick his own people, not have them dumped on him. A nothing night in the squadroom, me well outside the conversation as usual, when Dugal comes in and says, "Showtime."

"Good to go, LT," I say. Damned stupid reflex. Yeah, it's around I'm ex-army, but I know from day one that doesn't go down too well with these guys, any more than the fact that I'm there at all.

"Good, Ewing? Go where, Ewing? These men are geared up and you're not. Why is that, Ewing?"

Because none of you dickheads said anything about a mission, I think. "Making it happen now, sir," I say, sprinting off to the locker room. I put on a Kevlar vest, pull a black turtleneck on over it, open my lockbox and shoulder holster a most nonregulation weapon, slip into a black leather jacket. The rest: black Levis and black Chuck Taylor hightops, the white rubber edges blackened with a Sharpie. Then I run out to the parking lot.

There's a mean snickering when I scramble into the waiting van with Ice Box, two pumped dudes I don't even know and the LT, all of them wearing jeans or khakis and navy windbreakers with POLICE stenciled on the backs with white reflective paint. "Christ, Ewing, you think this is some kind of commando shit? Get your police coat," the LT snaps. The two unknowns are smirking, Ice Box's broad face is blank. Then Dugal looks at his watch. "Fuck it. We can't waste the time."

It seems there's enough of it to do the traffic crawl ten miles or so up York Road to Cockeysville, a warren of town houses, condos and apartments on what Ice Box says used to be all farmland. And then get lost for a while, driving slowly around crescents and circles. The LT's doing a slow burn on the driver, whose name turns out to be "Taggert You Fuck" in Dugal-speak. Finally we pull up behind a four-story brick condo and stop beside a Dumpster that hasn't been emptied for too long. Otherwise, the place looks pretty good, well maintained, solid citizens inside judging from the years and makes of the cars in the parking lot. Then we're through the unlocked steel service door and climbing the steel-railed service stairway, like the one in my apartment building, which I realize now isn't too far away. No need for Maglites. The stairwell's bright with floods in steel cages.

"Three B," the LT says as we ease out into a hallway and pad down beige carpet toward the target. There's thick, condo-grade patterned paper on the walls, bright white sconces between each anonymous beige apartment door. Outside 3B, the LT gives a hand signal, we draw our weapons, and suddenly everybody's looking at me like I've unzipped my pants and pulled my pecker out.

They're all holding cheap Ruger 9mm semis. In my right hand gleams a .50AE Desert Eagle, Israeli-made, wearing an Aimpoint. When the Aimpoint's red dot shows on whatever you want to hit, the Eagle hits exactly *there.* Awesome handgun. It'll punch through a car door, rip up the torsos of two men inside, and blast out the other door. Which makes any nine a limp dick by comparison.

The LT puts his lips so close to my ear it's almost a kiss. "Get that monstrosity on safe *now,* mister. You will not—repeat, not—fire that weapon no matter what goes down."

I nod assent. No way I'm following that order, though. "Clusterfuck," Gunny would've called this whole operation. I'm about to go through Alice's mirror with four men I have no reason to trust. I don't know how good their intelligence is, I've no idea if they're clear about what's on the other side. Only thing I'm confident of is that if 3B's the crib of stone gangsta drug dealers with Tec-9s, maybe Glocks or even full-auto mini-Uzis, I'm taking out at least two and more likely three with the Eagle before they can do anything but swiss-cheese the ceiling. I'm positive the guys inside and out don't know squat about fire discipline. Amateurs. Spray-and-pray. I've no intention of going down myself on some asshole's pure-chance shot.

Ice Box is through the door like it's wet cardboard, me right behind him spinning left into combat crouch, red dot already fixed on the chest of one of the dealers. Then I start laughing, really laughing, and Ice Box does too. The LT and Taggert You Fuck and the other guy come in like all their training's from watching old *Miami Vice* reruns. The LT glares at me and Ice Box. We're laughing so hard we're almost out of control, but he's covering the dealers while Taggert You Fuck and the other dude move to pat down and cuff our gangstas. I decock the Eagle and holster it.

"Freeze," screams Dugal. His timing's a little off tonight.

They've been frozen on a brown corduroy sofa, newest Pearl Jam cranked up on the stereo, since the door smashed down. Three pure white-bread suburban punks, no more than eighteen to twenty, in total shock. On the glass-topped coffee table before them there's a plastic salad-spinner bowl full of pills, and the kids' hands are suspended in the act of placing two pills each into tiny Ziplocs. There's maybe two dozen of them already filled and stacked at one end of the table. I pick one up. Ecstasy.

Taggert You Fuck and the other dude hustle the kids upright. One of them starts to piss himself. I can see the stain spreading fast down the billowy leg of cargo pants so huge they're gonna slide off his hips, the kind he's seen the black kids and rappers wearing on MTV but, my guess, never in his life face to face. Another starts to cry when he feels the steel snap closed on his wrists.

I catch Ice Box's eye, and we both erupt again.

"Shut up!" Dugal snarls, more to me and Ice Box than the weepy kid. We go off to toss the place. No more drugs, no weapons at all, unless you count some dull kitchen knives. The LT, after scooping the salad bowl, the pills and the pile of Ziplocs into an evidence baggy, turns on me.

"Hand over the piece, Ewing," he says. Taggert You Fuck and the other joker have taken the kids downstairs to the van. I unholster the Eagle and drop it into his outstretched hand from about an inch above the palm. He isn't ready for the weight and fumbles it, almost lets it fall to the floor. Recovering, he slides open the action and neatly catches the ejected cartridge. He tosses it up and down, slips a 9mm out of his spare clip and tosses the two of them together. "Ice Box, take a look at this," he says, dumping the cartridges into IB's massive hand while he looks over the Eagle. "Can't see shit through this laser thing," Dugal says. I don't mention it isn't turned on.

"Holy Christ," Ice Box says. "The round's almost a double 9. Bigger than a .44 Magnum. Say .50 caliber. They make pistols in .50? Ohhh, that's evil. Oughta be a law against it."

"I think maybe Ewing's confused about where he is," Dugal says. "You here, Ewing? Or you imagining you're still army? You believe you're some kind of *warrior*? We got no place for military *warriors*. We're in the law enforcement business."

"Eagle's a good gun, sir, in my experience," I blurt, knowing before I've finished that I've gotten too dumb to live.

"Do I care? Do I really give a shit about your experience? Is it meaningful to me in any conceivable way at all that you once ran around in the desert? I don't ever want to see this pistol again. Understood?"

"Yessir."

"Ice Box is now your partner . . ."

"You puttin' me with this Five-O crazy?" the big man interrupts.

"Your senior partner, Ewing. Your superior," Dugal goes on, ignoring IB. "You do what he says to do, when he says to do it. You do anything else, your ass is out of my squad, no matter how high up the brass who stuck me with you."

"Aw shit," Ice Box says. "Wait a minute, Lieutenant. I'm seeing *Lethal Weapon* movies here on my eyelids, and Ewing's the crazy Mel Gibson guy. I got some serious reservations about this."

"Live with 'em, Ice Box," the LT says and storms out of the condo.

Ice Box does. Ice Box susses I'm no pyscho, but not before he's told half the Department about Ewing's cannon, not before every half-ass is calling me Five-O and laughing as they say it.

"At least they're talking to you, acknowledging you exist, am I right?" Ice Box smiles a few days later. He's invited me for coffee at Teddy's. I take one sip of the grayish sludge in my cup and ask for a Coke instead. "They figure they've made you now, we know they haven't, but it'll relax the fucks. So you're not pissed, right?"

"What do you think?"

"I think you were thinking what I was thinking the other night. Too many cop movies. Lights, camera, action. They're going to go down looking real surprised one day, we hit anything bad."

"Yup."

"A fucking generation living TV and Hollywood referential," Ice Box says. He's starting to surprise me. "They got no idea what's real and what's not. They think the streets are some kind of set. Gotta watch your own back whenever you're out and about with any of these stumblefucks."

"You planning on watching real hard with me?"

"Do I need to?" Ice Box says. And for the first time I hear that high-pitched giggle.

He's saying the right things, but there's still payback due. He asks for it without knowing it. "Hey Luther, let me fire that Eagle thing on the range one day, huh?" he says as we're leaving Teddy's. He sees what he thinks is suspicion in my eyes. "C'mon, man. No set-up. You gotta let me try it out."

Early next Sunday morning we drive to the outdoor police range and Ice Box has the time of his life. He fires ten clips, grinning like a lunatic. "I *love* this piece, Five-O. I want one, with this red dot thing and all. Want one bad, bad, bad!"

I'm grinning Monday when he comes to work with an Ace bandage around his right wrist. "You shoulda told me about the fuckin' recoil, man," he whispers to me, mild reproach on his face, waving his wrist. "I think it's broke."

"Dude your size? Never crossed my mind it'd bother you," I say with a smile.

//

The fog's thick as wads of cotton wound-packing and Ice Box slows the Crown Vic to a crawl. "This guy we're going to see, he and I go back," IB says. "Almost no police record at all, just some juvenile stuff we both got popped for. We go back that far."

"And this slob is going to give up The Big Source?" I laugh.

"Never said that. But he called me. That's rare. Maybe he's got a name for us, we go see the name, maybe we get a couple more. Climbing the ladder. One rung at a time."

I sigh, take out my pistol, check the safety, drop the clip full of hollow points and rap it against my palm, then slip it home with a nice sharp click. I do this three or four times a day. Routine, but IB can't get used to it.

"Man, you handle that thing like it's your dick. In public. Don't you have any shame?"

"Riding with a human cube in a crappy Ford through middle-of-nowhere rain and fog is public? Have I done this in front of your wife? Ever see me do this in a mall, or your favorite pizza joint?" I wait 'til the wipers screech again. "So you never answered. Gonna be Tasmania and Chlorophyll or what?"

"I got two words for you. . . ."

"And this snitch you never mentioned before, tucked away up here in the boonies. Sure it isn't snatch?"

"Two words," Ice Box says. "And don't you go freaking out my friend, Chief, playing with your thing when we get there, anything like that."

"So you just want me checking out his trailer home, counting his pit bulls, see if his fourteen-year-old first cousin is flashing her little titties at us through the window?"

"Luther, how'm I ever gonna teach you anything when you get dumber every day? What I mean is, stay chill when you see what you see."

"I'm ice, IB. I'm so slick you could skate on me."

"It's The Big Source who's so slick. We got nothing," Ice Box says.

He's right. For about eighteen months after we took down the three kids in Cockeysville, Ecstasy only turned up once in a while. IB and I do a bunch of buy-and-busts that put away some addled crack-cocaine merchants, we nail some fairly big-time grass distributors—one asshole who's got maybe a hundred pounds neatly sealed in genuine two-pound potting soil bags stacked in his unlocked garage, claims he runs a little garden supply business for the local housewives. We even find a crazy high-school chemistry club president who's making methamphetamine in the basement of his parents' million-dollar, six-bedroom house in Hampton. Dugal lends me out to the City narc squad on some interjurisdictional traffic—heroin, on the eastern border of Baltimore and the County. It's copacetic. The City narcs I work with are serious spades, they're cool when I show up with the Eagle and pop some gangsta cribs with them. "You be forgettin' those County faggots, come hang with us, Luther," a detective lieutenant called Dog says to me. I'm tempted.

Then, suddenly, an avalanche of Ecstasy hits the County. We've busted twenty-six sellers, all of them pure white bread, just like the first three. The arrests make Dugal very happy, he sends glowing reports upstairs about how active and effective his squad is, he especially likes to personally count and recount each Ecstasy pill and put big numbers in the reports. But not one solid thing on the supplier. Which makes Dugal very unhappy and, though he tries to disguise it, tenser and tenser as the shit keeps coming.

Damn these wipers, making me crazy. "Confession, IB. I don't give a flying fuck about Ecstasy. It's nothing," I say. "Kids wanna drop this stuff in clubs, go all warm and fuzzy and cuddly for a while, who cares? It's only mommy-and-daddy money they're spending, not a crime wave."

"Ho, you haven't figured the priorities yet, slow learner? Make it simple for you. The mommys and daddys are very scared of this. Why? Because it's a new thing they never tried when they were kids. Hash, Thai sticks, a few lines of coke—no big deal, they've been there. Some of them probably still *are* there, recreationally. Ecstasy, wow! Don't want my kid on whatever that is. So the pressure comes down on the politicians, they slide it off on the Department Chief, he slides it off on Dugal. And Dugal creams himself whenever he gets his name in the papers."

Seems even more of a waste then, all that computer time collating everything the busted kids say about their supplier, trying to build a profile. All I'm sure of to date is it isn't the black city gang-bangers. These suburbans are too scared to deal with them. Anyway, the gangsta dealers can't be bothered with Ecstasy. It's too pussy, doesn't create its own inexorable demand. Old economy biz.

No trace of old-economy mafia, local or down from Philly or New York. Not a make on what seems most likely—a smart free-lance import man, using kids as mules to bring the pills in from Amsterdam or wherever, then using local kids to retail them.

Lately I'm worrying a lot, I admit, because the traffic's suddenly changed. Real bad news. Last four busts in a row, the kids are making what IB calls Bonus Packs. Inside each two-pill Ecstasy Ziploc, they put little glassine envelopes of super-pure heroin, meant to be snorted or smoked, not shot up, about two lines worth. Clever. Needles are too scary for these white kids. Dugal trys to stay cool about this. Dugal thinks his excellent leadership and police acumen keeps hard stuff out of the County. "We will never have a heroin problem here," Dugal says. He says the Bonus Packs are an aberration meaning absolutely nothing.

Nothing is what I've got on my iMac. A child's raggedy connect-the-dots drawing. All consistent, though. All the same, from twenty-six scared teenagers.

Two players. Man in his twenties, dresses Old Navy and J.Crew, hair buzzed short, bland face. And a chick who looks like nobody. Nobody to give our hormone-crazed teen dealers a hard-on, nobody who's in the mug files we make them all study forward and back. Like a coed at Towson State or Goucher, they say. You wouldn't look twice, detective. Not coyote-ugly or anything. Just not sexy. Totally average. She comes up to you in clubs, not on to you. Gets around to Ecstasy, gives free samples, asks if we want to make some easy money.

Hard to doubt twenty-six perfectly consistent stories.

"Wake up, Ewing, and start entertaining me," Ice Box says, "or you too busy having wet dreams about some merc action somewhere?" Another damned button, a bad one, but he doesn't know. He's hit it by accident. "There's the Congo, man. Hear they're hiring there again after all these years."

"Got just two words for you, IB." I laugh, but it feels like leather bands are tightening around my skull. I've got the shakes coming on. I need my medication but don't want to drop a tab until we get to where we're going and Ice Box is occupied with his snitch. I want to tell him fuck the fog, step on it and let's *get* there.

We're coming up on the first bridge over the reservoir. IB is steering with one hand and using the other to wipe the inside of the windshield because the defroster's dead. The pine forest is towering over both sides of the road. I clear a patch on my side window with my shirt sleeve and stare out. Rows of trees slipping by, like pages of a book you're riffling through from back to front. Everything blackened, dripping, branches sagging low down. Then, just an eyeblink, something so pale against the black it almost glows.

"Hey, brake it, IB," I say, twisting my head to try to keep whatever that was in sight, but losing it. "Saw something weird in the trees back a bit."

"Saw your own ghost, is all."

"No bullshit, man! Stop it and back up a hundred meters. I saw something."

"Rule one, always humor paranoids, for they just may be right," Ice Box mutters as he brakes, bounces the Crown Vic over the curb into the grassy strip between the road and the forest. He starts backing up. "Can't see," he complains, "rear window's all fogged."

I roll down mine and stick my head out. "Ease right a bit, okay, a little more. Now straight."

For what seems a long time I don't see anything but forest ghostly in the fog and begin to think Ice Box is right, about my own ghost. Then it's there, a pale spectral thing, down low against a trunk.

I'm out of the car and running before Ice Box stops. The verge hasn't been mowed in a long time and within ten strides my jeans are sopping up to my thighs. I hear Ice Box thudding along behind me. I reach the tree. And there, curled in the fetal position, is a naked little girl, can't be more than twelve or thirteen, blue-lipped, barely formed nipples puckered tight, flesh everywhere goose-bumped. Quick scan—no blood, no obvious marks or wounds.

"Dead?" I hear Ice Box call, voice strangely hollow in the fog, seeming to come from no particular direction.

I'm kneeling and taking her cold, cold hand in mine, finger searching urgently for a pulse in her thin, blue-veined wrist. I find it. It's shallow and much too fast. Suddenly her eyes open on me. I look deep into them. And I know she's not seeing me at all, but some image in her mind that sends tremors rippling down her poor frail body.

"Not yet," I say.

2

I've seen things nobody should have to. Never blinked. But I turn away from this girl's eyes. I stare at the pines until they're a blur. I lay the forefinger that searched for her pulse against the side of my skull, under my long hair. It fits perfectly, length and depth, into the dent there. Into the damage that demands four tabs of Klonopin every day to keep my brain from meltdown.

Ice Box, who can move, takes forever to slog back through the high grass and begin wrapping her in a silvery space blanket. "Called it in," he says.

I know he's fast, know it's only been moments. I know it's only for me time's gone all skewed and slow.

Then he's holding her hand. "Jesus, Mary and Joseph. It's okay, hon. You're safe. You're all right. You're safe, hon."

"Going hunting," I say and slip into the woods, casting around in broadening circles like Gunny's old setter. The drooping boughs force me to my hands and knees, shower me with chilly drops of water whenever my back brushes one. I go slow, careful as I can. Hyperalert for any sign at all—scrap of cloth, faint dent of a shoe print, broken twigs. All I find is slight smudges where the pine needles on the forest floor have been brushed lightly out of their natural pattern. I follow this a bit, keeping well to the side. The smudges are heading up from the reservoir. Somebody very light's been crawling. Nobody's walked this way. I back out exactly the way I came in.

When I emerge from the trees, the scene's lit up like a rock concert, the fog and low clouds reflecting and intensifying the revolving lights of two cruisers and an ambulance. The crime scene team has stretched its yellow-tape perimeter, and guys with empty plastic bags are systematically quartering the area. The EMS guys are hovering over the girl. I see Ice Box on the road by an unmarked talking to Detective Lieutenant Mason, head of the sex crimes unit.

"Yo, Ewing," she beckons me over. "When you've finished contaminating my scene, you want to share your insights? IB doesn't have any."

"Hey Annie," I say when I get to the road.

"So—bad date? Little girl out with some jerk too old for her, he fucks her, freaks, dumps her?"

"No."

"No?"

"When we got here, all the grass was standing tall. Me and Ice Box flattened two paths, see?" I point to the trails IB and I left from the Crown Vic. "Your herd trampled all the rest. No way anybody dragged or carried her from the road."

"Give me more," Annie says.

"She came up out of the woods. Alone. Crawling. Saw some signs in the needles. No footprints."

"That'd explain the little scratches on her forearms, belly and thighs," Annie says.

"Okay, so you tell me. How'd she get way down there in the woods?"

"Boat. Somebody dumps her from a boat."

"You know this part of the reservoir? What's down there?"

"Place called Hollow Point," Annie says. "Weird little cove with a pebble beach tucked in between two stone cliffs. You'd miss it if you didn't know it was there. From the water."

"Maybe somebody ought to go down there and poke around."

"Somebody's down there now, Luther," Annie says with a grin.

"Gee, happy I could be so much help," I say. Ice Box is shifting from foot to foot.

"So we done here, Loot? Luther and me, we got places to go, people to see."

"Hey," Annie says, holding up both hands. "Far from me to keep you from important engagements."

Ice Box heads off toward the Crown Vic. I hang for a moment. "One thing, Annie. Not your average mall rat. She's been well looked after."

"Instinct? Or evidence?"

"Her nails. Beautifully manicured. Buffed, polished and clear-coated, just like you get yours done every week. And the hair. Even soaked, a great cut. Like those $125 salon jobs you favor."

"You *notice* details like that, do you, Luther? You got a thing for female maintenance?"

"I appreciate it, Annie, that's all," I smile.

"Later, Luther?"

"Sure."

//

Ice Box is silent for a while. Just drives. Over the bridge, then off Dulaney Valley Road and up into the rolling hills toward Jacksonville. We tear free of the last lingering wisps of fog. The rain's eased too, and there's lots of action in the sky, storm clouds swirling and twisting, glimpses of blue from time to time. He kills the lights, sets the wipers on intermittent and somehow they aren't screeching anymore.

"Just when you think it's a nothing day," IB begins. "Can't tell you how much I hate shit like this. Poor little thing. What kinda world we living in, Luther?"

"Somebody's mistake?"

"Or worse. You know, I got shot once, when I was a uniform."

"Didn't know."

"Well, I did. And in the back of my mind ever since I've had the very weird notion I died on the operating table. And everything since then is some kind of afterlife—same people, same places, but all of it kinked, all of it just a little bit off."

"So you think you're in hell?"

"Nah, don't try to ID it. Something's just different now."

"You ever see things nobody else seems to see? Ever know in advance something's going to happen?"

"Nah, I only feel a little light-headed once in a while, and get bad heartburn."

"That's just your wife's cooking. You had me thinking for a minute you were into some very heavy-duty mystical shit."

"Just two words. . . ."

We're past Madonna and out on a two-lane country blacktop that rides the crests and troughs of the hills. Big pastures everywhere, maybe a mile between mailboxes at the heads of long drives that swing far from the road toward mansions, barns and stables. "Horse country," IB says. "Not exactly Kentucky, but some great thoroughbreds raised and trained out here."

He pulls into a drive flanked by two tall brick pillars with a wrought-iron double gate open between. There's a double row of yellow poplars along the drive, just inside a white post-and-plank fence that looks freshly painted. The drive takes a couple of curves until about two hundred meters out from this three-story red brick place with tall white columns from verandah to roof. There's a barn off to the left that looks brand-new, and a low U of brick, copper-roofed stables with a cobblestone courtyard, and behind all that acres of grass. I see three, maybe four tall, long-legged horses with proud heads gamboling around out there.

"So, your man the caretaker here or what? Shovels the shit out of the stables? His trailer tucked way out of sight, over in the tree line?"

"He takes care of it, yeah. Got some help, though," IB says.

Before we even pull into the gravel circle in front of the house, a tall guy wearing a suede blazer and green moleskin trousers tucked into paddock boots opens the door and comes skipping down the steps toward us, arms spread wide like he can't wait to give someone a hug. I should have noticed infrared security beams at the gate that signaled our entrance. Probably surveillance cameras in the trees along the drive too. You have a place like this, you pay attention to security.

As I climb out, the suede jacket's already got his arms as far around Ice Box as he can, which is only halfway, and they're patting each other. "Joey C, you old cocksucker. Joey man, it's been too long. How's it hangin', amico?" he's saying.

Ice Box is laughing. "Hey, don't muss my suit, Dee Dee. It's been too long 'cause you never call. Like all the dickheads from the old neighborhood who've made it. They don't want to know me no more. Afraid I'll embarrass 'em in front of their new old-money friends or some shit."

Dee Dee plants a big wet kiss on both of IB's cheeks, lets go and studies him. "You're right," he laughs. "I couldn't take you anywhere. You piss in your pants on the long drive or what?"

"That's another story," IB says.

"Joey C, Joey C. Listen, I thought it was gonna be you and me only?" He nods in my general direction.

"Just my partner, man. Luther, meet Dee Dee. We grew up on the same block. He parlayed a lot of luck at Pimlico into some shares in a couple of thoroughbreds, then parlayed that into full ownership and all this shit you're seeing."

"Hey Tonto," Dee Dee says. "That some new style, taking a shower in your clothes?"

"No," I say, giving him maybe a 75-watt smile with enough jitter in it to make him think there's a loose connection in my head. "We took an Italian submarine, on account of the weather. Leaky. You know the kind, goes 'Ping, guinea guinea wop wop wop' on sonar."

Dee Dee laughs. "Like his style, IB. He's okay. Now come on in where it's dry, have a cappuccino with a shot of grappa." He takes Ice Box by the arm and starts leading him up the stone steps. "C'mon, Luther, don't be shy," he calls back to me over his shoulder.

Perfectly polished wide-plank floors, Persian carpets worn and faded enough to be real antiques, lots of heavy mahogany furniture, lots of oil paintings of racehorses on the wall. We sit around a marble table in a half-octagon nook with a view out over the pastures where the horses are playing. There's logs blazing, never mind it's August, in a huge fieldstone fireplace behind us. No complaints from me—I've been shivering a little ever since we left the reservoir and it's great to feel my clothes drying. A dark girl with blue-black hair—I make her Sicilian with lots of Arab genes—comes in with a tray bearing three cups of cappuccino and a strange, stretched glass bottle. "Get the grappa from an *oenoteca* up in Friuli," Dee Dee says. I cover my cup with my hand when he tries to pour a shot. Ice Box doesn't. But it's damned good cappuccino. We sip.

//

"So Joey, to be honest I'm feeling a little agitato, no? 'Cause this is, what can I say, kind of sensitive?"

"If it's something Luther shouldn't hear, I shouldn't be hearing it either, Dee Dee."

"You cops. You fucking cops!" Dee Dee laughs, drains his cup, lights a cigarette. "This is maybe nothing at all, maybe you drove all this way for squat. But here it is.

"Two weeks ago, the biggest fuckin' Mercedes I've ever seen comes tooling up the drive without no invitation. I'm not worrying because what've I got to worry about? I don't owe a single soul a fuckin' nickel. I'm not mobbed up, as you know. And I got a couple of guys around the place you didn't see and they didn't see.

"These three dudes get out, big bulky guys so blond they look like they're fucking lifeguards down the Ocean except they're wearing very, very nice suits. Superfine cashmere, Italian linen, the best. Good shoes. They're smiling and waving and one dude says, 'Please excuse, Mr. DelVecchio, if we have dropped by at a bad time. We're in the area, we try to call, got a five-grand cellphone, but your line, nyet. If this time is bad, maybe we make an appointment, come back at your convenience.'

"Fuckin' Russians, talking like they do in James Bond movies. Now I'm curious, 'cause I've heard a few things from some guys downtown about Russians from up in Brighton fuckin' Beach, apparently some New York City slum, anyway coming down here and trying to do a little biz in what isn't their territory. They've been told the city's off limits. It's been made clear. They reply, 'Hey, no problem, we like suburbs, okay with you guys? We don't come near city. Maybe we cooperate with the import, we got great import like you can't believe. You got whole city for distribution and we stay out. You have any trouble with fucking Colombians, fucking Dominicans, fucking blackies, we take care of it for you. Ask around New York, you don't believe.'

"That's what the Russians tell the boys downtown. There's maybe some more talks on the agenda, the mob guys are fed up hassling with spics and nigger gangs who got no rules and no respect for nothin'. They want to step back, take life a little easier. This is what I hear, anyway.

"Now these Russian guys," Dee Dee says as he lights another cigarette, "they start telling me they're investors, very, very liquid, who want to get into the racing biz. I'm thinking money laundry thoughts right away. They're talking crazy prices for pieces of some horses. They want to buy a place like mine, all cash. They say Vinnie the Fish gave them my name, told them I could maybe steer them the right way. Big finder's fee, we don't have to mention that, of course. Very major fee.

"Fuck them! I want nothing to do with shit like this at all. I'm thinking I'm gonna kill the Fish with my bare hands first chance I get. But we're all gentlemen, we have a drink. I tell them I'll ask around, can't promise nothing, but I'll ask. They're fuckin' delighted, grinning like looney tunes. They give me their cell number. It's one of those fuckin' global satellite phones, reach 'em anywhere in the world."

Dee Dee slides a slip of paper across the table. Ice Box palms it. "That's it, Joey Baby. Do any good for you, I'm happy."

"No names?" I ask.

"Who can understand these crazy fucks?" Dee Dee replies. "Two of 'em are calling the other guy Vaseline or something."

I put on my 75-watter with the flicker. Only it isn't deliberate this time. Vassily. Jesus motherfuckin' Christ.

//

He's got this quirk, IB has, he likes to monologue it when he's mulling ideas, so I stay quiet on the long drive back to Towson. I really do not want to know this shit might be coming down. Can't be Vassily, not the one I knew. Can't be. "The Bonus Packs," IB's muttering. "Russians. Russian mob. Ah it's horseshit. But maybe it ain't. Maybe it is. Why? Why not? . . ." and on and on. I can't keep from tossing it all over too.

A tab at the station. I can't miss even one, unless I want to wind up on the floor, flailing and foaming at the mouth. At quitting time I walk over to meet Annie at Flannery's, a pub just off the square where the County Courthouse sits, a proud and well-kept example of nineteenth-century optimism with not a single one of the Towson buildings contemporary to it still standing. Flannery's draws a quiet mix—some lawyers and young government bureaucrats, some business folks from the high-rises down along York Road where the old two-story Victorian shops and the movie theater used to be, some students up from Towson State. No cops. I feel like dogshit when I slip into the corner booth Annie's occupied. Always do when I've skipped lunch and substituted coffee and cigarettes for the day's nourishment.

"Jesus, Luther, you've gotta take better care of yourself," she says, sipping a beer. I order a Coke from the waitress.

"That obvious, is it?"

"Well, if I were your doctor I'd lay down an ultimatum. Forget about modern medicine, pal, and go pick out a nice cemetery plot and a decent mortician."

She gives me that lopsided grin, the one she has no idea is the cutest thing going. Good-looking woman, Annie. Rangy, athletic, sandy hair, soft blue eyes and just a hint of a pout to her lower lip. She's changed out of the Anne Taylor suit that is her usual work wear—she keeps coveralls in the trunk of her car for the nasty calls—and she's now wearing an Orioles sweatshirt and Levis. Her eyes catch some light refracted from the big mirror behind the bar. We met when I first joined the Department. In fact, she came on to me, and I was thinking what luck until she made it clear within the first few sentences that it was purely professional interest. She was curious by nature, and I was the oddest thing to cross her path in a while. We got to be buddies. It's best that way, I know, but every once in a while, when the light hits her eyes like it just did, I think it's a damn shame.

"Hey, Luther, none of that now," she laughs, as if she's read my mind, which in a way she probably has. Then she goes serious. "The kid isn't a virgin anymore. Rape for sure, unless she picked the roughest, crudest asshole she could find to be her first lover."

"That sucks," I say. "Jesus, when she looked in my eyes when I found her . . ."

"You wanted to kill the guy that put her there," Annie frowns. "I know your reflexes by now, Luther. Anyway, the girl doesn't even seem to know she was raped. Claims she doen't remember a thing."

She studies me for a minute. "You well in control? 'Cause if you're not, this'll wait 'til another time."

"What'll wait?"

"The extra-shitty part." Annie's still scanning me in a way that's making me a little edgier than I like. Most cops don't trust Annie. They don't because she's too smart for them. She's got this weird double-major B.S. in biology and criminology from the University of Maryland at College Park, and an M.S. in psychology from there too. She's very young for her rank and they think she's a snitch for the Department psychologist. Also, she isn't a dyke. The muscleheads would've felt a lot easier around her if she'd been a dyke. Most of the males—and a hell of a lot of the female cops, too—like to keep their distance with Annie. They can't find any clearly labeled box to put her in, and that always makes cops uneasy.

"I'm cool," I say, having held her eyes through the scan. I'm not, really, since about seventy percent of my mind is going through hoops over Dee Dee's Vaseline. But the thirty on Annie's deal is on strong and tight.

"It goes like this. I track down her parents, both lawyers. Both 'in conference.' I leave messages. I hang around the hospital. Our guys do all they have to, the hospital does all it has to, the kid's ready to go home.

"The father takes an hour to make the callback. He's real curt when I tell him what's up. He sounds fucking annoyed. They don't exactly break speed records getting to the hospital, either. Then they take a quick look at their daughter, sort of pat her hands and say they're glad she's fine. Then I take them outside the room.

"They tell me, like it's an imposition they have to talk to me at all, that when she didn't come home at eight last night, they assumed she was sleeping over at a girlfriend's, and when she wasn't around when they left for work, they assumed she'd gone to school straight from the girlfriend's.

"Now I'm losing it big-time," Annie goes on. "'You never *phoned* her friend's parents to find out if she was there? You never thought to phone them in the morning? It never occurred to you to try the police?'

"The bitch gets all huffy and says, 'We're not under interrogation here. We're taking Emma home, now.' So the orderlies wheel her out in a hospital gown and robe, a nurse tells them they'll have to return the stuff. 'Where are her clothes?' the bitch snaps. I say, 'Didn't you hear a word I said? Your daughter was found completely nude, brutally raped, half-dead of exposure, in the woods near Loch Raven Reservoir.' And she says, 'If we had a decent police force in this county nothing like this would be allowed to happen. You'll be hearing from us!' "

"And you go?" I say. It's getting very overcrowded in my head.

" 'No way, honey. You're going to be paid a visit by me personally in a squad car with lights and sirens going, and by the county social welfare people. I'm filing a report naming you as unfit parents whose child needs to be removed from your custody for her own safety. I'll have a court order with me, count on it.' "

"Jesus Christ," I mutter. "Scumbags like that aren't fit to . . ."

"Whoa, Luther. Just let it go, before you make me sorry I told you. I had to tell somebody, had to vent. Don't make it a mistake for me to've picked you."

And remembering how she'd never made confession a mistake for me, I let it go.

3

I glide into Annie's office early next morning before the shift changeover. She's staring at what looks like a forensic report on her computer screen, hair still wet and rubberbanded into a ponytail. It's at least two minutes before she notices I'm there. Or lets me know she's noticed.

"Hey, Five-O," she says cheerfully, hitting the SAVE and STORE keys so the screen goes that wavery gray. "Sorry I laid all that on you last night. Didn't lose any sleep over it, did you?"

"Nah," I say. Double lie—the girl, and also a Russian I once knew but can't tell anyone about, not even Annie.

"Well," she says, facing me now, "check this. There's three messages on the machine when I get in today. All from the father. He's saying he and his wife were simply in total shock last night, they'd said a lot of things they realized were totally inappropriate, they're of course absolutely willing and eager to cooperate with my investigation. And I quote, 'This doesn't have to get into the newspapers, does it?' "

She's laughing before I am. "So which way did you go on them?"

"No way," Annie says. "I'm not calling the fuck back. He and his wife can shit bullets for a while."

I'm grinning but not saying anything.

"What's your read, Luther?"

"No case."

"Hey, we got the perp nailed. They checked her out with a colposcope. Then a Wood's lamp. Positive DNA ID."

"I'm not up to date on the tech, Annie."

"Oh, right. Colposcope's a magnifying lens medical examiners attach to a video camera, to check for tiny fibers and stuff. The Wood's gives the victim's body a purplish-blue glow. Drops or smudges from the perp's body fluids—skin oil, sweat, semen—show up under it. They swab, get DNA markers."

"Like I said, no case."

"What do you mean?"

"You gotta have a face, a name before you can pull somebody in and match the DNA. She give you that?"

"Uh, no. Not yet."

"So, zip. She may've been stoned, picked up someone, asked him to take her someplace . . ."

"She's only thirteen!"

"C'mon, Annie. Things like this have gone down with kids even younger. Maybe she was so whacked she decided to lose that virginity. Get back at her lousy parents that way or something."

Annie's frowning now. "Yeah, and she's the only one who can tell us how it went."

"When you asked her last night?"

"Said she couldn't remember anything after she walked out of Woodleigh Mall around seven-thirty. Shit," Annie snaps, "I gotta check again with toxicology, see if drugs are involved here."

"What for? Won't get you a face or a name."

Annie goes bad on me, which she only does when she's really upset. "Yeah, Luther, thanks for your ideas," she says curtly. "Now maybe you better get on with cleaning up the drug traffic. Got a pretty full agenda today."

Her last two words only echo off the walls, because I'm already gone. I know she'll come around all sorry after she finishes sticking it to the kid's parents and gets on the real problem. Way she is. It's why I love her.

There's a blue Post-It stuck on my computer screen when I walk into my cubicle. "See me when you get in, D."

No sweat. Dugals's done a 180. I'm one of his best boys now. A born asshole, the LT, always will be an asshole, but far from stupid, and very ambitious. He takes management courses at night in the continuing education department at Towson State, he wants a captaincy bad, a master's degree and one day his own county. Doesn't matter if it's this one or someplace else, just so he's chief of police there. He realized—once he got over being pissed off—that when your superiors hand you a wild child, a Luther Ewing type, what reflects best on you is taming the bastard, turning him into a great cop.

I made it easy for him. I began the day after that first Ecstasy raid.

//

That start—I rap on the frame of his open office door, stand at ease until he deigns to notice me. "What do you want, Ewing? You want to complain about something?" He swivels in his chair, beckoning me in.

"No sir. No complaints, sir. I want to apologize for the incident with the unauthorized weapon the other night."

"You do?"

"I failed to fully inform myself, sir. It won't happen again."

"Damn well better not," he says. "What made you think you'd need a piece like that anyway? Our Rugers are more than sufficient . . . when they're needed. Hell, in ten years I've only had to fire mine twice, both warning shots."

God watches over innocent bystanders, I'm thinking. Those P89s are the cheapest semi-autos Ruger makes. Christ, every rookie patrolman in the New York subways is carrying a good Glock. "I hope I never have to fire either, sir. Not my preferred way of dealing with a situation. Last resort, correct sir? But there is always a chance you get forced to."

The LT nods. "Yeah, in our business, that's true."

"I'd like to ask you a favor, LT. I can't shoot the Ruger for shit. I do have a personal pistol that I can use well, if I ever have to."

I hand him a black aluminum case. He places it on his desk and pops the latches. Inside, nestled in dimpled gray foam, is a matte-black semi-auto.

"Looks ordinary. Caliber?"

"Just .45ACP, sir. Standard issue in lots of places."

"I know that, Ewing. Capacity?"

"Ten rounds only."

"Hell, the Ruger carries ten too," Dugal says. "But you claim you're more comfortable with this, better shot with it?"

"Yessir."

"Let's check it out."

We go down to the range in the basement. Dugal calls over McKibbin, who gives me a nod and wink. I know him already, spend a half-hour on the range every day since I joined, to get back my groove after not shooting for almost a year. He's an Irish guy, Northern, ex–Royal Ulster Constabulary with some military cross-training, I'd bet on that, maybe even with the SAS, since he knows more about weapons than any cop I've ever met. One of the lucky lottery winners, he calls himself. He won a green card and here he is.

"Ah, a very lovely Heckler and Koch," McKibbin says as he handles the pistol Dugal's extended to him. "Did you just buy it, sir? Excellent purchase indeed."

"No, I did not buy it. It's the personal weapon of our new detective, Ewing. Ewing, meet McKibbin, our shooting instructor."

"Well, lad, can you use it?" McKibbin asks me with a broad smile as we shake. He puts my pistol back in its case, hands it to me.

"I'll go first," Dugal says. We all put on muffs, he steps into a booth, McKibbin sends the silhouette target racing down the wires to twenty-five yards, and steps behind the LT. Dugal draws his Ruger, takes maybe twenty-five seconds to settle himself into the isosceles stance, aiming for center of mass. He lets off three pretty deliberate rounds, then empties the clip as fast as he can. McKibbin hits the recall button and the target comes fluttering up to the bench.

"Good shooting, sir," I say. He's got two holes in the X-ring about two inches apart, a third just outside the ring, and then seven holes climbing up and right until the last two aren't even in the man-sized silhouette.

"Well, I'm rusty," Dugal says, "but it isn't the pistol's fault."

"With due respect, sir, ye've done what I warn everyone against. Pullin' the trigger too fast, without waitin' for recoil recovery. Muzzle climbs with each round. That's why ye've got this trail," McKibbin says as he sticks his pinky in the seven wild holes, "runnin' right off the target. Natural tendency, sir. Have to fight it until it's instinct."

"Well, I'm rusty," Dugal concedes.

"Right, then, Mr. Ewing," McKibbin says, clipping up a fresh target. "Twenty-five, is it?"

"Sighted in for thirty-five, if that's okay?" I say, fighting the temptation to send the target all the way out to fifty yards. But I don't want to humiliate the LT here, just get him to let me carry my own gun.

I take the HK Mark23 out of its case and slide home a clip. Dugal doesn't realize it's a SOCOM model I stole off a drunken SEAL in Kuwait City after the party there was over. He doesn't notice the small extension of the barrel, threaded to take a suppressor, though I know McKibbin spotted it immediately. Dugal's standing behind me with his arms folded across his chest, sure a thin guy like me is gonna splash rounds all over the place with a heavy-recoiling .45.

Fuck the isosceles, the Weaver, fuck even a two-handed grip, you never have time for that in combat. My eye's already zeroed on where I want to hit, and I raise the HK as if it's just an extension of my hand until the sights align with my spot. I squeeze off a round, pause a beat, squeeze off two more fast—a double tap. "He's dead," I call out. But then I put another three rounds rapid into the silhouette for good measure.

McKibbin's already laughing when he hits the recall button, and I hear Dugal start to chuckle too. He isn't seeing holes in the X-ring.

"Five-O," he says, in a tone that's close to jovial for him, "I think you need an hour a week down here with McKibbin."

"Nothing I can teach him," McKibbin says, holding the target up against his body so Dugal can take it all in. The first shot's taken out the tiny white X in the X-ring. The second's gone through the left eye, the third through the right, and the last three are clustered exactly between them, all holes touching and forming one big hole.

"Shit, Ewing! How the hell did you do that?" Dugal says, plainly annoyed.

"He shot deliberately, watching muzzle climb," McKibbin says.

"Army shooting team, sir. Not all-army, just the base team. The armorer does trigger jobs, jewels the feed ramp, drops in a match-grade barrel, accurizes, puts on tritium sights. You could shoot it as good as me."

"Yeah, well, another time maybe," Dugal says. "So is this legal and everything, McKibbin? Are we gonna have liability problems here?"

"Shouldn't think so, sir," McKibbin says easily. "Just a regular .45. A Maryland resident could buy one off the rack at a decently stocked gun store. Well within our guidelines, sir. And he certainly knows the weapon well enough."

"So I can carry this one, sir?" I ask.

"I'm thinking, I'm considering," Dugal says. God, the man hates to give in. "Okay. But no cowboy crap, Ewing. This pistol gets fired on duty, I'll be all over you. Understood?"

"Yessir. Thank you sir. I'll be happy if I never have to unholster it."

"Try hard to stay happy, Ewing," the LT says. He looks at the target again, shakes his head. He starts walking away. "Oh, all ammo's your personal expense, Ewing. We only supply standard 9 millimeter."

"Ah, Luther, ya devil," McKibbin starts laughing when Dugal's gone and I'm cleaning my piece. "Knackered him good, you did. Hey, I've got a rare one comin', a current-production AKSU-74 in 5.45x39. Murderous piece of work, official Russian issue. Wring it out on the outdoor range with me?"

"Just say when," I smile.

//

I keep making it easy for Dugal to turn ever since that day. IB and I build the best felony-conviction record of any team on the narc squad. Squeaky clean too; never a squeal about unnecessary force, about dubious evidence, about entrapment, about even the slightest violation of strict Department guidelines. The ADAs at the court just love to see me and IB coming to them with a case, 'cause they know they're gonna convict and they like looking good. Dugal likes looking good too, and we're pushing his ugly butt up the ladder for him.

So the 180. He doesn't like me personally, he isn't clever enough to suppress that vibe, he's almost certainly aware it's mutual, but we keep it muted. More than cordial on the job, gets off acting as if he and me and Ice Box are part of the same team. A real elite team, since it includes him. Pats on the back around the HQ, throws me a bone now and then, no "Taggert You Fuck" disrespect. I stay slick. Things go best that way sometimes, when you just stay slick and slide with the currents.

//

"Hey Luther, you're early," Dugal says with a smile when I get to his office. "Left a note for IB too. He not in yet?"

"Probably in the parking lot right now, eating a half-dozen Egg McMuffins he doesn't want us to see. We'll hear him coming." Teammates together, gives us the right to poor-mouth each other. Dugal likes this stuff.

"Got a nice note from Detective Mason, about your help on the reservoir girl squeal. Good job. Anything in it for us?"

"Don't know yet. Think she was doped up. With what hasn't come back from the lab yet."

"You see any ongoing problem? Any connections?"

"Too early."

"You and Mason are copacetic. Keep me up to date?"

"Sure thing, LT," I say, thinking the bastard smells, positively smells something bigger, full of photo-ops and sound bites, and he wants his talking head in the middle of it.

The frosted-glass interior walls of Dugal's office tremble slightly. "IB." Dugal grins as the man appears at the door.

"IB." I grin too.

"Get enough to eat, ready to start your day?" Dugal asks.

"Breakfast is the most important meal of the day," IB huffs, fitting himself pretty gracefully into one of Dugal's aluminum chairs, which cries softly with metal fatigue and unnatural stress anyway.

"How many today, IB?" Dugal asks.

"Say what?"

"Egg McMuffins?"

"Hey, I don't touch junk food. My wife makes me a wholesome breakfast each and every morning. Uh, yogurt, cereal with two-percent milk, couple of slices of dry whole wheat toast, like that." He looks offended, but there are muffin crumbs uncountable littering his shirt. "Now what are we here for, my diet or my report?"

"This Vaseline, this so-called Sovietski," Dugal says. "I do wish we had a make on this guy from more than a single source. Russian mafia? I am very doubtful."

"Why don't we have IB just call up," I say, and slip into a falsetto. "Hi, this here's Ice Box, Baltimore County Police, can I please speak to Mr. Vaseline? Got a horse for him in the seventh at Pimlico today."

"Oh fuck off, Luther," IB says.

"No, really," Dugal says, suppressing a laugh. "What should we be doing on just a description of three guys who may or may very well not be Russian mob but legit Polish or Czech or what-have-you businessmen?"

"We wait," I lie. "See if they contact IB's pal again. See if they contact anybody else in the horse game. Surely we got some vice squad undercovers who know the thoroughbred players. Maybe the City police have heard some things. Downtown's where IB's man heard his stuff—not from cops, of course."

"Our vice guys are still trying to figure out how to put coins in rubber dispensers," Dugal says. "They are not up to our standards in any way, shape or form. I don't know how they justify drawing their salaries. They wouldn't, if it was up to me, which as of yet it isn't."

I catch IB's eye. May that day never come, is what we read.

"I personally don't have a man downtown who would give me the time of day. Do you guys?" Dugal asks.

"Well, I could run it by Dog."

"Dog? They have a cop called Dog?"

"Detective Lieutenant Dog. Worked with him on those cross-line cases you lent me out for, remember?" I say. "He's cool, he's real, real smart. I think he'd hear before anyone if the Russian mob's trying to get in between the Italians and the black gangs for the drug market."

"Ice Box, should I be worried? Should I be seeing anything in this supposed Russian angle? Was my opinion of those Bonus Packs of yours overhasty? Was I unduly sarcastic about that?" Dugal says this as if he really wants to know.

"I'm with Luther. I say we wait, work a few connections downtown, check out the horsey set. See if my friend gets any callback," Ice Box says.

"Okay, okay. Midpriority only."

Ice Box leaves first. "Hey Luther," Dugal says in a low voice as I'm almost through the door. "Don't forget. You hear anything about the Reservoir girl that's drug related, you pass it on."

"Sure thing, LT."

//

Fuck waiting. I flash on punching up that cellphone number soon as I can. Things are starting to resonate for me in really nasty ways.

"Hey Ice Box, you wanna give me that worldwide number for Vaseline, the one with eleven-teen digits Dee Dee slipped you?" I say.

"No way. You rattle that cage, they're gonna know it came from Dee Dee. We gotta let a decent interval pass here, make sure they've given other guys the number."

"Okay. Had an idea, is all. When it's time, right?"

"Like what kind of idea?"

"Just make a call, see who answers. Big surprise for you, IB. I speak Russian. Even personally know six or seven Russians, drank a lot of vodka with 'em a few years back. Hundred-to-one Dee Dee's guys aren't my acquaintances, but you never know. Ain't my guys, I can back out easy. They'll never make Dee Dee."

"I do not like where this is going," Ice Box frowns. "I'm seeing implications that disturb me, Luther."

"Stay cool, man. Just give me the number when it's time, okay?"

"I'll consider it."

Back in our cubicles, Ice Box is soon twitching and sweating and cursing under his breath as he makes his usual struggle to keep his big fingertips from pressing two keys at the same time instead of just the one he wants. "This fucker is not ergonomic, unless they used Japs and young girls as the size parameter. Hell, they probably did just that, deliberately, to make a man suffer," he's saying.

"Yeah, there's a secret code at the keyboard factories in Taiwan. They got profiles on all the big men in America on a bank of supercomputers, and an extrasmall keyboard got your name on it, right at the factory."

"Aw, get outta here, Luther. First you're up kissin' Dugal's tush behind my back, now you're down here getting on my case. I'm not appreciating any of it, all I done for your bony ass."

"Don't believe me, go check out that big dude, what's his name, Radik, up in Homicide. His keyboard's twice the size of yours 'cause he requisitioned it under a chick's name, not his own."

"Two words: e-nough," Ice Box says. He is pissed at the world this morning. "The LT wants details about our talk with Dee Dee I'd have had to be wearing a wire to get. So shut up and let me think."

"I'm gone, boss."

I start looking at my arrest files. I catch one on a boy IB and I took down just last week. Had enough stuff, and yammered enough, for a sure felony conviction. But I remember him, maybe feel a little sorry for him. Son of a corporate gypsy named Halliday, been to six schools in six cities in twelve years, no friends here yet, probably never has made many. Reminds me of somebody else as a kid. I liked his parents when they came with their attorney to make bail the same night we busted him. They were concerned. They didn't want him spending even a night in jail. Said he'd always been good, never been in trouble. They all say that, of course. But these people didn't try any of that bullshit of blaming us, like most of the ones who come in.

Good people, it'd seemed to me.

Use 'em.

I call the father.

"Mr. Halliday, Detective Ewing. Yes, the one who arrested your son the other night. We talked at the station, yes.

"Sir, I may have a way to get this business changed from a felony to a misdemeanor. It would mean no jail time for James if that happens. Would you care to talk about the possibility?

"No sir, it's not necessary for you to come in with your son right away. This is all very preliminary and informal."

I tell the father that if James will agree to contact his supplier, claim he has a friend who wants to deal on a scale much larger than James was, and go with this "friend" to meet his supplier, my chief and I would encourage the DA's office to reduce the charges.

"We do this a lot. The DA's very supportive of it. The fact is, sir, we're not here to put away kids like James. We want the bigger guys, the ones who got James into trouble."

No danger, I tell him. The "friend" would be a narcotics officer, very highly trained. There'd be close backup. James would never be alone with the dealer, never out of our hearing or sight.

"Yes, I understand James may be fearful of his supplier, sir. That is natural, perfectly natural. But he'd be with us. No risk at all. It would, sir, clear his record and, most importantly, keep him out of jail.

"No, of course I don't need an answer now, sir. This is something you need to discuss with your family. I'd also suggest calling your attorney and informing him of everything I've said. If you decide you'd like to pursue this course, phone me anytime. You have my office and cell numbers, correct? Very good, sir.

"No, no trouble at all, sir. I hope to hear from you."

I put down the receiver and stare at James Halliday's file on my screen. I'm not really seeing anything. If his supplier is really connected, I think, the kid's gonna be in deep shit for ratting. But nobody has to know, we work it right. Anyway, James'd be dead meat in jail from the moment he walks in. Pretty boy like him . . . some hard-time dude's new wife before he can blink.

I call Dugal, tell him about Halliday. He isn't impressed.

"Hell, Luther, we made the same offer to a dozen or more of these little rats. All of them were too scared."

"Got a feeling about this one, LT," I say. "I think the dad really wants to do the right thing. I can feel it's going to happen."

"I'm not holding my breath," Dugal says.

"Just had an inspiration, made the call."

"Let me know if you ever get one back." Dugal hangs up.

//

On the way to the parking lot I give myself my routine pat-down. HK in a paddle holster on my right side, SIG-Sauer compact chambered for .357 SIG on my left ankle, spare clips for each, SOG knife belt-sheathed in the small of my back. Oh yeah, badge and ID in my shirt pocket. I feel like a clown in baggy khakis and a dobby-weave cotton shirt three sizes too big from Banana Republic, tails hanging down around my thighs. But I need all the billows I can get to cover up the hardware.

Out in Cockeysville, I stop at this overpricey pseudo-Italian deli. I like a treat now and again, and I've got one coming tonight. I buy some fresh figs and prosciutto di Parma, some local tomatoes I'll dice and sauté with garlic, some radicchio and mesclun, a loaf of Tuscan bread, a bottle of Pinot Grigio. I park the black Camaro I've had since I was seventeen, go up to my apartment. Dump my hardware, shuck those clothes, quick shower, slip into some soft jeans and a jersey T-shirt, put Sarah McLachlan in the sleek Sony mini-stereo. Then I stretch out on the sofa and look around. Could be anywhere. There isn't a truly personal thing in the place. Even the good books on the shelves are pretty generic, and the CD holder's full of whatever I liked when I heard it on the radio over the past three or four years. Say Luther Ewing lives there, and all you're saying is that some single guy in his late twenties, early thirties lives there. Except for this one thing.

I reach under the sofa, get my fingernail in the crack, and pry up a square of parquet flooring. I lift out a framed 8×10. I put the photo face down on my chest; I can't just look at it right away, I've got to have my mind squared and steady. Then I look. My monster dune buggy in the Iraqi sands, oh so loaded, twin .50s mounted on the roll bar, a rack of Stingers along one side. There's Snake up behind the .50s, no shirt, just a flack vest, head wrapped in a blue bandana, like a pirate. There's JoeBoy, no Kevlar beanie either, behind the wheel, wearing night-vision goggles up on his head and looking like some killer insect, waving his M4. And there's the Comanche, full warpaint and long black hair blowing, a ferocious Franchi SPAS 12-gauge Velcro'd to the dash in front of him, an HK MP5 submachine gun fitted with sound suppressor in each hand, pointing right at the camera. And we're grinning our asses off. There's four or five other buggies with three-man teams parked close around us.

I look at Snake and JoeBoy for a few moments, scan some of the fainter, grainier faces of men on other buggies—there's Radar, Ricky B, Tark, Loose Bruce, The Duke, Squeaky, Chris, Tony Ducks, Matty—then glance quickly again at mine. Brothers once. Fuck it. I slip the photo back in its cache and replace the parquet square.

//

I'm way down the hole, deep into the dark and paralyzed, REM in control. I imagine a ringing. How the fuck did it get here? Another, sucking me up from sleep. Another, then another.

"Yeah," I mutter, picking up the phone beside the bed.

"It's me," I hear. I check my watch: 2:47.

"No kidding."

"Sorry I went all bitchy on you this morning," Annie says.

"S'okay."

"You were just . . ."

"Don't explain. I get it."

"Luther?"

"Huh?"

"What if I come over to your apartment, put a little something in your drink, do anything I want to? And when you wake up, you'll never even remember me or the drink, never mind the dirty stuff. Total amnesia."

"Sounds shitty."

"What?"

"I'd wanna remember every dirty detail, with you."

"Yeah, well, the dope the reservoir girl got put a nine-hour blank spot in her head that could be there forever."

The girl next to me shifts, murmurs, "Luther, why you on the phone, babe?"

"Whoops," Annie says, catching it. I can't tell if the little giggle she lets out is amused or sort of disappointed. "Five-O's busy. Sorry. Bye."

"Just police crap. They never care what time it is when they phone," I say to the girl, who's crawled up under my armpit and draped a smooth, smooth leg languorously over mine.

"Yeah . . . seen that on *NYPD Blue.* Get an unlisted number, hmmm?"

"Great idea. Back to sleep now, pretty."

4

Waking next morning, I have the sense I'm looking at some digital page from an Ikea catalog, one they only release in Sweden. There's a naked girl in it, though I don't notice right away. I see a Stromstad sofa in gray chenille ($699) facing two bright blue Arjang easy chairs ($49 each) across a Morke wool pile rug (six-by-nine, $149). In between is a plain pine Krokshult coffee table ($149), and over by the kitchen nook an Igesund dining table and four chairs. Near the bed, in the Nyland standing mirror in a blue-stained spruce frame ($179), I see a pair of endless legs and a flawless ass, toned by years of tennis and riding, slipping away from me into a pair of tight black cotton capri pants, a taut but softly modeled back and just the slightest curve of one small breast vanishing under a black sleeveless cotton blouse with a spread collar.

She's only twenty; she'll never look exactly this perfect again.

Sascha roman blinds mute the daylight. Full set of glasses, knives, forks, spoons, plates, towels, sheets and blankets in their appointed places. Assorted table and floor lamps. Bought it all in one day—took me five trips to get it home.

The girl wasn't part of the package.

There'll be a day, I think then, when a catalogue or a DVD may be the only place I'll see a woman this fine. And feel idiotic grieving over a loss far in a future I don't even believe I'll have. Christ, I'm only thirty.

I need my morning tab.

Helen—yeah, the old-fashionedness of her name suits her so well—Helen's back from summer break only yesterday, ready to start her final year at Goucher College. There'll be plenty of mornings like this. Keep your horizons short, Ewing, I remind myself. You live in the present tense only. Don't let yourself go the way you did a couple of mornings last June, just before Helen was going home for the summer to New Canaan or whatever rich Yankee enclave she comes from. Don't start imagining what it'd be like to see Annie's legs slide into those pants, Annie dressing fresh from your bed . . .

Helen tosses her honey hair and glances over her shoulder as she bends to slip on her sandals. "Jammin' night, Luther," she smiles. "Hadn't realized how much I've been missing you."

"So come on back here. Linger a while. I'm not going any particular place."

"Gotta book," Helen says. "Dorm rat stuff, see my adviser, make some plans on what classes to take this semester."

"It's Saturday, for Christ's sake."

"Hard-working college people don't enjoy the luxury of leisure our police apparently do. Have to register first thing Monday morning," she says, laughing, leaning over me for a kiss. I slip my hand into the gaping neck of her shirt, kiss her hard, feel her body tauten. She breaks away, just a little bit flushed.

"Oh, did I miss you," she says, grabbing her bag and heading for the door. "Call you later?"

"Use the cell, in case I'm out wandering."

"I'll track you down, babe. Maybe I'll just handcuff you to the bed, so I know you'll be here when I get back."

Door closes. I sit up. Damn. She *has* handcuffed my left wrist to one of the bedrails. The key's on the bedside table, sitting pertly on a white piece of paper that bears the imprint of her lips in pale red.

When she's gone, Helen's all gone. Like most everybody in my life. I grind up some beans I buy at Starbucks, put 'em in the gold filter of my coffee machine, and smoke a cigarette while it brews up. I start thinking of calling Annie, find out what she was up to last night. The coffee's done. I microwave some cream in my mug, pour in strong, dark Sumatran, add a spoon of sugar.

Then I light another cigarette, take a deep draw and a first deep sip of coffee. Immediately I feel semihuman. I lay my finger into the dent along the side of my head, open the prescription bottle and down a Klonopin with a second smooth sip of coffee. Two, maybe three cups with one or two cigarettes each, I know I can face the day. Caffeine, nicotine, modern pharmacology already doing good, good.

Too good, maybe. Start zeroing on Vassily, more pixels in the picture than Sony or Toshiba dare dream of, it's that sharp: how I met him, what we did together. How damn good he was. One of the best I ever saw. That's the baddest news, if Vaseline is my Vassily and we're on opposite sides in this tussle, instead of comrades in close-quarters combat.

Shut it down, Luther. Now.

I clean up last night's dishes, put fresh sheets on the bed, tidy up here and there. Then I sit at the table again, smoking and fidgeting and restless as hell. I call McKibbin, ask if he wants to go out to the range, shoot a little. He'd love to, but he's taking the kids to the Aquarium. I think of calling Ice Box, but the man doesn't really like firearms, doesn't dig the aesthetics of firing fine weapons. Pure curiosity made him want to shoot the Eagle. I go down to the basement, where every tenant has a padlocked wire cage for overflow possessions. Mine's filled with a 1,500-pound gun safe. I sprayed over the "Winchester" logo with black, no need to alarm anyone, but it's still faintly visible after three coats. I work the combination dial, bolts thicker than your thumb slide back into the door when I move the lever. There's only five or six guns in there—it's built to hold sixteen. I pull out a cased rifle, two boxes of shells, a spotting scope, a handful of targets. Then I go out to the Camaro, put it all in the trunk and head for the outdoor range.

It's nice there, far from any road, forest all around, grass neatly mowed. Nobody shooting, ten o'clock on a Saturday morning. I pin up my targets down at the butts, then walk back and keep going another 100 meters past the 100-meter bench. I open the case and withdraw the Weatherby Accumark in .270 Weatherby Mag with a Leupold 3x9 scope. I bought it a few years ago, thinking I'd go out to the Mescalero Apache Reservation in New Mexico, ride into the mountains twenty or thirty miles from any road with just a Mescalero guide, and get a monster elk. With a flat-shooting round like the .270 screaming out of a 26-inch heavy fluted barrel, the Weatherby's deadly out to 400 meters in expert hands.

Never did it, though. Never hunted any animal anywhere. Only men.

I slip three rounds in the magazine and one up the spout. The rifle's ready. Then I lean against an old oak for a while, just getting into it, just smelling the scent of the forest, settling, calming.

Gunny used to always tell me the Crotch attracted the few, the proud, the crazed. In most marine units, he claimed, but always in the spooky ones like Recon, you could count on finding at least one guy deep into some esoteric shit, working his way through some kind of mystical internal labyrinth. He knew one dude in Nam who was a Nietzsche freak, intensely into the uebermensch ideas. He read and reread, just absorbed until it was part of him. There was only one other guy in the unit who had a clue what he'd be talking about, and that was the CO, a major. So night after night, when ops weren't on, you'd see this sergeant huddled over joints with this major, discussing Nietzsche. Sometimes they'd talk all night, Gunny said.

Same in Special Forces. I knew a couple of Zen masters, one had even spent a year as a monk in a monastery up in the mountains in Japan. They were wiggy, they seemed AWOL from this world a lot of the time. Until shit happened. Then they were concentrated like you could not believe.

"Give you the story short and sweet," one of them said to me. "Do a lot of archery in Zen, dig? And you know for sure you finally understand the first time you shoot and *feel you are the arrow.* Become one with the arrow. That's what's happenin', man."

I never did get that into it, but the idea never left my mind. When I squeeze off, I'm like outside myself, my vision's a very narrow tunnel or a tube headed straight to what I want to hit. The bullet just travels along that tube and hits the spot I'm staring at.

It's a gift. It's why I won all those shooting competitions. It's why I've got more than a hundred scalps on my belt that I'd like to be rid of, but never can.

It isn't happening today. After three magazines, the best I manage is a three-hole group just over an inch center to center. There have been days when I've put eight bullets into almost the same hole with this rifle at two hundred meters. I quit.

//

Half-hour later, the Camaro rumbles up to the curb in front of Ice Box's house, a red-shingled ranch on the usual quarter acre. He's out there in the driveway, wearing a guinea-T and too-tight shorts, hosing down a vehicle that's some computer-generated shade of deep, unearthly purple. It's a Dodge or Plymouth minivan, wearing temporary tags, but that's no reason in IB's mind not to gently and lovingly dry the thing with a big piece of real chamois. I'm within ten feet when he moves fast and gets the hose on me. Just a splash. Then he cuts the water.

"What are you doing, showin' up at my home uninvited? Trying to scare my neighbors, get me a bad reputation, get them calling the cops about suspicious characters hanging around 1302 Knollton Road?" He grins. "Thought I told you to come only after dark, and park a couple of blocks away, so nobody would see you."

"Me and my vehicle not quite up to neighborhood taste levels, that it? What are they gonna think about this . . . purple space turd you're massaging."

"I told him," I hear Mary Jo's voice from behind the screen door, "to go for the white one. But he saw his beautiful face reflecting back at him in metallic purple and fell right in love. Couldn't persuade him. Tried some pressures too. Didn't work either."

"Sure you did your best, MJ. If you couldn't make it happen, nobody could."

She's backing out the screen door using her butt, both hands holding a big wooden cutting board with a submarine sandwich on it that has to be nearly two feet long, balancing the board on her huge, protruding stomach.

"Looking real good, MJ," I say. She's a pretty brunette with liquid eyes, just a hint of a hook in her nose, hardly any varicose veins in the backs of her shapely legs.

"Lunch!" Ice Box says. "At last."

"Luther, you have always been so full of it," Mary Jo says to me. "I'm looking and walking like a hippo. Feeling like one too."

"How much longer?" I ask, reaching out to take the cutting board.

"Hey, don't you let that weasel near my lunch," IB calls.

"Six more weeks, if I live that long," she smiles at me. "Don't move, Luther. I'll be right back."

She lets the screen door slam behind her. Ice Box is headed my way. Then she's out again, a beer and a Coke in one hand and a big bread knife in the other.

"Hey, don't do that," IB says plaintively, but his wife makes a diagonal cut through the middle of the sub. "Put the board right here on the step, Luther, and eat something."

"Thanks, MJ."

"Yeah, thanks, giving away my food. I needed that," IB says.

"Ice Box, if they locked you in a cell for two weeks and only allowed you a glass of water a day, I doubt you'd come out more than a pound or two lighter," MJ smirks at him. He tries to pat her ass, but she slides away. She moves real well for a big woman.

IB thuds down next to me and we begin to eat the subs: salami, provelone, shredded lettuce, thin-sliced onions, some olive oil. He takes delicate bites all around the edges and then works into the center, but I've still got half of mine to go when he's finished. He looks at it.

"You want this, IB?"

"Nah, you eat it. She gave it to you."

"I'm full, man. You take it."

"Nah, finish it up. Don't want it."

"It's just gonna go to waste."

"You eat it."

I put it down on the cutting board. "Can't do it, dude. I'm full."

"You sure?"

"Oh yeah, IB. Couldn't take another bite."

So he polishes it off, then sucks on his beer. "Don't tell MJ I ate part of yours, right?"

I nod, light a cigarette.

"You know, I hate to see you doin' that, Luther. It's committing slow suicide."

"Easiest kind for everyone involved."

"Don't even go there, you fuck," Ice Box says. "I ain't talking with you about philosophies of life and death and so forth and so on. Why spoil a great day? C'mon, have a look at my new toy. Just picked it up this morning."

"And it got so soiled on the drive home you felt the need to wash it?"

"Gotta keep this clear-coat paint spotless, my man. I want it shining, really shining when I bring those twins home from the hospital."

"Got any names yet?"

"Two words for you. Just two words. . . ."

"Hey Luther," Mary Jo calls from inside. "How does 'Chloroform' and 'Cholera' grab you?"

She's laughing. "You *told* her about all that?" I say, grabbing a fold of IB's T.

"Sure," he says. "Why not?"

"I was only being a smart-ass with that stuff, MJ," I call. "I never meant any of it."

"Really?" She's still laughing. "Too bad. I sort of liked the ideas you were coming up with."

"Check this action, Five-O," IB says, pointing the key ring at the minivan and pressing a tiny red button. The whole side slides back slick and silently until both front and rear seats are exposed. In the back I see two top-of-the-line infant car seats already snugged in tight. "Cool, yeah? You come strolling up, your arms are full of kids or groceries or whatnot, you touch your button, and just glide right into that very roomy and comfortable interior."

I laugh, pat him on the back. "Jammin'," I say. "Well, except maybe for the color choice."

"Do I ever criticize that junker making the whole street look like a slum?" IB says.

"Some, yeah."

MJ comes butt first through the screen door once more, carrying a light aluminum-and-webbing lawn chair. She sets up the chair facing us, and we start talking about the twins and how her family's going to go nuts and what IB's folks are going to do and on into imagined futures for lives that haven't even started yet. She looks so peaceful, even if she has to keep shifting her weight to stay comfortable.

I feel my head going jagged. IB's my age, Mary Jo's twenty-eight, married four years, nice house, nice life, lots of close relatives who stay in close touch, their own kids on the way, plans for more—all connected somehow with a world I can't grasp. I can see they're very happy in their state of being, see a deeper contentedness that counters all the small, shitty irritations of living day to day. 'Cause they aren't living day to day, I decide. It's a path they're on, which, barring bad luck or disaster, will take them all the way out to the end.

So what's missing in me? Why does my life start fresh every morning when I wake up, and die when I fall asleep at night?

I hang out happily with Ice Box and Mary Jo until just before dinnertime, sticking to what they got like a fucking leech.

//

I answer my apartment door that night wearing only my yakuta. It's a lovely thing, falls all the way to my feet. From any little distance the superfine cotton appears to be blue-and-white checked, but when you look closer you see each bit of blue and each bit of white is actually a crane with wings spread, interlocking. Gunny got it for me in Japan. I've worn it maybe three times in my life.

Helen's there, smiling a big one, string bag with a change of clothing slung over one shoulder, baggy gangbanger shorts riding low on her hips so I can see her navel. She looks me up and down with approval, but before she can say anything I've got her in my arms and my lips locked on hers. She's cool about it, she wants to slide with me, I can tell by the way her body melts into mine.

So we slide, right there on the dining table. And later, in bed.

I jerk awake about four, dream-image in my brain—but so hi-rez it seems realer than real—of the last time I saw Vassily. Bloodred's the dominant color, corpses torn and leaking the smell. Got to get smooth again. I slip under the covers and begin blowing softly on the blonde hairs of Helen's pubis. They float and shimmer, just barely visible in the little light from the parking lot that edges around the shades and into the room. I blow this way, then that way until she shifts her hips in her sleep. Then I lick once or twice, and blow again. Her hips are moving a bit, but she's pretending to be asleep. I'm sure she's awake, though she keeps her eyes closed when I penetrate her. She moans softly, arms and legs stretched wide. She comes so quickly, but I can't get off.

"Oh God, Luther. I'm so far gone," she murmurs.

I keep at it, looking down at her spread-eagled, just letting things happen to her.

Nothing happens for me.

5

Hate Sundays. Have since I was a little kid, so little I hadn't even started school yet. Woke depressed and got more depressed as the day wore on until the very last hours of light, when it got almost unbearable. It was worse in the autumn and winter, when the days were so short. My mother used to hold me then and ask why I was so sad.

I never had any answer. Not even a lie. Just, "Hate Sundays."

I take Helen for brunch at Le Petite Marmot. Yeah, it's in a mall, but everything out here is in a mall, and at least this is an upscale mall and the Marmot owners are trying. They bake their own croissants and muffins, they make really dark, rich coffee, they can sling together decent eggs Benedict if you remind them to go light on the hollandaise.

"Today I get to be a cop," she says when we're walking back toward my apartment.

"What piece you gonna carry, Smith and Wesson?"

"A clipboard!" she says. "The seniors have to show all the freshies around, get 'em into their dorms okay, explain the rules, give some tours of campus facilities, that crap."

"Cool," I say. "How about we switch? I go guide all the new girls, the really nervous and impressionable ones, and you take the day off? I can be very reassuring."

"You know, I had a Lab like you once, Luther, he'd hump . . ."

"Can't believe I'm hearing this from the product of a fine women's educational institution," I say.

"You believe it when I suck your cock, though," Helen laughs, sliding into the new lime-green Volkswagen Bug she got over the summer. Her change of clothes turned out to be lime-green capri pants.

"It's a pandemic, capris and Bugs." I smile at her. "Who fixes things so thousands of girls all want the same thing at the same time?"

"We all get together over the Internet and take a vote on what boys are going to like seeing us in best."

She's bright, she's shiny, she's a happy kid. I wonder if any of that is due to me, or if she's just naturally this way all the time. Never any Sunday blues for her. She waves as she drives off.

I decide it's natural. All I give anyone is grief and sorrow. Or much worse, if I don't like them. I decide to go to work. Just jump in the Camaro and drive. The SIG's already on my ankle and I don't need anything else, off-duty on an August Sunday.

The engine stutters, then grumbles to life. Sounds like it's got grit in its cylinders. Used to love driving that car, used to love the low rumble it made. Now it just irritates me.

A lot of things I used to feel okay about just irritate me now. Mostly my brain. My damaged brain. Running ragged as the Camaro's engine too many days, these days. The Swiss doctors warned me that could happen, that there could be deterioration.

Should get a new one.

But no trade-in value on either. They're junkers only.

Cruising down York Road in moderate traffic. Nothing but garbage on the radio, static in my head. Do I feel one fucking thing that isn't physical? Am I alive emotionally, or just going through the motions? Basic inventory: Hate? Oh yeah, plenty. Love? No, just lust really. Well-being? Maybe sometimes in the old days with the team, in the old days with Gunny and Momma, sometimes with IB and Mary Jo, sometimes with Annie. But I always feel like I'm taking and never giving anything back. Joy? Only if you can call the rush of rattling some dude's bones on full-auto that. And you can't call it that and be sane.

Fucking Sundays.

//

The front desk's manned, there's a couple of uniforms lounging around in the back, joking with a couple of plainclothes cops. They stop laughing when they see me. I nod and pass through to the detectives' area. One guy's in the Homicide squad room, there's nobody in Sex Crimes, and Narcotics is empty.

I pad in and know instantly that's wrong. No lights on anywhere, but I think I hear the soft tapping of a computer keyboard coming from somewhere among the warren of cubicles. I can't see any heads above the partitions, nobody's murmuring into a phone. Just a little tapping. It stops. Maybe just imagination. But there's a presence I feel. Then I hear the hushed whirr of a laser printer.

I check the room fast but quiet, cubicle by cubicle: Taggert You Fuck's, empty; Gus the Greek's, empty; little Petey K.'s, empty; Bimbo the weight freak's, empty; Tommy Weinberg's, empty; IB's, empty.

Mine.

I see the back of a head swiveling between my Mac screen and the HP laser printer. I see my drug dealer profiles coming page by page out of the printer.

"Interesting way to spend a Sunday, Annie," I say. If I've startled her, she's not giving anything away.

"Hey, Luther," she says, not turning. "Just looking for some possible correlations here with the reservoir girl."

Christ. She's wearing lime-green capri pants. Do they really sense the buttons and push 'em on us when they feel like it? Women, I mean? Too uncanny to dwell on.

"So how'd you get past my security? Password and all," I say.

Now she turns and smiles innocently. "Why, I'm a policewoman. But any half-ass hacker can crack a password. Your file system isn't even coded. No ice around your stuff. No problem."

"Problem one, I don't really expect anyone to come sneaking around my data. Problem two is I don't really *appreciate* it."

"Hey, sorry. I needed a look. I needed to see if any of your dealers might have connections with the drugs that blanked the reservoir girl. Hoping for matches, hoping to show her some mugshots. Maybe jolt her, fill in that memory hole."

"I'd have shown you all I got, Annie. You only had to ask."

"Was going to, the other night when I phoned you late. But you were . . . occupied?" She laughs.

I don't say a word.

"And I was in a hurry. Couldn't wait around all weekend," she says. "So who's the student of the month? That Cate kid again?"

"Cate graduated June before last. It's Helen. Met her last fall. You've heard me speak of her. She's just back from summer vacation, starting her senior year."

"Well, excuse me if I don't keep track of your private pupils. You know, Luther, you skate awfully close to the statutory laws with these kids."

"Helen's twenty. So was Cate when I met her."

"Okay, so you're clear legally. Always puzzles me, though, this thing you have for kids."

"Would you have tolerated being called a kid when you were twenty and earning your degrees?"

"No, not then. I'd have been pissed, claimed I was a woman, not a girl, and if I wanted to sleep down and sleep old it was nobody's business but mine," Annie says. "Now I'm twenty-eight, though, and I know better. I *was* a kid back then. A pretty foolish one at times, too. I got taken advantage of more than once."

"Sleep down, Annie?" There's an edge to my voice I don't like but can't control. "Sleep down and old?"

"I didn't mean it to sound as hard as it does. But ten years is a lot when you're nineteen or twenty. And I never notice any of your students inviting you home to meet Mom and Dad. They're having their delicious little adventure, their faintly illicit fling. Then they graduate and go back to their real world and you never hear from them again. You never do, do you?"

"That's just the way I want it. No fuss, no mess."

"And no future. Ever think of the future, Luther? With a woman? Maybe live together, have some babies, build a real life?"

"No." Might learn how with you, though, I think.

"Gotcha."

"No, I got you, Annie. Nobody serious since I've known you. No hint of any urges for a union with some guy, maybe having some babies, building a real life. If that's what you mean by 'real.' "

"Career, Luther," she says. That slightly crooked smile again. "Still comes first for a while. Then we'll see. But you don't even have that excuse. I hear Dugal wants to make you detective sergeant, help you start climbing the ladder. You turn him down, refuse to take the exam."

"I like things just as they are. I'm content with my lot."

Annie laughs. "No way, Luther. You haven't had a content day since you lost the army. I *know* you, pal."

"Big mistake, being that sure you understand someone."

"Could be, except that it doesn't matter if I'm wrong in this case, because I'd damned well prefer to be wrong. I care about you, Five-O."

"There it is. Annie goes all slippery and obtuse on me again."

"Ever hear of anomie?"

"No."

"It's a psych term. You got it bad. You got it early and you kept it. Made you a good soldier, makes you a good cop. But it'll ruin you for living, if you don't bust out of it."

"Explain, professor."

"Gotta split now. Maybe tomorrow night at Flannery's? Unless

Cate or Helen or whoever's already booked you?" Annie says, gathering up fifty or sixty sheets of printout, tapping them into a neat stack. She stands up. She's as tall as me, she looks terrific with no makeup, fetching in her jersey T and those capris. "Catch me tomorrow," she says and walks away.

"Have to be Tuesday," I call after her.

"Okay," I hear as she just keeps walking. "Get that semester off to a fast start, Luther."

It isn't 'til she's almost out of the squad room that I click on what's gone down. Clever bitch diverted me and walked off with all my files, never gave up the drugs they found in the reservoir girl. Way she is, I think. Gotta love her for it.

Bright idea then.

"Get your butt back here, Annie," I call. "You owe me."

I slip into IB's cubicle and turn on the Mac, wait for the password rectangle to appear. When it does, I type in Ice Box. "Invalid password," the Mac admonishes me. "Try again." The synthetic girl's voice is chilling, gives me the creeps. Too cheerful and too unhuman at the same time. I type in IB; invalid. I try refrigerator; invalid.

"You're not putting yourself in IB's head," Annie says, peering over the partition. "Try, uhhmm, 'chill.' "

I type in "chill," and the screen opens up. I see a folder labeled CONTACTS and double-click on it. A page opens up with a long list, seems to be mostly nicknames. I scroll down. There it is: Vaseline. This is a shitty thing to do to IB, I know. But I can't wait on him. I scribble down the cell number on a pad and move to shut down the machine.

"Don't," Annie admonishes me. "If you do, when IB turns it on it'll open just where you are now. Backtrack, closing each file, then click on SHUT DOWN, under the SPECIAL menu at the top."

I do it.

"I'm not even asking why you're breaking into IB's stuff," Annie says.

"Just needed something and he's not here . . . like I wasn't here a few minutes ago."

"No see, no hear. It's unethical and unconscionable, what you just did." She laughs. "If you tell me any more, I'll be an accessory. So shut up."

//

I get on my Mac, call up the dictionary. Check Annie's word, then go to the Web, checking psychology sites. The search engine's a literal-minded bastard, almost useless. But at last I get an article that looks right. I read it but don't print it.

Then I get a truly whacked notion.

I call Helen, leave a message on her machine that if she can get out, I'll be home around ten-thirty. I leave the station, start driving, pick up a six-pack of Grolsch at a convenience store, and head around the Beltway to Jones Falls Expressway, into the city.

Federal Hill's this old neighborhood with wonderful views of the harbor. First it turned into a gross fucking slum, then it got so bad even the dealers and hookers and the die-hard squatters fled. Then, years ago, the first cohort of baby-boom yuppies started urban homesteading. It worked. Some got fed up halfway through—we're talking gutting the places down to the bare brick walls and redoing everything—and sold out. Annie got hers about three-quarters done and planned to do the last quarter herself, since she was mortgaged up to the eyeballs. That was four years ago or so. She's still got an eighth to go. She works on the place every free moment she has.

So I'm not surprised when she answers the doorbell in an athletic bra and cut-off overalls, plaster splashed all over her. She's got a bandana wrapped around her head, like some babushka. I hand her the six-pack and she unhinges the ceramic top of a bottle, guzzles, then takes the pack and puts it in the fridge. There's a drop cloth on the parlor floor, a tall wooden ladder 'cause the ceiling must be fourteen feet high, and trowel marks in fresh plaster on the ceiling.

"Gotta smooth those out before they dry," she says, climbing up the ladder with a bottle of beer in one hand and a trowel in the other. "So," she says, taking a pretty smooth stroke across the plaster, "thanks for the beer. I needed one. Why'd you bother coming all this way, though, unless you want to rant at me for breaking into your computer?"

"Hey Annie, get fucked, you computer thief," I say.

"That's it?"

"I ranted, didn't I?" It feels awkward, craning your neck to talk to someone eight or ten feet above you. Her skin, and I can see a lot more of it than I ever have before, is shining with sweat.

"You call that a rant?" She laughs. "Shit. Where were you raised? Try something like 'Annie Mason, you're a lowlife bitch, pretending to be my friend and then raping my private stuff. Then having the balls to brush it off as if you had every right to do that. You're a faithless, untrustworthy cunt, and I hope you fall off that ladder and break your fuckin' neck.' That's a decent rant."

"Hey Annie, since you brought up that body part, you know I can see right up the legs of your overalls and you're not wearing any underpants, and how come your pubic hair is a lot darker than the hair on your head?"

She starts giggling, the ladder starts shaking, and she slings a glob of plaster off the trowel down at me. I take the hit on my left foot.

"Sorry 'bout that, Ewing," she says, stepping easily down the ladder, swigging beer as she comes.

"Want a beer? Nah, you don't want a beer," she says when she's down and facing me. "I'll make you some good coffee, right. And then you tell me why you came?"

"Deal."

"So I can assume we're still on friendly terms?" she says as I follow her through the huge, rambling house to the kitchen. Late-afternoon sun is slanting through crisp gingham curtains on the windows there. I sit at a red lacquered table that fits into a nook in the window bay. She grinds some beans, starts some water boiling, takes cream out of the fridge and puts it before me, with a mug. A sugar bowl's already sitting on the table.

"What are you doing Labor Day weekend?" I ask when the coffee's in front of me and I've taken a few sips.

"Working here, I guess. Damn if I'm going down to Pompano to see my parents."

"Want to come with me to Virginia and meet mine?"

It's the first thing I've ever said that stops Annie cold. She looks at the sweat beading on her green glass beer bottle for a beat too long, then puts her famous scan on my eyes.

"What's this all about, Luther?" she asks at last.

"Maybe anomie. I looked it up. Not too pretty. Thinking maybe you'll see something, notice something. Point it out to me."

"Christ, you're putting me in a very odd place with this."

I just keep meeting her gaze.

"Luther, I'm not a therapist."

"I know. Don't want one. Not yet, anyway."

"So what do you want?"

"Gotta tell you, my father's refused to see me for a bunch of years. I did something he hated. So I want a friend at my side. A little backup if I need it."

Annie reaches across the table and lays a plaster-crusted hand on top of one of mine. No scan now.

"Yeah," she says quickly. "I can do that."

//

I drop my dime, using the cell, stuck in the traffic crawl on York Road on the way home. The number has a 39 prefix. Italy? Those worldwide cells can have a home number anywhere, so why not Italy? After four rings, I hear it click on.

Absolute silence.

"Vassily," I say.

"A mistake, I think. Who is speaking, please?" I don't recognize the voice.

"Tell Vassily it's Shooter."

"Yes, wrong number you have. Goodbye."

"Tell Vassily it's Shooter," I say, harder and in Russian. "Tell Vassily Café de la Paix on Suleiman Boulevard. Shooter and Mikla."

"Give your number."

I recite my apartment phone. The connection's broken almost as soon as the last digit's spoken.

When I pull up in front of my apartment, there's a lime-green Bug already parked there, front door open and a pair of long legs stretched out. Those gangbanger shorts.

"They were such a hit last time, thought I'd wear them again," Helen says as we go inside. "Your table ready?"

It isn't. I never bothered to move the cardboard and plastic containers coated with the remnants of our Thai dinner.

"Ewing, you're a pig," Helen says when she sees the mess.

But I just flick off the lights, pop an old tape—*Nirvana Unplugged*—into the Sony, lead her into the bedroom, and duplicate the table trick on the bed. She doesn't seem to mind at all.

Afterward, she just wants to lie on her side with me pressed up against her from behind. Fitting like two spoons in a drawer. It's pleasant, peaceful. Soon I drift off.

I see she's awake when I come jumping out of sleep on the first ring of my phone about three A.M.

"What?"

"Maybe you go to pay phone, lots of quarters, you call 718-555-8912, Shooter."

"Fucking now? You're crazy."

"The number's 718-555-8912."

The phone goes dead.

Helen doesn't say a thing. She stirs, pretends to go back to sleep. I pretend too. I repeat that number over and over until I'm sure it's engraved nice and deep in my head. Then lots of other thoughts start sprinting around, and a few bad images too, only they run in slow motion. Like sitting with Mikla at the Café de la Paix in Sarajevo and seeing Vassily come walking by with his men, smelling the powder and blood about him when he sits down to join us and orders a brandy, even though it's just past dawn. It's a long couple of hours before Helen feels she can decently slip out of bed, brew up some coffee and come back with two cups of it. She kisses me hard.

"'Tis the lark, love," she says. "I must away. Got an eight o'clock today."

//

I'm jittery. I take my morning tab plus a couple of Ativans to make it easier not to start moving on the day too fast. I take a long, long shower. I force myself to dress slowly, slowly strap on my guns, slowly check around the house to make sure I haven't left a stove burner on or the coffee machine either. I don't leave. Can't use a pay phone; the only ones around are in plazas and malls that aren't open yet. Fuck, I gave out my home phone in the first place anyway. So, I decide, I'll call from home. That area code, 718. Brooklyn?

"Very smooth, my friend, your call," I say in English when there's a pickup and silence. "Fucking middle of the night. I don't keep those kinds of hours anymore. Scared the hell out of my girlfriend and almost put me in cardiac arrest."

"Ah, Shooter." A voice laughs. It *is* Vassily, it's the laugh I recognize, not the voice. "Only way your heart stop is if someone puts bullet in your head. Me, mine almost stopped when this guy calls himself Shooter phones me sometime. I'm thinking you never made it out of that hospital they fly you to."

"Made it out, made it home. Now I'm making some things happen."

"What things? Things like some man with a farm I meet?"

"You been giving out your number to lots of slobs and lowlifes. I got some racehorses now. I hear you like horses."

"For sure. And some other things too. We got to see each other, I think. Telephones I hate."

"Me to you, or you to me?"

"Maybe you like to visit New York? Think about it. I call you back, a few days maybe."

"Great, but listen, you fuck," I say. "My office hours end at eleven P.M."

"Okay, okay," Vassily laughs. "Soft life you are living. I don't call middle of the night."

"Good," I say.

"Better idea I have. Thursday I am in Baltimore. You buy me dinner, da?"

"Sure. You know Hausner's?"

"Very famous old seafood place, correct?"

"Say eight o'clock."

"*Da. Da.* I find the place, I find you there, Shooter," Vassily says and hangs up.

I check my tape. It's fine. I make a copy on my sound system deck, put the original in my lockbox, pocket the copy. Then I check my apartment again, pat my wallet pocket and my guns like an obsessive-compulsive, and leave for work. Calmer now. It's always first contact that jukes me. Once the action starts I'm the iceman.

The action's started. But nobody knows that yet except me. I make the right moves, nobody's ever going to know anything. Even when I finish it.

6

The Camaro takes a mortal hit and goes down hard on York Road about halfway to HQ Monday morning. There's a sharp whang, a dull whump like a mortar going off, and I just manage to get the car into a mall parking lot, crawling on six of its eight cylinders, before the remaining six lock up too. KIA.

I take a bus the rest of the way to work. I'm not pissed or irritated or depressed at all, which sort of surprises me. In fact, I feel a little excited.

It's a nothing morning. I start typing up my conversation with Mr. Halliday for the file. The room fills, the usual bitchin' and moanin' that passes for greetings on Monday. It's a while before I notice the absence of Ice Box. Have about ten seconds of bad thoughts and reach for the phone when I remember he and MJ are down the Ocean—that's how "Bawlmer" people say it—taking the week before the Labor Day holiday for beach-time at Rehobeth. Means I'm solo 'til Friday night, then off for the long weekend in Virginia. Maybe. With Annie. Maybe.

Takes me two cups of coffee and a tab before I can start dialing the Virginia number. Haven't seen Gunny or Momma since I went overseas again in '94. Gunny'd reamed me out about what I was doing then, said if I did it don't ever think about coming home after. Went anyway, naturally, did a good job for maybe ten months, and then my little bonus pack turned out to be ten months in a Swiss hospital. I left with that dent in my skull and a need for those tabs. Since then, a few calls and letters from Momma. Not a word from Gunny. The man always had truly meant whatever he said, I guess.

I feel chickenshit when I notice my pulse speed up with every ring. I'm in luck. Momma answers, starts crying when she hears my voice, manages to tell me Gunny's out fishing.

I say, "Momma, I'd like to come on home Labor Day. Bring a friend. We can stay at a motel and meet somewhere, if Gunny won't have me in the house."

No more tears. "That Gunny, you not worry, comprendez?" Still got the Viet accent, still loving her French. "My house, too. You will stay here."

"Am I gonna have to get physical with Gunny?"

"Hah! I take care of this man. He be *un petit chien,* tail between his legs. He won't say, too much pride, but he is missing you almost so much as me, Luther. I catch him some nights, drinking whiskey, looking at my box of photos of you. You come. No damn motel. My house. You don't worry for your papa, n'est-ce pas?"

"Okay, Mom. See you maybe nine or ten Friday night?"

She's crying a little when she says goodbye.

I lean way back in my chair, feeling lighter than I have in a long, long time. No illusions. I know Gunny and I are gonna go at it. Maybe, when we've exhausted each other, he'll bear-hug me and lift me right off the ground, the way he used to. Maybe he'll listen, actually hear me when I tell him why I did it, actually understand.

It could happen. It could.

Car. Fuck. Annie'd drive, but I don't want that and I need wheels anyway. I unlock one of my file cabinets, take a small gray steel lockbox out of the bottom space, put it on my desk.

Not a lot in it. My honorable discharge, my medals, my old Virginia state trooper badge and ID, receipts for my guns with serial numbers, title to the Camaro, a little slip of paper with a thirteen-digit number on it but no hint it's for an account at a Lichtenstein bank where my blood money sits. And my local checking and savings account statements. I take out those.

I see I've got $55,289 and change in my Equitable Trust money market fund, and $11,015 in my Equitable checking account. Most of it's pretty old money. I never spent much when I was in the army, saved all my combat pay and a good portion of my regular salary. Saved a bit as a trooper, too, and operate now always at a surplus. Pay off credit cards bills in full each month. Don't owe anybody anything.

I take a neat titanium calculator, parting gift from Cate, out of its leather case. Multiply my weekly take-home pay by four, add up my fixed monthly expenses. Shit, I could afford $400 to $500 a month payments on a car and still have more walking-around money than I'm likely to spend. Good to fuckin' go, Luther.

Lunchtime, I go over to an Equitable branch and get a bank check for ten grand.

After lunch, I get a call from Mr. Halliday. They want to come in, talk it over. I tell him what I've got to do now is give his number to my chief and the DA. They'll call him, arrange a meeting, work the deal. I remind him to bring his lawyer to any meeting. The man actually thanks me. Solid citizen. I had the feeling.

I call Dugal, fill him in.

"This surprises me very much," he says. "You sure you didn't promise anything we can't deliver. Or use a little pressure?"

"Yup. I even reminded him to check everything I said with his lawyer. And to make sure the lawyer's part of the talks with you and the DA. All you got to do is call the man, LT, have the meeting. This is going to fly. Then I'm gonna take that kid and nail the fuck. And when I nail him, he's gonna give up his boss. We're gonna go all the way up on this one, LT."

"You're sounding overexcited, Luther. You're using the personal pronoun too emphatically. Don't leave me thinking I have to remind you we're going to work this—if we get something to work—as a team."

"Sorry, LT. I'm just revved. You know I'm a team player."

"So far, Luther, that's true," Dugal says mildly. "I do get alarmed, though, when I hear a lot of 'I's."

"Hey, LT, I'm thinking the usual way. You and the DA cut the deal, then you and me and Ice Box make the plan, the Halliday kid arranges the meet, we all converge and nail this fuck."

"Right. We *all* converge and pop him. Clean, solid, hard evidence, airtight bust."

"We'll make it happen, LT."

"Great. But Luther, do me a big favor? Stop using those Gulf War clichés, won't you? They date you. And they get on my balls."

"I'll make it happen. Sir!" I say. Dugal laughs and hangs up.

//

I E-mail the Halliday file and notes on the deal and my conversation with Dugal to Ice Box, so he'll be up to date soon as he gets back from vacation. Then I figure I've done a day's work and slip out, even though it's only three. I catch a bus toward Cockeysville.

Out past the old Timonium Fair Grounds, with its hog sheds and cattle barns for the annual state fair, and its racetrack for thoroughbreds, there's all kinds of auto dealerships tucked in among the malls. Subaru, Ford–Lincoln–Mercury, Chevy, Volkswagen, Saab and Volvo, Acura and Lexus. I'm thinking go inexpensive. I'm no kid, I'm not going to get more dates 'cause I'm driving overpriced wheels. Maybe something low mileage, just in off a two-year lease and still under warranty. Then I'm thinking, would I buy a Ruger instead of an HK to save some bucks? Never mind that in that analogy there are serious professional reasons to prefer the HK. I get off the bus where there's an Audi dealership on one side of York and a BMW facing it on the other side.

I wander into the BMW showroom, clownish in baggy shirt and khakis again, hair in a ponytail. Salesmen look up briefly from their desks and then get real busy with bogus paperwork. Fuck 'em.

I walk into the Audi dealership, pretty much the same reaction from the salesmen. But then I see it: a two-seat TT, hardtop, Audi silver with slick black leather interior. A real unique shape, businesslike, no doo-dahs, super-clean lines. This thing's gotta be way out of my league, I think. I look at the sticker, expecting $60 or $70K. Surprise: $33,980. Comfortable number of thousands below my annual salary. With the ten grand in my pocket as a downpayment, how much could monthly payments be?

A salesman comes over. "Like it?" he asks. "It's a rocket."

"I'm gonna buy this one right here, the silver one, today," I say. I see greed in his eyes.

"That's the price, there on the window?" I ask. I've never bought a new car before. Thirty years old and never bought a car from a dealer. But I'm not as dumb as I'm acting.

"Sticker only," he says, getting into gear. "We can work with you on it, naturally."

I pull out my bank check, show it to him. "This down, you finance."

"Yessir. Got some very attractive rates, especially on a thirty-six-monther."

"Ballpark on the payments?"

"Well, come on over to my desk, we'll do some math," he says. "That one is really loaded, just came in this week. There's not a lot of them on the road. Production's pretty limited, we even got waiting lists for buyers who want particular colors and options. Hey, let's take it for a drive first?"

"Nah, let's talk money first," I say. I know I'm gonna pay more than I have to, but I don't give a damn.

"Okay. Now, I'll have to clear this with my manager, but I think I can let it go for about $850 off the sticker, say $33,100 to keep the numbers round. Ten K down, that leaves $23,100 at thirty-six months, five and a half percent if we finance." He uses a pencil to punch buttons on his calculator. "I'm getting monthly payments of about $600."

"I don't like that. Say I put another ten down. What then?"

"Ah, let me see, now we're looking at $460 over thirty-six."

"Close."

"But no cigar? C'mon, let's drive it. The TT'll rock you."

I pull out onto York Road, run up fast through all five gears until we hit 100. The salesman starts sweating. "Listen sir, you gotta slow down. I mean this is trouble, it's illegal, it's fucking dangerous."

"No sweat. I'm a cop," I say, fishtailing off onto a side road that runs around and behind the fairgrounds, just gliding through the loops and the curves. The gear shift and clutch are smooth and flawless as the trigger and action on my HK, the little TT seems to love the road. I'm in love. I gear down, get back onto York, and pull into the dealership like a little old lady.

The salesman's shook up. I show him my badge and photo ID. "I want the car."

"Gotta talk to the manager." He disappears into an office. A few minutes later he pokes his head out and beckons me over. "This is Sam Limbaugh, our sales manager, Mr. . . . ?"

"Detective Ewing, Luther Ewing, BCPD. How ya doing?" I shake Limbaugh's hand. He grins. "Like that little baby, do you, Detective? Gave it a pretty good workout?"

"Yup."

"Numbers Pete here gave me sound doable. Gotta run a credit check, of course you understand that, Detective? So I need some ID, your social security number, your bank, your employer. No problems?"

"None," I say. I give him what's needed.

"If you wouldn't mind stepping out for a moment and letting Pete show you all the features of the TT . . ."

Limbaugh comes over about ten minutes later. "We got a deal, Detective. All you have to do is sign a few papers. Leave us the check, but you'll need a certified check for $13,250 tomorrow. That extra three grand is tax, title and tag fees. You come by at 6 P.M. with that, sign the loan agreement and you drive away. We'll have it all cleaned up, temp tags on, everything ready to go."

Shit. I'd forgotten about taxes and stuff. The hell with it. I'm doing it.

//

Back in my apartment, I take off the HK and the SIG. No Helen tonight. So I put two Stouffer's meatloaf dinners into the microwave, let the molecules collide as long as the package says they have to. Meanwhile I get a John Lee Hooker CD going, pick up the Dave Robicheaux mystery I've been reading and put it on the table. When the microwave buzzes, I peel off the plastic wrap, burning my fingers a bit. I pour a glass of Coke. Then I dump both meatloaf dinners onto one Ikea plate, sprinkle garlic salt all over everything and begin to eat.

Then I think about what kind of dinner I'll be having Thursday. I push the food away.

The phone rings. "What?" I say.

"Robbed your files for nothing." It's Annie. "Toxicology found just two things in the girl's blood—Valium and chloralhydrate. Chloralhydrate's been around forever, it's what they used, I don't know, sixty or eighty years ago to dope somebody in a bar. The old Mickey Finn, they called it. You slip some drops into somebody's drink, he passes out, the bad guys drag him out into an alley and steal everything he's got. He wakes up a few hours later and can't remember a thing."

"So it's none of my guys then," I say.

"Probably not. I was thinking some brand-new designer drug,

hard to come by, which would limit the field to medical people, pharmaceutical people. Or much more likely, one of your dealers. But any housewife in the county can find a doc who'll write a script for Valium. And chloralhydrate's even easier. It's prescription, but not a four-parter, not a controlled substance. No way to track down buyers of that."

"So a dead end?"

"Yeah, dead end."

7

When I hit the squad room next morning—late—Tommy and Gus are juked up and jamming.

"It's double-bonus time now," Tommy says, grinning. Turns out last night they popped a young Ecstasy merchant they'd been watching for a week or so outside the Cineplex at Dulaney Mall. Not a huge haul, maybe twenty-five Ziplocs in his backpack. Two pills, as usual, but two glassines of smack, four good lines.

"The asshole'd been sampling his own wares," Gus says, laughing. "A line was missing from one Ziploc. Just one line and the punk's practically asleep on his feet. I don't think he even realized we cuffed him, put him in the car and brought him here. He couldn't get a coherent word out for at least an hour. And when he could he didn't know where the fuck he was."

"You should've seen the look on his face when it dawned on him, Luther," Tommy rattles. "It was like, Say what? I'm sitting here with *cops*! I'm busted! How the fuck did that happen?"

"Complete moron," Gus says. "Naturally he spills his guts."

"And?" I ask.

"Same old same old," Tommy says. "Some guy he met at a club. Can't remember what he looked like, only ordinary, real short hair. Gave him an Ecstasy tab, though. Talked a little biz. They meet two nights later, he gives him five hundred dollars and he gives him the twenty-five Ziplocs. Claims he never got the chance to sell even one before we popped him. Said since he paid twenty dollars a bag, he was figuring on retailing at fifty dollars.

"'But hey,' he goes, 'I never sold one. So like, how come I'm busted?'" Gus says. "Tells us we can go ahead and count 'em and we'll see all twenty-five are there. Said he was sorry he snorted that one line and he wasn't going to get into trouble or anything for that, was he?"

"Dumbest fuck yet," Tommy says, shaking his head in disbelief.

They walk away laughing way too loud.

I'm thinking we've got someone very savvy out there. Very smart, good business plan. Introduce new product to your consumers a taste at a time. Totally nonscary—hey, you can't get addicted from snorting a couple of lines every now and then. The kids get comfortable with it. Then add a couple more lines. Hey, this is cool. We can handle this, no problem. Big problem. 'Cause they get used to it, they imagine they're handling it, and then a day or two goes by and they can't get any and they find out they *need* it. Pretty soon they need it bad. Pretty soon they'll do anything to get it.

Don't want to think about that, so I stop.

The room starts to empty out around lunchtime. I remember I need that check today for the TT, so I run over to the bank, get it, pick up a ham and swiss on rye at the deli and come back to the squad room. It's empty. I go back to my own cubicle. Annie settles into the other chair there. She's looking sleek and groomed, but not at all pleased with herself.

"Could be another dead end," she says. "The girl's parents are giving me grief about talking to her again."

"Tell 'em we're issuing a press release otherwise."

"I did. They're going to get back to me, but the tone's changed. I'm not sure they'll cave. Ah, I don't know, Luther. I feel like I've got to get this bastard quick. I think maybe I've got to stay on it. No weekend in Virginia."

"Listen, Annie. You know very well you're not going to nail anyone in the next three days. You've got your team on the case, they know their business or they wouldn't still be on your team, right?"

"Yeah, but I feel I need to be here."

"When's the last time you had a vacation?"

"Um, last March, I think. I took a week."

"Where'd you go?"

"Well, nowhere actually. I worked on my house."

"Give your brain a break. You need a little distance maybe. Maybe pieces'll come together when you're not so consciously concentrated on making them come together. Meanwhile, you've got your people out doing all the scut work, trying to find witnesses, checking the car angle, all that."

"Yeah, but I feel—"

"Friday around six, unless you get a sudden breakthrough, you drive down to Virginia with me. Just like we planned. Anything happens over the weekend, your people can reach you and we'll be back here in three hours. Okay?"

"Ah Luther, I don't know."

"C'mon Annie. I'm right about this."

"Maybe you are. Let's see what happens in the next few days."

"Good enough."

"I'll try to make it happen." Annie smiles. It's low on the scale of her range of smiles.

"Do me a favor? Drop the Gulf War clichés you learned from me." I grin. "They date you."

//

I'm at the Audi dealership at six. The car looks like a dream. Limbaugh's beaming when I've signed the last of the forms, hands me the keys like they're the keys to heaven. The man must believe in his product. "Let 'er rip, Detective. Drive her hard, she wants it that way. But don't forget the scheduled maintenance. That's very, very important."

I'm as smooth as I've been in a long, long time when I pull out of the dealership. The TT feels good, it smells good, it sounds good, it moves good. I spend the next four hours driving around, just cruising past spots where we know some dealing goes down, checking out the malls, watching the young girls leaving stores and cinemas. Then I take it out on the expressway and push it up to 125, just touching that for a moment, than easing back down to the speed limit.

I feel like I want to take the TT into the apartment with me, park it right in the main room and just stare at it. But I lock it up, go in alone and go to bed. Sleep's a while coming; my legs are still, but I can feel them moving clutch and accelerator pedal. It's some time before I realize my mind's been blanked, not a thought about Bonus Packs, Russians, the Reservoir girl, even my Alpha homies in Iraq. I just forgot the fucking world for at least fifteen minutes. For the first time in years.

Over a goddamn car. I pay for that when it all floods back, hours of images moving on fast-forward into one long stream, images tough enough to bear when they only come one at a time. Then, finally, a freeze-frame that kills any chance I had for sleep: Vassily's face, eyes fixed on mine.

8

Hausner's: hi-rez. Tang of Old Bay seasoning filling my nostrils, sharp crack of crab claws and shells bursting loud and distinct out of the low rumble of talk and laughter. The wood of the tables and chairs has been waxed and rewaxed for so many years it looks black. On the walls are old but almost grainless and glowing photographs of fleets of Chesapeake skipjacks under sail dredging for oysters, Bay watermen tonging from skiffs or hauling in wood-and-wire pots full of blue channel crabs, armadas of log canoes heeling hard during a race. A lost world. I get lost in it for a minute. Slack. I go to superscan, checking every face, hearing every sound, totally alert to movement, to comings and goings.

Not alert enough. Strong, thick-fingered hands seize my head before I sense the presence behind me, pull it back almost as far as my neck will bend. I feel my hand moving for the HK, just manage to freeze the reflex. The fingers are probing all around my skull. One finds the dent. Almost strokes it for a moment. Then the hands are gone. Somebody's laughing.

"Shooter! A lot you changed, these years. I don't recognize you." I turn and see Vassily beaming down at me. He's wearing a navy linen suit, hair's cropped so close it's just a white-blond stubble, face round as round can be except that his cheeks are bulging 'cause he's grinning so broadly. "But hole in the head, I know it's you. So, they put a plate in there, yes? You more crazy now than then?"

"Guess about as crazy as you." I stand up. "You scared the shit out of me just now."

"Oh sure, I see how you tremble." He chuckles. "Very frightened man." He seizes my head again and plants a big kiss on the top. No trick, since he's about 6′6″. Then the big Russian hug, meaty arms almost cracking my ribs. "Thin like a bird. Nobody would believe little guy like you could do some things I see with my own eyes. Nobody!"

Then that laugh again. Eyes cold blue like a Siberian husky. And shiny, a little wet. He releases me, rubs his eyes with those huge hands. "Excuse me please, too much emotional. So much time . . ."

"The river flows, Vassily," I say, moving the talk into Russian. He follows my lead.

"Ah, it's like some miracle, our paths crossing again," he says, moving around the table and sitting down. "Never did I think to see you again, my friend. It is too good. Some times we had, no? Remember the night we go up that hill? . . ."

"We did that. In another life."

"Da, da. So no history," Vassily says, eyes dampening again. I feel something close to affection for the man, despite what he was, and probably still is. But then what am I, if not the same? "No history. We drink, we eat, we celebrate new life, okay?

"But fuck God, it's so damn good to see my little brother," he says, waving over one of the waitresses, an aging lady with stiff hair the most unnatural shade of platinum I've seen.

"What'll it be, hon?" she says, smiling at Vassily. There's a little bit of bright red lipstick on one of her front teeth.

"Vodka, you beauty," Vassily roars in English.

"Vodka? You mean like just a straight glass of vodka, hon?"

"I mean bottle, big bottle, very cold." Vassily beams at her.

She lowers her order pad, the little stub of pencil in her right hand bobbing up and down. Then she laughs. "A bottle, hon? Sure thing. You look like a man who can handle a bottle."

When it comes I have to explain to Vassily why I can only have a sip, not match him shot for shot. He looks dismayed. "This is some damn shame," he says, shaking his massive head. "So. I drink for you, my friend. In honor of you!"

He does. He also slurps down three of the four dozen Chincoteagues on the half shell I order. They taste of the clean salt sea. He cracks his way through two of the three dozen steamed crabs, bright red and crusty with Old Bay. He polishes off most of the whole baked rockfish, plus massive portions of cole slaw, potato salad and sliced tomatoes.

"Ah, this I love, Shooter," he says. "This sort of life. No more field rations! Never again! A peaceful life. Food, vodka, plenty of pussy. We earned all this, no?"

"We earned it all right," I say. We're sticking to Russian only. "But what the fuck are you doing here, my friend? How the hell did you ever wind up over here?"

"Ha! Who wouldn't come to best place there is?" Vassily grins. "A simple story. I only stay around that shitty place we were together maybe six months after you left. Then I go back to Moscow, no more military crap for me, and get into some business with friends. But Moscow, hey! It's like your Wild West. Completely crazy. Bribe this official, bribe that one, everything's supposed to be fixed. You relax, maybe even make the mistake of counting your money before it's in your hands. Then out of nowhere some punk kid pops up and tries to shoot you. Always misses. But still, this is insane. I get tired of this pretty fast, although I'm making lot of money. More than I could believe."

"So then?"

"So then, I get in touch with some friends in New York. They tell me there is good business to be done there. Easy business, because they've got rules there. No worries some stupid crazy kid will take a shot at you for no a reason you can think of. I sell off some of my Moscow enterprises. I get on a plane to New York with some capital. Very quickly I find my friends were not lying."

"But the word here is you're interested in horses, Vassily. Not that great a business, I can tell you."

"Just a sideline," he laughs. "I got lot of interests now. First, I got this big nightclub in Brighton Beach. Full of people every night, people with lots of cash. We got food, vodka, dancing girls, the works. The place is making me rich. Horses? That's more like a hobby. But what about you?"

"Not getting rich," I say. "I own some pieces of a few thoroughbreds, they do all right for me. Then I have a couple of sidelines—between you and me, not exactly legal, but pretty safe. I sleep sound. I get by."

"Ah, my friend," Vassily grins. "Maybe we should do a little business together sometime. What I really have first, and big hopes for, is some import–export. Import merchandise, export cash to Caymen Islands banks. That's the idea. So far, great! Maybe I need to help you get rich too."

"Or maybe I'll help you. I retail merchandise around here. How is your retail network?"

"In New York, almost perfect. Here, not too bad so far. This is pretty new market for us. Not even six months down here."

Shit, I think. He's the one.

"I like to start cautiously. Too small just yet for you, I guess. But if things go well, who knows?"

"I'll be here. I'm interested in building my business cautiously too. And peacefully."

"You think I want any problem when life is so sweet? So. You let me know if you hear of any good opportunities with horses. I let you know when I get something going we can do together. Any interest in pharmaceuticals? Could be big. Very big, I think."

"Seems we're thinking very much alike. My sense too that there are great growth possibilities," I say.

Vassily grins, cocks his head. We're both probing, and we both know it. We know this isn't the time or place to take it any further. So we slide into reminiscence, over coffee, about the old days, remember a few mutual friends who never made it out. Vassily kills the bottle of vodka with a toast to them. And he almost rips the check, grabbing it from me, pays in cash and leaves a $100 bill for a tip.

Outside, in the humid air of a Baltimore night, another kiss on the head and a rib-cracker of a hug before he slips into a big Mercedes that I figure must have been waiting outside the whole time. I glimpse a heavy in the back seat. The driver looks like a heavy too.

"Shooter, you I love. Let's do some things together soon. Okay, little brother?" Vassily calls. I wave. Then his window glides silently closed and the Merc pulls away.

Pharmaceuticals my ass, I'm thinking as I drive home. Vassily is our man. The one we have to take down. The magnitude of that task hits me hard.

//

"Love ya to pieces and all that, Luther, but no way I'm taking a felony fall with you," Annie says in the parking lot outside HQ Friday night. "You steal this off the street, or put a gun to a drug dealer's head and make a little offer—he gives you the car, and you let him slide by not planting a half-kilo bag of smack in there and then busting him for it?"

She's got her old leather Gladstone hanging from her shoulder, her head's cocked to one side, and she takes a long step back as I slip in the key, pop the TT's trunk, and reach for the bag to cram it in.

"Hey, the car's mine," I say. "Bought it a couple of days ago. The Camaro died."

"You *bought* this? This midlife crisis toy? You went into debt for this? Aren't you a little young for midlife crisis craziness?"

"Came on early and real sudden. Must be my high-pressure existence. Or an old soul." I grin at her. "What's that they say, 'Live fast, die young, and leave a good-lookin' corpse'?"

"You think I'm buying into that one, think again. I'm not planning on reaching my peak for at least another ten years, and then the decline's gonna be so gradual and graceful nobody'll even notice."

She's laughing when she hands me the Gladstone and then eases her slim self into the TT. When I climb in on the other side, I see her slyly stroking the black leather, checking out the cool instrument panel, sort of form-fitting herself into the seat. "Have to admit, it's a nice piece of work," she says, when I start the engine and she hears the very muted growl as I ease out of the lot and onto the road.

The past three days had yielded zero progress on the Reservoir girl, so Annie kept her promise about the long weekend in Virginia, though I knew she'd have her cell clipped to her belt, or be otherwise within reach twenty-four hours a day. I slip into the heavy traffic on the Beltway toward Annapolis, then break free of it and head down the more lightly traveled Route 301 through Anne Arundel, Prince George's and Charles Counties. I punch the TT up very fast just once south of La Plata. "Oh, I'm digging this," Annie says, doing her version of a twenty-year-old college girl. "I adore speed."

So I ease off and we cruise just above the limits, cross the Potomac over the Governor Nice Memorial Bridge, and head southeast into the Tidewater country of Virginia. I like to make custom tapes, choosing favorite songs from bunches of CDs and putting them together in moods. Nothing sophisticated—a tape of opera arias with easy stuff like that wonderful duet from *Lakmé;* a tape of ballad-rock by guys like Vic Chestnutt, Van Morrison, Mark Knopfler; my great chick tape: the Sineads, O'Conner and Lohan, some Sarah, early Björk, acoustic Chrissie Hynde, Joan Osborne, that girl with the Bosendorfer, Tori Amos. We don't talk much until we're within thirty miles or so of Tyding's Landing, a little town on one of the creeks off the Rappahannock River, where Gunny and Momma have retired.

"So do I need a briefing before we get into the bear pit, Luther? Rules of engagement, preferred behavior, anything like that?" Annie asks.

"Just Annie being Annie, that's all. Get into it as much or as little as you like," I say. "Mom's gonna be great. It's been five years. Gunny? I don't know. He's gonna love you even though you're with me. Me? Well, like I told you, when I went overseas in '94, he said he was through with me for good."

"You maybe want to tell me exactly why that was? Or where the hell it was you went, maybe some hint about what you did?"

"Classified." I laugh, but I don't feel too humorous now. "I could tell you, but then I'd have to kill you."

"Damn, Luther. That's two huge, lame clichés in one breath. Well above your usual quota."

I realize I'm more scared of losing Annie's good opinion than I am even of facing Gunny. How to tell her and not lose that, though? Straight and true, I conclude, after considering how easily she'd see through any bullshit story.

"I'm out of the army, working Virginia State Police, as you know," I start, not real sure if I'll make it all the way. "Guy comes around, 'Mr. Westley' he calls himself. Represents certain parties with an interest in the former Yugoslavia. CIA might as well have been tattoo'd on his forehead."

"He made you an offer?"

"Call it recruitment. This is '94, remember. The Serbs are practicing genocide in Bosnia . . . damn, you know how horrible that shit was. His principals are seeking trained special ops soldiers with combat experience to go to Sarajevo and maybe put some big hurt on the Serbs. Political angle I see right away—the Bosnian Muslims have already got Afghani mujahedeen helping 'em out. They're getting Saudi money for arms. Time for the West to weigh in. Nobody wants a radical Muslim state in the Balkans if Bosnia hangs on and survives."

"So you go mercenary? That it? That's what turned your father against you?"

"He hated what was happening there. He wanted the fucking First Marine Division, maybe with support from the 82nd Airborne, to go in and kick Serb ass. Refused to understand why that was never gonna happen."

"But he's got something against mercs, even when they're doing what he wants regular U.S. troops to do?"

"Something like that. Soldierly code of honor thing."

"I'm going to be real interested to hear his views about that," Annie says. "Going to try real hard to follow the logic. If there is any."

I don't say anything, I'm just listening to the TT purring, feeling the car in perfect synchronicity with the road. Damn dark on this two-laner, maybe a gas station or a convenience store every five or six miles, otherwise hemmed in by forest and marsh.

"Care to say what you did in Sarajevo?" Annie asks.

Oh, Christ. Oh fuck. Guess I have to go all the way with it, now that I've gone as far as I have.

"Shot eighty-four Serb soldiers," I say softly. "Confirmed kills anyway. Could've been quite a few more. I was a sniper. It was my job. Then a Serb sniped me. In the head."

"Jesus," Annie hisses. I can't tell if she's revolted, appalled at me or just freaked by the whole story.

Presently I'm off the two-lane blacktop and the TT's crunching over a long, twisty driveway of crushed oyster shells. No stars, no moon, nothing ahead in the halogen high beams but loblolly pines, oaks and tulip poplar forest. Then there's a white clapboard house, lights on in a few windows upstairs and down, and the black sheen of water behind it giving back a wavery version of the place. When I stop the car and Annie and I get out, I can scarcely hear the front door open and Momma calling to me for the riot of tree frogs. Mom comes up and hugs me hard, nods repeatedly as I introduce Annie, greets her with air kisses near both cheeks, French style. Then we're into that house. "Your father," Momma says, "one full bottle of Jack Daniels he drink, waiting. You know what that means, Luther."

I do. Annie doesn't but stays cool. Momma leads us toward the kitchen, where I can see a dozen or more plates of Vietnamese delicacies she's spent all day preparing, no easy feat considering the necessary ingredients are rare commodities in the Tidewater.

I lag behind. I hear Gunny's voice rumbling and rolling out of the little room off the living room he calls an office, but that's more a personal museum, archive and library. It was in that room I received my banishment. Two of the walls are covered with photos, frame jammed to frame, from every stage and every tour of his thirty-year marine career. Homemade floor-to-ceiling pine bookshelves on the other two walls sag under the weight of nearly everything ever written that's worth reading on war, from Sun T'zu, Clausewitz and Moltke the Elder to the great modern military historian John Keegan's books, and even *A Bright Shining Lie.* The number of common foot soldiers like Gunny who're serious scholars of their trade would amaze most civilians.

"Throughout history," he's rolling on, "the profession of arms has been an honorable and honored one. The professional soldier has sacrificied the ease and luxuries of civil life to protect and defend that very life, that very society."

Jesus, he's a preacher tonight, for sure.

"I speak only of the professional man of arms, naturally. I do not include irregulars, partisans, conditierri, mercenaries, all nothing more than assassins. Under pressure from the ruling national bodies, the professional military has frequently stooped, to its discredit, to make use of such bandits as auxiliaries. Or in cases such as the later Roman Empire and the Venetian Republic, because the civil populace had grown too effete to look to their own defense and preferred to hire protection. Always, the results were disastrous. The brotherhood of arms . . ."

Lecturing the fucking walls, fluency enhanced by that fifth of Black Jack. Discoursing on soldiering in ways he never could as a soldier. What jarhead marine would have a clue what he was saying? What officer would expect Gunny to be anything but a man whose basic job was to turn young men into "maggots"—that favorite DI word—and then, their humanity erased, re-create them as trained killers? And when the shit hits, lead them by personal example through the killing grounds?

I feel sorry for him as I go into the kitchen, where Mom is busy quizzing Annie and getting absolutely nowhere since Annie does know a thing or two about interrogation techniques. It goes on as I eat. Still, I can tell Momma is liking her and that Annie is amused by it all.

Gunny's voice is only an almost subsonic drone in the kitchen. When we've finished eating, Momma suggests we turn in early, face Gunny in the morning. She leads us upstairs. Awkward minute: She's only made up my old room. I put Annie in there and go down the end of the hall to a smaller room, where there's nothing but an unmade bed. Momma wants to fuss and fix it up. I convince her all I need is a light blanket and a pillow.

Lights out. Low vocal vibrations from Gunny's office go on, but pretty soon I'm not hearing them anymore. Pretty soon, klicks away from sleep, I'm watching surround-sound, high-definition eyelid movies.

//

Sarajevo. Winter. A new kind of cold for me, somehow *ancient,* malevolent, as if its source is somewhere far off in the Asian steppes of Attila, Genghis, Tamerlane. Buses flipped on their sides, end to end, in largely futile efforts to make safe passages through the fields of fire of the Serb snipers in the hills. Shattered buildings of reinforced concrete, the rusty iron rebar twisted as tentacles. Low-intensity action: the high whistle of a howitzer round coming in, then the pressure wave in your ears from the explosion. Once in a while a sharp crack of a passing bullet, followed by a rifle report far away. Sometimes fifteen or twenty minutes of heavy small arms and mortar crashes, as Bosnian squads and platoons try to drive wedges into Serb positions high up the slopes. The sweet reek and disgusting, cough-syrupy taste of the local plum brandy, raffia or something. A lot of us drink a lot of it every night.

Us is several dozen Americans—ex–Special Forces, ex–Deltas, ex–Marine Recon, ex–Army Airborne, ex–Popeyes, as Navy SEALs are known because they all tend to be overpumped in the muscle category. Us is several dozen Brits—ex–SAS, ex–Special Boat Unit, ex-things so secret we've never heard about it. Us is a couple of dozen Russians, all ex–Spetsnaz, their version of Special Forces. Us is a dozen Germans, all former members of that elite antiterrorist unit, the one that greased the Muslim fanatics who highjacked a Lufthansa plane to Mogadishu some years back. Us is two companies of the French Foreign Legion—who probably aren't ex- at all, but here secretly with French government approval and support.

We've all got our separate missions, we're all split up. Some marines and some Germans are training Bosnian assault infantry. Some SAS and some Germans are training and leading Bosnian infiltration units behind Serb lines. Most of the Spetsnaz guys aren't into training, but leading hit-and-run raids on Serb advance posts, then going in to take out an artillery emplacement if they can. The Foreign Legionnaires and SEALs get into this action too.

Maybe twenty of us, the best shots of the lot, are snipers and countersnipers, each working in a two-man team with a Bosnian shooter. My partner is a woman who won a bronze medal for the Yugoslav team in the '92 Olympics. She uses a Sako TRG-21 in NATO .308, and she's good out to 600 meters with it. I spot for her at those ranges, she puts the lights out on any Serb who exposes his head. She calls herself Mikla, never talks much, and when she does it's always shop—ranges, windage, bullet-drop comp. Her little secret: Geneva rules call for full-metal-jacket bullets only, which usually go in clean and come out the other side. Supposed to be more humane, and unless it's a head or heart shot, whoever gets hit does have a chance of surviving the wound. Mikla uses hunting bullets, long hollowpoints designed to expand on impact and destroy as much tissue as possible to drop an elk or a moose or bear in its tracks. They greatly extend her kill zone on men.

I don't need that advantage. I use a Barrett 82A1, which fires .50 bullets, the same cartridge heavy machineguns use. Semi-auto, mil-spec Heinsoldt scope, 10-round magazine. Got my choice of loads—FMJ, incendiary, tracer, armor piercing. My effective range is 600 to 2,500 meters, with good luck and perfect conditions maybe 3,000 meters. I can blast through Serb bunkers, destroy Serb jeeps, kill every man inside an armored car, penetrate the steel shield of artillery pieces and kill whoever's behind it.

At first, when my main targets are Serb officers who think they're well out of range, I blow them in half with FMJ rounds. It's a grin. The guy's head explodes, everybody around him is dripping blood and gray brain matter, Mikla laughing as she watches through the spotting scope. Then they all duck a few seconds later when the boom of the Barrett reaches them! Mikla laughs harder. The bullets travel much faster than sound. Nobody hears the rifle fire until somebody's already dead.

I get off on it. I'm hurling thunderbolts like Zeus. Mikla has a little leather notebook, and she writes down date, place, time and, if possible, rank of each kill. She takes a slug of plum brandy from her canteen each time she or I take out a Serb, makes me take one too. I only do because it would insult her if I didn't.

Later, as I get more bitter about the little kids and old ladies lying in pools of blood on Sarajevo streets, I get more inventive. I use state-of-the-art night-vision goggles, which won't reach out to the Barrett's full range but allow me to smack Serbs who've left their trenches for a safe and peaceful midnight piss at six hundred meters. I imagine this makes their buddies piss their pants. Or shit in them.

I do better, make it more brutal. My best—three Serbs way out, scanning down on the city with binoculars, presumably artillery officers, maybe even bigger brass. I'm tucked away in the rear of a blown-up apartment, Mikla's spotting with a 60-power scope, my Barrett's solid on a tripod nailed to the flooring. One of the Serbs takes a step, the angle's absolutely perfect, the crosshairs touch my point of aim. Juke 'em! An incendiary round tears through the bellies of all fuckin' three of the shits. Mikla's like a sports announcer. The Serbs are down, writhing, their clothes are on fire, their intestines are curled all over each other, roasting! Their flunkies are running this way and that like madmen, some are puking their guts out. . . .

Best shot I ever made. Never told a soul. Only Mikla saw it, recorded it in her little book. She's dead.

Somebody—I suspect Vassily—sends me her little notebook in Lausanne. Brain still not clear, I think three or four pages have been stuck together with some cheap brown glue. Realize later it's dried blood. Mikla's blood.

Mornings I hang at Café de la Paix on Suileman Boulevard, drinking what passes for coffee. Sometimes Mikla joins me before we go out to set up for the day's work. A couple of times I see this big blond Spetsnaz guy come by, a squad behind him, just back from inflicting some all-night terror on Serb positions. We start nodding, next we're waving, next I'm calling him over for a drink.

After that we start hanging pretty regularly. His English is good, my Russian's even better thanks to the Army Language School. Eventually I even go out with him and his team one night. He's a pro. We're into a Serb bunker complex without being seen and then we're frying their asses with white phosphorous grenades, hosing them down with AKs and my favorite HK MP5. I reckon we do about twenty-five of the fucks in no more than three minutes, then scramble back down the mountain with Serb machinegun tracers flaming way over our heads.

Friends for life after that. He's Vassily; I'm Shooter. Nobody has a real name in this business.

Ten months or so. Vassily and me, we eat togther, we get drunk together, we laugh, we screw some women, sometimes we go out killing together. Then I don't see him for a couple of days. Mikla and I are set up in another ruined apartment building. She's the shooter, I'm the spotter. Just after Mikla headshots a Serb, some lucky fuck of a countersniper clips me in the head. Mikla thinks I'm gonna die. So do I. Tears on her face—first time I've seen an emotion from her except elation whenever we downed a Serb. But the organization that got me to Sarajevo surprises me by getting me out, via Italy, to a hospital in Switzerland. Ten more months. The dent in my head. The antiseizure drugs. The trip home on a false passport. A little help with resettlement, rehabilitation. Then the job in Baltimore County.

//

Way past dawn. I smell breakfast cooking. I hear Gunny rumbling at Mom downstairs. Annie, wearing jeans and an Orioles sweatshirt, pops my door without knocking, hands me a big cup of coffee light with cream. "Get your butt downstairs pronteaux, Ewing," she says with a laugh. "I've been libeling you to Gunny and the man wants to talk."

9

Slip into the jeans I wore last night, pull on a fresh T-shirt—bright red, Corps emblem on the chest in gold, below that the slogan "When it absolutely, positively has to be destroyed overnight—U.S. Marines." Gunny will love it or hate it, no in-between. Nothing to lose, I figure, padding downstairs and back toward the kitchen.

Annie, at the table with Gunny, laughing about something he's just said, looking younger than she is, hair pulled back in a ponytail, no makeup at all. Pop drinking coffee from the personalized mug he's had for twenty years, Corps emblem, Gunnery Sergeant Thomas "One Way" Ewing, letters and crest beginning to fade though he always, always washes it by hand himself. Momma at the stove, in one of her favored flowered housedresses, looking over her shoulder at me and saying, "Eggs over easy, bacon not so crisp for my boy, n'est-ce pas?"

At that Gunny's eyes move from Annie's to mine. He puts his cup down on the table, places both hands palm down there too.

"Yo, maggot, you been making your momma awful sad, never coming around," he rumbles. He's in his jovial NCO mode, not his military philosopher one. No doubt Annie—and sleeping off the bourbon—put him there. He's wearing khakis—not GI, Wal-Mart—and a white T-shirt. Starched. He's always made Momma starch his fucking T-shirts.

"Haven't gotten too many invitations, sir," I reply.

"Shit for brains, I warned you," he says to Annie with a grin. "Maggots know better than to call a sergeant 'sir.' And since when does a son need an *in-VI-tation* to visit his momma? I'm damned, double goddamned and rammed up the butt if I ever heard such bullshit."

Back to me, eyes to eyes, me braced for more insane Corps virtuosity in insult and invective. Or a total freeze. Or dismissmal, orders to get out. Instead, "With your permission, Lieutenant," eye flick to Annie, then back. "Luther, get your bird-boned ass over here and shake your poppa's hand."

When I do, he pins mine in his huge one, rises so fast his chair flys over backward, and slings on a chokehold that could strangle, or snap a neck. "Goddammit Luther." He laughs. "How you survive in the world I don't know. You not only little, you slow. Now I want you to apologize to your momma this instant, and you do it knowing this morning she's happier than she's been since fuckin' '94. Now do it, Lubejob!"

Gunny tightens the choke. It's getting a little hard to breathe. "Sorry, Momma," I gasp.

Gunny lets go, spins me, claps me on both shoulders. "Lame, Lubejob, piss-poor. I've heard Jap geishas who sounded more sincere, and they only talkin' toys, not people. You go over and hug your momma right. But first you tell me how glad you are to see your poppa, 'cause your pop is shit-sure pleased to see his son, even if his son was also one of Uncle Sam's most mis-fuckin'-guided children."

"Ah Gunny, you numbah ten, Luther numbah one GI," Momma grins, deliberately dropping into Nam pidgin English. "Luther, you sit, numbah one chow for you. Gunny, you sit. Nothing for you. You too fat already."

"Fat?" Gunny laughs deeply. "You see my moves on this so-called trained warrior we got ourselves?"

"I see fat man play tricky-tricky, that all. Luther, you sit, I bring chow."

Then we're all at the table, I'm nuts wondering what Annie's making of this. Everybody's eaten but me, Momma's sipping her green tea and can't keep her eyes off me, can't keep the smile off her face, can't stop the tears leaking slowly from her black almond eyes.

Gunny refills Annie's coffee from the big Thermos, then tops off his own cup. "Move it, Luther. Get that plate clean fast. We got things to do, crabs to catch, they ain't gonna wait all day," Gunny says. "Your lieutenant here's given me a fine fitness report on you, an outstanding evaluation. Ain't that so, LT?"

Annie just grins. "He does okay. Not sure he's officer material."

"Thank god for that! No disrespect intended, LT, but as everyone knows, any outfit's nothin' but a clusterfuck without good NCOs," Gunny says. "The brass, they'd rather sip fine whiskey and smoke big cee-gars than go out and kick butt. Speaking of which, I think I will now have myself a fine cee-gar."

He drops from near roar to near whisper. "Offer you one, LT? Prime. Real Cuban, straight from Habana. Still got friends in Guantanamo."

Annie nods. Gunny's off to his office, back in a moment with two big Monte Cristos or some such. I never had the taste for cigars. He carefully trims the ends of both, uses his Zippo to light Annie up with the delicate wavey sweeps of the flame connoisseurs favor, gets his own going. I'm mopping up egg yolk with a scrap of toast while Annie draws on her cigar, nods appreciatively at Gunny, and says, "I do believe you've obtained some outstanding contraband here."

Gunny puffs and chortles. He gives me an affectionate slap on the back, but so unexpected and so powerful the yolk-soaked bit of toast pops out of my mouth. Momma's still looking, still smiling, still teary.

"Luther, you home now. You finally home," she says.

I'm sure Annie thinks it's more an asylum for the criminally insane.

//

We're on the creaky little dock built out from Gunny's narrow water frontage. There's a fiberglass Boston Whaler moored at the end, rubbing against bald old tires he uses for bumpers. The man's been busy early. Coiled in a proficient military manner at the base of each piling is a length of cord with a chicken neck tied to one end. Gunny weaves from piling to piling, tossing the baited strings into the murky creek waters. Annie's watching, bemused. She's from Ohio, she's eaten crabs before like everyone else around Baltimore, but she doesn't know squat about the water, about oystering and crabbing. Gunny shows her the drill. The cords are slack, but when one tightens up, you ever so slowly begin pulling it up. Those blue channel crabs, the big jimmys, don't like to let go of their meal. But if they spot you, they'll bolt. The trick is getting them near enough to the surface so someone beside you with a long-handled net can get it beneath and scoop 'em up.

It's about a 50-50 deal, usually. Annie misses the first half-dozen, then nets four in a row. She tries to grab her first catch from the front instead of from behind and gets a nasty claw nip on one of her fingers.

"Aw fuck," Annie snaps.

"Improvise, adapt, overcome. Surrender is not in our creed," Gunny says.

"You know, Gunny, you talk like you watched that Clint Eastwood movie—what was it, *Heartbreak Ridge*?—two or three too many times." Annie grins.

"Huh!" Gunny grunts. "I *taught* those Hollywood pussies Corps talk. That's why Eastwood sounds *authentic.*"

Mom fetches a Band-Aid. Annie isn't fazed. The baits go back in, we watch the lines, we pull when one goes tight, we dip the net. Annie grabs a netted crab from behind, sneaks up on Gunny while he's pulling a line, and waves those snapping claws a half inch from his nose. "Goddamn!" he bellows.

Before lunch, we've got three dozen in a Styrofoam chest full of ice and creek water.

We eat Smithfield ham sandwiches and drink cold beer from the bottle, sitting in Gibson Island chairs under a big old oak. I drift off into a doze, Annie and Momma and Pop talking. Late afternoon, we rebait and cast the lines. We net another dozen before it gets too dark. Mom steams them with Old Bay, and we eat on the little screened-in porch—crabs, cole slaw, sliced tomatos, potato salad with lots of mayo, choice of beer or iced tea with lots of sugar and lemon. I have the tea.

It doesn't quite feel real. My head gets jagged, but an easy jagged, not a scary one. Still, I slip a tab under my tongue when no one's watching, then wash it down with tea. We all watch a nice moonrise.

Late that night in Gunny's office, Annie and Momma gone to bed, Gunny sipping whiskey and me a single beer, Gunny turns serious. "That silver bullet out there, that come from blood money, Luther?"

"Negative."

"Don't bullshit me, Lubejob!"

"I didn't do it for the money. I tried to tell you that when I was leaving, but you wouldn't hear."

"I wouldn't then. Damn straight. I'm hearing now, though, if you got anything but shit to say."

"Won't insult your intelligence by claiming I did it entirely for a fucking cause. It was partly wanting to be on the right side, but it was also partly wanting very badly to practice my profession."

"Which you lost in Kuwait. Which I understood. You weren't the first and won't be the last soldier who refused to accept the enemy's surrender. I refused, mostly always, in Nam."

"But I got caught, you didn't. I lost it all. When the Sarajevo offer came along, money was never part of the equation."

I pull out a plain buff envelope with a return address of "Postfach 480, 0101 Vaduz" printed discreetly in the upper-left-hand corner, with a Lichtenstein postmark on the upper right. It's been in my jeans pocket all day. I take out the bank statement it contains and hand it to Gunny.

"That's all? What've you been spending on, besides that fancy car?"

"You sure you're hearing? I already told you no about the car. What you're seeing is my *entire* salary and my wound bonus. The whole damn thing. I haven't touched a dime. I get a statement once a year. This is this year's. The money's been sitting there since '95. Probably sit there forever," I say.

"Christ, this is chickenshit!" Gunny's looking at the numbers. "This isn't much more than a sergeant's yearly salary with combat pay, if there was any combat around anymore."

"Yeah, well, there was free room and board, you know. PX privileges too, if there'd been a PX, which there wasn't."

Gunny's laughter rolls through the room. "Oh Lordy, Lordy, I do hate to admit it, but I had you wrong. I figured you were going for big-time bucks. Never imagined mercs worked so cheap. Goddammit, I still say we should've sent in the First Marines and cleaned the Serb clocks! Greased every swinging dick they could muster in Bosnia, then gone on into Serbia proper and taken Belgrade and executed that goddamn Slobo what's-his-name and all the other war criminals."

"Ah, you're just jealous because your thirty years were up in '90 and you missed Desert Storm. And because we pissed away that win by stopping too soon."

"Fuckin' right!" Gunny was still laughing. Then serious again. "Are you gonna forgive your old man? He'd be most pleased if you could do that. He feels like dogshit for the way he treated you."

"Ah you know." I'm not truly trusting this, but I go with it. "Burned-out old jarheads, they can't think straight. They're all too concussed. Hard to blame the pathetic fucks when they're out of line. They know not what they do."

Poppa smiles at me in a way he hadn't since I finished my Special Forces training. He doesn't say any more for a while. Then he raises his glass and shouts, "Here's to us and them like us. Most of the poor motherfucks are dead."

If Annie'd been there, she'd have said he was stealing movie lines again.

//

We leave Sunday after lunch because the traffic's going to be hellish on Labor Day Monday. Mom gets a bit teary again. Gunny shakes Annie's hand very solemnly. "Do me a favor, LT," he says just before I start the TT down the oystershell driveway. "Make sure my boy gets his butt back down here. Soon, and often. Semper Fi?"

"No problem, Gunny," she says.

I feel a little like I'm being sweated on a felony charge as we head north. Details—who, when, what, why? Annie wants details, more details. Annie says my folks are great, says I'm wrong about Gunny, says the problem's mine, not his, if I still think I'm unwanted down there. "He's genuine, Luther," she tells me. "Not acting to please your mother. My read on all this is pretty simple. He regrets a lot of wasted years. He wants to do what he can to make up for that. He wants to see his son just as bad as your mother does. He just can't express that any way but rough and jokey. Don't blow it off, Luther."

"I'm not. I'm just doubtful."

"Your standard condition. Part of your anomie."

"That again?"

"It comes with certain professions. Cops, soldiers. We're asked to protect society, but to do that properly we sometimes have to break the society's rules. We feel our leaders are unreliable, society's basically unpredictable and without order. Natural conflict, don't you see? Leads to anger and total frustration."

"I get that, but what about the rest?"

"Easy. We're not hardwired to believe killing is wrong. That's software. In some people it never gets loaded properly, and you get drive-by shooters, mob hit men, cold-blooded murderers."

"Yeah? I didn't get the right software, is that it? Shit."

"Maybe you got it, but it was taken away. What good's a soldier who'd crumple up and weep every time he shot an enemy? For that matter, what good's a cop who couldn't pull the trigger when a perp was about to shoot his partner?"

"So then why'd Gunny hate me for going to Sarajevo?"

"Because when they erase the killing inhibition, they try to substitute certain protocols to control the killing. Your father has a very rigid set of principles. No doubt he's been developing them and dressing them up with notions like honor and ideas that war should be conducted according to certain rules. Total contradiction right there. The soldier is ordered to destroy the enemy. No way around it. You do lots of pyschological gymnastics so you can live with it.

"Shit, I'm running off at the mouth," Annie says. "Short answer, Luther, is that mercenary work violates your father's artificial construction. He hates that, because he knows down deep his own rules are pretty flimsy. Now he's sorry. End of story."

End of conversation, too, for a while. More than enough to mull. Then, as we head north through Maryland, her cell rings just moments before mine. We're each listening hard to our separate callers, talking fast. I push down a bit on the TT's accelerator pedal. We click off almost simultaneously.

"You go first, Luther," Annie says, a little hitch in her voice that worries me.

"Just Ice Box. He's got a live one for tomorrow night. Buy-and-bust. Medium-good, he says. Nothing major. You?"

Annie's staring way down the highway, her right knee bobbing up and down. She won't look at me.

"Major," she says at last.

"C'mon, give," I say.

"Old lady, living alone near Madonna. About sixty-seven years old. Son of a bitch breaks in, rapes her."

"Aw shit."

"But then he feels obliged to rearrange her face with his fists. She's in the hospital now, major reconstructive surgery." Annie sighs.

"Oh man, that's bad."

"On a lighter note," she manages, "get this. Those asshole parents of the reservoir girl? They've shipped her off to some boarding school way up in New England somewhere."

//

Annie's just closed the TT's door and is loping off toward her house when my cell chirps again.

"What?"

"It's not eleven yet, little brother. Still office hours, yes?"

"I'm not exactly busy at the moment, Vassily."

"Why not come see me then? I'm down here. We talk a little, I show you something funny. Like old times."

That I do not like the sound of, but the address he gives me is on Charles Street, not ten minutes from where I am and on my way home anyway. Turns out to be a row house on a good block just south of Johns Hopkins University. A wirey guy with black hair slicked back greets me at the door. "Shooter you must be," he says, grinning. Russian. "Vassily, he tells me all about you. Me, I am Nick. You come with me."

We go along some corridors. The place is nicely furnished, but there's no sense of a home to it. It's like a room at a Marriott. Near the back of the house Nick leads me down the stairs into the basement, then through a steel door. Through a time warp too.

One bright light on the ceiling, circling a naked black kid tied to a steel chair. He's got a gang tattoo on one corded bicep, and a face from a nightmare. Somebody's been massaging it, most likely with lead-lined gloves. His eyes are so swollen they're just slits, his mouth looks like ground beef.

"Hey Shooter!" Vassily calls from the shadows outside the circle of light, then steps into it and puts a hand on the kid's shoulder. The kid flinches. "Remind you of old times, except here we got no fucking Serb pig. Here we got a thief. This blackie and his friends, they been robbing our pharmaceutical retail operation. Right, Nick?"

"Da, Vassily. For sure."

"But he won't admit it," Vassily goes into Russian. "Pretty tough, this blackie. You want to give it a try, Shooter?"

"Fuck no! I'm finished with that shit," I say, feeling a shakiness and a nausea I know I can't show. "He didn't steal from me."

"Ah little brother, America's made you soft," Vassily laughs. "Okay, Nick. Next step."

Nicks waves his arm, and another guy, Russian for sure, steps into the light and triple-wraps duct tape around the kid's mouth and head. Then he produces another steel chair, puts the kid's legs up on the seat so his knees are just at the edge, and duct-tapes his ankles real tight. The kid starts to squirm and buck, so the guy sits down on the chair, pinning him. His thighs are like a bridge between the two chairs.

Fuck me. I know what's coming.

Vassily suddenly swings down as hard as he can on the kid's thighs with a baseball bat. Dull meaty thud mainly, but a definite chilling snap as both thigh bones facture. The kid's head snaps back, the scream's silent.

"You know, Shooter, this game of baseball, it's really boring. I go to a game once in Yankee Stadium, I fucking fall asleep it's so boring." Vassily laughs. "But this," he says as he hefts the Louisville Slugger, "this is nice little tool."

"You drag me over here just to see this shit?" I say. It's taking all I got to keep my voice steady, normal.

"Sure, why not? Like old times, right? This doesn't amuse you?"

"Fuck no, Vassily. Told you I was past that shit."

He moves in close, scanning my eyes. "This is maybe troubling you, Shooter?"

"Fuck off, you Soviet slob." I laugh. I'm pretty sure I make it sound genuine. "Think I really give a shit if you put the hurt on some thief? It's just boring. Like baseball. I'm out of here. Before I fall asleep."

Vassily laughs in his old way, slings an arm around my shoulder, walks me back upstairs. "Hey, sorry if I wasted your time. A little ego maybe. Maybe I just wanted to show I still know my work. Pretty stupid. You and me, we don't have to show each other anything. We already did that, didn't we?"

It was war then, man, I'm thinking. There was a reason. Certain things had to be done. This is just sick.

"Sure. Listen, we'll go have dinner again or something," I say, leaving.

I get pulled over doing ninety-five on the Jones Falls Expressway by a City cop who only sneers at my badge and writes me a $150 ticket.

10

"So I misspoke myself," Ice Box says, shrugging, Monday night in the squadroom. "So it's not a buy-and-bust, it's a door-popper. Same old same old. Ecstasy. Maybe a Bonus Pack. Hell, Dugal isn't even coming along."

"Just you and me and a warrant to toss some condo again?" I ask.

"Yeah, except it isn't a condo. That's the only hinky thing here. I checked it out this morning. Big mock-Tudor on a bunch of acres between Pots Spring and Dulaney Valley. Owners are Dr. Stuart Reigel, heart surgeon, and Dr. Mumtaz Singh Reigel, psychopharmacology specialist. They happen to be spending a week at their vacation house on St. Bart's. Their little girl Hannah, she's home alone. Hell, not so little. She's eighteen, graduated from Mercy High last June. Taking a break before starting college, I guess."

"Boring, IB. Very boring. This the best you could come up with while I was away?"

"First, you were only gone two days. Second, I'm not making it happen, it's just happening. A couple of her ex-schoolmates got stopped on a traffic violation a week ago. Arresting patrolman found maybe ten Ecstasy tabs in the car. The girl driving ratted Hannah in an eyeblink. Said all her friends got stuff from Hannah. Dugal got the warrant, gave it to me just after you left for your long weekend, said wait for you to get back, we could handle it ourselves. Like I said, no biggie."

"Oh, the LT does love us, Ice Box," I laugh.

"Yeah, and it's mostly your fault, being so sweet to the asshole, Luther. On the other hand, thank you for being such a great suck-up with Dugal. I like jobs like this. Hell, we can probably just carry water pistols. Knock on the door, little Hannah answers, we say, 'Hello, young lady, we're your friendly neighborhood police officers and we'd love to talk to you,' and she wets her pants."

"And the ace crime fighters IB and Five-O nail another menace to society. I get so proud of myself, helping keep suburbia free of dangerous criminals."

"Hey, be grateful. Two City narcs got killed Sunday. I like to keep myself in one piece."

"Shit!" I say. "Anybody I know?"

"Doubt it," IB says. "It was in South Baltimore, not up in your pal Dog's territory."

We head out in the Crown Vic, Ice Box driving, and I get on my cell, trying to reach Dog. He's out, but one of the guys in his squad I know confirms IB's story.

"Shit, sorry 'bout that," I say. "Gangbangers?"

"Here's the weird," the City narc tells me. "*Supposed* to be a buy-and-bust from some Crips. It goes down. Our dudes got two Crips on the ground, cuffing them, and then some whitey in a suit slips out of a doorway and clips our guys. Kills 'em in the head. Silenced weapon. He runs with the drugs, and the money."

"This confirmed?"

"We got five citizens tellin' the same story. The two Crips got sidewalk skidmarks on their faces and are lying there cuffed when back-up arrives. The Crips claim the same as the citizens, only they say they don't know dick about no drugs, they was just hangin' and two cops shook 'em down for no reason. The Crips' pieces hadn't been fired. We're waitin' for forensics to figure out what hit our guys. Three shots in the face. Some strange shit."

I do not like what I'm hearing. "Hey, ask Dog to give me a call when he gets back, okay?"

"No problem. Oh, 'nother weird thing. The bangers claim the

shooter took one of their homeboys away with him. Crazy shit, man."

Ice Box looks over at me and almost smashes a row of mailboxes when the Crown Vic swerves. He rights it. "You spooked, Luther? You know the cops that went down?"

"Nah," I say, telling the truth. But I don't say what's shook me.

Our bust goes just as Ice Box called it—except Hannah is way cool about it. She answers the door wearing a cropped top and a spandex mini, little silver navel ring shining against light coffee skin. Tall, slim, drop-dead gorgeous with huge eyes, full lips, a straight little nose with a ruby stud in one fine nostril. She smiles as if she's glad to see us—Academy Award talent, this half-Sikh, half-American girl. Just laughs when IB asks her where she keeps her stash. Flirts with me: "Do you really think I'd sell drugs, Detective?" The girl's been around the block a few times, even if she's only eighteen. Stays calm when Ice Box opens up a shoe box—Manolo Blanik—from her bedroom closet and finds it full of Ecstasy tabs. I snap out of my little crush and realize she's so cool and so warm because she's floating on her own dope. Still, when we put her in the car and head back to HQ, I can't stop delicious little thoughts of what she'd be like in Helen's place, what she'd taste like and what she'd do. You're a sick old dog, Luther, I tell myself. No good. I never can believe myself.

IB reaches her parents in St. Bart's, there's a good lawyer at the station in an hour, he and the judge agree that because she's only eighteen she should spend the night in the juvenile detention facility, with a bail hearing tomorrow if her parents get back from the Caribbean in time.

"She'll make bail, go home with her folks," Ice Box says as we wrap the paperwork. I'm still thinking of that flat smooth stomach and her dark eyes. Ice Box had pumped her for her source on the way to the station and got nothing. My guess is that when we formally interrogate her, attorney present, the best we'll get is the same sketchy description we'd always gotten from these kids. And no way is slut-in-training Hannah going to be one to help us set up any buy-and-bust. Not that it matters.

We got James Halliday on deck.

//

Late next day, Hannah walks as IB predicted. She isn't high now, leaving the courtroom, but she gives me this smile. No future for you, I think, and it's kind of a sad idea, a pretty thing like her well on the way to fucking up her own life. But I smile back. "Catch you later, Hannah," I say. Her well-tanned, beautifully dressed parents glare, her lawyer starts to move on me, courtroom-macho ass who wouldn't last a minute in anything physical, but I just turn and walk away.

Two nights later, me and Ice Box take a twenty-one-year-old plainclothes out to do a buy-and-bust on a whitebread we know's been peddling Ecstasy. We can't do this ourselves, we're too old and too scary. It's got to be kid to kid, not like the city, where even the fourteen-year-olds haven't been kids since they were so small they could still ride the buses for free. The plainclothes is a smart one. We've got him acting like a highschool jock with a wild streak, he handles the buy slick but looks jittered when IB and I move in and make the bust. Maybe it's because we cuff and mock-arrest him too, so we can use him again. He isn't enjoying it, getting tossed into a holding cell with the dealer.

The dealer surprisingly chooses to shut up until his lawyer gets here, unlike every other Ecstasy kid we've popped. The plainclothes out of his cell and with us, we find out why he got that look. His purchase is on my desk, I'm about to open the brown paper bag and tag what's inside.

"He wanted five times the usual money, said I'd be able to double it easy. Don't think that's Ecstasy, sir," he says.

Right. The usual Ziplocs but no pills, just glassine envelopes, the kind postage stamps used to come in.

"So you already sample the shit or what, kid? Naughty, naughty," IB laughs, sticking a big finger into one of the little envelopes. He takes a delicate taste of the powder that's stuck to his fingertip. "Fuck me," he shrills, then mutes it. "Pure horse, Five-O. Oh man, I can't stand it when shit like this happens."

I take a taste too. IB's on the money. Good heroin. Goddamn good heroin. I just know the lab's gonna come up with a purity percentage that's off the fucking charts.

"Dugal's gonna have our asses on every kind of overtime, he finds out about this," Ice Box complains.

"Good to go. Sir!" I grin at him.

"Aw, cut that shit out. Makes my balls ache, just thinking about what's heading our way. I need it easy for a while, MJ about to pop and all."

"Yeah, and that van you gotta wash every day." I'm staying light as I can about this, but I do not like the signs I see flashing up ahead. Unless this buy is a freak, which I can't believe for a minute, we got a major problem developing.

It isn't a freak. Taggert You Fuck next Tuesday night and Tommy Weinberg on Wednesday night come in from planned Ecstasy busts with exactly what me and Ice Box scored. I call Dog again, finally reach him. We agree to meet. Dugal calls a war council next morning.

"So what is this all about, gentlemen?" he starts off, the whole narc squad crammed into his office. "What is happening here?"

"Well sir, our Ecstasy kids are selling heroin. . . ."

"Taggert You Fuck, I *know* that. What I wanna know is why now, why the change, how come these punks aren't spilling their guts but calling lawyers, who is it that scares them more than we do, where's the smack coming from, how is it coming, how big is it?"

"Started with the Bonus Packs," IB says.

"Yeah, and I said bullshit, they're no problem. I take it back, IB," Dugal says. "First thing, every one of you that made a Bonus Pack bust, print out your interrogation files and give 'em to Ice Box and Luther. All information centers to them. IB, you and Luther are going to find me a trail here, some sort of pattern. We backtrack 'til we get something, anything, and then we follow it forward. Anybody got vacation planned, cancel."

There's a couple of groans in the room.

"Anything from the city?" Dugal asks.

"I'm seeing my man tomorrow," I say.

"Why not tonight? These tough city guys afraid to go out after dark?"

"The meet's tomorrow, LT. You want it around that it's panic time out here?"

"You're right, Luther. I don't want anything around. Biz as usual. Nobody talks to the press. Nobody talks to anybody outside this room until we get some better information. Understood?"

Guys nod, guys grunt.

"Anybody got any busts planned, just make 'em as usual. Talk to your snitches, we're still looking for Ecstasy. Anybody mentions smack, act surprised. Then get curious. Anything you see or hear or find, pass it to IB and Luther. IB, Luther, make your move with the Halliday kid as soon as you can set it up."

"Already on it, LT. He's calling his man. Meet could be in a couple of days, maybe a week," I say.

"Daily updates, please. The rest of you, get going now."

"Aw shit, what'd I tell you. What'd I say," IB moans when we're back in my cubicle. "Why's he pick us to do the grunt work?"

"'Cause you know and I know Dugal doesn't have anybody else near good enough to do it," I say.

//

I see Dog sitting on a bench in Mt. Vernon Park, legs stretched out across the walkway, eating a cannoli, drawing uneasy looks from the suits, male and female, who're passing by. I know what they're thinking: trouble, danger. This is safe Baltimore, a safe white island, with the Peabody Conservatory on one side, the Walters Art Gallery on the other, a monument to George Washington rising up in the middle of the little park. Small law firms, architects' offices, some doctors' offices in expensively renovated row houses round about. Dog takes a big bite out of his cannoli and smiles hugely to himself, staring out at nothing.

Dog's an odd one. Put him in a suit, and nobody here would look twice. They'd be right not to. He's got a BS from Maryland, his family's solid. Dad's been earning good money at a union job at Bethlehem Steel since before Dog was born, mom's active in their neighborhood Baptist Church. But the city's the city. Dog's older brother went bad early, ran wild with some gangstas, wound up all wet and messy on a sidewalk, shot dead in a drug deal gone bad.

The man was skeptical of me, first meet back when Dugal lent me out to the city. Not that I gave a shit. He turned anyway on the second bust we did. Dog and his team got four guys of a crew on the floor of their crack crib, enough evidence lying around to send them all away for ten to twenty. I'm easy, leaning against the wall next to the kitchen door. Peripheral only; fifth crew member slips out, Tec-9 cocked and locked, Dog and his guys swivel, know they're dead. I stop that. No biggie. All training, all instinct. Before anybody can blink I've broken the fuck's gun arm so bad there's a jagged point of bone sticking through the skin of his forearm, he's down, the Tec-9's skittering across the floor, I've got my boot on his thorax, and he'd have been dead as he lay if Dog hadn't moved fast and pulled me off him.

Pure instinct, from the training. Don't remember what moves I used. They just happened. Muscle memory. Don't really remember moving at all. Dog remembers, though. His homies remember. We get fairly tight after that. Dinner every couple of weeks or so at this Chinese place that specializes in Peking duck. Dog's a fiend for that, heaping on the hoisin and shredded scallions. A few times he has me over to his mother's for fried chicken and greens. "Doesn't get any better than this, Mamma," Dog says the first time.

"Now Lincoln, you just have another thigh," his mother replies. Lincoln. Dog's real name is Lincoln. But he gives me a look that makes it real clear I'd best never call him that, or tell anybody.

I ease down next to him, I see the suits pick up their pace as they pass us. "What you know good, home?" Dog says, not looking at me, not asking a question either. He's wearing baggy jeans and a real loose Tommy Hilfiger athletic-style shirt, sleeves pushed up his corded forearms. Six small gold hoops adorn his left ear.

"Jammin', Dog," I say. "What's goin' down?"

"You heard that already from my man."

"I heard two narcs, in South. White shooter."

"You ignorant? Or you be playin' dumb?"

"I'm real stupid," I say. A shadow falls across us. Look up, there's a young uniform, trying to be cool, but having a lot of trouble keeping his right hand a decent distance from his holster. He's black but he's still scared. The suits really start scurrying now. Dog flips open his gold shield. "Sorry," the uniform says, backing up a step and turning to move on.

"You wanna be watchin' that racial profiling, dig, Officer?" Dog says softly, then takes another bite of his cannoli.

"Nosir, it wasn't . . . I mean yessir," the young patrolman says, scuttling off. Dog permits himself a small chuckle. He's not a laughing sort of man.

"So you dumb, Luther? Here's what it is," he says, crumpling up the paper that cradled the cannoli and stuffing the little wad into one of the many pockets of his jeans. "Besides two cops down on a buy-and-bust with two gangbangers."

"Bad?"

"Whacked, man. Past week, we got three Crips killed in the head, two Bloods killed in the head. One Crip we make as an LA import, the other two local recruits. One Blood's from LA, one's another local."

"So it's turf?"

"Wish it was. Here's what's whacked. The Bloods and the Crips, far as we can take it, ain't shooting each other. They've had their territories marked off clean for nearly a year. Lookin' like we got a white shooter on these five. Lookin' like the same shooter, or motherfuckers who went to the same school as the motherfucker tapped our two guys."

"That is whacked. You thinkin' the Italians figure the bangers are rippin' them off? Lesson time?"

"Fuck no. The Italians, they all too fat and happy. They don't have the stones for no war no more. Shit, they all living out your way in big houses now, takin' life easy. They got the gamblin', the track, the loansharkin', and they sourcin' the crack and smack the niggers be street-sellin'. Why they want trouble?"

"Like I said, maybe the Crips and Bloods are shortin' them."

"Easy answer. But wrong. Doesn't tell me why they'd hit two of our guys, leave two niggers alive. Never been a hit on a cop by a mob guy in my twenty years on this shit-ass job. And the hits are weird, man."

"Weird?"

"Everybody uses 9-millie hollows here. Dome shots, usually from behind. Bone and brains splashed everwhere, looking all shitty. But all seven of these shootees was tapped in the face by three very small pills, like .22 size small. No mess at all. And forensics, they can't even *find* these pills. So you tell me, soldier boy, what we dealin' with here?"

AKSU-74s, submachine guns not much larger than a big pistol like the Eagle. Standard set-up: 3-round burst, full-auto rock 'n' roll. Slightly longer, thinner bullet, shorter and fatter cartridge than our 5.56mm M16 round. Russian.

"Hey Dog, mystery to me," I say. "Don't sound like anything I've ever seen."

Dog gets up, looks down at me. "Give it some of your fine, fine thought, Luther. Then give me what I know damn well you know, jive motherfuck," he says, chill. Then he walks away.

I'm twisted, driving back to Towson. Have to face what I was trying hard to keep in denial. It's Vassily. No way there's two Russian crews on the same turf. And Russians are all muscle, crude boys, no nice rules against cop killing. I'm thinking I can't let IB anywhere near this—got to keep him and MJ safely out of the way. How the hell will I manage that, unless I cut out Dugal and the squad entirely, go freelance? Or go just with Dog. Either way, it means stepping straight into the deepest shit in the world.

11

The digital flash on my answering machine, the one I've ignored all week, is up to number five. Last thing I feel like doing, but I check the messages out.

One: "Hey, Luther, I'm back. Are you? Call me." It's Helen.

Two: "Missing you, babe. Still not back? Awfully long holiday. Love ya." Helen again.

Three: "O that I knew he were but in by the week! How I would make him fawn, and beg, and seek. . . ." English Lit major. Sounds like Shakespeare or someone like him. The girl loves her poesy.

Four: "Luther, it's me, Helen. Listen, I'm getting really worried about you. Are you okay? Call me soon as you can, or I'm calling the police."

Five: "Fuck yourself, Luther. I'm sure not going to anymore, if you don't call me in the next twelve minutes. Goodbye."

Yeah, well. I would miss that. I spend a long time in the shower, though. Wash my hair twice with some herbal Body Shop shampoo Helen left last June, before she went home for the summer. Shave, which I really only need to do every three or four days, thanks to those Vietnamese genes. Deodorant. Then I slip into my yukata and call Helen back.

"Damn, Luther! Where've you been? Why didn't you call?" she says.

"Tell you all about it, if you come over."

"Give me an hour," she says. "And you better have some good excuses." She giggles. "You better be all-around good to me tonight, as a matter of fact."

I put on a tape I'd made—a mix of Crash Test Dummies, Nirvana, new Pearl Jam, and easing off with a lot of tracks from Dido and Sinéad Lohan—and lie down on the sofa to wait. Thinking a lot about 5.45s. Mean little bastards got a small air pocket behind the tip, do horrendous damage when they hit flesh, ten times worse than our 5.56s. Afghans called 'em "poison bullets" because any man hit by one, anyplace on his body, was almost certain to die of the wound.

Kill that thinking. Start trying to picture Helen. Hannah the baby vixen shows up instead. Wicked. Wonderful images. I'm asleep when Helen rings the bell.

She comes striding long-legged into the place like she owns it, I see her eyes quarter the room almost like a trained investigator. Looking for what?

"So, babe," she grins, "How'd it go with your parents and your little cop-ette friend? Good times roll? Was it, like, what you expected, or a sweet surprise?"

Did I tell her I was taking Annie to Tyding's Landing? Did I even tell her I was going there at all? How much had I told her about the rift between Gunny and me, if I'd told her anything at all? Damn tabs. They grease your memory so things slide away, but there's no pattern, no structure to it, you can't tell what'll go and what'll stick in the Save file. And even stuff you're sure is saved and stored sometimes just won't call up. Then when you aren't looking for it, it'll often pop open.

The girl's got me off-balance in less than a minute. Plus she's looking terrific in a thin white linen shirt—Club Monaco, I guess—hanging loose over tight black linen pants that flair a bit at the bottom. I can just make out slightly darker points where her nipples press the shirt, and the way the shirt moves when her breasts do.

I wrap her up tight, body to body, and run my tongue over her lips. Her mouth opens slightly. She pushes me away after a moment, stands hip-shot, one arm bent and hand grasping her waist, head cocked so her hair sways a bit to one side and hangs there.

"Well?" she says. "Account for your whereabouts and your goings-on. Where were you on the nights of September fifth, sixth and seventh? Anything you say can and will be held against you."

She's grinning but she wants some answers. I give her the short version—Tyding's, my job. No details on what was said, just things went okay, I was hopeful. No mention of Dog. Or Vassily.

"So. You have an alibi, except about the cop-ette. Are you messing around with her or what, Luther?"

"Hell no." I laugh. Then I make a tactical mistake. "Though I admit it might be fun. If she'd have anything to do with me, which she won't.

"She's got a real tight body, like this one here," I add, touching her in a couple of crucial places.

"At her age?" Helen says. "Cellulite time already for that woman, I bet. And she's way old for you—given your kinky tastes, Luther."

But Helen loosens up, no serious jealousy trip, she's just yanking my chain for fun. We drink some wine she'd brought down from her father's cache, a Chateau Trotanoy, maybe $80 a bottle. Then we indulge some of those kinky tastes. Hard to tell which are mine and which are hers, they're such a slick fit. I catch myself wondering where the hell she got her training, since I never taught her a thing. Stifle that brainwave quick. Luther's rule—don't ask, don't tell.

//

The Halliday kid sets up the meet. A Friday afternoon, the light soft and buttery but still strong enough and hot enough to send up wavery mirages off the black asphalt of the parking lot. It's going to be a drive-by, this first contact. We decide to drop the young plainclothes idea, I'm doing it myself. The buyer has to look like someone serious, not just another local kid.

James's man is no rookie. Crowded mall lot, hundreds of cars, shoppers picking up things for the weekend flowing back and forth from the stores to their rides. The kid's man will cruise the lot until he sees the TT, with me in the driver's seat and Halliday outside sitting on the hood. He'll stop if he feels safe, roll down his window as I roll down mine, exchange a few words, drive off. Nobody notices a thing, no citizen even registers what goes down.

It does go down, just like that. The guy's in his twenties, blond hair buzz cut, sunglasses with thick, black plastic frames, blue T-shirt. His car's too common to make, the sort of generic sedan that could be a Toyota, a Nissan, a Mitsubishi, a Honda. Who the hell knows? It's beige, though the maker probably calls it Desert Moon or Pearl Taupe or something. It needs a wash.

"Your bud?" Buzz Cut says to Halliday. Voice as beige and generic as the car. The kid nods. Buzz Cut turns his head to me, though I can't see where his eyes are focused, with those glasses. "What's your name?"

"People call me Snake," I say.

"Weird name, man. Nasty connotations. You ever think of encouraging people to call you something less provocative?"

"Nah," I say. I'm not wearing shades, I want him to see my eyes. People get nervous when they can't see your eyes.

"I would. I wouldn't want to be known by that."

"Does it make a difference?"

"Not really. Whatever you can live with."

"I live with it just fine."

"Just fine, right. What else would be just fine?"

"Some of what makes Jimmy fine. But a fuck of a lot more of it. Plus a fuck of a lot more of those little surprises in glassine envelopes that come with it."

"Very vague, man. Fuck of a lot? What's that supposed to tell me?"

"About fifty times what Jimmy got last go. About five hundred times of the surpise packs. Just to get started."

"Unusual proportion. This maybe sounds like the beginning of competition, not a deal."

"I don't do biz around here. From Rockville and Gaithersburg way out toward Frederick, Hagerstown. Lot of high schools out that way," I say. "Had a wholesaler in D.C. Need a new one."

"What happened to your D.C. man?"

"Somebody with more juice did him. Changed the whole corporate structure."

Buzz Cut laughs. "The story of the whole economy, man. Hostile takeovers, mergers and acquisitions."

"So. You want a new client? Check with your boss, see if he can handle the weight. If the service is good, lots of repeat business."

"Boss? I'm an independent entrepreneur. I can handle whatever the market demands. Terms are cash on delivery. Ballpark figure on what you said you wanted . . . oh, say ten thousand dollars. No hundred-dollar bills. Your wallet big enough?"

"Much bigger. Except that's just—ballpark now—multiplying what Jimmy pays by fifty and five hundred. Generally there's a discount on larger orders."

"My usual practice, on repeat biz. First time out, it's manufacturer's suggested retail only." Buzz Cut grins.

"Hey, nobody pays sticker price anymore. I could go downtown, get at least a grand or two off."

"So go downtown. But since you're from the sticks and shut down in D.C., really think that, first, you'll connect? And second, that the downtown dudes won't just take your money and do you?"

"That could happen there. Could happen here too."

"Look at me. Does it appear that I conduct biz that way? Anything giving you any thoughts along those lines? Jimmy's standing fine, right? So are all the rest of my clientele. Naturally a few fuck up, but their troubles come only from the BCPD narcs, not me. I run a safe, reliable, and fair operation."

"Make it nine K, you've got a new customer. And pretty soon regular orders, in the twenty-five to forty large range."

"Very attractive prospect. Also very ambitious. Why should I believe you can make the weight?"

"Why not? Nice operating environment out in the sticks. No competition worth mentioning. The demographics are great, getting better all the time. I like to build my business. Don't you?"

"A businessman's always got to be alert to opportunities for growth."

"Here's one for you. I'm looking for a long-term, secure supplier. I am not looking for problems. Jimmy's got my address and phone. Have somebody check me out."

"Being done even as we speak," Buzz Cut says. "If things are like you say, I could go to nine thousand dollars on the first, with volume discounts on further orders."

"Fair enough," I say.

"I'll be in touch. But mind if I call you something else than Snake? I don't like reptiles. Bob? How about Bob? I just watched some *Twin Peaks* videos. Ever seen any? Long-haired man's named Bob." Buzz Cut smiles. I nod. I think this is going off perfect. Then I get jolted. Buzz Cut says, "James, get in. I'm giving you a ride. Later, *Bob.*"

I can't say a thing. The kid climbs into the sedan, and Buzz Cut waves as his window closes and he drives sedately off. I'm down so low in the TT I can't make the license plate before the car disappears in the mall maze. Jimmy snatched, no way to track Buzz Cut. Fuck me!

//

I drive down York Road about five miles toward Towson, pull into a Dunkin' Donuts, slip into the booth where Ice Box is drinking coffee.

"Uh oh," he says when he hears how it went. "What's your instinct? The kid stand-up? Or is he going to rat?"

"Gut feeling, James is more scared of us and jail time than he is of Buzz Cut right now. The man's just tough enough. No way he's into messin' the kid up. He'll have a conversation, very calm but very clever, because he's a pro and he's cautious. If he gets anything from James it'll be because he tricked the kid. Then he'll just drop him off at home or someplace."

"Then why is it," IB says after slurping some coffee, "that you're so wired? You're doin' that jive with your fingers you always do when you're nervous, and you don't even know it."

IB's right. The hand tic is happening, trigger finger making pulling moves over and over on the yellow Formica of the table top. I hate when that happens. Christ, by now I ought to know to keep my hands in my pockets.

"It's nothing, man."

"Oh, Luther, Luther. Luther." Ice Box grins.

"What?"

"Nothing." He's laughing a little now, he shifts a little in his seat and I swear the whole booth moves. "Can I say something, partner to partner, no offense? Don't answer, I'm saying it anyway. First, you are too worried about the kid. You hate the idea that he got snatched by this Buzz Cut, and you know damn well that Buzz Cut might be dangerous."

"Maybe."

"Other thing is, your mind's working two cases at the same time. Helen, and this secret thing for Annie, man, and it's making you a little crazy."

"Aw bullshit, Ice Box!"

"Hey, you think you're the only one? I got this secret little thing for Annie too. There's four or five guys got this secret little thing for Annie. But we all know it's just a head thing, nothing ever gonna happen. I think you don't really know that yet. I think in there somewhere, Five-O's got some kind of feeling there's some slight chance something nice could happen with Annie one of these days."

"Shove it up your ass. She's a good friend. End of story."

Ice Box laughs harder. "Give it up, Luther."

"Nothing to give up."

"Okay. The man's spoken. But how about giving up the tape so I can go get it transcribed? I can't sit here all day being your therapist."

"IB, you go walking on ice that's mighty thin for a dude your size," I say, easing the Nagra recorder—old-tech tape but still the best quality in the world—out of my pocket and slipping him the cassette under the table.

"I'm outta here. You coming?" Ice Box says.

"No, I'm going to have some of that delicious coffee and scarf half a dozen jelly donuts. I'm thinking maybe if I get as fat as you I'll get as smart too."

"Okay. I'll get you on your cell if the kid calls in," Ice Box says, working a bit to get his bulk out of the booth. I wait 'til he's driven off, notice he's stuck me with his tab—two coffees and three French crullers—pay up, and cruise the reservoir road once, pushing the TT hard through the curves just for the fuck of it. I'm chill when I get back to the station. IB's gone home already. There's a note from Annie on my desk, asking me to join her at Flannery's.

//

She's alone at a little table tucked back near the serving station, two empty shotglasses and one half-golden with tequila, two empty bottles of Dos Equis before her, and one to her lips when I sit down.

"Hey, don't look so judgmental, Luther," she says, giving me one of those smiles. I wasn't aware I'd given her any sort of look of the kind. "This is my last round. Know my limits. And you know I do."

"Also getting a strong impression you're not real happy tonight," I say.

"Little stressed these days, is all."

"You got reasons. Not like you're making it up."

"Ah, I'm whining. Got to stop whining. I keep telling myself, forget the Department bullshit and concentrate on the cases."

"You can do that."

"I *could* do that. It's not working too well right now."

"You can handle it."

"Sure. But the damned cases. There's almost nothing to handle, nothing to zero in on." Annie knocks back the last of her tequila, slams the shotglass down, chases with beer. "I've never been so fucking frustrated in my life, Luther! I'm beginning to think I'm no good at this."

"Hey, you know that's not true. You don't make lieutenant on nothing."

"Maybe I just had some easy cases, and the chief likes my legs and ass." Annie laughs, but there is no true laughter in it. "Sorry, Luther. Whining again. Seems to be getting habitual. Not a trait I admire in anyone, least of all myself."

"So I'll whine a little, give you someone else to dislike for very little reason besides yourself," I say, and tell her how I lost my kid at the meet earlier.

Not that it does much good. Annie seems as moody when we leave as she was when I came in.

//

I was fretting and sweating it for nothing. James calls on the cell when I'm driving home around ten. Tells me Buzz Cut asked pretty much the questions I'd told him he'd ask. James says he gave the answers I told him to give. He swears he wasn't nervous, swears he wasn't scared of Buzz Cut and didn't give a thing away by acting kinked or anxious. "It was cool, Luther," James says. "It was kinda fun. Like being in a movie or something."

I can feel muscles in various parts of my body loosen up after James hangs up. Then I have to watch where I'm going pretty closely, because I'm not going to my Cockeysville place. Just in case Buzz Cut has the resources to check me out, I'm staying at an apartment in Randallstown. It's one of the Department's safe houses, but hardly ever used. It's due to be retired, so Dugal got it for this one last thing. We changed and backdated the lease, the phone and gas and electric to the name of William Chase. That's me for now. William Chase. Driver's license, credit cards, all that stuff. The name James gave to Buzz Cut. The address and phone.

The place is a dump. Until I hear from Buzz Cut, I've got to go there at nights, park the TT right out front, sleep there. I take out garbage, let myself be seen around. I watch for tails when I go to work. There aren't any. But still I park the TT in a different place in Towson far away from headquarters, and on two days drive to Frederick and Hagerstown, park, and get lost in the tiny downtowns of those little cities for a few hours.

It's tedious. It's a pain in the butt. But it only lasts four or five days.

Then James gets me on my cell. He says tomorrow night, at eight, come alone with the money in a Gap shopping bag, walk down the east corridor of Dulaney Mall, and Buzz Cut'll meet me inside near the main entrance.

Be there at eight, James tells me, but you may have to wait a while. The man's funny about time, about showing up when he says he will.

12

Dugal wants a major scene: plainclothes, uniforms, even fucking tacticals with black masks and CAR15s. He's so revved it takes me and IB close to a half hour to convince him how bad that shit's going to go down in a crowded mall. "Guys in hoods with assault rifles? Mass panic. Newspapers'll go nuts," from IB clinches it. Dugal backs off.

No way this is going to be like the movies, though I can feel some of the more impressionable fucks on the squad rerunning great bust scenes in their heads. Big black Mercedes pulls up behind an abandoned warehouse, a couple of muscle guys with Uzis leap out and scan the littered alley, the buyer opens a Vuitton briefcase filled with perfect stacks of crisp hundred-dollar bills. . . .

No hundreds, for one thing. That's what Buzz Cut said. I'm threading my way through the crowds in Dulaney Mall around eight, dressed suburban white-boy fly—baggy cargo pants, acid-green T, $175 Reeboks—carrying $9,000 in that blue Gap bag with the drawstrings pulled tight. I'm near the big fountain that dominates the mall's entry lobby when I see Buzz Cut ambling toward me along the opposite spoke, looking very J.Crew, carrying a Barnes & Noble bag. We touch right fists when we meet. "Hey, Bob," he says, "who'd you roll for those pants? You need a wardrobe consultant."

"It's what's happening with my young friends," I say. "Embarrassing. But whatever it takes, right?"

"The things we do for biz." Buzz Cut shakes his head. He puts his hand on my shoulder and very gently steers me toward the automatic doors that open to the outside. Moment I feel that hand I want to shoot the fuck.

Just outside, in full view of the citizens coming and going, I open my bag a little, say, "Hey, check this out, man." Buzz Cut looks in, opens his bag too. I see the merchandise, neatly taped baggies. "Looks like we both got the weight," Buzz Cut says. We turn toward the parking lot, quick switch with the bags, and before we're another full step I snap on the cuffs. Ice Box is almost instantly on Buzz Cut's left, massive hand locked like a vice on his bicep. Tommy appears in front of us, two female plainclothes move in on the flanks, and Dugal pops up from behind the first row of cars and strides toward us.

"Oh *Bob.*" Buzz Cut sighs. "Don't even tell me. Let me guess. I'm under arrest, right?"

"Fuckin' A." Ice Box laughs. I start to Miranda him, but I'm slow off the mark because Buzz Cut is so cool about this he's kinked my rhythm. He's too damned chill, like he believes, really believes, that all this is just a little waste of his time.

So Dugal butts up and reads him his rights, then he and Tommy and the plainclothes girls take Buzz Cut off toward the LT's car. Me and Ice Box are left standing there, like we've just been robbed or something. "See you later, *Bob,*" Buzz Cut calls back over his shoulder.

"The fuck's smiling at me, IB. Dig him," I say.

"Yeah, Jesus, what an asshole," Ice Box says. "See how long that smile stays in place when we get him in the sweatroom. See if he keeps grinning while we grind him down."

We go off to get the TT. "This doesn't feel right. Perfect bust, and it don't fuckin' feel right," I say.

"Forget that! How in the hell am I supposed to fit in this toy?" Ice Box says, looking very dubiously at the TT. Of course he's seen me driving the thing out of the Department parking lot, but he's never been right next to it before, and when I scan the car and scan him side by side, my heart sinks. The man's going to crush my beautiful machine.

"Slow and easy, IB. Watch how heavy you come down. Just sort of slide right in, the way you do with MJ," I say, but I'm anxious.

"Shut up, small boy. Aw fuck!" Ice Box cracks his head on the outside edge of the roof. He's sort of stuck, his legs and half his ass inside, the rest outside.

"You gotta bend more, IB, and slip sideways. Watch the leather, though."

"I can't bend anymore. You think I'm some kind of circus contortionist?" IB complains. Backing and filling like an eighteen-wheeler in a crowded truck stop, he manages to get in and even close the door. Of course his head's near the dashboard instead of back against the seat, and his shoulders and torso are so far over toward me I have to punch him every time I shift gears. He bitches all the way to Towson, a running stream of abuse that would excite admiration among the most inventive drill instructors in the Corps.

"You're paying the chiropractor bills," he says when he pops out like a jack-in-the-box once we park at HQ.

"Yeah, yeah," I say. My mind's in the near future, I can't muster the usual comeback.

"Good, clean arrest, men," Dugal says when we come in. "Outstanding. You're going to love this, Luther. Our man's agreed to have a little casual conversation with you while he waits for his lawyer to get here. Says he'd enjoy a nice chat. That's a quote, his exact words. Your man's self-possession under the circumstances is extraordinary."

Good, clean bust only because I convinced you, asshole, not to fuck it up.

//

"I'm glad you want to see me, Peter," I say. "Did you see James in the holding cell? He's very angry with me. Won't say a word. Feels betrayed, I think."

"Oh, no hard feelings, Bob. None at all."

"Generous of you."

"I know you're just doing your job, Bob. I know you have to do your little thing for your little paycheck."

"What's your job, Peter? Do you like it? Like your employer?"

"Actually, I don't have either, Bob. I have investments."

"Oh? Trust fund from a rich uncle or something?"

"A bit more complex than that, Bob."

"Interesting. You must have some very interesting friends, Peter," I say. We're in the sweatroom, nothing sinister about it, just a very plain room with a table and three chairs, a large one-way mirror on a side wall, and the name on Buzz Cut's Maryland driver's license is Peter Raskin. That's being checked out. So are his fingerprints.

"No, Bob. I wouldn't call them interesting. I wouldn't call them friends." Buzz Cut smiles.

"Well, they impress me. I've seen a lot of horse, but never seen any as pure as yours. Our lab people are jumping up and down with excitement. Your friends gave you something very special. Don't you find that interesting?"

"Actually, Bob, I'm not quite following you here. Horse?" he laughs. No shades on now, I'm seeing his eyes for the first time; they're a pale arctic blue. "Jargon, Bob."

"Cut the crap, scumbag," Ice Box says. "Horse. Smack. Heroin. You handed it right over. Dumb move."

"Is that right? I find your big friend here interesting, Bob. Italian-American, I'd guess. Lasagna or baked ziti are his favorites, but he likes his mother's more than he likes what his wife makes. A little tension in the household? The wife hates going to his mother's for Sunday dinner sort of thing? I love the little details of little lives."

"Fuck you," Ice Box says. A minute into it and he's already on the edge of losing his cool. Not the usual IB.

"Oh, I like his mother's better too," I say, smiling. "IB's got good taste. The fact is his wife's a lousy cook."

"Now Bob, you can do better than that. So far the good cop–bad cop act is lame. I'd expected better."

"You want bad?" IB says. "I can give you real bad. You like a little pain, huh Pete? I'm thinking I've got this nice, heavy sap just waiting to meet your kidneys. You could be pissing blood for a week, not even a bruise to show how it happened."

"Please officer, not that." Buzz Cut laughs. "Bob, restrain your big friend, I beg you. You wouldn't want to blow your case by letting him do anything illegal, would you?"

"I'll do just that. Peter," I say. "I'm a very legal-type guy."

"Bob, that's not what I've heard. I've heard some shocking things."

The fuck's playing with me, he's having fun here.

"It's the other way around, Peter, isn't it?"

He laughs again. He laughs in this totally controlled way that is sending all sorts of signals to me now. "Did you see that great movie where Gary Oldman's a crooked DEA agent, he and his team bust into the apartment of some guy who's been short-weighting them and shoot him and his wife and kids? And when he hears the police sirens, he calmly starts to leave, except he orders one agent, who looks like some kind of hippy, to stay. And this hippy DEA says to Oldman, 'What do I tell the cops?' And Oldman says, very coolly, 'Tell them we were *doing our job*!' "

"Short-weighting? Jargon, Peter," I say. "Now you've gotten me all confused. This short-weighting sounds very bad, whatever it is. Now what if your friends found out, some way or other, that *you* have been short-weighting them? I mean, I know it's only Hollywood hyperbole you were talking about. But even if it was only half that bad. Oh Peter, I wouldn't want to be you."

"I'm not clear on what you mean, but is that some sort of threat? Are you threatening me in a veiled way, Snake?" Buzz Cut says, a little less cool now. "Now what is your boss, who's looking and listening on the other side of that mirror over there, going to say to you later? Is he going to say 'Snake, you asshole! I thought you knew how to interrogate suspects'?"

Then he's laughing again. "Oh Bob, you're not living up to my expectations at all. I was looking forward to a really interesting chat."

"I'm sorry if this is boring you, Peter. Let's start over. Where'd you get the heroin you tried to sell to me tonight? Name some names."

"Sell? I never tried to sell anything, you know that. I was simply carrying a bag someone I never saw before handed me, and you snatched it from me outside the mall. Good thing there were police around. An attempted robbery, in front of hundreds of witnesses. And you're so distinctive-looking, Bob. Anyone could identify you."

Now I laugh.

"Bob, let me ask you a serious question. Are you a crooked cop, the sort you sometimes read about in the newspapers, robbing and stealing and things?"

"Aw fuck this," IB snorts, getting up from his chair and moving behind Buzz Cut. "Stand up, shithead. I'm going to work on your kidneys."

"Your big friend watch a lot of television, Bob? Lot of movies, like Harvey Keitel in *The Bad Lieutenant*?" Buzz Cut says, standing. He turns his head back toward IB, gives him a big smile. "Well? You going to start this hitting shit or what?"

Ice Box puts his hands on Buzz Cut's shoulders and pushes him down into the chair, gently. "Not just now, faggot. Maybe later, after you've been gang-raped in your cell tonight."

IB gives me a hand signal, and we both start to leave the sweatroom. "I think I'll be going home before anything like that could happen," Buzz Cut says. "In fact, I guarantee it."

//

"Oh, very fruitful. Very useful. Really going to help a lot," Dugal says to me and IB.

The LT decides to let Buzz Cut stew a while. The LT goes off to have some coffee, maybe a snack. When he enters the interrogation room maybe an hour later, Peter Raskin is flanked by Harvey Eckhaus, the best criminal attorney in the county. Eckhaus is smart and fast as a weasel, he's beaten us more times than we can count. No questioning Raskin at all. Eckhaus says charge my client or release him. Dugal charges him with major felonies, Eckhaus gets hold of a judge and sets up a bail hearing that same night, and Buzz Cut walks on a $250,000 bond. It's so smooth I'm stunned.

Raskin checks clean. Born in Brooklyn, moved to Maryland three years ago, no outstanding warrants anywhere, no prior arrest record.

I'm standing by the door when Raskin's leaving with Eckhaus. Some flash out of nowhere hits me. I blurt, "Son of a horse-fucking whore!" in Russian. Raskin whirls and snarls, "Lick my balls!" In Russian. Eckhaus hustles him away.

Last doubts vanish. Definitely time to get next to Vassily. Time to sic the Dog.

13

I see Helen's Bug in the parking lot. I see her sitting on the corridor floor, leaning back against my door, legs sprawled. Her head's nodding in an odd way. Panic second. Then I see the tiny earphones, the thin wire snaking down to the slim silver CD player not much bigger than a CD itself resting on her lap. Her eyes are closed. I put my mouth close to her ear and call out, "Jammin'!"

She starts, grins up at me, pulls out the 'phones. I can hear the tinny sound of music from them. "You're going to go deaf, listening at that volume," I say.

"New Moby. Have to play it loud to get it all," she says, standing up.

"Get what, besides electronic drone? Don't know where you got your taste in music." I shake my head.

"Must have been the same place I got my taste in men." She kisses me. "About time you showed up."

"I don't recall we'd made a date for tonight."

"We didn't, but I was feeling needy so I came over."

"How long were you going to sit there waiting?"

"Oh, just 'til that song was finished. Then I was going to write you a heart-breaking note that'd make you feel guilty for hours, leave it leaning against your door so your neighbors would see it, and leave."

"Oh?"

"Well, I think nearly an hour was long enough sitting here waiting."

"You're a very whacked young lady, Helen," I say, keying the door and pushing it open, watching her slip in.

"No, just horny." She laughs.

She means it. We don't even make it to the sofa, we don't get any of our clothes off, just her skirt lifted and my fly unzipped and then it's happening on the living room rug. Quick but sweet. She rolls out from under me almost as soon as its over.

"Much better now," she says brightly. "See you later."

She gets up, but makes no move to go. Instead, she fetches a couple of beers from the fridge, hands me one, then curls herself up on the sofa, graceful as a cat. She watches me like a cat, too, for a while. An unblinking, concentrated gaze, impossible to read. Then she starts laughing.

"I'm trying to decide who you are, Luther," she says. "It's a bitch."

Normally I'd click off any conversation that weighted at its start, but I'm cool about it now. Seeing her so lovely and looking like she so belongs exactly there, content on my sofa, is better than a tab. It smoothes and soothes me. I can bear some girl talk in this state.

"Just what you see," I said.

"Can't see character, that's got to be revealed in words and actions," Helen says. "I thought I had a fix on you by last spring, but then three months apart, and I've lost it. Actually it's as much fun as it is a bitch, like I'm getting to learn you all over again. You know how you read a good book once, and then when you read it the second time after an interval, you find all kinds of new things and think, 'How'd I miss *that* the first time?' It's like that."

"So put me on the curriculum, let some of your classmates see if they have the same reaction."

"No way! No sharing. One or two of those sluts would make a try for that. Even though you're so old. And *you'd* probably go right along—even if they're kind of overweight and not great looking—'cause that's your character."

"Thought you hadn't figured out my character yet?"

"That part, for sure. It's the more complex bits. Can't decide if you're more like Faulconbridge the Bastard, Hotspur or Prince Hal, with weird bits of Mercutio, Hamlet and Iago all mixed in."

"What is it with you and Shakespeare?"

"Aside from writing the most beautiful English ever written by anyone? It's that all his characters *change* their characters. They don't stay the same all through the play. They shift and change like real people."

"Okay. Like real people, if you say so. But if you're right, you'll never figure out me or anyone else, because plays end and lives don't. Well, they do, but you don't usually get to see anyone's go all the way through to the end."

"I knew I was right about you, Luther! You want people—your audience—to think you're just a tough guy with street smarts and that's it. Like you said, what you see. But you can talk about ideas, relate to Shakespeare even if you've never read his work."

"Have read it. Well, we had to read *Julius Caesar* in high school. I liked the big stabbing scene best. Great knife work for a bunch of pansies dressed in sheets."

"Oh, kiss my ass, you cynic." Helen laughs, draining her beer and going for another.

"Now that wouldn't be any change, would it? Kiss that and a lot else in the vicinity every chance I get, don't I?"

"I suppose if that changes, I'll know it's over."

Later, drowsy in a rumpled bed, Helen in the shower, the phone jerks me wide awake.

"My little friend! You okay?" Vassily's drunk. He's also either clairvoyant or Buzz Cut's his man. I rule out the first immediately.

"Never better. Just got laid really, really well."

"Hah! So you got woman after all. I'm a little worried when I see you. You don't look so happy. I'm thinking, something missing in Shooter's life. So you getting taken care of?"

"Sure, Vassily. And you?"

"You need to ask, little brother? Knowing me like you do?" He laughs. "You take little vacation, come up here for a few days. We have some party."

"Not interested, if it's going to be anything like Charles Street."

"No, no, no. I'm thinking about sweet, sweet pussy. Lots of caviar, champagne. Nothing boring about that, is there?"

"Sounds much better. Yeah, I'll come up. Pretty busy right now, but soon."

"Promise me?"

"Sure."

"Because also maybe something is coming along we can do together. Some business."

"I'm listening."

"When you come, we talk. Guy I got down there where you are, I begin to think he's the wrong guy. Little stupid. He's giving me some damn headache."

"Think it's the vodka did that."

Vassily's laugh booms over the line. "Not since I stopped sucking my mother's tit! Vodka! No such thing as too much. Same with women. So I let you get back to yours. She got a sweet ass? I let you go then. Until we meet, little brother. World is nothing without friends."

"Until we meet." I hang up. My mind runs replays even after Helen slides in next to me, smelling sweet and good enough to eat. Why's it got to be Vassily? Why couldn't it be someone else?

//

Next morning, warrant all official, IB and Tommy and I go toss Buzz Cut's crib. Nice place. Saporiti sofa and chairs, Nakamichi sound system, lots of Italian style. Clean as an old bone too, which I expected. No dope anywhere, naturally. No papers, no ledgers, no cash stash, no address book. Got his numbers in his head, I figure, or in a Palm Pilot he carried out of jail when Eckhaus sprung him.

IB's rummaging through kitchen cabinets, Tommy's prodding and poking and lifting cushions on all that nice oxblood Saporiti leather. I'm in the bedroom, just scanning. Confident boy, Buzz Cut, I'm thinking. Smart. Knows there's no way to hide anything that any competent pro burglar won't find. So why bother? There's a night table, steel and blond wood with a Berenice lamp on top. I slide open the drawer. Like I figured: a driver's license in the name of Peter Raskolnik. Platinum Visa, MasterCard and Amex Blue with the same name and expiration dates a few years down the road. I don't reach for an evidence baggy. It's illegal as hell, but I just pocket the license and the cards. They might be useful sometime. I toss the stuff in his closet and his armoire for appearance's sake, then just stretch out on the bed. A lot more comfortable than my Ikea number. Lot of thoughts shuffling around while I listen to IB and Tommy chattering and banging around in the other room. I only notice I've started thinking in Russian when IB appears in the doorway and says, "What the fuck? You figure it's nap time already?"

"The room's clean," I say. "Not a single thing worth bagging."

"Shit!" IB says. "We got the big zero too."

"What'd you expect, Ice? The guy's a pro. He's gonna have scales and heat sealers and a couple of kilos of smack lying around? You don't shit where you eat, right? He don't work where he lives. Bet you five large he's got a little very anonymous and very secure crib someplace. A business address."

"Which we'll never get unless he gives it up."

"IB, you're a genius."

"Kiss my guinea ass."

//

Most everybody calls out some greeting when we get back to the squadroom. Except Taggert. Taggert has his nose deep into some paperwork, keeps his head down, doesn't look up or look at me.

Ice Box comes over and sits on the extra chair in my cubicle. The chair squeals and creaks. "Great morning. I hate zeros," he says. "So, man, you going to tell me what that little exchange between you and Buzz Cut when he walked was all about? Start simply—like with what language you two were talking."

"Russian. But never mind about that, IB."

"Russian? You thinking Russian mafia? You considering asking me for that cell number Dee Dee gave me?"

"Don't have to. Got it a long time ago."

"What?"

"Well, I broke into your computer and took it. It was easy. You had it filed under 'Contacts' as 'Vaseline.' "

"You lowlife fuck! I resent that, man. That's really going too far."

"Oh, chill, IB. You so tense about the birth you losing your sense of humor or what?"

IB leans toward me, lowers his voice. "Luther, I'm scared shitless. From no kids to twins? Aw Jesus, it's shaking me up. Suppose something happens to MJ? I get bad thoughts like that sometimes."

"Nothing's going to happen," I say. "Except that when she and the kids get home from the hospital, the Ice Box is going to learn what sleep deprivation means, and experience many times day and night the great aroma of dirty Pampers."

"You know what, Luther," IB says, getting up to leave, "every time I get woke in the middle of the night for a feeding, every time MJ forces me to change a diaper, I'm gonna phone you and give you the play-by-play. Call it payback, thief. You won't like it, but you'll be grateful to me later, when your turn comes."

I can hear IB laughing to himself even when he's back in his cubicle.

I call Annie. Voice mail. I leave a dinner invitation for tonight. Then I start thinking about Buzz Cut. We've got nothing at all on his girl counterpart, and I don't believe he's going to give her up. I'm thinking she must be scarier than Buzz Cut too, because none of the kids we've busted who dealt with her are willing to do what Jimmy Halliday did. I'm wondering how tight she is with Vassily. Could be very tight.

//

"So what's got you down, Luther? Helen cutting out on you or something?" Annie asks. "For a man who just pulled off a major bust very cleanly and neatly, you don't seem to be exhibiting appropriate responses."

"Which would be?"

"Well, a little excitement, maybe. Even exhilaration. Some self-satisfaction would be in order. Some boasting and bragging would even be understandable. You look like your brother died or something."

Oh, that's too close, I think. It's my own fault. I've been staring at rather than eating the plate of linguine with pesto before me at Bocca, where Annie and I met for dinner.

"Anomie, maybe?" I mumble. "Or maybe letdown. Sort of like the post–Christmas depression I always had as a kid."

Annie just laughs, shakes her head.

"So I'm too fucked up to live, right?" I say.

"I hate to be the one to say it, but yeah." She smiles. "Do you want me to shoot you, or would you prefer to do it yourself? I've tried, but I can't think of any other solution. You're a terminal case."

"Will you do it for me, Annie? Will you? But please, not in the face. Make it a heart shot, okay?"

"Sure, but I'd like to finish this veal, it's delicious," Annie says. "And then I'd like a tiramisu for dessert and a double espresso. Can you wait?"

"Oh yeah. No rush at all. I can handle my miserable existence for another half hour at least."

Annie goes back to enjoying her meal. I start in on the linguine, but I don't have much appetite. Annie's the one person in the world who'd understand exactly how complicated my situation's getting. She'd see that no matter how I go after Vassily—strictly by the book, which doesn't seem to me to be either sure or safe, or freelance, which'd give me a better chance of surviving—I'm going to *look* dirty, even if I'm spotless as an angel. It's going to come out we know each other, that I've been seeing him, probably too that I was a merc in Bosnia.

I can't tell her a thing about Vassily. And I definitely can't mention the only clean solution I've come up with—a totally covert mission. Shit. The only thing worse than letting yourself get fucked is fucking yourself.

"You know what it is, Annie? Buzz Cut's nobody. I shouldn't have moved on him. I should have used my head, got close to him, let him lead me up the ladder toward the guys who really count, then popped them all. If Buzz Cut's put away, he'll just be replaced by his boss. And I don't have one single clue who that boss is. That arrest was a goatfuck," I lie. "So I'm having a self-esteem problem here."

"That's a first!" Annie says. "Welcome to the club. Maybe now you've got a hint of how I've been feeling lately."

14

Dog's on the phone next morning before I even get the lid off my cardboard cup of bitter, burned coffee.

"What is it, home?" I say.

"Got something real pretty to show you, Luther. You'll dig it. Just go down Greenmount Avenue to Thirty-fourth Street, make a right. Can't miss the house. Lots of yellow tape, lots of cruisers with lights flashing. You got maybe twenty minutes before the good stuff gets taken away."

Dog's right. Crime scene tape has an old two-story house with crappy aluminum siding that once was white and now's a dingy neutral wrapped like a Christmas present. There's at least three meat wagons in addition to four patrol cars and two unmarked. Lots of uniforms standing in the tiny front yard that's mostly beaten earth with a few clumps of weed, or peering at the immaculate red Dodge Viper, a V-10 exotic worth $80,000 and change, in the cracked concrete driveway. Beyond that's a new silver Lincoln Navigator. A uniform trys to growl me away, straight Police Academy style, but one of Dog's men comes out on the porch, sees this action and calls me through.

This place hasn't seen much in the way of maintenance in a long time. The wood steps up to the porch are warped and dry-rotted. Forensics team is hanging out there, waiting their turn inside. Paint's peeling off the wood front door, but there's a fairly new and heavy-duty steel grill backing it. The first-floor windows are well barred too. The door's open. I'm expecting to smell what happened here before I step in, expecting that heavy, oddly sweetish odor of blood pools not yet congealed. Instead there's just the stale breath of a house long lived in, never kept too clean. Musty. Mousey. Then I see a little kid lying in the foyer face down in a little puddle that's part blood and part some other fluids. Can't tell if it was a boy or a girl, in those superbaggy nylon cargoes, the Polo top, the Nikes. But I guess about five or six years old by the body size.

Two suits—homicide, they're wearing surgical gloves, there's evidence baggies hanging out of their jacket pockets—come into the corridor from a side room, muttering to each other. One, an older guy with dark bags under his eyes and not much hair left, glances at me and stiffens. "Who the fuck are you? Some DEA freak?" he shouts.

"It's okay, dude. One of mine," Dog says, moving out of the room opposite.

"Don't touch a thing. Don't neither of you touch one goddamn thing, or I'll have your ass," the homicide detective says, way too loud. Either he's got a hearing problem he doesn't know about or he's just a real dick.

"What you know?" Dog says, beckoning me down the hall.

"No good," I say. "You indicated I was going to enjoy this."

Dog laughs, mean edge to it. "You will. This definitely your kind of thing, man. Check it out, check it out."

In Dog's room, the kitchen, there's a body sitting on the floor, back propped against the cabinets under the sink. Three small holes you couldn't fit a pencil into, crusting around the edges but still oozing, in her swollen face. Young woman, judging by her shape and the skin and muscles of her legs, which I see almost all the way up to her crotch because her skirt's so short and tight.

Across the corridor, where the Homicide suits had been, I count three men—one draped over a big dining table, one sprawled on the floor near a china cabinet, one still remarkably on his knees, with a hand gripping a window bar. Heads all turned toward the door, three small holes in each face.

Dog leads me up the stairs to the second floor. Just at the top there's another young woman, and three steps away a fat old lady in a quilted robe. No blood pools. Faces intact. But their clothes are soaked around the abdomens. Zoom in. Three little holes in each. The rear bedroom has a steel door. Inside there's a big gun safe, a steel table with scales, a box of heavy plastic bags and one of those machines for heat-sealing them when they've been filled. White powder lightly dusts one pan of the scales.

"Smack or coke?" I ask.

"Her-O-in," Dog says.

The safe's open. No drugs, no money. Two Tech-9s, two Mossberg assault shotguns, one AR15 carbine still racked. A body with one arm reaching for them, another male body under the table. Three in the face for both.

In the bathroom, a woman sitting on the toilet, naked, rubber tubing wrapped tight on her right bicep and a hypo still stuck in the vein. Three in the face. In one front bedroom, two kids in one bed, coverlet soaked pinkish in the belly area. In the other, a young man fucking a girl, bodies still joined. Three holes in her side, between the hip and the ribs. Three in his, same place. Oozing.

"Some neighbor get pissed off because these people playing music real loud, or what?" I say. I'm not liking what the scene's telling me.

"Watch what you sayin', nigger. Dead kids some joke to you?" Dog snaps.

"I've seen worse. Innocent kids."

"Implyin' these kids *deserved* this shit?"

"No, I didn't mean . . ."

"Fuck you didn't. You thinkin' they just nigger brats of drug-dealing slobs, what they get is what it is. Like they had some choice who their mammas and pappas was. Don't be giving me no war stories either, dude. You got no idea how bad the parents of the kids you saw wherever the fuck you saw 'em were. Torturers, rapists, stone killers for all you know."

"You're misunderstanding me, Dog. I didn't mean what you seem to be hearing."

"Fuck that, Luther. I didn't call you 'cause I like you. I ain't been liking you much since you held out on me when those two cops got the same face jobs as this crew. You know something. I want it."

"Hey man, I don't know a thing about this shit."

"You lying to me, nigger."

"Take it down a notch, Dog—now," I say sharply.

"Yeah, yeah," Dog nods, but the anger doesn't leave his eyes. "Here's how it is. Crib of the Trey Four Crew, cap-poppin' bangers. You right about the loud music. The neighbors say they hearing a lot of Ice T, stuff like that, 'til about two A.M. Then they hearin' nothing. No gunfire, nothing. And they do know the sound of shots 'round here. Start with that."

"Suppressed weapons. You don't need me to tell you."

"No, I do not. But the heads? My guess is the autopsy report's gonna say the same as the two cops."

"Yeah. So what? You got some shooters with the same weapons, is all that means. Maybe it's the start of a trend."

"What fucking weapons, Luther? Check the bodies. Not a single exit wound. Not one bullet hole in a wall or a door. How come nothing went through a head and came out the other side? How is that possible? And why three, always three holes?"

Choice time. Do I gain anything by keeping the Russians to myself? Negative. I'll need Dog. Go deeper. Is it personal with Vassily? Could be, but can't let it be. Unfuck it, Luther. Give.

"I'm thinking 5.45mm, in a short-barreled sub called an AKSU. Three-round bursts. Cartridges loaded with frangible bullets."

"Say what?"

"Shit, Dog. You use hollow points, Cor-Bons probably, in your pistols because they expand, make bigger wounds, have more stopping power, right? But they've got enough mass still to pass through a man and hole the walls or whatever. You know what happens with a high-velocity rifle bullet, any caliber—small hole in the forehead, the entire back of the skull blown away by the exit. Holes in the walls again. Wet and messy, worse than 9-millie dome shots."

"Right. Keep goin'."

"Frangible bullets disintegrate, man. Very light, very fragile. They just barely penetrate and then explode. No exit wounds."

"Keep on, man."

"Regular NATO 5.56 ain't anything but a super-juiced .22, has a steel penetrator core, 62-grain bullet leaves the barrel at over three thousand feet per second. Major high velocity. Little hole going in, pressure wave cavitation and big hole leaving. These people wouldn't have any heads if it was that. Frangibles, 5.45, loaded subsonic, just go *pffft.* But they mush everything inside. Autopsy these stiffs, their brains or abdomens are gonna look like somebody put 'em in a Cuisinart. Run a really sensitive metal detector over the mush, you'll get a reading. Tiny fragments of copper mixed in with the tissue."

"I follow. Plenty of speed, but the bullet breaks up and stays inside. Why no blood pools?"

"Bleeding's mostly internal. The holes just ooze, unless a major artery very near the surface gets clipped. Then you'd get a real hosing. Red rain, man."

"Gimme it all, Luther."

I take Dog back to the steel-doored drug room, we kneel beside one of the bodies. "First, nobody got shot above the eyebrows or anywhere in the cranium. No dome shots with frangibles. They might not get all the way through skull bone before fragmenting, just scoop out a chunk of scalp and chips. Guy might even live. So the first shot goes in the cheek, just above the jaw bone. Notice how the next two are slightly higher and angle up toward the right? Means you got a right-handed shooter with the weapon set for three-round bursts, hits rising because of muzzle-climb. You'll see the same left-to-right climb on the belly shots, unless one of the shooters was left-handed. Then the pattern would reverse."

"Why? Tell me the fuck why? Why not just come in with a silenced nine and kill 'em all in the head?"

"Faster, cleaner, much quieter. Just *pffft, pffft, pffft.* No bullets to get dug out of the walls or woodwork for ballistics to examine," I say. "And a style."

"Whose style?"

"Dog, this place," I wave my arm around to indicate the whole house, "was taken out by Russians. Ex-military, probably former Soviet Special Forces. It's their signature. Very, very ugly. Meant to scare the shit out of everyone who hears about it. So when they come callin', folks'll act nice and cooperative."

"Fresh, man. Going postal," Dog says. Funny look in his eyes now, anger gone and something like excitement lighting them up. "Every gangsta in town gonna know about this. They already jumped-up about the dead Crips and Bloods. They think they real bad, but they learning maybe there's dudes much badder movin' into the 'hood."

"Oh, much badder."

"Now I know why you been jivin' me, Luther. You after these fucks. I think you *know* these fucks. Your boss aware you cruisin' out on this?"

Forensics is swarming all over the house now, dusting for prints, scavenging fibers, the usual. The first of the bodies is being bagged and taken out to the meat wagon. "You gonna tell *your* boss what I told you, Dog?"

"Not today. When, depends," Dog says, smiling somewhere in between evil and friendly. "You and me, we together on this? We tight?"

"Could be. But just you. Not your crew."

"You don't trust your County homies, so you goin' solo, right, Luther?"

"It isn't trust. I just don't think they're up to it."

"My guys are. Russian fuckin' mafia. Shit!"

"You do some crack this morning or what, Dog?" I say. "Seein' what you see here, hearing what I just told you? These aren't spray-and-pray gangstas. These are pros who could take out your whole squad before any one of them could even draw his tool."

"So they take your sorry ass out, too."

"They're never gonna see me coming. If they do, I know everything they know about this particular line of work. Plus some."

"You got the mouth. Ain't seen the moves . . . except that one arm breaker."

"Maybe I'll let you watch, things come down that way."

"Shit. So you sayin' it's just you and me? That it, Luther?"

"That's the deal."

Dog raises his fist. I raise mine. We punch knuckles. Deal done.

15

Scut work the rest of the week. The high point is Hannah day. Her lawyer brings her in around ten-thirty one morning. We sit around the table in one of the interrogation rooms, but there's no tension. Ice Box and I aren't working her hard, that's clear even to her attorney, who's alert but relaxed. He looks curiously at the photos of Buzz Cut and the composite sketch of the female dealer we slide in front of his client.

Hannah's playing. She read me from the first moment she saw me. She likes to push the buttons on men. She's wearing a cropped jersey top that molds and cups her buffed little breasts like second skin, her nipples tight and pressing against the thin fabric as soon as she slinks into the room. Just the air conditioning, I know, but she gives me this look that almost seems to say she's making this happen deliberately. She's got a new navel ring, this one with a tiny gold spider dangling from it, her spandex skirt comes barely to mid-thigh, and her bare legs go a long way before they disappear into russet suede ankle boots.

It's all wasted on Ice Box. She might be a fourteen-year-old virgin in a Catholic schoolgirl's uniform, the way he speaks to her. Maybe, I think, he's got a switch in his head that he flicks, and that's exactly what he sees before him. Not that she gives a damn. She's the clever one, she knows exactly who to toy with. One day, I think, she'll do this with the wrong guy in the wrong place and wind up damaged. What a waste.

My mind is nowhere near to being on my work. I'm falling in ruinous, dangerous love—a little deeper every time she feels my appraising eyes on her, which she never fails to no matter how subtle

I try to be about it, and responds with a smile so full of promise it's hard to credit it's only a game. A little playtime.

People have been telling me for years I need professional help. I know they've all been right.

"Never saw this boy in my life," she says when Ice Box asks her about the Buzz Cut pix.

"You're absolutely sure?" IB presses.

"Oh, I'd remember. I always remember, don't I?"

"I wouldn't know, Hannah," IB says evenly.

"I bet Detective Ewing knows," the little bitch smiles. "He knows I'm the girl who remembers everything."

IB glances sharply at me. I shrug denial. He's maybe not buying it.

"How about the girl?" IB asks her. "She look at all familiar to you, Hannah?"

"Girls I remember too. Not this one, though," she says. She's under her lawyer's instructions not to make any mention of drug buying or implicate herself in any drug-related matters. "But someone a little like her. Around the malls and stuff, the clubs. Only the one I'm thinking of has eyes a bit larger, set farther apart. And her upper lip is fuller than her lower. Kind of pouty, you know? Like mine."

"So this sketch is close to someone you've seen, except for the eyes and that lip?" IB says. "Remember anything about that girl? Where you saw her, how frequently, how she dressed? Her car? You ever see her car?"

"A couple of clubs in Towson, where the college students hang," Hannah says. She knows we don't give a shit about her slipping underage into bars for drinks and dancing. "Streamers and, like, that other place that plays a lot of house music, with twin DJs? Shit, what's the name?"

"Thought you had this great memory, Hannah. You go to this place a lot, don't remember the name?" IB says, holding her eyes with his. I'm watching her breasts move like live creatures as she shifts and stretches her arms over her head as if that was a mnemonic aid of hers.

"Bodies and faces are my specialty, so maybe I never saw anyone I really got into there," she says coolly. "Give me a sec or two."

"Take your time," I say. Hannah lowers her arms, crosses them under her breasts, a completely unnecessary gesture since she's got my undivided attention.

"Think, think, think." She smiles. "Something techie, sort of sci-fi. Internet-y. Yeah, Ethernet! That's the place. Ethernet."

IB glances at me again. Both clubs were big with Ecstasy users. "And the car, Hannah?"

"One of those new Bugs. Yeah, a few times I saw her driving a Bug. Took a boy with her, too, but always a different one. Not this jerk," she says, pushing Buzz Cut's photo away from her with one long, bloodred fingernail.

On some instinct I open another file and slide an 8×10 across the table. Hannah takes one quick look and smiles. "Him I know," she says. "I mean, I don't *know* him, but he's around a lot. He's always asking everybody if they want some Ecstasy." She jerks very slightly. Probably her lawyer tapped her knee with his under the table. "I never bought any from him, though," she says. "Lots of people did, but not me."

The photo's of Jimmy Halliday. I get an instant bad vibe on that. Maybe Jimmy's more than we thought.

"Okay, great. You're sure, Hannah? Anything else you can tell us?" IB asks. She shakes her head no.

"So, gentlemen, if that's it we'll be on our way," the girl's lawyer says, standing up. As they're leaving, Hannah sings a low line from that Fiona Apple disc: "I been a bad, bad girl . . . ," which is as far as she gets before her lawyer grips her arm and propels her out the door.

I lean back in my chair. "Life is sweet for certain. But too fucking short. Just imagine how that girl could rock your world, IB."

"You're sicker than shit, Five-O. Drooling over kids. You're gonna get busted by Annie's people one of these days, you ever act on your perverted notions."

"Chill on that, IB," I say. "Down-to-business time. You read anything into her being so quick to finger Jimmy?"

"Yeah. It raises some questions, doesn't it? Like maybe he's a badder actor than we thought?"

"My take exactly."

"Which means, you realize, he's walking a much more dangerous line than we set him up to walk."

"That occurs to me too."

"More protection?"

"What more can we do? We kept him in the holding cell for eight hours after Buzz Cut walked on bail. Then we had him walk out with his lawyer, just in case there were any eyes out there watching. As far as Buzz Cut and his bosses are concerned, Jimmy's busted bad as Buzz Cut."

"I don't know, just don't know. This shit is getting way too complicated for me." IB sighs. "It was simpler in the old days. Everybody snorting lines of coke in the bathrooms. Easy busts. Now the kids drop Ecstasy before they go into the clubs. Nobody's carrying anything. You send a plainclothes or two into a club now and draw a zero. Just a lot of spaced-out kids dancing. All into some kind of mental cyberspace. Wonder what it feels like? Like being stoned on grass, do you think?"

"I hear it's more like LSD, minus the hallucinations. And no bad trips."

"This makes me feel old, Luther." IB sighs again. "Very old."

Friday night, sheet lightning flashing and thunder cracking the sky beyond the hills to the north. I pick up Helen and we go downtown to one of the movie theaters that feature foreign films. *Burnt by the Sun* is playing. We'd both seen it when it first got released in the States, but Helen loved it and I wanted mainly to brush up on my Russian.

I dug the story. It was believable, except for the young guy killing himself at the end. He was much too hard, much too cold, much too much a suvivor to do that. Shit, it was just one more betrayal. Why get juked by that, when betrayal's your trade? But Helen's in tears after the aging colonel makes love to his young wife for the last time, then leaves her and his adorable little daughter behind the gate of their dacha to drive away with the secret police.

"So sad," she says when we're driving out to my place afterward. "Really cracks my heart."

"Just what the filmmaker hoped would happen. You're his ideal audience."

"Oh, it didn't touch you? Where's your heart?"

"In the present. Who cares what happened in Stalin's time?"

"Are you saying the past isn't worth grieving over?"

"Yeah, basically."

"Liar."

"What's hard to believe about that? What's done is done. You just move on."

"You don't know that you talk in your sleep?" Helen says. "You really don't?"

"I never talk in my sleep."

"Yeah, then who was Mikla, and why do I know that name? What was she to you and what happened that makes you whimper over her some nights?"

"You must have dreamed that yourself." I feel suddenly very, very shaky. "Is that even a name? Doesn't sound like a name."

"You say it often enough in your sleep. You say it like she was someone very close and you've got loads of grief about her."

"No way."

"Oh, maybe she's your imaginary friend, then. And sometimes you dream about her. Except you're a little mature to have imaginary friends, don't you think?"

"I still think it's you that's dreaming," I say. Gotta get out of this somehow. Can't let it go any further. So I take a step so ruthless it makes my stomach flip.

"I'll tell you what I grieve over, what I might be dreaming about for a while," I say, and give her a semisanitized but still graphic version of what I saw in that house on Thirty-fourth Street.

"Oh my God, Luther," she says. She looks stricken. "I saw that on TV. Only the cameras didn't get inside the house."

"The fucking vultures tried hard enough, even though they knew damn well the gory stuff would never air. The station news directors censor the hell out of bang-bang. Don't want to upset the viewers with too much reality."

"Those poor, poor kids. Why did they have to shoot the kids? Why would anyone do that?" is about all that Helen can manage. She doesn't really want an answer, so I don't give her one. We ride in silence the rest of the way.

Inside my apartment, Helen fusses around in her purse and then holds a palm before me. On it are two Ecstasy tabs.

"Not you too," I say. "Where'd you get that?"

"You're the narc, you ought to know." She smiles. "Luther, it's everywhere. Don't go all stern about it. The pills you take, the dope you've smoked and the coke you've snorted . . . and don't dare deny *that.* Maybe you've narrowed it down to some pills now, but sometime when you were younger I *know* you did your share of smoke and coke."

"The pills are prescription, for a medical condition."

"So you say, and so what? Lighten up a little, babe. Take one of these with me. I need you to. World's looking a bit too nasty for me just now."

We drop the Ecstasy, put Sinéad Lohan on the sound system, cuddle up on the sofa. It's my first time. I keep waiting for something to kick in. Nothing does. Helen goes so soft and dreamy, so peaceful, that I wish I could be where she is. Nothing, though. Yet I find I can't be bothered to get up and change the tunes when Sinéad's finished, but just let the tape loop again and again.

When Helen, who's been stroking and nuzzling me, murmurs "Who's Mikla, Luther? What happened to her?" I say, "She was a girl not much older than you, in the wrong place at the wrong time, and she got shot."

It feels like Helen's warm arms are enfolding my soul when I begin to weep.

16

My brain still feels like it's cradled in velvet when I hit my cubicle the next morning. Though I'm late, it seems too early. The sky's lowering, dark and dense, and what light there is dim, diffuse, a sickly gray tinged with yellow. The office fluorescents barely cut the gloom.

Ice Box looks wasted, as if he'd been on a bad drunk last night. But he says, "Man, you look very weird, especially around the eyes. You get any sleep, Luther?"

"I was about to ask you that."

"I didn't. Not much anyway. Had a bad scare. MJ shakes me awake around two, says the babies are coming. So I'm up quick, you know, putting clothes on, ready to rush her to the hospital."

"Bad scare? What's wrong with you, IB? You should be joyous. So did it happen? No, wait, that's stupid. You'd be at the hospital, not here, if you were a new dad."

"Nothing happened. Except two more times MJ did the same fucking thing, and I get dressed, and then she says false alarm. Hard on the nerves, Luther. I didn't get a wink. I mean, let's get it over with. I'm ready."

"Guess God and MJ aren't quite ready." I laugh. "And neither of them are about to time things just to please you."

"Go ahead and laugh. It ain't funny. I can't fuckin' wait 'til it's your turn, Five-O. Jittery as you tend to be in your normal state, you're gonna go berserk in a situation like this. Then I'll be doing the laughing."

"My turn? You'll be drooling in some nursing home, with your kids too scared to bring their kids over to see their crazy granddad, before it's my turn."

"Oh we'll see about that. You might have an accident with one of your little lovers one of these nights, and actually have the integrity to do the right thing."

"I'll have the integrity to see she has the safest abortion money can buy, my treat," I say. "Anything beyond that, forget it. I make my rules of engagement very, very clear at the start."

"That is truly fucked up. Do you have any awareness at all how warped you are?" Ice Box laughs, but he cuts it short, a really odd expression crossing his face. "Luther, I think whatever you got must be contagious. Otherwise, why am I here talking to you on a fucking Saturday morning when it's not our shift?"

"What?"

"It's Saturday, Five-O. Sometimes we work Saturdays and sometimes we don't, you idiot. This is not—repeat, not—a duty Saturday."

"But we're here. Right?"

"Exactly. Jesus, what did you do to your head last night? I've got an excuse for confusion, but I'd love to know what explains your crazed state of mind. No, scratch that. I don't want to know. It's probably something I'll find offensive. Or illegal."

"Uh, maybe we'd better talk deal here, IB. Let's quietly slip out, separately so we create as little disturbance as possible, and forget we had this conversation. In fact, this encounter does not exist, nor did it ever exist. Agreed?"

Ice Box nods. "I'll go first," he says, and moves off. Before he's taken two steps he turns. "MJ says why don't you come to dinner tomorrow night?"

"Little late for dinner parties, isn't it? After last night and all?"

"I'm doing the cooking. Baked ziti, salad, garlic bread. Nothing fancy. MJ says nothing's going to happen for at least a week now."

"How's she know that?"

"Hell if I know. She just says she knows."

"Well, right. Love to come," I say. IB takes another step, then turns his face back to me.

"Oh, MJ says bring your girl. Not that Hannah, the real one you claim you got. Says she's tired of seeing your ugly face solo."

"I'll make it happen," I say, but regret the words instantly. "Around seven?"

IB nods and leaves the squad room.

I sit for what seems a long while staring at my phone. Images of my night start to jostle and shove for attention. I remember the weeping, Helen's embrace. God, the girl's wise beyond her years, I'm thinking. She understood completely, didn't judge, offered comfort. Even Annie couldn't have handled me better. I could live with that kind of woman. . . .

I could live with Helen, we could have a real life, fuck the age and class difference. I care for her more than I cared for anyone else I've ever been with. . . .

Then I snap back. Dangerous shit, that Ecstasy, I decide. I call Annie. "I'm up on an eight-foot stepladder scraping paint off crown moldings with a small propane torch and a table knife. I'll call you back when I'm done," her recorded voice says after the fifth ring. Damn.

I drive out to Loch Raven, make my way down through the piney woods. I hate it, hate the dark monotony of the trees, the spooky whishing of millions of needles stroked by the wind. But I want to see this Hollow Point. It isn't much; a little cove with a pebble beach flanked by tall rock outcroppings. I scale the one on the right. It's an easy climb, but at the end I'm almost ten meters above the water, the rock's sheared away so cleanly it might have been quarried, except there's no drill marks in the stone. I can see up and down the reservoir for maybe a mile, the water a steely gray and the distant peninsulas looking deep, dull black in the storm light.

I squat on the granite for maybe thirty minutes, maybe an hour, waiting for rain, waiting for thunder, a little exercise in not remembering, a little drill in putting feelings down so deep inside it's as if they never existed. Used to do this before combat—if there was time. "You gotta get your head cold and clear," Gunny used to tell me when I was young. "You don't want to be having to think. You want to let your training, your instincts take over completely. You want it like you as a person don't exist. You make yourself a machine, with faster relexes and faster responses than any man could have. Thoughts, emotions, they just slow you down, make you a target. Always go in cold and clear and empty, you wanna win and live to tell about it."

Except there's nothing much to tell, afterward. You're so cold and clear and slick everything slides off you—the sounds, the sights, just exactly what you did. All you know after is there are dead people around you, it's gone all quiet again, and you're still standing and breathing. All you check is who else on your team's still standing and breathing. That's the only victory.

I slip down off the rock and up through the forest like I'm a ghost, and get the TT back to my apartment on autopilot, not a thought in my head. When I park and slip out of the car, I get drenched to the skin by a downpour I'd never noticed before I can make the ten-meter dash into the building lobby.

Maybe you got trouble with rules of engagement of every variety, I think to myself. But you're number one at disengagement, for sure.

I drop a tab to help keep it that way, call Helen. She'll be over by eight tonight. And Sunday dinner with IB and MJ is fine by her. I call Annie. She's still up her ladder with the propane torch. Or wants everybody to think she is.

//

"So, Luther. How come, for the first time ever, you're taking me public?" Helen asks when we're driving to IB's house.

"MJ told Ice Box to tell me to bring my girl. Said she's tired of my ugly face solo. So . . . orders."

"MJ's about to have twins, right? Her hormones are running amok. She's got a thing about you, Luther. She wants to see if you've really got a girl, or if you're a gay boy."

"That's truly whacked. You're talking about my partner's wife, for God's sake, who happens to be the most centered, self-secure person I know."

Helen's laughing harder now. "Cro-Magnon, babe. You *really* don't know how women's minds work, do you?"

"There isn't a girl in town who wouldn't be scared to death to get involved with me if they knew how well I *do* know them."

"The ego on you really stuns me," Helen manages, still laughing. "Tell you a truth right now. You've got sweaty palms about this. You're praying I don't go all girly, since you already feel like a cradle robber. You're scared I'm going to find out lots of your secrets. MJ's gonna give them up."

"No way. Negative." I smile. But, dammit, my palms are sweaty, a little at least. Within an hour even I can see Helen's in the X-ring. MJ treats her exactly like a contemporary, not a schoolgirl, and Helen makes a bond. They're an instant team, and they're amusing themselves with their boys. They're out in the backyard lying in lounge chairs, taking the last of the September sun, and laughing excessively, in my opinion.

"How is it women get away with this shit?" Ice Box says. We're in the kitchen, him laboring over the food and me a neutral observer. "Like bugs under a microscope, you and me."

"Affirmative. Got to face one fact, IB. They're smarter than us."

"But how is it they get so tuned in to each other so quick? If they click at all, they click as soon as they meet. Never works that way with men."

"No, never does."

"Helen's so sharp it's scary," IB says, removing a foil-lined baking dish from the oven. The kitchen's immediately awash in aromas of oregano, Parmesan, ricotta, provelone and other good things. I hear more laughter outside. "I underestimated you on this one, Five-O. I admit it. Imagine what she's going to be like in a few years, once she's been out in the world and picked up some experience."

"Isn't it about chow time, IB?" I want off this subject. It's reminded me about those thoughts of Helen I squelched after our Ecstasy night.

"Yeah. Go get 'em, will you?"

Over the baked ziti and salad and a decent red Merlot from the Veneto, IB and I are face-to-face with female complicity.

"I tried making this dish once. Just once," MJ says to Helen.

"I can guess what happened," Helen says. "IB claimed it was no way near as good as what his mom makes. Though it was probably a lot better."

"Now that's not exactly what . . ." IB tries.

"Exactly," MJ says to Helen, tossing IB a wicked grin. "God bless the sacred Italian momma. Once he complained that his mom even washed his underpants better than I could. How, I asked? Don't know exactly, he said, they just feel better, the way Mom does it."

Helen nearly spews a mouthful of wine across the table, convulsed with laughter.

IB's looking stricken, staring alternately at his food and at Helen. I can feel he's hoping I'll wade into this.

"What about women and their doting dads, spoiling their darling girls rotten? We must be a real comedown for you," I say.

"That the best you can do?" IB mutters.

"Not at all," MJ says. "No sensible woman wants some kind of gentle patriarch for her man, once she's past puberty. On the other hand, we do appreciate a little maturity."

"Like what, exactly, are you talking about here?" IB says.

"Well, it would be nice if you didn't strut around the house with your big gun in your shoulder holster, and make some kind of drama out of taking the rig off when we get undressed for bed," MJ says. "Luther like that, Helen?"

"Worse. Sometimes he looks like Keanu Reeves in that scene in *Matrix,* armed head to ankle. Real bad actor." She laughs.

"Just tools," I say.

"Do carpenters and plumbers wear their hammers or plunger things in fancy leather harnesses at home? Do they carefully arrange them on the night table?" MJ grins. "You guys are frustrated movie stars."

"Not me," IB says weakly.

But over espresso and panettone, they display mercy. No more teasing, no more analysis. The talk turns toward the dailiness of life—what Helen's studying, what MJ studied, how long she'll stay at home with the kids before going back to work, that sort of thing.

"Got the names yet?" I venture.

"I do. But IB's bridling. He wants—get this, Helen—one of them named after his momma."

"Now wait a sec. Have I made an issue of this?" IB says, so obviously defensive we all start to laugh, for it's clear he's at least been wheedling about it.

"And that would be . . . ?" Helen asks.

"Maria Annunciata." MJ grins. "Might as well put 'Sister' in front of that on the damn birth certificate."

"So we call her Maria. That's a pretty name. Find any fault with that name?" IB says.

"What'll they actually be, MJ?" Helen asks.

"Allison and Sarah."

"Sweet," Helen says.

Ice Box catches me aside when we're about to leave and hisses in my ear. "Goddammit, Luther! You know what's happened? Now they're gonna be friends, calling each other up all the time and badmouthing us, giving each other ammo to use against us."

"Hey man, remember who told who to bring who. I'm clean here. Not my fault."

"But you let 'em get away with it, you pussy."

"Didn't see you wading in and containing things, big man. All I saw was the Ice Box doing a large cringe routine."

But back home I half expect Helen, who slipped an Ecstasy tab down in the car when she thought I wasn't seeing her moves, to go a bit dreamy, maybe drop some hints about a future.

"MJ's terrific, and they're a solid couple," she says. "But Jesus, no way in the world I'd want to be in her place, with anyone. Husband, kids? The absolute pits."

Light recoil.

17

Heavy recoil.

"Five-O. Where've you been, man?," IB almost snarls when I hit the squad room a little late next morning. "Out cruising the high schools for young snatch?"

"Oh, hostile, IB. Kind of aggressive. You're not still brooding on last night, are you? 'Cause that'd be really immature."

"Last night, yeah. But not why you think." IB takes a deep breath. "Jimmy Halliday bit it last night," he says.

"What?"

"Stupid little fuck took his old man's SLK to the limit on Route 83, lost it, rolled at least six times." Ice Box slams his fist into the cubicle wall. "Dead meat, man. Roadkill."

"You're shitting me!"

"State troopers hit the scene first. Say the car was flat as a pancake. When they pried it apart, Jimmy was mostly jelly. They had to *shovel* the goop into a body bag."

"Where'd you get all this?"

"Local BCPD went to the scene when they heard the troopers radio for the meat wagon. Guy I know who responded called me this morning. They managed to find his license in the goo. Saw the address, saw it was our territory, phoned to ask if somebody down here wanted to break it to his parents, or let the troopers do it."

"Christ! Dugal know?"

"Of course."

"So what's he doing?"

"Nothing."

"Fuckin' nothing!" I explode.

"Hey, what's he supposed to do? It was a car crash. They checked blood. Alcohol about twice the drunk percentage, man."

I crash into Dugal's office. "We gotta get that car, LT."

"You might knock, Luther," Dugal says, not looking up from an open file on his desk. "Now, are you possibly speaking of the Mercedes James Halliday managed to kill himself in?"

"Shit, what else, LT? We gotta get that car, check it out!"

"What for? Anyway, the state police have it. Hell, I understand it's not really recognizable as a motor vehicle anymore."

"Cross your mind, LT, that somebody took Jimmy out? Somebody figured he gave us Buzz Cut and did a sure-to-crash number on that car?"

"As a point of fact, it did cross my mind, Ewing. Crossed and recrossed, not that I'm obliged to explain myself to you. But the kid was so drunk he'd probably have come very close to dying from alcohol poisoning, if he hadn't crashed the car. You really think we're going to find anything at all in the wreckage that might confirm a murder attempt? Some sort of cut hydraulic line, some tampering with the brakes or the accelerator? The troopers say there's no way in hell to tell a goddamn thing of the sort, the car's so totaled. I asked, for your information, Ewing."

I don't say a thing.

"The troopers are about ready to close the file on this one already. Kid with extraordinarily high levels of alcohol in his blood loses control of a car traveling an estimated 125 miles per hour. End of story. Now what is it, exactly, you want from me on this? We've lost a key fucking witness. End of the second story."

"I just don't buy it, LT. Something's kinked here, I can smell it."

"Oh, you can? Well, please give me a full report when it dawns on you just what you smell. But do not—repeat, do not—waste your time and mine following your nose. The case against Buzz Cut is still solid gold. He sold smack to you, remember? In full view of four other cops."

"We promised the kid and his father this was a no-risk deal," I say.

"And so it was. Nobody killed Halliday. Halliday offed himself. Nothing we could have done to protect anyone from that. Now, if you've got it all off your chest, get the fuck out of my office, will you? I got work to do."

I leave.

"Well?" IB says.

"Well shit. But I just don't read Jimmy as the type to do something like that. Do you?"

"On one level, no," Ice Box says. "He wasn't like that. But I've seen so many kids change practically overnight into somebody you wouldn't recognize that I'm not real surprised. Something snaps, they go wild. Jimmy just had worse luck than most."

"Too pat, too easy. If they didn't fuck with the car, they fucked with his head. It was a hit, IB. I feel it, man. Buzz Cut's people took him out."

"Maybe, maybe not. I know this, though. No way in hell you'll ever prove it, not if you spend your entire life on that single case."

I leave the station, go across the street to the shitty deli that makes the shitty coffee that always turns my stomach acid and sour, and buy two take-out cups. I go back to my cubicle, gulp them down, scorching the taste buds on my tongue. If I'm gonna feel bad, I may as well feel worse, I figure. But there's a window on my brain screen with one word typed on it: Vassily.

After a while Ice Box glides over. "You okay now, Luther? You got your grip?" he asks.

"Da, durak," I say.

"Say what?"

"Yes, I'm fine. I'm cruising, man."

"Listen, Luther. Timing's kind of shitty, I know, but I got something I gotta run by you, okay? That you're maybe not gonna like much."

"Everything's copacetic, IB. Hit me."

"Well, after Hannah the other day, I asked the police artist to make a second sketch from the first, with the changes she talked about." He puts the sketch of the girl dealer on my desk.

"So? What?" I say.

"Look close, Luther. Check the eyes, the lip. Like Hannah described. What do you see?"

Double fucking recoil.

The sketch is Helen.

"Oh get fucked, IB. You cocksucker."

"Easy, Luther. Remember I just saw Helen for the first time yesterday. No bells rang. Then I'm looking at this sketch today and—shit, this sucks—I see it, with Hannah's changes. And you see it, too. You just gave it away."

"Fuck off. So what? It's a lousy sketch. Any resemblance is just coincidence. You could pull in three dozen girls this age, line 'em up, and never make a match on one, even if the real one was among them."

"Yeah, sure. You're right, I know you're right. It's just kind of weird, is all," IB says, unusually softly. "Uhh, what kind of car does Helen drive, Luther?"

"A Bug, you dumb fuck," I say, start to rise into a combat stance, but get a grip before my butt's three inches off the chair and slump down.

I hit the button to start my Mac. "Get away from here, IB—now," I say, crumpling the sketch with my left hand and tossing it back over my shoulder at him. Silence, except for the ping and pong the Mac makes as it boots up. I know IB's gone. His fucking shadow's still looming over me, though.

//

It gets darker. Peter Raskin, known as Buzz Cut, drug dealer from Brooklyn of Russian parentage, fails to show up for his grand jury that afternoon. Eckhaus goes ballistic on the steps of the courthouse.

"Little stupid," Vassily had called Buzz Cut.

Right.

Little dead is more like it. Radik up in homicide gives me a call around five-thirty. A headless, handless body was found early this morning in a dumpster behind an Acme supermarket in Pikesville. The medical examiner and forensics guys agree that judging from maggot activity on the corpse, it's only three or four days old. They also agree—seeing burns on the genitals and other marks—that whoever the fucking corpse was, he was tortured very, very systematically for a long time before he died. Since there's no sign of any mortal injury on the body, they conclude he was killed in the head.

I conclude a three-round burst of 5.45s. In the face. Which was probably, along with the hands, dissolved in a tub of acid. They'll never identify this corpse. Vassily's guys made sure of that.

Could it be any of my dealers, Radik wants to know?

No, I tell him.

And no point, no point at all, in mentioning this to Dugal. Let him figure it out for himself.

18

I most definitely do not feel good to go about anything, or willing to make anything happen.

Taggert You Fuck makes it happen.

Big surprise, the meeting in Dugal's office the following morning. Major buy-and-bust, on for that night. Not a kid like Buzz Cut. "Serious players," that asshole Taggert calls them. Deal for $25,000. I hear Taggert made the connection in Jugs, a sleazy topless bar just across from the Timonium racetrack. Taggert liked to hang there on his own time, liked a table dancer when he was feeling flush. He had a snitch who worked there, never produced anything before. All of a sudden, the snitch gets Taggert close to two guys in their late thirties maybe, and Taggert—the dumbest, clumsiest and meanest guy on the squad—passes himself off as a major customer, for the right goods at the right price.

Dugal takes it from there. "All right, girls. My reading is whoever was backing Buzz Cut has stepped in personally since we've removed their man from the action. My reading is they want to accelerate their growth in our area quickly, while they think we're still congratulating ourselves on eliminating the biggest trafficker we've ever seen and not paying much attention. My reading is they are in for a major surprise. Am I right?"

Not as big a surprise as you're likely to get, LT, I think. It's Vassily pulling all our strings now.

"Of course I'm right, so nobody needs to answer," Dugal runs on. "This is going to be easier, logistically and public safetywise, than Buzz Cut. No meet in a crowded mall. Taggert will roll in solo on that little road behind the track, the one they use for the horse trailers. He will stop where the road ends at the stables. It's off-season, stables are empty, no real security around except maybe a rent-a-cop asleep in his office near the grandstand entry. Taggert's sellers will arrive at two A.M. You know what happens then. As soon as Taggert shows the cash and they show the goods, we move in."

I flash on Poppa's Nam jive: world of hurt. I do not like this. I can't find any holes in Dugal's dispositions—me and Ice Box concealed in the stables, Tommy and Gus with shotguns back in the entrance to the grandstand, a few tacticals with AR15s a level up, the LT with Petey K. and Bimbo in a plain car, and three cruisers with two uniforms in each ready to roll down the few hundred meters of road as soon as they hear Taggert say, "Got the cash. You got the goods?" Taggert wired, naturally, with a transmitter.

World of hurt. It keeps looping in my head. The LT's plan is standard, solid. If we were dealing with a real deal. Taggert set it up? This doesn't feel like a real deal.

After the briefing I want to talk to IB about this, but we aren't talking much since the sketch thing, barely nodding at one another when our paths cross. Unfuck it, Luther. But I don't.

//

After lunch I drop by Annie's office. "Hey, Luther," she says.

"So how come I haven't heard from you?"

"There hasn't been anything to tell. I'm nowhere on all my cases."

"And so you're nowhere to your friends? Always up a ladder plastering your ceiling? Can't answer your phone?"

"Don't you ever need some downtime?" She looks at me with those eyes. Then I know I can't tell her what I feel almost desperate to tell—about Thirty-fourth Street, Halliday, Vassily, the bad feeling I have about tonight.

"From the job, sure." I say. "But I could've come around, bought you a beer, maybe listened if you felt like talking."

"Just the point. I didn't feel like talking."

"Hey." I shrug. "Your life."

"But you'd be around if I needed you, wouldn't you, Luther?"

Sure I would. I'd be beside this woman all day and all night . . . in another life, maybe. "You know it, LT babe. Nowhere else."

//

Except, that night, in a world of hurt.

It's chilly in the stables. I'm shivering. IB and I moved into place an hour before the scheduled meet, coming up on foot through some woods out back. Tommy and Gus and the tactical shooters came in with us and ducked into the grandstand entrance. I don't much like the setup once I see it. The few security floodlights don't overlap their coverage, there are too many dark spots. When Taggert pulls up at one forty-five I like it even less. He's just at the edge of a circle of light, the stupid shit. The dealers, if they're pros, will stop outside the circle. All I'll see of them is silhouettes against another distant flood.

"This is fucked," I hear IB mutter. He's picked up on it too. What I need is an MP5 with a night-vision scope. What I've got is my HK .45. Some instinct, some intuition caused me to slip its long, fat sound suppressor into one of the cargo pockets of my pants. If I have to shoot, I don't want the targets knowing where the hits are coming from. I want to hit quietly, out of nowhere, like the finger of God. I screw the silencer on now. And then I move.

"What the fuck, Five-O?" IB hisses as I crawl crabwise out of the stable cover, trying to stay out of the light, and slide under Taggert's car. He doesn't hear me coming. I don't let him know I'm there.

I do my breathing drill, breathing myself cold and clear and empty. "On the way," I hear Dugal in my earphone. I see a silver BMW coming down the road, swinging around in a tight arc and stopping just out of the circle of light facing the way it came in. Ten meters from Taggert's car. HK's cocked, full clip of hollow points and one up the spout, tritium sights glowing faintly. It feels part of me, an extension of my hand. The way it should.

It happens fast, it happens slow-motion. Two men exit the rear doors of the BMW, move in on Taggert. All I can see now is three sets of legs. I hear two snaps. Taggert must be opening the brief case. I hear him say, "Here's the cash. Show me the goods." I hear another voice say, "Not tonight, my friend." Then the legs start a weird shuffle, I hear a quick sound like cloth ripping, Taggert saying "Fuck this!" I hear Dugal over my earphone. "What's happening? What's happening, dammit?" I hear IB say, "Can't see. Two guys, close up with Taggert."

I hear "I'm coming in" from Dugal, but before he gets it all out there's three coughs so rapid it sounds like a pulled zipper. Taggert's body smacks the dirt. I've got no shot, only legs. I roll over on my back, arch my neck, see everything upside down: one guy standing with an AKSU, wisp of smoke rising from the silencer's business end, one bending for the briefcase full of cash. I pop two caps on the standing guy. He falls instantly, puppet whose strings got cut. Split-second eye contact with the bender as he's straightening up, looking real surprised. I double-tap. The back of his head explodes.

I roll out from under Taggert's car on the side away from the BMW. I hear fire behind me, probably IB coming on, and two shotgun blasts from the grandstand entrance. I see the driver's out of the BMW with an AK shortie, night-scoped. A three-round burst snaps past my left shoulder, he swings and empties full-auto toward the grandstand. He's sliding back into the driver's seat as I bring the HK up. Pop two caps before his head gets below the roof line, double-tap through the passenger window. Glass shatters, shards go spinning, glimmering. He's slammed back against the open door, he glides down to the ground.

Bright lights, flashing cruisers blinding me, sirens deafening.

Dugal shouting shit in the earphone. I put the HK on the trunk of Taggert's car, raise my hands high over my head, move slowly into the light so everyone can see it's me. Still, there's a shotgun blast and the rear window of Taggert's car shatters. "Don't shoot, you assholes! Fuck, it's me! It's Luther! Don't fire! It's over!" I bellow.

Dugal sprints up, Ruger drawn. Tommy comes limping from the grandstand. Uniforms swarm around the BMW. "Holy shit," I hear one of them say. Then I hear someone puking his guts out.

"Aw fuck me, fuck me," Dugal says, his Maglite freezing on Taggert, face down in the dirt. No apparent wounds, but I know he's dead. I know there'll be three little holes in his face when they turn him over. Dugal shouts for an ambulance, kneels, places his fingers on Taggert's neck, desperate to find a pulse. "Aw fuck! Fuck me."

I lean against Taggert's car. Other Maglites are flicking the scene. Thick pools of blood, gleaming rich red so dark it's close to black, spread slowly around the heads of the two dealers. Two suppressed AKSUs in the dirt. The dealers' faces are pretty much intact, but there's nothing left behind their ears. Skull and brains, all blown away. People are stepping in that shit, cursing when they feel the squish under their shoe soles. I hear another cop gag, then puke.

I walk around to the BMW. Driver's head the same, but the blood pool's bigger because he also caught two in the chest. The window shots, I figure. Dugal's got me by the arm, asking things I don't understand. Then I hear Tommy's voice. "IB's down, LT! IB's hit!"

I scream at the sky. Just one lung-searing scream. Then I breathe real deep, once, and start to walk slowly toward a big man flat on his back maybe five meters in front of the stables. Others are running there.

Cold, clear, moving on autopilot. A machine.

"Juked those motherfuckers! Dome shots!" I hear myself say. I feel the rush then, and smile. I'm unaware Dugal's still got me by the arm until he drops it like it was a hot wire and backs off a step. I turn to look at him. Fear's twisting his face. Seen that before.

I walk on.

//

People manhandle me into an ambulance. Tommy's already inside, moaning. An EMS guy slits the right leg of his pants from cuff to groin. A piece of his calf about the size of an orange looks like fresh hamburger. No hemorrhage, no other wounds. But he's pale, so the EMS guy rams a needle into the crook of his elbow and starts a saline drip, then straps an oxygen mask over his face.

Another EMS guy's feeling me up like I was a girl. "You hit, you hit?" he keeps asking.

"Fuck no," I say. "Leave me alone." He doesn't. Standard procedure—a cop who's just been in a shooting gets trauma treatment. I let the EMS dude attach a pulse meter to one thumb, blood pressure band on one arm. When he tries to stick me for an intravenous, I hit him just below the breast bone with two knuckles. He sits down suddenly, looking greenish, gulping air.

The transmitters are still live, the 'phone's still in my ear. I hear Ice Box's voice: "Oh man, I feel like I ran into a wall. Gotta get my breath, just gotta get my breath. . . ." then nothing. They must be giving him oxygen. He sounded chest-shot. Oh Jesus, not chest-shot.

"They gonna do a dust-off to the Trauma Center?" I ask the EMS guy I knuckled, who's got his breath back now.

"Fuck man, why'd you hit me?"

"Shut up and answer," I snarl. "They gonna dust-off for the Trauma Center?" One of the best in the world is at a hospital downtown.

"I don't dig what you're saying, man," the EMS guy says.

"Are they going to chopper the shot cop to the Trauma Center?" I shout. *"Get that?"*

"I don't know, man. Just stay cool. There's another team with him. They'll get him through. Just stay cool, okay?"

"I am cool, you asshole. Why don't you help your buddy there with Tommy instead of sittin' on your ass? Tommy's the one with the leg wound. Right behind you, numbnuts."

"Okay, okay. Just chill, man. We're taking care of him."

He turns, starts helping his teammate with Tommy. I pull two tabs out of my shirt pocket and drop 'em. Hate doing it dry. I see a bottle of water, grab it, take a big swig. Better.

Then I think, Bad habit, Luther, dropping like that. I don't feel jagged at all. I feel smooth, real smooth.

Sirens blurping, lights flashing, some cool high-speed weaves through traffic to the Greater Baltimore Medical Center. They gurney Tommy into the emergency room. Before they can try that on me, I pull off the pulse meter, rip off the blood pressure band, and walk in. They want me to lie down, but I sit on the edge of the bed next to Tommy's. They want to put in a drip. I tell them to get off my case. A doctor pleads with me, so I let them attach another pulse meter and blood pressure band. I sit quietly for five minutes. Then I wave the doctor over. "Read the numbers," I say. "Out loud."

"Pulse rate 72, and steady. Blood pressure 118 over 80. Jesus."

"Right, I'm outta here," I say, removing the monitors.

"But the psychologist is coming. You can't just walk away."

"No? Watch me." I stand up and go. When I hit the corridor they're wheeling Ice Box in fast, passing the triage room and heading straight for the operating theater. His face, what I can see of it around the oxygen mask, is swollen and purple, like somebody's used it as a punching bag. The front of his jacket is in shreds. I trot after his gurney, but they slam the doors to the OR in my face. I sit down on the floor, back against the beige tiled wall.

I start thinking what I'm going to say to MJ. I start wondering if I've got the balls to go to her and say what's got to be said. I shiver. Time goes nowhere. Then Dugal's sitting next to me.

"Give, Luther."

"Taggert got himself set up. Those dudes were just going to rip off his cash. He wasn't credible, LT."

"Yeah," Dugal murmers. "No drugs. They had no drugs."

"I'm under the car, I don't see much. From what I hear, I figure Taggert is stupid enough to go for his gun, never gets it out of the holster."

"He didn't. Half out," Dugal says.

"So they did him. They might not have done it if he hadn't gone for his piece."

Dugal gives me a kinked look. "A man's dead, Luther."

"'Cause he made a stupid move. He didn't stay cool."

"So you did them. With this," Dugal says, holding the HK. "Couldn't hear your shots. Now I see why. And why were you under Taggert's car when you should have been back in the stables with Ice Box?"

"It felt like a goatfuck, LT. I had no good field of fire from the stables, saw that as soon as I saw Taggert put his car too close to the edge of the floodlight circle. So I bellied over and slid under. Taggert didn't hear me, didn't know I was there. If I hadn't done that, I never could have capped those dudes."

"Yeah, you dropped the three all right."

A surgeon comes out of the OR and waves Dugal over. They walk off down the corridor, beyond my hearing. They huddle. I'm thinking how in the hell am I going to face MJ. I feel sick to my stomach all of a sudden.

Dugal comes back, face blank. I stand up. I say, "You want to tell his wife, LT? Or you want me to go over to his house and do it?"

Dugal suddenly grins. "You're their friend. Why don't you go over and bring her here so she can talk to her man, Five-O?"

"What?"

He shakes his head, he's almost chuckling. "I never used to believe in miracles, but I'm close to changing my opinion. God, I am changing my opinion. Ice Box got hit by three bullets not an inch apart right over his heart. But the bullets just exploded on his vest! They just disintegrated! That Kevlar was never meant to stop high-velocity rifle rounds. FMJs should've punched through IB's vest like paper and killed him instantly."

"His face looked real bad when they brought him in. He looked like a dead man who didn't know it yet," I say.

"Good God, Luther! All he's got is about two dozen small cuts on his face from the bullet fragments. They've got most of the metal out already. Surgeon tells me the pieces are smaller than fingernail clippings. They won't even have to stitch most of the cuts. He's just going to look funny for a while, like he had a real bad shaving day, nicked himself a lot. Thank God!"

Yeah, thank the fuck for frangibles, I think. Russian assholes. I should have figured. I shouldn't have sweated over IB.

"Struck dumb, are you, Luther? Amazed and relieved? Well, shake out of it," Dugal puts his hand on my shoulder, "and drive that fancy silver bullet of yours like hell and bring his wife back here."

I'm ringing the bell in less than fifteen minutes. I wait a while. It's almost four A.M. MJ eyes me through the peephole. I can hear a sharp intake of breath, a muffled "Oh God, don't let this be." I put my arms around her as soon as she opens the door. "Don't say it, Luther. Don't tell me. It isn't true. It can't be true."

"IB's fine, MJ! He's absolutely fine!"

"Don't lie to me either, you bastard! If he's fine, why isn't he here?" Her legs are shaking.

"He didn't want to scare you. He's got some scratches on his face, he looks like the bogeyman. That's all. I swear it. C'mon, I'll take you to see him right now. Don't get dressed. Just throw a raincoat on."

She does. She's laughing and crying at the same time, and then cursing me and the TT when she has almost as hard a time fitting into it as IB did. "It went bad, didn't it?" she says when we're rolling. "There was shooting, wasn't there?"

"Oh, just a little, MJ," I say. "Nothing serious. I did most of it. Everybody's pissed at me for it."

"You're a lying son of a bitch, Luther, and I love you lots." MJ laughs. "So IB just tripped and fell into a thorn bush or something?"

"Yeah, sort of."

"You lovely lying bastard. I'll get the truth out of IB soon as I see him. I know just how to pull his chain, scaring me like this."

"I bet you do, MJ," I say, grinning.

"You can wipe that off your face, mister. I'll be pulling yours, too. Showing up like a spook in the middle of the night."

Dugal and a doctor take MJ by either elbow and lead her to the private room where they've moved IB. I stick my head in for a peek, see IB's got little white butterfly bandages all over his face, also got a tray in his lap with a half-eaten stack of pancakes and bacon, and a full mouth. The tray goes clattering to the floor when MJ moves to the bed with her arms outstretched. I duck back out. I get a rush. I hear some crying, some laughing, some sort of stern lecture-sounding talk from MJ. Dugal, standing next to me, starts to laugh.

Jolt—the bedside alarm goes off. Ice Box is shouting. A doctor and two nurses dash into the room. One nurse hustles out almost immediately, rounds a corner of the corridor, and rolls back into the room with two orderlies pushing a gurney. Dugal grabs my arm. Then the gurney appears with MJ propped up on it. She waves and tosses a smile at us.

"Stick around a little while, you'll get to meet Allison and Sarah, Luther," she calls as they wheel her away.

19

I stand in the shower a long time. Usual drill, but this time doing what a wiggy spook with twenty years in Special Forces once taught me—concentrating on one muscle group, deliberately tightening it, then relaxing it, going on to the next. Toes first, moving up to calf and thigh, same with the other leg. Then groin, abdomen, pecs and lats. Fingers, forearms, biceps, triceps, deltoids. Finally, rotating my neck until that little grinding noise quits, flexing my jaws wide as I can before going slack mouthed. I feel totally loose and limp at the finish. That's supposed to be the point.

But it's an effort then to wash my hair and scrub my skin with the loofah. Dipshit, I think. Got it backward. Wash first in a precise, orderly military fashion, *then* do the muscle thing.

When the steam half-clears, I look at myself in the mirror and feel like I'm looking at a police sketch. Face sort of familiar, but it isn't me—or anyone real. My hair's down to my nipples. Never noticed it'd gotten so long, since I usually keep it in a ponytail. Time for the Comanche to go back to the reservation, I decide. I pad naked out to the kitchen, find some scissors in the knife drawer, pad back to the bathroom, grab a handful of hair, and shear it off a quarter-inch from my scalp. I'm down to the last lock, I look like a marine recruit, the face in the mirror's suddenly me. One more snip.

Then I punch in Vassily's number. It rings a bunch of times before I hear a groggy *"Da?"*

"My friend. Too much vodka last night, eh," I say in Russian.

"Ah, little brother, never too much. But this is not my office hours."

"Sorry, but something funny is all over the news this morning. Three white drug dealers shot and killed a cop last night."

"So?"

"The cops kill all three. They're from Brooklyn, it turns out. Since you said something about little stupids, thought you ought to know. You need any help?"

"Me?" Vassily's alert as hell. "I'm good, good. That changes, I will let you know. But thanks for the call. *Spasiba,* little brother."

I'm just off when there's pounding on my door. Pulse instantly up fifteen beats per minute, no more, no less. My standard adrenaline reaction, I don't have to finger it to know it. I move fast to the bed, press the number code to open the lockbox duct-taped under the frame, take out the Desert Eagle, flick off the safety. No need to check—it's always loaded. More pounding, louder now.

I put my back against the wall next to the door. "What?" I shout."

"It's Annie! I've been ringing your bell and knocking for ten minutes. I'm about to call for backup and break in. You gone deaf or something?"

I peer through the peephole. It is Annie. Unchain the door then, swing it open, and in she strides.

"Great haircut! But, uh, they do it to you for electroshock therapy or something?" She smiles. I follow her gaze down to the Eagle. She's ignoring the fact that I'm naked, dick swinging in the breeze. "'Cause it seems like you could use some."

"This?" I decock the Eagle. "Sorry. Dugal took my guns last night."

"I know what happened last night, Luther." She's still smiling. "I'm wondering why you come to the door with a weapon at all."

"Don't . . . usually."

"So this is an aberration of some sort?"

"Yeah."

"Impulsive act, like the hair? Which you obviously chopped off yourself, without professional assistance."

"Yeah."

"I guess I know that. Guess that's why I came calling at, what is it now, six forty-five A.M.?"

"I was just going to ask you about that."

"Don't you think, before we continue here, it'd be polite if you first put your pistol back where it belongs, and cover up the rest of your equipment with a bathrobe or maybe, if it's not too much trouble, some clothes?"

"Uh, yeah, yeah. Be right back." I flee to the bedroom, slam the door behind me.

When I come out in my robe, Annie's made coffee, she's at the table sipping a cup. She pours me one as I sit down.

"Now," she says. "Are you really okay?"

"Hell yes. Why shouldn't I be?"

"Last night."

"That wasn't much."

"It was too much, way too much. The story's all over the Department. I got a call from a friend on nightshift forty-five minutes ago. IB and Tommy wounded, four men dead."

"It happens. It's part of the job."

Annie shakes her head. "You're worrying me a little here, Luther. Okay, I understand you need to stay cool, you want to seem calm, seem chill. But it's just me here. Your friend. You can let it go a little."

"Let what go? I'm fine."

"Luther, you blew away three guys. Yeah, they were bad, they shot back. But you killed three men."

"I'm *supposed* to do that. In a situation."

There's a pleading look in Annie's eyes I don't recall ever seeing there before. "Oh Luther, you are wrapped so very, very tight. What did they do to you in the army, to get you this way?"

"They trained me to do my job and walk away when the job was done. Any problem with that? You seem to have one."

"So humor me. Answer one question."

"Okay."

"Don't you feel anything?"

"Sure. I feel real bad Ice Box got hit, but real good he got off with scratches. I feel pissed I'm assigned to desk duty until those IA assholes finish their investigation."

"Nothing else?"

"Like what?"

"Never mind," Annie sighs, sips her coffee. She just stares at me a while. Then she lays her hand on top of one of mine. I think I see the beginnings of tears at the corners of her eyes. "Poor, poor Luther. Somehow, someway, some people fucked you up bad."

"Okay. I believe I should feel bad 'cause I shot those fucks. All I feel is weird because I don't. So I don't think about it. I've never even dreamed about all the people I've killed. Not once."

"Remember our talk on the way back from your folks' place?" Annie says. "Maybe the military training you got was too good, too effective in erasing the no-kill program. That's what it's designed to do, isn't it? But it usually doesn't work real well, does it?"

"Yeah, it fails. Most guys, if they hit combat, hate it. If they kill—but it's really rare to be sure, everybody all around you is shooting as fast as they can and who knows afterward whose bullet took anybody down?—they don't dig it. A lot get haunted by it."

"But it didn't fail, with you?"

"Appears that way, I guess. I don't know."

"You ever been really crazy in love with a girl?"

"What's that got to do with anything?"

"You'll see. Have you?"

"I guess not."

"You ever cried because a woman dumped you? Because someone you cared about got killed?"

"Can't remember. Don't think so."

"Luther, I know you won't like this idea. But with some help, a really good shrink, maybe an ex-military guy, you could get your feelings back. You could have a life, be able to really love a woman, really love your friends. Really get close to good people."

"No way, Annie. Too late."

"But why, Luther?"

"Because if I really *felt,* I don't think I could bear the weight. Couldn't pretend all I've done never happened. Couldn't live with feeling it. Could you?"

//

Hi-rez. Perfectly clear. Perfectly cold.

Desert Storm's almost blown out, our armored divisions have smashed the Iraqi army, our planes have made the road out of Kuwait City the Highway of Death. My job finished when the tanks shattered the lines we'd been operating behind. Me and my guys on the buggy had hit a dozen installations or communications posts or defensive positions, we'd wasted a lot of ragheads, scared the living shit out of a lot more, before the armor assault. Same as all the buggy teams. Swinging back now southeast out of Iraq toward Kuwait City. Mission complete.

Perfectly clear: cold gray light just before a desert dawn. We come up over a rise maybe three hundred meters away from a stucco building by a little back road. No traffic, no people in sight. Two Iraqi army vehicles outside.

Juke 'em.

JoeBoy floors it, Snake sprays the building with the twin-50s on the way in. Dust and stucco and all kinds of shit's flying all over the place. One vehicle explodes. Can't tell if we're taking fire back. We stop maybe twenty-five meters from a door, I roll out with an MP5SD in each hand. Adrenaline at 100 percent. Duck and dodge inside. There's a dozen Iraqi soldiers, huddled and shivering, their AKs on the ground, hands clasped on top of their heads. Lots of babbling, sounds like begging. Perfectly clear: the bloodshot eyes full of terror, the unshaven whiskers on each face, the torn and filthy uniforms. One dude's holding up a piece of paper. A surrender leaflet. The air force dropped tons of them all over the desert.

Fuck it. Waste the cocksuckers. I squeeze both triggers, hose 'em down with 9mm FMJs. Two full clips, sixty rounds, all my strength keeping down muzzle rise. All the ragheads dead or twitching wounded, five seconds max. I drop one MP5, slip a fresh, full clip into the other, pop three-round bursts into anyone still moving or screaming. Snake comes through the door with an M4, JoeBoy with the SPAS while I'm doing this.

"Holy fuckin' shit, Luther. Oh man, you stepped in it," JoeBoy says. "How we gonna explain this? We weren't taking no fire. We're fucked, man." He's about to hit me when Snake shouts from the second room. We go over, see two girls, clothes all stuffed around their heads, bloody and ripped up between the legs from a gangrape, one bullet hole in each of their tits.

"Fucks you wasted deserved it. But you didn't fuckin' even know it, Luther. You just did it, man," Snake says. "Cover-up time."

Snake and JoeBoy move gingerly among the Iraqi bodies, place AKs in their hands, press dead fingers against triggers, fire whatever's in the clips into the walls, the doors, out the window into our buggy. So it looks like a firefight. Then I'm standing in the doorway, looking at the holes in the buggy. I hear a click and turn. JoeBoy's kneeling, very carefully sighting an AK. Bam. A sledgehammer knocks my right leg out from under me.

"You crazy motherfuck! You asshole!" I scream. "You fuckin' shot me!"

"Hey, not me, man," JoeBoy grins. "A raghead did it. Firefight here, remember."

"Fuck you! Fuck you! I can't believe you shot me!"

Snake's beside me, slits open my camo pants. "Beautiful, Joe-Boy," he says. "Right through the calf, clean exit. All meat, no bone. You could stick a pencil straight through, all the way."

"Sure looks like a firefight here," JoeBoy smiles.

Sort of. We radio, our CO arrives maybe an hour later, sees right through our shit. Just scans body positions, entry and exit wounds, buggy damage, hole in my leg, and *knows.* He just knows. But he doesn't want an atrocity on his unit's record, the army doesn't want any stains on its clean, glorious victory. I tell the CO the truth, clear Snake and JoeBoy. They skate, they get to stay in. No court martial for me, either. I'm just told to keep my mouth shut. I'm just told I do not exist, never did exist. Except they're rigging an honorable discharge soon as my wound heals. That's the cover-up.

//

I tell Annie all of it. She never flinches. She keeps her eyes steady on mine, while I'm having a hell of a time keeping mine on hers.

"They turned you into the guy who did that, Luther," she says when I quit talking. "They psyched you and tuned you and played with your mind and sent you into that shit cocked, with a hair-trigger. You *can* walk away from it."

"I have. Fuck the dudes I wasted. Only thing I regret is losing my career."

"No, no. I mean you can absolve yourself, you don't have to stay like you were on that one day in the desert. That wasn't really you, that day. You can get back to the real, you can get on with a real life instead of the movie you're living."

"Like I said, Annie. Too late now."

"*They* fucked you up, Luther. Like I've heard you say, unfuck it. Unfuck yourself."

I can't tell her the whole truth. About the rush. I can't tell her I like it when I drop someone, I get off on it. It wouldn't be cool. I'd lose her.

//

When Annie's left, I get dressed carefully, nice clean white shirt, clean jeans, suede chukkas. I drive down to the GBMC.

Soon as I walk into IB's room he starts laughing like a lunatic, smile so broad a couple of the butterflies on his face rip. "Who in the hell scalped you, Chief?" he says. "Man, I'm glad to see you. But not like this. You look like a nightmare. Listen up, I've got two beauties upstairs in the maternity ward. They're perfect, man. You never saw such beautiful kids. You go up there to see them and MJ, I swear on my life I'll crush your bones. 'Cause you'll scare 'em silly, the way you look."

Back and forth with IB like this for maybe ten minutes, he's so high on surviving and his new babies he's babbling stuff he'll never remember and be absolutely convinced he never said if I ever claim he did. Stuff about saving his life by capping those dealers. You know, just shit. He got hit anyway, didn't he?

I leave him and go see MJ. She looks wrung out but high and happy too. She babbles some nonsense she must have got from IB. I just smile a lot, tell her Allison and Sarah are beautiful and so is she, leave her some flowers.

Then I hit the station. Lots of uniforms looking at me funny and I know it isn't the haircut. The atmosphere in the squadroom's a little sour because of Taggert, nobody ever wants a fellow cop to go down even if he was an asshole, and there's always the shock factor—you know, "Christ, if it happened to him it could happen to me" thinking. But it's half-balanced by the good news about

Tommy and IB. Funny eye action behind the smiles and nods of greeting, though. It ain't just the haircut.

I sit in my cubicle, switch on the Mac and call up a file to make it seem like I'm doing something besides staring into space. Annie at my place starts auto-replay in my mind. It hurts. Stop button doesn't work. I drop two tabs with that bitter deli coffee I can't stand but drink every day anyway. I don't feel like doing anything or talking to anyone.

The phone fucks that.

Dog first. "Shit goes down even in the Valley, huh? Oh, you bad, Luther."

"You're vergin' on disrepect, Dog. Sure you got the stones to diss me?"

"Get down, shortie. Hear you lost one, popped three. Nobody fucks with my man, huh?"

"Deal goes bad, what you expect? What you think the guns are for?"

"You nice with your hands, too."

"That what you hear?"

"Saw. A while back, remember? What I wanna hear now, home, is what heaters the gangstas was packin'?"

"Same as the dudes who made that house call down where you hang. AK 5.45s. And they whities. We don't let no nigger gang-bangers move in our 'hood."

"Hey Luther, what say you and I drop the street mouths? It's funny for a while but it gets old. Agreed? Have you got identification yet?"

"Not confirmed, just driver's licenses. Our print people are working on it."

"Are you gonna pass it on, once you get solid IDs?"

"Don't need to wait on that. Russians. And I called the Russian they worked for this morning. I think he'll be calling me back real soon."

Dog laughs. "No frontin', nigger. I'm beginning to like you again. Maybe you a homie after all."

"Get off my shit, nigger. I thought we were dropping the street jive."

Dog laughs again. "Can't seem to help myself. Too many years on that street, in the lane. And, oh yeah, you got me scared. Capped three. I dig it, homie. I'm around, you get callback."

"Later, Dog."

Dugal next. I suppose he doesn't want to start talk in the squadroom by hauling me into his office, so he calls instead.

"You fit, Luther? You are feeling right about what went down? Do you feel the need for counseling? Posttrauma?"

"Nah, LT. I'm good. Everything's cool. You, sir?"

"I've been better. I don't like a bust going bad. I hate losing a man. In fact, I never lost anyone before. This escalation to city-style violence is very disturbing."

"Affirmative, LT."

"We'll deal with it. In an orderly fashion. But the pressure is coming down from up top very quickly. Very powerfully."

"That's the way it usually comes."

Then it's Helen. "Hey, babe. I just heard on the radio about the cop getting shot last night. Got worried. You weren't involved or anything?"

"I was there."

"Oh my God! I didn't think things like that happened out here, only downtown. You're okay? You're sure you're okay?"

"I'm fine. Really. It wasn't such a big deal. You know how the media makes everything seem more dramatic. It's show business for them."

"If you're okay, prove it."

Suddenly I flash on that sketch. "How?" I ask.

"Invite me over to your place tonight."

"Can't tonight. But hey, pretty, how about stopping by my place tomorrow night? If you're free? We'll watch a DVD, maybe fool around a little?"

Helen laughs. "What time?"

"Say, seven-thirty?"

"I'll be there. Take care, babe. Okay?"

20

Nighttime, I'm home alone. Not brooding, just on low simmer. Sometimes it all gets too much for my fucked brain—the people, the connections, the way the world turns. Skewed, all of it. Panic flashes that I might be losing it. Fucking neurologists can't even tell me what exactly that dead gray matter controls, so they can't say if anything really weird is suddenly going to pop up, take over. Only thing they're sure of is the seizures. It's the uncertainty that freaks me.

Annie'd say I'm wallowing, sitting all by myself watching *The Professional,* starring that same French guy who played Victor the Cleaner in *La Femme Nikita.* In this one he's Leon, deadly assassin for the New York mafia, calls himself a cleaner. I like that. "Cleaner." Got a certain je ne sais quoi cool I appreciate. Doesn't matter that it's a movie maker's made-up term nobody ever used on the street. Young guys coming up in the trade will probably adopt it.

Phone rings just when Leon is doing an only-in-Hollywood job of taking out DEA agents in full military combat mode while hanging from a bar on the ceiling of his apartment, with a twelve-year-old girl as his backup.

I press PAUSE, pick up. "What?"

"My friend, you are good?" It's Vassily. "Time, I think, we see each other."

"What I was thinking this morning."

Vassily laughs. "I got an idea for something we can do together. Some good friends of mine, they run into a little trouble down in the place you are."

"Friends of yours? Then I'm sure they know how to take care of any little trouble."

"Same thought for me! But the trouble for them, it was final. You were right."

"And you call it little?"

"Da. In the big scheme of things. Anyway, what I have in mind . . . let's have a talk."

"So. My place or yours?"

"Take a vacation, why not? Come up here."

"Where and when?"

"Oh, say tomorrow? Anytime you like. What kind of car you drive?"

I tell Vassily a TT. He's never seen one. I describe it.

"You just park on Brighton Boulevard, across street from Palace nightclub. We find you, if you find place."

"I'll get a map. If I get lost, I'll just ask a cop for directions."

Vassily laughs. "Ah, little brother, always the humor. This is good. Too serious men, I don't trust. They break easy. Brittle, no?"

"More or less."

I hit PLAY and see Leon the Cleaner take out a few more DEA guys with his pistols. Surround sound. Almost sounds real. But not quite.

Then I call Dog.

//

Around midnight I'm walking the Dog down Greenmount Avenue in the Waverly neighborhood. A movie theater, a supermarket that should be cleaner, lots of cheap stores selling clothes, mattresses, shoes, CDs and tapes. A pharmacy chain branch that stocks lots of hair-care products and too few pharmaceuticals to fill the Medicaid presciptions old folks bring in. A few blocks to the west is the perfectly manicured campus of Johns Hopkins University, world-class institution. To the east are the long streets of row houses, front lawns the size of a large blanket, backyards slightly larger and all ending in alleys. Walk down any of them for a while, you'll pass at least one place that's a gangsta crib.

"This was all whitie turf until the seventies," Dog says. "Working class, gettin' old. A few black families who're doing well move in 'cause they want their kids in a safe neighborhood, all the whities move out. Then my own people fuck it up, the schools get bad, the place ain't so safe anymore. I lived a while over on Old York Road, in a row house my daddy bought from a white man who'd just retired. I *watched* everything turn to shit."

"Same old same old," I say. "Tell me something I don't know."

"Russian mob definitely takin' over the dope business down here. Popped caps on six more gangstas who didn't want to get down with them in the last week. I got an undercover guy in a crew. Anything happen to him, I'll cap you for rattin', 'cause nobody, not even dudes on my team, know about this undercover but me. It stays that way, dig it?"

"Fuck off. Who do you think you're talking to?"

"Yeah, I think I know, but man, what I've seen, you *never* know."

"You got any doubts here, stop talking. I'll go back out to where I stay."

"Stay chill, man."

"Like I said, Russians I capped out there. Made guys, if the Russian mob's got old-time mafia-style shit like that."

"Uh-huh."

"Their boss called me back tonight. Dude named Vassily. He thinks I'm in his line of business."

"Uh-huh."

"I've been invited to Brooklyn tomorrow. He wants to talk."

"Uh-huh."

"Will you please stop saying uh-huh, man! It's getting on my nerves."

"Hunh."

"That's better. So, you want to ride up to Brooklyn with me, in a nice fast car, see what you see?"

"Uh-huh."

"Think you can find the intersection of York Road and Seminary Avenue? Give you a hint, it's outside the city line, just north of the Beltway. I'll be driving by about seven A.M. If you're there, I'll give you a ride."

"Goin' to where the shit goes down, am I? Uh-huh."

"Later, Dog."

Tuesday morning, early. Take the TT slow through the York Road–Seminary Avenue intersection. Dog, on the southwest corner, sticks his thumb out like a hitcher.

We're going in.

21

"First time I been in a city where I feel conspicuous," Dog says. We've been parked on Brighton Boulevard for maybe a half hour, and he's talking for the first time since we got here. Mostly he's just been staring.

"Yeah? How come?"

"How come? How come? You blind or something? You seen any people of color anywhere around here? You seen any niggers, besides us?"

"What's this 'us' shit? Only one I see is you, Dog."

"Nothin' but white folks. Young, old, tall, short, fat, skinny whities, all of 'em givin' us bad looks, man. What kind of city is this? Shit."

"They probably think we're New York cops, man. Everybody in this 'hood is Russian. Call it 'Little Odessa,' I heard. Ever meet any black Russians?"

"Fuck no. That why they used to call the old country White Russia, am I right? Like they needed to spell it out?"

"Not exactly. Think they called it that because of the snow. Lots of snow there. Snow you can't even imagine."

"You really funny, man. I feel like I'm stuck in a blizzard, all these fuckin' flakes blowin' by me."

"I could drop you down in Bed-Stuy. That's where all the homies stay. Problem is, when I come to pick you up later, you wouldn't be there. A meat wagon would've collected your body already. Killed in the head, dig it?"

"What the fuck you know about this New York City? Shit, trouble you had gettin' us here, I know it's your first visit."

"Some dudes I was tight with in the service, they were from Bed-Stuy. They said it was a bad 'hood."

"And you believed their jive? Probably they just actin' bad."

"Oh, I seen them do some things. They weren't *acting.*"

"Uh-huh," Dog grunts.

"Now don't start in with that again. Makes my head ache."

"Hunh."

End of conversation. No need for any. Dog got the whole story on me and Vassily coming up the New Jersey Turnpike. Wasn't easy for me to start, but he needed to know if he was going to be in on this with me. It took my mind off the crap I was seeing all around me. I spent most of my life in small, clean, pretty places, like Camp Lejeune and around Parris Island and Quantico. Some ugly strips nearby, but short ones. Even the worst parts of Baltimore seemed small and relatively clean compared with the disgusting sprawl you hit miles south of Newark and stay in for an hour or so. I don't know if New York metro ever ends. Maybe it just stays ugly all the way to Boston. I don't know how so many people can live in this shitpile. They must be like fuckin' dung beetles. They must feed off it. Makes me feel sick.

I watch the crowds moving along this boulevard. They look normal enough. Like Dog'd said, short, tall, fat, skinny and white. Some ugly, some pretty. Some dressed with style, some slobs. No beggars, no gangsta kids. Only thing that's off at all is that almost every shop sign is in Cyrillic. I look to see who's packing. With some training, it's pretty easy to tell if a man's carrying a weapon. Man with a pistol walks a little funny, subtle but clear once you know what to look for—a slight list to the weapon side, a different way of holding the arms, a reflex pat every now and again, unconscious, no matter if it's shoulder-holstered, side-carry, tucked in the belt behind the back. I haven't seen anyone yet I think is armed. Only a couple of beefy guys in leather jackets who look like they should be, or want to be.

Sharp rap on my window. See a flash of blue cloth in my peripheral. Figure it's a uniformed patrolman, going to give us some static. Out of state plates on the TT, sitting here for a long time. Reason enough. Hit the button, the window glides silently down. "Any problem . . ." I start to say, still looking straight ahead.

"Out, out! We go across street, little brother, we eat, we drink vodka, we talk. Only who is this with you? I am not expecting anybody else."

"My partner," I say, getting out of the car. Vassily wraps me in a bear hug. The fuck is so strong. I see he's got one man in back of the TT, another just behind Dog's window, real close.

"No trust? You can't come alone?" Vassily whispers in my ear. "You gotta bring this blackie?"

"No trust? You got backup around my car? Is that any way to greet your brother?" I reply, also in Russian. Then I imitate his English. "Shooter you are not trusting, Vassily my friend? Making me sad, this not trusting."

He breaks the embrace, laughs, nods to his men, lays an arm on my shoulder. "Be happy," he says. "I am a little nervous after Baltimore trouble, that's all. Please don't take offense."

I tell Dog to get out of the car. Vassily's man backs away to let him. The five of us go over to the Palace, where another man swings open the service door from the inside. He moves to pat us down, but Vassily halts him by holding up a big palm.

"Don't bother," he laughs. "Shooter's armed, I know for sure, the blackie too. It doesn't matter." Then, to me: "What you got there under your arm? Glock 17?"

"Plastic toy like that? You should know better, Vassily."

He grins. "Okay, I'll guess. HK .45, military issue. And you'll say to me 'Vassily, 9 millie is pussy round.' Still the same Shooter. You're like me, the same. Remember what we do with the phosphorous grenades that night? I know you do. One great night, yes? Ah, you know, sometimes I miss these things."

"Not me. You want some more, you know plenty of places to go. Half-a-dozen countries in Africa, for starters."

"No, no. Is not same there. Not civilized. Blackies running around in jungle? All the time everybody switching sides? Anyway, now I want to have peaceful life, make a little money, get laid every night. Normal life, you know? I love this place! America I love."

Dog's lost, standing there flanked by four Russians, not understanding one word. "Can we go to English, Vassily? My partner?"

"Sure thing. I lose my manners. Come, come."

Vassily leads us through the club. Lots of red velvet on the walls, carpet so thick it's like walking in beach sand, huge crystal chandeliers hanging high above, chairs around the tables gilded and gaudy. But it smells like somebody's sour breath on the morning after. A cleaning crew is working on that, spraying and vacuuming and wiping tables and chairs with Pledge or something.

Back in his office, we sit around a table on velvet-covered sofas and overstuffed chairs. One of Vassily's guys pours Stoli into shotglasses, passes them around. Vassily stands, holds out his glass, shouts "Good health!" in Russian and we all shoot the vodka. There's plates of black bread, pickled vegetables, hardboiled eggs, caviar, smoked sturgeon on the table. "Eat something. Eat," Vassily urges. I put a spoon of Beluga on a piece of toast, savor it. The others help themselves to this and that. Except Dog. There's nothing visible on his face, but he's giving off a bad vibe. I begin to think big mistake, bringing him here. But Vassily extends his hand, and Dog takes it. "So, you are partner of my old friend here? So then you are my friend also. How do they call you?"

Dog returns the shake, manages a smile that looks real enough. "Dawg," he drawls.

"Hah!" Vassily laughs. "You Americans, this I love. These crazy names. Crazy I like."

"So, comrade," I say. "What's happening?"

"Hey, no 'comrade' shit, Shooter. You make me think you some kind of fucking Communist or something." All the Russians laugh.

"Nah, it's never been the same since Stalin died."

"Before any of us got born, thank God." Vassily smiles. "Okay. I stop with the joking. What's happening, you ask. Up here, good. Everything very, very good. Now, as I told you, I'm building some little business other places. Baltimore place, for one. Only I got some troubles."

"Such as?"

"Blackie gangs. Crazy wild, these fucks. They are not businessmen. We got to liquidate some. No trust. Bang."

"Ah, my friend, you owe us already but you don't know it," I say. Vassily looks puzzled. "My partner, he's got an experienced crew. Finds himself in a little war with these young punks, these imports from LA. The fucks who trouble you."

"So? Please to explain," Vassily says.

"Put it this way. At first we didn't know it was you guys, just Russians down from New York, taking over from the Italian mob."

"Those fat shits! Old, tired and lazy," Vassily says and nods.

"But Dog figures Russians are the next thing. He figures he can do business with Russians. So he lets you get rid of the gang bangers."

"Lets us? This is not my impression."

"Why do you think it's been so fuckin' easy? Why do you think somebody, for instance, just gave your guys that address on Thirty-fourth Street?"

"Hah! Hah hah! Damn god, Shooter. It *was* easy. Made me wonder a little. Da, da, da. So now I see." Vassily spasms with laughter, then stabilizes. "So you still like to play, little brother. You still like the action. Hah!"

"Never mind that," I say.

"Well, thank you for the help, Mr. Dog. But outside the city, rich kids everywhere, what a market that can be, correct? We go in very gentle, very careful. Boom. Fucked up. My starter gets caught, little stupid. I send three guys, more experienced. Stupids too. Decide maybe they make a little money for themselves behind my back. They make a stupid deal, going to rip some fuck off. Big surpise! He's a cop, they kill him, cops kill them. What you phone me about, Shooter. Ahh," Vassily shaking his head, "fault all their own. I spit on their corpses, the mess they leave me."

"So maybe you need some local partners?"

"So maybe local partners I need. Guides, you know? Like in Sarajevo? Any interest you got in that?"

"Not as guides. I'm not walking point up the mountainside."

"So you not gone crazy after all," Vassily concedes, grinning. "Is reasonable, this attitude. For certain."

"You understand 'joint venture'?"

"Sure."

"How are you shipping now?"

"Not bulk. Quick drive down when demand is there."

"Okay, think about this. Get some bulk down there, Dog and me will buy it, let it sit awhile. We'll put your guys together with Dog's lieutenants. When the time comes, flood the city and the county. If we leave little signs it comes from a local stockpile, but nobody knows exactly where, the cops will think it's coming in by ship direct to Baltimore. They won't see a trail back to here."

"Clever boy, Shooter. But for the county, the rich kids?"

"They hate downtown. Won't go there. Somebody brings something nice to them out there, nobody gets scared, nobody gets burned? Pretty quick they'll all be wanting a taste. You've been trying that yourself, so I know you've figured this out. I've got local guys who can do that job. They are not little stupids."

"This I see. Good sense."

"There's a catch, though."

"Explain, please. Money?"

"'Course not. This is between friends, right? It's tactics. Right now your guys are wholesaling to what, maybe a dozen different crew leaders? Half of them Crips, half Bloods? They compete, they don't like each other, it gets violent sometimes, drive-by shootings just like LA, that sort of thing. A big mess, am I right? Bad for business, draws too much heat."

"No discipline, they got. Big mess, true."

"So we clean it up. We fuck the gangbangers. You come down with the bulk, you introduce your guys to Dog and his guys, me and my guys. From then on, you're the wholesalers, we're the retailers, we all know each other face to face. You tell your guys they deal only with us, forget all those crazy gangsta kids. Dog handles the city, I handle the suburbs. Cleaner, neater, safer for all of us."

Vassily ponders this a moment. "Cleaner, neater, safer. Yes, for me. But tell me please, why you so ready to handle these crazies, these gangbangers?"

"Dog doesn't like them."

"Cocksucker! You wanna liquidate these crazies? One reason only. Money! For sure."

"Money? Never crossed our minds. We believe in the cause, Vassily."

He laughs. "Sure, like fucking Bosnia. You more crazy than before, I knew it. But smarter now than then. Both of us smarter now than then."

"Smarter *and* richer than before."

"*Da, da.* Okay. I like clean and neat. Me and my guys, and you guys only. I think all my problems go away. Any problems, you solve them, if we do this."

"You think I can't handle a little trouble? Maybe I'll stop any trouble before it even starts."

"This I believe, Shooter! Okay. Okay. We do it. Money details, what's money between friends? We all get rich! No problem. We work the split out later, okay?"

"Okay by me. Dog?"

Dog nods.

Vassily stands up, spreads his arms wide, comes over and bear hugs me again. Then he bear hugs Dog. "Hey." He laughs. "How come your partner Dog carry pussy 9 Glock? Only joke, only joke. Damn god, we do some good together, Shooter. You want to stay up here tonight? We drink a little, we talk a lot about old days, then you get brains fucked out by some hot young Russki girls, yes? These I got, fresh from Ukraine. Much better than Bosnian pussy, you won't believe until you try. Guarantee!"

I beg off, too much biz to deal with, make it another time for sure. Vassily seems a little disappointed, but I ease our way out, saying all this in Russian, my arm draped around Vassily's shoulder. We get over to the TT, the man plants a kiss on my forehead. Looks almost like he's going to cry. Vassily and two of his men stand right there on the sidewalk, grinning and waving us off.

Dog slumps down far as he can manage when we're out of sight. "Some kind of fag, your dude?" he says.

"Aw yeah, I swing that way too. I been admiring your sweet ass for a long time, Dog. Think we could make it?"

That loosens him up finally, enough to start a laugh. Once going, he laughs a long time. "Jesus, Luther. You slick as shit, man. We got names, we got numbers, we call in the big smack load when we want to, we bag all the motherfuckers."

"Maybe," I say.

"Fuck maybe. They're good as nailed right now. Christ, I gotta take a leak. Where am I gonna take a leak?"

"Got a place up ahead where you'll feel real at home, Dog. Vince Lombardi Rest Stop, first one on the Jersey Turnpike."

"How the fuck you know anything about that?"

"Vassily. He said I want to keep this fine car, get home safe, whatever I do don't stop there."

22

Fast. It has got to happen fast.

My mind won't move fast as I need it to, that night in my apartment. So I give up trying. Can't do anything tonight anyway. I put on a Dvorak string quartet CD, lie on my sofa and do the muscle-relax drill. Then I do the mind-clear exercise. Cold and clear pretty soon.

Doorbell. Check my watch, seven-thirty. Helen's on time. I get up from the sofa, smooth the fabric where I've been sitting, go and let her in.

"Cool," she says, looking me up and down. "Hair's sort of radical, but cool. Tell me about the other night."

"No." I wouldn't tell her details in any circumstances, but I'm extra alert now. That sketch. Then a fresh jolt. Helen seems to have turned up just before and after every single move, from the Vassily dinner, most of my busts, the Buzz Cut murder, now Brighton Beach.

"Why not?" She grins. "Tell me, babe."

"Nothing to tell," I say easily, trying to read her eyes. Nothing the least sinister there. I'm getting fucking paranoid, I decide. "Thai okay? Tod man pla, some of that spicy chicken, lemon grass soup?"

"Sure, if you've got some beer in the fridge."

"Got some. Have one while I call the restaurant."

I overtip the delivery boy when he shows up with the food. As we eat, Helen starts telling me about a girl in her class she's sure is fucking an English Lit professor who's married and has four kids. And he, she says, isn't doing a decent job of disguising it.

"He practically drools when he looks at her in class," she says.

"It's really disgusting. I mean, she does have award-winning tits and a tight butt, but is that any reason to be so uncool?"

"I'd have to see them to judge that."

"Them?"

"The award-winning tits and butt, of course."

"You are so predictable, you dog," Helen laughs. "Sometimes I think your brain's not in your skull, but your balls."

"Well that's okay with you, isn't it? Seems to be, so far."

"Wow, I'm just noticing something here. You have a big dent in the side of your head, Luther. How'd that happen?"

Right. Like I'm going to tell her about getting shot.

"Backyard football. I was maybe ten or twelve. Went out for a pass, all my attention on the ball, hit the house corner full speed."

"Ouch! I didn't think you could actually *dent* a skull. Wouldn't it just fracture?"

"Did fracture. They had to operate, take some bone out. Put in a little metal plate in its place. Bother you?"

"Gross. Not the dent, not that. It's hard to see, only at a certain angle. It's not ugly or anything. The idea of it, though. . . ."

So how would the idea of a high-velocity bullet slamming into a head strike you, girl? Or maybe you have some idea if you're the sketch. Got some lines out, to check that out. Time to slip away from this.

"Got two DVDs, one for you, one for me. *Much Ado About Nothing,* the Branagh–Emma Thompson version, and *Pulp Fiction.* You choose."

Pulp Fiction! Helen laughs. "I love that scene where John Travolta and the other guy ram that huge hypodermic between Uma Thurman's tits after she's overdosed. And she jumps up and scares the shit out of them."

"So let's play it," I say, getting up from the table and going over to the TV. Helen's already on the sofa by the time I've got the disk going. Her palm's out, two Ecstasy pills lying there.

"So let's get off too, okay?"

"Hey, Helen. How often do you do this stuff? Can't be good for your brain, you know. Weird chemicals."

"Only on special occasions. Not even once a week. I just loved the way we were together that one time we did it. C'mon. Don't be such a cop, babe. We'll have fun."

We do. We watch the disk, we play so sweetly in bed after. Helen's drifting off to sleep. I'm not. Adrenaline's cutting right through the Ecstasy cloud.

Take one step. Take the next, and the next.

The bulk has to come soon, Vassily's guys have to meet me and Dog soon. Because it won't be long, in the city, before a gang crew leader goes to his personal Russian and asks where the fuck's the shit he needs? We're blown then.

Vassily has to be personally present with the bulk. We scoop it and his men up without nailing Vassily, Dog and me are stone blown. For good.

And, maybe toughest, tomorrow I've got to explain this whole business, leaving out lots of details that have to stay secret, well enough to convince Dugal to lend me four guys. Can't be narc squaders. I'll need four tough young guys, the smartest the BCPD's got, to go undercover with me. All on trust, because I won't have time to personally train them.

I wonder if all this has hit Dog's cerebrum yet. It must have. He was so high on the way home he wasn't hearing shit, wasn't registering what I was saying about all this. Now, probably, he's home, thinking just what I am.

I slip silently out of bed, close myself in the bathroom, cell Dog. "Yeah, I know," he says before I say anything but hi. "We got trouble, this don't go down quick. I'm talking days, man, not weeks. I'm working on it."

"Later, man."

"Not much later, man," Dog hangs up.

Hits me then, how stupid I am. Simple fix—one part of it, anyway. I call the Brooklyn number. "One thing, my friend," I say in Russian when I get Vassily on the line. "Don't tell the guys you already got working down here a thing until me and Dog and you and the product all get together. Business as usual, right? Don't want to upset the gangbangers unnecessarily, do we? Gotta be biz as usual until me and Dog step in."

"You drunk or something? Too much celebration?" Vassily laughs. "How else you think I do this thing? Put an ad in newspaper? Say all blackie gangsters, you have new source now. And put in your phone number? And then let my team down there get shot by blackies? Never mind. Stay drunk. Celebrate. Me, that's what I'm doing. You should see what I got sitting in my lap right now. Young, fresh from Ukraine. I call you when I got arrangements made. Be a little patient, you're too excited. Meanwhile, business as usual. So celebrate!"

What?

//

Three hours and thirty-eight minutes. That's how long I'm in Dugal's office next morning. I follow the prime rule of successful lying. Stick as close to the truth as you possibly can, give up as much information as you possibly can without compromising what you need to keep hidden. He goes from being pissed off I've done a deal with that City narc Dog without telling him to very skeptical about the magnitude of the possible bust to very excited about making the biggest catch ever. He's relentless in pursuit of details, implacable in demanding he personally be involved in every planning session I have with Dog, in every single step I take. In the end he's good to go but can't promise he'll be able to get me the guys I need. Says he understands why I don't want to use narc squad members, why I need young patrolmen, but he's going to have to come up with a pretty good line of bullshit to convince the chief to let him have men who aren't under his command. Says he'll do his best. I know he will. If this comes off, he will definitely score big—a captaincy, maybe even a jump two or three rungs up the ladder, not just one.

I'm wasted when I leave his office. I figure it's gone as well as it could have. I call Dog. He's good to go. He's already got some smart young guys on his team who aren't overexposed, and he's going to use them. He's got no problems. Business as usual until he hears from me.

Then a real bad thought. Was Buzz Cut's memory sharp enough for him to have given up the one detail that could link me to his bust—the quick blast of Russian curses when he walked out after the bail hearing? Would it have come up in the torture session? Would he have suddenly remembered the one strange thing about "Bob"? Would he have dribbled it out between screams, in some desperate hope that'd make the pain stop?

No way, I decide. He'd describe a big cop built like a refrigerator, a skinny cop with a long ponytail, Jimmy Halliday. His mind would be too fucked up by what they were doing to his body for him to reach down and pull out that flash, instinctive reaction to my totally unexpected Russian insult.

If he had, I wouldn't have walked out of the Palace in Little Odessa. Vassily would've had me hit, taken Dog out too. Vassily would've known everything Buzz Cut gave up. I must be clear.

But damn if I feel sure of that.

//

I roll into the office Friday feeling just right, balanced and calm. I love these Maryland Octobers—nights just this side of frosty, brilliant sunny days, hardly ever any rain, not until November anyway. And there's Ice Box, hulking in his cubicle. The man's back on the case. All right!

"Hey, IB. Looks like you been sparring with a cat. That cat cleaned your clock for you," I say. There's lots of little scars on his face, bright pink still but they'll fade.

"Just two words for you, Five-O," he grins.

"Everything okay? You fit? MJ and the kids? You dig gettin' up in the middle of the night, smelling diapers, all that good stuff?"

"Matter of fact, I do. It's beautiful, man. *They're* beautiful. What can I say? I musta been made for this."

"Now that's real hard to believe."

"No shit. Surprises me too, but it's the truth." He can't stop grinning. "So, I miss anything cool?"

"Nothing cool goes down without the Ice Box. Tommy's still out, gonna take a long time for that hole in his calf to heal up. Things've been slow. Kinda boring."

"Oh yeah."

"Lunch?" I say.

We go to IB's favorite, Marco Polo Ristorante. I'm hesitant on this, watching him shovel down something heaped with tomato sauce. Fuck it, I decide. He's my best. I spill everything all in a rush, every little detail from my early jolt when Dee Dee ID'd one of the Russians as Vaseline, my history with Vassily, my contacts with him these past few weeks, the deal with Dog, Brighton Beach, the deal with Dugal.

IB keeps shoveling down the pasta, apparently as unconcerned as if I'm telling him some woeful tale about trouble with Helen or something. After he's mopped the plate with the last piece of bread, chewed and swallowed, he pulls off the napkin he's had tucked into his shirt collar and throws it at me.

"You fucking asshole," he says, but mildly, like it's all some kind of joke. "What'd I say to Dugal when he made us partners? Something about seeing *Lethal Weapon* movies on my eyelids with you as the Mel Gibson psycho? I was wrong. You're fuckin' crazier than that."

"I'm just doing my job, IB."

"Bull fucking shit. You're on some kind of vendetta or something. You've gone way beyond our job description here. You ain't being professional. Wake up, Five-O. This is not a movie. You are not Mel fucking Gibson."

"Hey, man! I know what I'm doing. It's a legitimate operation. It's all clear with Dugal."

"That asshole. You always could make him believe any lies you dreamed up. You must have really turned it on to get him to go for this. I know, I fuckin' know you never told him what you just told me. You made up a bunch of shit so he wouldn't see how far over the line you went to get to where you are. Otherwise he'd have never bought it."

"Well, let's say I got a little creative with certain facts."

"Jesus Christ, Luther. How the hell do you expect me to keep you alive, let alone out of jail, you go doing shit like this?" Then IB grins hugely. "So what're we doing, exactly, next?"

"You're not doing anything, Ice," I say. He frowns. "You never heard one word of what I told you. You even give a hint you know any of this shit to Dugal or anybody else, you will get me tossed in jail or killed."

"Fuck that," IB laughs. "I'm gonna kill you myself, just to save a lot of time and bother."

"MJ would not be pleased with you. MJ likes me a lot, IB."

"Shit. That is a problem. I gotta think about this."

"Think all you want. Just remember it's going to go down, and when Dugal explains the bust to the squad, it's hot fucking news to you, right?"

"I'm not promising nothing, Luther. I'm feeling a little hurt here, you keeping all these secrets and shit from me."

"IB?"

"Yeah, yeah. You had reasons. I'm pissed. But I'll get over it."

//

Next afternoon I drive to the station, park the TT, go up to my cubicle. Can't concentrate. On impulse I call McKibbin. Sure, he's up for wringing out that Kalashnikov. "Meet you at the range," he says.

We probably go through five hundred rounds each, slow singles, three-round bursts, full-auto. Ranges from ten feet to a hundred meters. The little monster shoots buckets, it gets fouled and dirty and hot, but it's still willing to go without a hitch or hang when McKibbin shreds a silhouette full-auto, thirty-round clip.

"Mean little weapon," I say.

"Very, very mean, indeed," he says, looking admiringly at it.

I drive home, edgy. No Helen tonight—she's got some school thing. Time's moving too slow. About eight, Annie shows up at my door, lopsided grin as broad as I've ever seen it, a nearly empty bottle of tequila in her hand. She stumbles as she comes in, starts giggling.

"Kind of festive, kind of early," I say.

"Yeah, goddammit, I am," she says, taking a swig from the bottle, offering it to me, then remembering and clutching it between her breasts. "Festive, yeah. I'm just gonna flop here on your sofa and get a little more that way."

"Wanna tell me the occasion? Or do I have to guess?"

"Guess. Go ahead, Five-O. Guess." She's giggling still between sips of tequila, her long legs sprawling.

"You finished plastering your ceiling."

"Wrong! Wrong! If it was that, I'd be on my sofa looking at my beautiful work."

"So what then? I give up."

"My beautiful work, what else? My excellent, really excellent work."

"That's no answer."

Annie knocks back the last of the Añejo Patron. "Luther, you're very thick sometimes. That fuck who raped and beat the old lady in Madonna? I busted his ass today. Nailed him to the wall. A for-sure conviction, I know it. Just waiting for DNA confirmation. I got him so good I don't even need that. The prosecutor's wetting his pants to try this shit, just on what I already got."

"Excellent work, LT. You share that bottle with the prosecutor, or kill it all by yourself?"

"It's mine. Deserve to celebrate. Nailed that fuck to the wall." Annie's head is wobbling on her long neck. I give her three minutes to pass-out time. I carry her into the bedroom, take off her shoes, sit her down on the bed.

"Gotta get home," she slurs, tries to get up, collapses back. "What'd you do to me now, dammit?"

"Nothing, and you know it. You were hyped on your bust and you got drunk."

"Guess I was. Guess I did," she admits.

I help her up. She stumbles stepping out of her skirt, sits on the bed and fumbles with the buttons of her blouse. She gets it off, and shrugs off her bra before she seems to realize I'm still standing there.

"Get away you." She smiles. "Not sleeping with you."

"I never sleep with drunks," I say with a laugh, laying her down and covering her up. "See you in the morning."

Flick off the light and close the door almost in one motion. I hear her mutter something. I lie down on the sofa. I watch *La Double Vie de Veronique.* I'm awake for a long time after, thinking about Veronique and her double, and if the world ever really works that way. Then I'm hoping Annie will call to me from the bedroom, how sweet that'd be. It doesn't happen.

Next morning Annie's shy and awkward as a girl. She can hardly meet my eyes over coffee, can't stop apologizing for getting so drunk. She's gone before nine.

Boring fucking day. I can't stand waiting for action to start. I phone Helen. She comes around early that evening equipped with Ecstasy for two. I'm beginning to like this a little too much, I'm thinking, just before it kicks in. Then things go sour. I remember her fucking sketch. What shakes me is that's exactly how I think of it now: *Helen's* sketch.

23

It starts.

Dugal huddles with the head of uniformed patrolmen, gives him my specifications—young, smart, cool-headed, tough but in a way only a pro would recognize, not pumped and mean-looking, not obvious muscle like barroom bouncers. Military background a plus. The guys approached are only to be asked if they're interested in being detached from patrol duties for a while to do some undercover work. In a few days Dugal begins sending me the pick of the litter. I meet them at Teddy's Gyro, an Arby's on York Road, the seats around the fountain in the atrium of Dulaney Mall. One at a time. Different times and different places. They don't know who I am or what the mission is, they're made to swear our meeting never happened.

Not bad, overall. Better than your average company of baby marines, which has always got its share of gung-ho assholes and angry, resentful skulkers. I dismiss a few of the first type—overeager, wrapped too tight. Likely to go postal if it gets real tense. I don't get any of the second type, but some don't make the cut because they aren't cool enough under my questions. They can't disguise their nervousness. If I can spot their edge so easily, so will Vassily.

Three days, seventeen guys, I get my four. One's a Mexican, actually born here of Mexican parents, did his bit for the Corps. A hitch in the 1st Battalion, 2nd Division. Recon. Well trained. Stays chilled, smooth when I try to provoke him, insult him. We look like compadres. Other three are white boys, college boys who have ambitions—detective, or maybe DEA or FBI—but ready to take it step by step. Calm, cool. I judge they're all nice with their hands, cool with their tools, comes down to it. It won't. Not the way I want this to go off.

All from different units. Word in their units is, they're on two-week vacations. We put them in a safe house, keep 'em off the streets and out of sight. We all gather at the outdoor range, in the building there, when there's no regular police activity scheduled. We get to know each other. I drill 'em on a number of possible scenarios. I make sure they know what to do if the deal goes bad, but mostly I train them how to act like experienced drug dealers, how to handle a deal so it goes down clean and simple. I make them all take a taste of smack, just a little snort, so they'll know what it's like. They have to seem authentic, they gotta know the shit.

Pretty soon, they're good to go. I'm only sweating that Vassily won't move fast enough, that my guys'll get restless and stale, waiting. I check in with Dog. His team's ready, too.

Little hitch, finding time to see Helen at least as often as our usual routine, maybe even slightly more often. Can't let her know anything special's going on at work. Wouldn't be wise under any circumstances. Lots of conflict in my head, lots of creeping paranoia. Shit.

//

Vassily does move, faster than I'd hoped. I love that insane Russki, I'm not going to take any pleasure at all in this. That's what I think after I get his call.

"The stuff's down there, my friend," he says. It's early evening, less than ten days after the Brighton Beach talk, I'm alone at home, Helen due to come by later on. "Okay? You ready?"

"Hell yes, man. Just like we said, our guys meet your guys, everybody loves each other, friends for life?"

He laughs. "For sure. You are going to love us more, you see what we have for you. You want to bring a chemist, feel free. I invite you to bring your chemist."

"Do I need to?"

"No, I think not. I think you have a little taste, you know. But I got no objections."

"Trust, my friend. No chemist. Just me and Dog, and our guys. We'll be ten, all of us together, okay?

"Only me and five, that's it for our side. That's my team."

"You want to bring a few more, make it even, that's cool."

"What for? Trust, like you say." Vassily laughs again. "Not tomorrow night, but two nights after. You bring 750 large."

Christ, he means $750,000. Step once on that many keys at the going wholesale rate, that's $1.5 million worth maybe $6 to $8 million on the street. Large enough.

Vassily laughs once more, like he's just pulled off a great joke on me. "I'm not hearing anything, my friend. Too big surprise? Any problem?"

"Wonderful surprise," I say. "Good as it gets. The best."

"No hundreds, though."

"Naturally. Gave up on those long time ago."

"We do this early, have some dinner someplace after, just you and me, okay? Make it seven o'clock. Listen, there is phone booth on corner of Gay Street and Edmonton Avenue. Fucking phone don't work. Never mind, address will be scratched on the glass by three in afternoon that day."

"Okay."

"But, my friend, better go yourself. Don't send your blackies. This address, they can't read it. I am very sure of this."

Yeah, I think, it'll be in Cyrillic.

"Genius, you are, my friend. See you soon."

"Da. After, you take me for some of these crabcakes, oysters, good stuff, okay? Good, good."

//

First thing next morning, Dugal and I drive into the city, take a walk around Lake Montebello with Dog and his boss. We talk backup, how to coordinate, when they'll break in on the meet and make the bust. Dog's boss reluctantly agrees we'll use County tacticals only if the meet's outside the city, to avoid fuck-ups since County and City teams have never trained together. But he'll be there with City narcs alongside Dugal's County narcs. More likely the meet's in the city, so it'll be the reverse. Copacetic. There's some dispute, though, about how many should go into the meet wired.

"Nobody but me," I say. "They probably won't be checking for wires. If I'm wrong and they do, I'm the only one they won't pat down. Vassily won't let that happen. So it's gotta be me, and me only, wearing a transmitter."

Lots of jive from the other three over that, only one transmitter, suppose it breaks down, whatever. But they're finally convinced, accept it under one caveat—they stop hearing from me inside for even two seconds, the SWAT boys storm the place.

"Dumb motherfucker," Dog says to me when we've fallen far enough behind our bosses as we head back toward our cars. "Thought you was finished with this hero shit."

"You got anything under your dome but air, man? Ain't gonna be pat-downs, no problems, no shooting. When it goes down, Vassily's just gonna raise his hands high, like you and me, and we all let ourselves get busted. He's a long-time close-quarters combat man. Why do you think he's still alive?"

"Fuck if I know dick about this military shit."

"Because he ain't suicidal. He'll see instantly there's no way to shoot his way out. So he'll let his lawyer take care of springing him later."

"I believe that shit when I see it."

"You ain't got long to wait."

We're all dumb motherfuckers. I know that as soon as I copy the address scratched on that phone booth. We all been watching too many movies, it's warped all of us even though we're on the streets and see it for real every day. We've been thinking, mainly, some old warehouse down in that rat's nest of them at harborside, the working harbor east of the Inner Harbor showplace. Dark alleys, wind rustling the rubbish, half the lights busted or burned out.

It isn't going to happen that way. The address is maybe two miles down the road from Dee Dee's horse farm. A fucking horse farm—house and stables at least a hundred meters in from the road, security cameras, infrared beams, could even be tripwires and claymoor mines. Nah, that's paranoid, the mines anyway. Get clear, get cold, Luther. Only got a couple hours to get it together. I'm on the cell soon as I get in the TT and heading back to the county. Alert Dog, alert Dugal.

Thinking, thinking. Hit it. When I see the product and Vassily sees the cash, I say "Comrade!" like I'm real happy. Dugal has some guys from the electric company kill all power for exactly sixty seconds. My job is to chill everybody inside when the lights go, the back-up team's job is to use those sixty seconds to get past the disabled security and right up against the house or stables, I'll clue them which one we're in soon as I'm in. They wait another two minutes after the lights go back on, give anybody who's drawn a weapon time to calm down, untense, lower it.

Dugal isn't happy. "The risk ratio is going up very fast here, Luther. I do not like it. I do not want a firefight. Killing the lights, goddammit, sounds about as intelligent as striking a match when you're standing in a pool of gasoline."

"You have a better idea?" I ask.

"Yeah, we just wait until your team leaves with the drugs, and then we roll in and roll up the Russians."

"Negative, LT. That's how you'll get your firefight. At first they'll think it's a rip-off by us, not cops coming in. They'll go full-auto, 'til Vassily realizes it isn't us, but cops. He'll quit then. But it may be too late for a lot of cops."

"Maybe," Dugal says, sounding very dubious.

"Second, and this is crucial, I gotta be in there with my guys, we gotta be *seen* by the Russians getting busted right along with them. Otherwise we're blown, we're known as cops, we're walking targets ever after."

"I'm feeling a slow turn from win-win to lose-lose here, Luther," Dugal says. "Just a feeling. Analyze it rationally, any operation this size has sizable risks. It would have been easier in close quarters, downtown. Now it's harder."

"It is. But doable. Definitely. If we stick exactly to plan."

"I'll see to that. You have the harder task."

"What?"

"Keeping yourself and your men alive in those sixty seconds of darkness."

24

It goes down.

Blue twilight, thoroughbreds moving ghostlike here and there in distant pastures. We pull up to the gate of Vassily's place—it's almost twin to Dee Dee's—in two Ford vans. I say, in Russian, "It's Shooter and Dog" to the speaker embedded in one of the brick columns. Whirring, a steely click, the gate swings open. Along a tree-lined drive to a graveled area between house and stables. We get out slowly. A wiry Russian, the one who answered the door at the Charles Street house, strolls easily toward us.

"Shooter," he calls in English. I'm sure he's being covered, I'm sure somebody I can't see has his scope reticle on my face. "Your boys all carrying, yes?"

"Sure, wanna see?" I say, tell Dog and both teams to slowly open their jackets or windbreakers, let their pistols be seen.

"No problem with this, Shooter," the Russian says. "Our guys too. Is normal. We meet before, remember? Charles Street?"

"Yeah, it's Nick, right?" I say, taking his outstretched hand, shaking it firmly. "Where's Vassily?"

"Come on in. To stables. You, all your guys." Nick smiles.

"Hell of a welcome, Nick. Stepping in horseshit in the fuckin' stables," I say. Now Dugal and the back-up know where we'll be.

Nick laughs. "Stables like this, you never seen. Cleaner than house, where nobody lives," he says, leading us into a big round structure—it covers a dirt riding ring—with three wings of stalls radiating from it. Bright spots on the ceiling, light's as bright as a circus ring. I see two rough wooden packing cases in the middle, tops off. I see five Russians standing in a casual semicircle around the crates.

Quick scan around. No way to tell if there are others hidden down the stall-ways, or up in the rafters; the light's blinding from there.

"Who are your friends, Nick? I didn't see them at the Palace," I say in Russian.

"Of course not," Nick says. "They are the boys who live down here now. The whole idea, right? Your boys meet our boys, everybody gets to be friends? Better to use English. Some of these boys, they're Russian all right but born in Brighton. Their Russian isn't so good as yours. A shame, but hey, this is America. Come see what we have for you in crates. It's going to give you a hard-on, you're going to love it at first sight."

"Sure. And you look at what we got for you, you're going to come in your pants," I say, motioning Dog to come up with two big Halliburton cases, pop them open. It takes two to carry $750,000 when you can't use hundreds. "But Nick, one thing. One big thing. Where is my friend Vassily? He going to jump out of one of those crates, just to surprise me?"

"Like Vassily said, a good sense of humor you got, Shooter. Vassily, he's very, very sorry. He tells me to make to you a thousand apologies, but he has to go out of town in a hurry."

"Then the deal doesn't happen."

"Shooter, Shooter. Vassily said you would be upset, and please to forgive him. We're here, the product's here, you got the money. We should all be happy, yes?"

Happy? This is the worst. The fucking worst. We do this bust without nailing Vassily, all we got to look forward to is Vassily coming back at us. Christ, I'm hoping Dugal's picked up my hint.

"Deal can't happen without my friend Vassily," I say, tossing another plea to Dugal. Please God, let him get it. Don't let him come on with the backup.

"Be reasonable, Shooter. Vassily, he got to go. For the future, yes! Because this is just the start, you understand?"

"Where the fuck did he go? He told me he'd be here." I am not going to say "Comrade." We're going to walk on this.

"Moscow, then Kazakhstan. He go to *source.* That's how much he trust you. He go to source, make arrangements for much more of what we got here," Nick says. He puts his arm around my shoulder. "Everything is perfect. Such a waste, all this trouble we all go to, everything is perfect, and you walk away just because Vassily is working for future? Don't do this, Shooter."

Nick steers me to the crates. Goddamn. Key upon key of smack. Nick nods at one of the Russians, who flicks a switchblade, makes a small slice in one bag, carries over a tiny pinch of white powder on the knife blade, which he points at my face. "You taste that, Luther. Then you know why Vassily go where he go, and can't be here."

I taste it. Rocks me. Pure, pure shit. I can't stop a grin from spreading across my face. Nick sees that, reads it in a way I never intended, gives me a hug, says, "Okay, comrade . . ."

Fuck. Pitch black. I seize Nick, scream, "No guns, no guns anybody. It's not a rip. Not a rip!" A lot to say, real fast, in English and in Russian. I almost piss myself when I hear one of the Russian boys call, "Fucking power loss! Stay cool. Happens a lot out here. Stay cool! Shit, I live in this place for two months, happens all the time."

Then we're blinking hard, almost blinded when the lights hit us full force. I look at Nick. He looks at me, serious, agitated. Everybody in my view has a hand on a weapon. Then Nick laughs, slowly at first, then in big Russian-style bursts.

"Big scare, huh, Shooter? Jesus Christ. Man, make me shake, shit like this. Come on now. Get your boys to take crates to your vans. Me, I'll take briefcases. Let's do it before the fucking power goes again. Shit, that happens, we all be shooting each other. Big fucking mistake. Big fucking shame, yes? And look." Nick waves. "Afterward, party like Vassily said. Everybody gets to know everybody, man to man."

I see—how could I have missed it on the first scan?—a long table draped with white linen at the far side of the ring. Silver ice buckets, bottles of vodka and champagne peeking out the tops. Big plates of food.

"We all get drunk together, get friendly. Our boys, your boys," Nick says.

Dog latches the cases, looks up at me. I nod. He stands and hands them to Nick. Then he waves our guys over to the cases. The Russians are nailing the lids back on. Except for one, who comes over and takes the cases from Nick. "Count?" he asks.

"Fuck no. Here we got trust. Any little bit short by mistake, hey, honest mistake. We make it up later, right, Shooter?"

Got to've been two minutes since the lights went back on. Maybe we're not fucked. Maybe Dugal got the hint. God, I'm too dumb to live. They did the lights on Nick's "comrade." It's gonna go down. Now?

Now!

It's like I'm struck deaf, hearing only the blood roaring in my ears. Tacticals all in black, black-hooded, swarming in from all directions. Assault shotguns, CAR15s, red laser dots butterflying across our chests, flicking back and holding. My arms go straight up in the air. Nick sees two red dots on his stomach, doesn't notice the one steady on his forehead. His arms go straight up too. Swarms of tacticals and city narcs and county narcs wearing blue police windbreakers are on us, shoving us, ripping our jackets, pulling our guns away, kicking our legs out from under us, putting muzzles to our heads as we lie in the dirt. Nick's cursing a hurricane of the worst Russian obscenities I've ever heard. Bullhorns, orders. I realize I'm hearing again. "Any motherfucker twitches, grease him," some asshole bullhorns. These fucks are feeling the rush, they're kicking and yanking us to our feet now. A boot catches me on my way up. I feel one, maybe two ribs crack. Overkill, overreaction, too fucking psyched, moving too fucking fast, somebody's gonna make a mistake.

Freeze-frame. Silence. One of the Russians has Dugal's arm twisted behind his back, switchblade at his throat. I see a tactical in the dirt, geyser of blood from a severed carotid. "Keep the fuck away, keep the fuck away," the Russian kid's screaming, his eyes wild and crazy. A little blood's starting to trickle down Dugal's neck. But the LT's face is blank.

"Let it go, let it go now," Nick roars at the kid, who's edging himself toward the main door, Dugal in front of him as a shield.

"Keep away! Keep away! I'll slit the fuck's throat," the kid screams. Nobody's moving. Except the kid and the LT, slowly edging backward.

PopPopPop. Like three bottles of champagne uncorked almost, but not quite, simultaneously.

The kid drops, dead before he hits the ground. Dugal swings away, hand going automatically to his throat. Hand comes away, he stares at the blood, expressionless. I see it's minor, the kid was only pressing the blade too hard, not slashing.

"Calm, please, gentlemen," a voice comes from outside. "One of yours, coming in."

Then McKibbin walks through that wide door, AKSU-74 with night scope slung over his shoulder, muzzle down, his hands in the air. "Gentlemen, please remove the laser sights from me. It's very distressing, you know. Thank you."

Ulster Constabulary, my ass, I'm thinking as we're led, cuffed, to police vans. Ex–SAS, for sure. Cool.

//

That three-round burst of McKibbin's is the only thing that's cool. I don't mind spending the night and the next day in a holding cell with Dog and our guys, in full view, deliberately, of Nick and his guys in the cell opposite. I don't mind that Nick and his guys almost miraculously make bail before the day's end, while we still sit there. I don't mind the bad, suspicious look disguised with a grin Nick gives me when he walks. Minor inconvenience. Part of the show.

Like hell it is.

It's the sit-down with Dugal that night that is so fucking uncool I can't believe it. Because he can't believe we're fucked. He's convinced we've won a famous victory. He's already seen his face on the TV news, bandage on his little neck nick bigger than it needs to be, announcing the biggest drug bust in Baltimore County's history, seen his photo and his direct quotes in the newspaper, taken calls of congratulation from the county executive, the department chief and who knows what other big swinging dicks, maybe the fucking governor. The man's so high on all this he just will not hear me.

No consolation, feeling sure Dog's eating the same shit as me with his boss downtown at this very moment.

"We fuckin' blew it!" I explode.

"Take it easy, Luther. I understand you've been under tremendous stress. I empathize. Under a little stress myself for a moment," he says easily, brushing the bandage on his neck. "We got the drugs, we got the players. Perfect. Except for that SWAT man we lost, it would be one for the textbooks. We've hit these guys so hard they've been knocked all the way back to Brighton Beach. They won't come down here again."

"Wrong!"

"C'mon, Luther. Ease off. You're getting excessive here."

"LT, we missed Vassily. He's still operative. Without him in lockdown, we have not—repeat, not—turned off the faucet."

"You're not thinking clearly, Detective. Just because this Vassily wasn't at the scene does not mean he's not ours. We'll get him through his men, during the grand jury process. We'll turn one of them, make a deal, offer him witness protection. We will, I promise you, get this Vassily. The DEA and FBI have been alerted. So what is your problem?"

"His men will not—repeat, not—give him up. Sir. He will not—repeat, not—be found by the DEA or the FBI or even the fuckin' CIA. Sir. *Nobody knows who he is!* Sir. Nobody knows his real name, nobody's got his fingerprints, nobody's gonna catch him at JFK or any other airport he chooses to fly back into because he's probably got six different perfectly forged passports. Sir."

"I don't believe I'm hearing this from an experienced man like you, Luther. What makes you so sure a drug dealer of this magnitude can come in under the radar of every law enforcement agency we have in this country? It's impossible. He will be found. He will be arrested. Unless he stays in Russia, which, if I were him, I would seriously consider."

"You're not him, LT. I don't know who he is, but I do know very well what he can do, what his capabilities are. Even if the Feds manage to find him, he's untouchable. So we're fucked."

"We will get him . . ."

"For what? We don't have any reason to arrest him because he wasn't there. We have no connection between him and the drugs! He never got fucking near them. All he did was talk with me and Dog. He's clean. His hands aren't dirty. He's taken a slight loss, is all. Everything he lost—men, dope, money—he can replace. I guarantee he will."

"I'm convinced otherwise, Luther. We'll just have to agree to disagree. Let's leave it at that for now. I don't want to get into a disagreement with a man who's just done some of the finest policework I've ever seen. You have done that. Congratulations."

Dugal extends his hand. For a moment I hesitate to take it. For a moment I feel like going ballistic. But I take a deep breath, meet his eyes, shake his hand. "Little advice, Luther," he says as I'm leaving his office. "Don't be thinking failure. Don't be thinking the bad guy got away. Start thinking commendations, promotions. That's what's coming your way."

"Sir," I say.

All that's coming my way, I think on the traffic crawl out York Road toward Cockeysville, is a three-round burst some time, some place when I least expect it. Or maybe something worse.

25

If Nick wasn't lying—and every instinct says he wasn't, that Vassily really did go to Russia to keep himself clear of the action, if not to actually do that Kazakh business—I figure I've got maybe a week or more of grace. Damn if I'm going to just sit on my butt, waiting. There's lots to prepare, war gaming that needs doing. I'm going to find out some things I need to know.

So Friday night the TT's hustling down Route 301 toward the Nice Bridge over the Potomac and into Tidewater country. Everlast on the tape player. "Gotta watch how you act, watch what you say, 'cause they ain't no stallin' when death comes callin'. . . ."

"This is neat," Helen says. "Taking me to meet the parents. That hasn't happened since high school days."

"All that long ago? Really? Nobody from Towson State or Loyola or Hopkins ever take you home, show you off?"

"I *never* dated college boys. You should know my tastes don't run that way, babe."

"I should. I do. So which ways do they run? The cop, I know." Oh, very uncool, Luther, I'm thinking as soon as the words have left my mouth.

"Let's see. There was a bouncer at some club, maybe it was Ethernet. A couple firemen—you know they're always the cutest things going. And, oh yeah, this drug dealer, he had a gun and everything, when I was a freshman."

I laugh. Then my own rule jerks me a little. When you lie, stick as close to the truth as you can. "Must be the danger thing, right?" I say.

"Must be. Can't be *muscles* or I wouldn't have looked at you."

"Not even once," I say, then shift fast to cover my error. "Gotta tell you that you might be a little surprised when we get where we're going."

"Love surprises. But I'm wondering if I should read anything into this. Any intentions. Because, you know, my time horizon's pretty limited. A few months at most. Anything further out, I can't see until I get nearer to it."

"Think it's any different for me?"

"It'd be flattering if it was, but scary as hell. Eight, nine months and I'm gone, remember?"

"Super clear. Nothing symbolic in this. The trip's just for me. Gotta take a break."

"That huge heroin bust? Wrung you out, did it?"

"Little bit."

"Guess it would. Guess it wasn't like being in a movie or anything. Really Russian mafia, like the media says?"

I just shrug. "I thought we might have some fun down here. I do need some fun about now."

"Now that sounds much better. I was getting kind of nervous, you know?"

"Hey, if it's not fun, just say so. We'll bolt."

"Okay, babe," she says, laying a hand on my thigh, stroking, grinning.

I can feel Helen's curiosity, she's radiating it, as the car crunches over the oyster shell drive walled in by forest, as we stop before the lit-up house, as my mother and father together step out of the front door before we can even exit the TT.

"Ho, Luther," Gunny booms out into the night. "Hey there, Lieutenant Annie. Get your butts over here! Momma's got food on the table."

"Uh, Luther . . ." Helen says.

"Excuse me, ma'am," Gunny says when we enter the light and he sees his mistake. "Little confusion on my part, old eyes in bad light. Call me Gunny, please. I'm Luther's poppa, but you know that, don't you?"

"Hi, I'm Helen."

"Well, hello Helen. Don't stand here in the chill, c'mon inside," Gunny says, ushering her and my mother, who are introducing themselves, through the door. They head toward the kitchen. He lingers by the door while I fetch the bags from the TT's trunk.

"Who said my dog won't hunt? Luther, you are one devious hound," he murmurs to me as I enter. "How many of these sweet young things are you pointing on, anyway? No, don't tell me. Envy is inappropriate for a man of my age and position. But Jesus fuckin' Christ! You say you're bringing a friend when you phone, but you don't say *this* type of friend. My assumption of kind is correct, right?"

"Yessir. All the way." I grin.

"Well, your momma's going to be a little flustered, because she made up both bedrooms this time, remembering last time. And you're not going to use but one, are you?"

"That was the intention."

"Then get in there and get things smooth, maggot," he laughs. "Before I whup your sorry ass."

There's nothing to smooth. Pop always did underestimate Momma. She's doing fine with Helen. It's Helen who's a little flustered as we sit down to eat, but she makes a real nice recovery, impresses me again with her cool. Beyond her years, I think. Then I think I tend to do to Helen what Gunny does to Momma, otherwise I'd just be taking her ability to improvise and adapt for granted. Hell. Gunny and me, both of us dumb grunts who maybe chewed too much dirt in the wrong places at the wrong times and lost forever good judgment and sense of proportion about the world and the women in it.

Adaptation is the order of the night, it seems. Gunny tones

down the corps lifer act he played so well for Annie, Momma behaves more motherly to Helen than the woman-to-woman connection she made with Annie. Fine, friendly dinner, light conversation, but Momma's face goes impassive when she shows us up to the bedrooms and I steer Helen into mine. Nothing Helen would notice, but I know Momma's mask of disapproval.

"Wow!" Helen laughs once we're together under the sheets and a thick wool blanket. Only early in October yet, but it feels like there might be frost before morning. "Megasurprises, Luther. What are the acoustics like in this place? Do I have to whisper? And keep real still when we fuck?"

"Solid. They can't hear a thing in their bedroom. It's downstairs on the other side of the house."

"So start explaining."

"Why don't you tell me what you expected?"

"Maybe just some resemblance between parents and child. I never imagined your dad'd be a black man and your mother Vietnamese. You don't look anything like either of them. You adopted or something?"

"Sure, I was a Chinese orphan."

She laughs. "C'mon. Really."

"I'm just what happens when there's some fairly radical mixing in the gene pool. Anything you feel funnny about?"

"You mean do I care? And—what I think you really mean but don't dare say directly—is my WASPy sensibility at all perturbed? I resent your little test, yes. Otherwise, it's a pretty cool surprise."

"I wasn't trying to test you."

"The hell you weren't. Somewhere inside that mad mind of yours, you were going, 'Let's see how rich bitch Helen handles *this.*' It's okay, though. I can see where that would come from. I've shown you enough frivolous, bratty, spoiled sides of me to spark that. But the test's over. I pass. So get fucked."

"All by myself?"

"Well, I won't be that severe. Let me see what I can do to help you out a little."

She helps out a lot. Afterward, watching her sleep, I'm thinking smart girl, so very clever, she would have been right on target in an ordinary situation. She'd have probably been on target—a different one—if she knew what I was really about with her. And Gunny and Momma. If she knew I always check my back real good, then say a silent goodbye to those I care about before I go into a place I might not come out of.

Bad thought then. Maybe she does know. Maybe she's always known.

//

I'm up at dawn, out on the jetty, watching the early light on the creek, listening to the woods. A fish jumps, ripples spread in a perfect circle behind the slight splash. Perfect fall morning, clear and clean, the smell of cold tidal water and leaves going from green to brief, dry colorful death. I twitch when the cell in the TT starts chirping.

"So. What your guys call a goatfuck, yes?" Vassily's Russian is even, controlled. "Very, very bad, little brother. Very, very bad, that's what I hear from Nick."

"We got ratted out, Vassily. And I'm fucking pissed."

"Pissed? Who took the big loss here, little brother?"

"Who took just as big a loss and is facing trial and jail maybe? Not you. You didn't show, Vassily. You weren't fucking there. Why weren't you there?"

"Because I was here. Not here in Moscow, like I am right now, but over here someplace taking care of business. Nick told you all about it. He says he told you all about it."

"Yeah, he told me. Maybe you should've told me in advance, put off the meet. Maybe Nick's got a big mouth, maybe he tells lots of people lots of things. Maybe that's why we got fucked."

"Or maybe your blackies, eh? I will find out about my own people pretty damn quick. I'm leaving here, coming back there in a couple days. I'll find out, count on it. You better be finding out about your team."

"We got to talk when you get back, Vassily."

"Oh yes, little brother. We talk. Just you and me." What does he know, I'm wondering. Could he have made me and Dog for cops? "Just you and me. We figure out who fucked us."

"And then?"

"We fuck them dead, what else? Whoever they are," Vassily says laughing. "I call you as soon as I get to New York. Go carefully, little brother."

Then I'm staring at a dead phone in my hand.

Back inside, quietly, I get coffee going before Momma or Helen wakes. Helen. Paranoia shakes. Would I be so juked over this if I hadn't taken that head shot? It's so goddamn implausible, her having anything to do with Buzz Cut and Vassily. Her story's solid. I know because I checked. Rich white girl with rich white parents in rich white Westport, Connecticut. Just like she said. How would she ever get connected with the Russians?

It could happen. Sure.

But how could she possibly get so fucking good at it?

Gunny comes into the kitchen, buttoning a plaid flannel shirt, sniffing. "Java, hoo-ah!" he says, helping himself to some. "Lifer juice."

We stand there sipping. He's looking me over. "You're about to do something wiggy, Luther. You're about to go into a hot LZ locked and loaded. Aren't you?"

"No."

"Can't bullshit me, boy. It's in your eyes. You gotta do this?"

"Yeah."

"Is it an authorized mission?"

"Sure."

"Not some outlaw stunt you just wanna do?"

"Negative. Recon behind some lines. Orders."

"Then grease 'em all if that's what it takes to get out again. But, goddammit, don't you let your momma see what I'm seeing."

"She won't."

"She will, damn smart lady that she is, if you don't get your eyes straight and your party face on. Do it."

"Aye-aye, Gunny." I smile.

Momma comes in, starts cooking. Helen trails her by just a few minutes. Long, slow breakfast of ham and eggs, grits, toast. Helen's bright and cheerful, asks for seconds. Momma's warm enough, but I know she's not completely relaxed because she doesn't spar with Gunny in her put-on Viet girl talk. She keeps to her best English, with a little French thrown in here and there. Gunny finally slides out of his chair, leaves the kitchen, comes back cradling an old M16.

"Luther and I are gonna go play in the woods. You're welcome to come, Helen. Unless you don't like the look of this." He smiles.

"Can I shoot it?" she asks.

"Surely can," Gunny says.

"Cool. Let me just run upstairs and get my jacket."

"You numbah ten, Marine," Momma says to Gunny when she's gone. She looks hard at me. "Don't let him scare her, Luther. She just a kid."

"Oh, I don't think anybody's gonna scare her, Mom," I say. I'm believing that more and more.

"Too young, I say."

"Don't worry, Momma."

Gunny, Helen and I walk down the driveway to the highway, cross it and trek into some swampy pinelands. Gunny's carrying a bag of something and the M16. "Now, about half a klick in, there's this pond," he says. "In this pond is the great-granddaddy of all snapping turtles. Huge beyond belief. I've seen him take not just ducklings, but a full-grown female mallard."

"Sounds a little exaggerated. Sounds a little like your bass stories," I say.

"Ho! You'll see, you'll see. I been trying to nail this monster for two, three seasons now. But he's too fast, too smart. He's the Victor Charlie sapper of snapping turtles."

"What's that mean?" Helen asks.

"Means he's so slick he could sneak up on Gunny, and Gunny's toes would be bitten off before he ever knew what hit him," I say.

"You must be speaking about your own self, Luther. I got all my toes. I just haven't got this turtle yet. Today could be the day."

The pond's almost dead black, a few bleached stumps still standing here and there, and a long, bark-stripped deadfall reaching maybe three meters out into the water from the shore. Gunny hands me the 16, edges carefully out along the fallen trunk, reaches into his bag and puts a fat, two-foot-long dead eel in a little notch where a branch broke off, about a foot above the waterline. We find a firm, dry patch of pine needles about thirty meters off and sit down.

"Now, Miss Helen, we get this snapper's attention," Gunny says. He takes sections of eel about six inches long, sticks a bunch of corks in the gullets. "We toss these in the pond, the snapper tries to grab some lunch. No use in shooting when he grabs them, I've tried two dozen times and he's too quick. But after a while, he'll edge himself up on that log to get the big meal. And that's where we get him."

I see the wood around the notch is holed and punky. "Hell, all you ever got is wood."

"Yeah, well, today could be the day."

Helen's laughing. "You guys are crazy."

"Yeah? Watch this." Gunny heaves a piece of eel out into the pond. There's a splash when it hits, but the corks keep it afloat. And damn, a couple of minutes later a big, reptilian head with a gaping, horny beak pops up and snatches the eel.

"Jesus Christ! That looked like some kind of dinosaur or something. Creature from the Black Lagoon!" Helen cries. "It is a monster. You sure it's a turtle? I've never seen any turtle like that thing."

"He's a snapper, sweetheart," Gunny says. "The great-granddaddy of all snappers. Watch again."

He tosses another slab of eel. A few minutes go by. Then a flash of a hideous beak and the eel's gone. I'm getting creeped by this thing, but Helen's laughing. "Holy shit! Holy shit!" she says.

"Let's wait for him to get interested in the main course. You want the first shot, Helen?" Gunny says.

"Hell yes," she says.

Gunny drops the clip, checks to make sure the chamber's empty, then moves around behind Helen and gets her and the 16 into shooting position. "Now," he says, "see the ghost ring up close to your eye? Ignore it. See the post at the end of the barrel? Just concentrate on that. Snapper comes up on the log, all you got to do is move a little until the post is on him, then squeeze the trigger. You ever shot before?"

"Sporting clays with my dad. Twelve-gauge Beretta over-and-under. I wasn't very good," Helen says.

"Well, if you've fired a 12-gauge, you'll hardly think this is a gun at all. No kick."

Gunny takes the 16, slips in the clip, pulls the charger, lets it snap. Gives the rifle back to Helen. "It's live now. Do not, please, put your finger on the trigger until you see the turtle. It'll fire if you touch the trigger."

"Gotcha," Helen says, settling in, rifle butt tucked into her shoulder, cheek on the stock. *Like she's done it before.* "When's he going to come?"

"Well . . ." Gunny says, "that depends. Could be a while. Best to rest your left arm on your knees."

We wait. We wait. The pond's still, water flat as glass. "I can't believe I'm sitting here in some Virgina swamp with an army rifle, trying to shoot a turtle!" Helen says, chuckling. "Spend a lot of time just sitting here like this, do you, Gunny?"

"Fair amount. My goal in life is to waste that snapper. I can't stand him eating all those baby ducks. And this would be a good place to catch panfish, if he wasn't eating them all."

She laughs. "Sure, it's perfectly logical."

I'm not paying much attention anymore. I'm liking the sun warming my face, but my mind's eye is seeing gray, gritty city streets more than water, trees, sky and clouds. I'm looking Vassily in the eye. He's looking back. Who's going to see whose soul first? That'll make the difference.

"Holy shit!" Helen hisses. I scan the fallen tree. The biggest, ugliest, scariest snapper I've ever seen is edging himself slowly out of the water and onto the log, just left of the notch where the eel's draped. His head looks as big as a grapefruit. He stretches his neck, and that beak . . . Jesus.

"Pop his shit," Gunny whispers. Helen squeezes off, drops the 16, jumps up.

"Gawwwd damn!" Gunny shouts. Helen's bullet has taken the snapper near the base of his neck, right where there's a gap between his shell and his belly plate. The thing's jolted hard, but he's so heavy he just slides into the notch instead of being blown back into the water. "Gawwd damn!" Gunny's hustling down to the log and out on it, Ka-Bar knife out just in case. He prods the turtle's neck with the point of his knife. Nothing. "You greased him good!" he shouts. He tries to lift the snapper by the tail with one hand, has a little trouble. The bastard must weigh an unbelievable amount. Gunny's grin is strained as he lugs the thing back toward us.

"You see that, Luther? You see me shoot the monster? Creature from the Black Lagoon. Blam!" Helen's sort of hopping up and down. "That was way cool! Now I know why you guys like guns."

Gunny plops the thing on the ground near us, shakes his arm. "Hoo-ah! Heavy duty. Look what he could do." He levers open the snapper's beak and has no trouble slipping his wrist in.

"Oh man, he could bite your hand off easy," Helen says. "This is unbelievable. Wish I'd brought my camera."

"We got one at home. If we can carry him that far, we'll take some pictures. Just try picking him up, though."

Helen takes the tail with both hands, pulls hard as she can, and only gets the creature halfway off the ground before she gives up.

The old man and me drag the thing home, rope him up on a thick oak branch. Momma comes out the door. Her eyes widen. She puts her hand over her mouth. "Get the camera, will you, please?" Gunny calls to her. She does. Then Helen poses next to the slain monster, its shell big enough to cover her from tits to hips, cradling the M16. Gunny goes through a whole twenty-four-frame roll.

"Can't wait to see the pics. I'm going to really gross out all my girlfriends with them," Helen says.

Then we sit in the outdoor chairs. Mom brings us each a beer. Air's cool, but the sun's hot now. Great autumn day. Except that snapper is spooking me. Don't know why, I've killed plenty of snappers, starting when I was a kid with a little .22. Gunny's slit the snapper's throat with his Ka-Bar to bleed it out. There's a slow, steady dripping into the grass.

"So," Helen says, halfway through her beer in two gulps. "Do we eat this thing? Or what?"

"*Some* folks eat snapper. Southern folks. Mostly *poor* Southern folks. I personally wouldn't take a single bite if you put a gun to my head. Eat a thing that ugly? No way, young lady," Gunny says.

"You just going to throw it away, then?" Helen sounds disappointed.

"No. It's your snapper, you made a fine shot. You want to eat some, be my guest," Gunny says. "Momma knows some turtle recipes."

Helen looks over at the thing, wrinkles her brow a little. "Uh, I think maybe I'll try it some other time, if that's okay."

"Outstanding. Because I know some folks down the road about five miles, nice white folks even if they are rednecks. Don't have much money. They'd be real glad to have that snapper. It'll feed them and their three little kids for four days, easy. I'll run it on down to them in the pickup in a little bit."

After lunch, Gunny and Helen do that. I sit outside with Momma. She's sipping green tea. "What you up to, Luther?" she asks after a while. "With this young girl?"

"Not a thing. She's just a girlfriend. Don't you like her?"

"She too young for you. Short time, okay. But she's not in love with you. Girlfriend only. Comes to wife, you take that Annie."

"First, Mom, I don't want a wife. Second, Annie'll never be in love with me."

"Already is. I see that. Just she doesn't know it yet and she never let you know it once she knows it. Unless you show her you in love with her first."

"Oh, beaucoup good advice."

"Why you so cruel, Luther? Your poppa, he talks a little rough sometimes but his heart is always tender. So you don't get it from him. Tell me, why you have this cruelness?"

"I didn't mean to upset you, Momma. Just that you don't really know or understand my life."

"I got feelings I trust, Luther. Bad ones now about something you doing, or going to do. With this girl or not this girl, Annie or not Annie. More likely some bad people, number ten people. Just stop, please. Think. Every time you ever in trouble in your life, it because you not stop to think before you do something. So you promise your mother you think. Or you are a very cruel boy."

"I promise I'm not doing anything wrong to anybody, and yes, I'll stop and think hard before I act on anything, good or bad."

"That's okay, then," she says, patting my arm. "You make your old mother happy if you do that."

//

In bed that night, Helen's smooth and supersweet. "You delivered," she murmurs, when her lips aren't busy with other things.

"Delivered what?"

"You said it would be fun. Don't think I've ever had so much fun. Except, maybe, what I'm about to have right now."

26

"We fuck them dead, what else?" Vassily's laugh in Moscow had bounced off a satellite and reached me in Tyding's. It keeps looping through my head.

Stuck on desk duty, I start trying to reach out to a lot of old friends—military mainly. It's a slog. All the homies I used to bang with are scattered, some new base or some new place, hard to track down by phone. I keep on it, call after frustrating call. There's some hardware I know I'm going to need, and they're the only ones with access. Got to make this happen. Getting edgier by the hour.

I can't let anyone know what I'm up to, but people won't leave me alone. Even Ice Box gets on my case. "You don't trust me?" he complains first day I'm back on duty. Okay, he's feeling abandoned, a little hurt that he'd been left out of the entire Russian setup except that mad assault on the stables, but I do not need this, not now. "That's why I got no part of the Russian Rattle?"

That's what everybody's calling the bust. They're talking about it too damn much. They got the Dugal point of view. A famous victory. They just don't get it.

"Bullshit," I snap, meaner than I want to be. "Did I or did I not tell you everything in advance, big man? Anyway, I blew the thing. Why is it none of you fuckers can comprehend that missing Vassily means we missed everything?"

"We'll get him," IB says. Even he won't get it, dammit. So I lie.

"I wanted you in with me, but the only deal I could get Dog to agree to was him and me, just him and me. He had like this obsession. Him and me. Total secrecy until the last minute. Dude's been out in the badlands down there too long. It's made him crazed."

"Well," IB concedes, "guess you had to do what you had to do. But goddamn! The score we made out there. The biggest ever. You should be thinking about that. Instead you're all kinked about old Vaseline. That's whacked, man."

I don't even try to explain what's going to come down, hard and fast, on me and Dog. I just grunt, "I know the man, is all."

"Great. Meanwhile, Five-O, it's lonely out there by myself. There's nothing much happening. Never seen so little action."

"That's a good thing, not a bad one, you dumb fuck."

"True, true. But it's making me real torpid."

I look him up and down, grinning fake but large. "Your natural state, isn't it, IB?"

"Just two words, Luther . . ." We both laugh.

Annie makes the obligatory drop-by, gives me the CAT scan look, decides all synapses are flashing in an orderly fashion, invites me to Bocca for dinner. I say yes.

She asks the obligatory questions about the Russian deal, and then some more acute ones that could mean trouble, so she gets some slick evasions with just enough fact and truth to tell her not to go there. She's wise enough to read that, heed that. She's even easy—though it brings on the very first blush I've ever seen on her face—when I steer talk to that little drunken episode at my place.

"So what's the big deal?" She laughs. "So you saw my tits. Plenty of guys have. Probably you've seen a lot better."

"Never! Best pair going."

"You are so full of shit, Luther." She giggles.

Nearly every day, picking times when there're no training sessions on the schedule and I'm getting no callbacks, I go down in the basement and work out with the SIG, the HK, the Eagle. Also a beautiful little Walther PPKS in classic .380ACP, points and shoots like its barrel is my forefinger. I just couldn't resist buying the piece.

I've taken to wearing it in a Fobus holster tucked into my pants at the small of my back.

First time McKibbin sees that, he laughs at me. "Planning on a situation where we need to do a New York reload, are we, then?"

"What?"

"Much faster to pull another pistol than drop a clip and slip in a fresh one," he says. "Or so they believe in New York. I've me doubts, but what do I know? Personally, I feel if you haven't solved your problem with the standard seventeen rounds in the Glocks they carry, you must already be dead. Makes reloads moot, wouldn't you say?"

When I'm finished shooting, stripping and cleaning the weapons, and nobody's around but him and me, I say, "SAS. I figured that out a long time ago, you know?"

"Wild imagination you have, lad. Or ye've gone mad." He laughs. "Just a copper walkin' the beat in Belfast. Twenty-five years as a constable, I was."

"Un-huh."

"Just another copper on the beat." He grins.

"Takes more than that to make a shot like you made at the stables."

"Get lots of time on the range, don't I, lad? A child could've made that shot, provided he'd sufficient range time."

"If you say so. What were you doing out there, anyway?"

"Oh, a wee bird spoke to me. A wee bird, a lieutenant bird I think, who'd bought himself a new weapon and came to me every day for a week or so for a bit of advice and instruction. You would have been interested to see his weapon, Luther, bright as a new penny. Very nice Heckler in .45. Exactly, by chance, the same model as you're cleanin' this very moment."

"Fucking Dugal?"

"I'm shocked, Luther. Namin' a name. Suggestin' any such thing. A man of your experience! Truly shockin' lapse, I must say."

"So he let you tag along? No idea, naturally, of what you'd be carrying, or that you'd feel any need, let's say, to use it?"

"Actually, invited meself, so to speak. Gets a bit borin', you know, handholdin' young wankers day after day, despairin' over whether they will ever learn to shoot properly, despite my best efforts. Thought it would make a nice change. Fresh air, good company and so forth."

He's got me laughing now.

"By the bye, the wee bird's become quite proficient with his HK. Not yet up to *our* standard, mind. But well above the norm. Exceded my expectations, I don't mind tellin' ye."

//

On the twelfth night after the Russian Rattle—Helen the English major would get off on the irony, it occurs to me later, but at the moment she's deeply stoned and deeply asleep, her breasts pressing my back and one arm draped over my hip—one ring of the bedside phone.

"Trust, little brother. Honor." Vassily's voice is cold as Siberia in January. "I trust you like a brother and you fuck me."

"Fuck you! You know what charges I'm facing? You know what I had to go through to make bail?"

"Sure. But you fucked me. Me! Your brother!"

"Unfuck it, Russki. You set the meet, your responsibility to make it safe. Was it safe? Where the fuck was your security? You got a leak."

"My organization, it has no leaks. Yours, I'm not so sure of."

"Bullshit, Vassily. My crew is solid. But one of your guys is talking to the Baltimore cops or the Feds. One of your guys may *be* DEA. That's the only way we could have got busted."

"Not only way."

"I'm telling you, you got a leaker. You got someone who gave us away to the cops."

"No, and I tell you why I'm so sure. The only people who knew time and place were me, Nick and five guys we had in Baltimore. So as soon as I get back, I talk to them, one at a time. Very private conversations." Oh shit. Terror flash. "I talk to them in a way I know I am going to get truth. Like father to son, for start. Nothing. Nothing from any of them. So then I talk another way. The way Spetsnaz interrogator once talked to captured Afghanis. Or Charles Street way, if that makes it clearer for you."

"Tough boys. One of them's holding out on you, Vassily."

"I think not, little brother. A man going through that who doesn't talk, who doesn't even start babbling crazy lies so it'll stop . . . it is only because he doesn't know nothing.

"So make your conclusions, little brother," he goes on. "None of them said one word. Not one fucking word."

"Then you better talk with Nick again, my friend."

"Ah, is not possible." Vassily laughs. It's not a laugh I recognize. "Nick, he doesn't have tongue anymore. He doesn't have lots of things. Toes, fingers, balls. Even head. All gone. Same for five boys. Not one ever admitted one thing when they still had heads and tongues. They would have by then, this I am absolutely certain of. If they had any errors at all to confess. So is one of yours, my friend. Have you spoken to Dog and all the rest in serious way?"

I say nothing.

"Too soft, eh? You surprise me, little brother. So quick to place blame on me without checking your own team seriously. I think you have to do what I did very, very fast. Then I think you and me, we got to talk."

"Don't like your idea of conversation, asshole. You wanna see me, you come and get me."

"Personal insults now, on top of everything else? So you do have something to hide, I think. Oh, then I'll be coming. Count on it, little brother. I'm coming."

Helen hasn't stirred. But I slip off, lock myself in the bathroom, then call Dog at home. Tell him word for word what's just gone on with Vassily. "Watch your back, man," I say. "Like starting tonight, you down with that?"

"He frontin', man. He never did his own crew," he says.

"Vassily says he did, then Vassily did."

"So I got homies can handle whatever," he says.

"Don't underestimate, Dog. Our friend's ex-Spetsnaz, as you know. When he shows, he'll show Spetsnaz-style. With Spetsnaz boys."

"Spets-shit, they come around where I stay, they be cheese."

Damn. That Dog just won't take the warning. Too much street time. He thinks it can't happen. Like the gangbangers. Always look real surprised when they're lying there all wet and messy and dead.

First thing next morning, I go into Dugal's office. Not much point in playing my tape, it's in Russian and he won't understand, but I play it anyway, translate simultaneously. Dugal's only mildly impressed.

"You've had no way of knowing, Luther, but the FBI and the DEA have been onto this guy for a long time, even before I called them after our bust," he says. "We just got the first punch in, before they were ready to move on him. Well, they're moving now. Had guys from both agencies come by to see me. They've got copies of everything we've got on the case."

"All those assholes'll do is read-and-file. Or snitch. Shit."

"Mind telling me just why it is, Luther, you have such contempt for federal agencies? Is it some leftover bitterness from your own experience in the military? You shouldn't allow that to creep into your thinking on this. We are talking FBI and DEA here, not the U.S. Army."

"One, LT, there is nothing in anything of ours that directly links Vassily to the deal, or links him enough to call for an arrest. I wasn't wearing a wire when I went to Brighton, remember? The best they can hope for is a racketeering indictment. Two, how long did it take the Feds to get John fucking Gotti, even though they knew beyond a shadow of a doubt he was capo of the New York mafia?

"*Years!* That's how long. And only then because his right-hand man entered the witness protection program and ratted him out."

Dugal's just looking at me blankly, like what he's hearing is beyond his cognitive range.

"Three, the DEA and the FBI don't give a shit if Vassily takes out me and everybody who was with me. They might even like it. Might help those limp dicks build a case. That answer your question?"

"I think that's an overly severe assessment, Luther."

"They let Vassily back into the States, didn't they? The fuck's up in Brooklyn right now. He's still in business. He's making fucking phone calls, personally. Want me to play the tape again?"

"Did it occur to you that they wanted Vassily to come back from Russia? That they eased him right through customs and passport control just so he would get back to Brooklyn, where they have jurisdiction and can go after him?"

"It ocurred to me the FBI and your DEA don't even fucking know he's here. Call your new pals up, LT. See if you can surprise them with the news."

//

I go to my locker, then down to the range, where I pop the latches on a dull black aluminum case. Nestled in the gray foam are twin MP5Ks, a loaded 30-round clip beside each. Poppa and I are both Uncle Sam's misguided children. We robbed the dumb old bastard blind—Poppa with his M16 and who knows what else, me with my HK and the MP subs and some other really good shit, like about a kilo of C4. All kinds of great toys.

"Ohhh, very sweet," McKibbin says over my shoulder. Before I can move he's lifted one from the case, slipped in a clip, clicked to full-auto, and emptied all 30 rounds into a silhouette, every fucking hole in the center of mass. A nearly impossible thing to do.

"Ah, the very finest tool of its kind ever made." He sort of sighs, dumping the clip into his left hand and placing it and the gun back in the case almost reverently. "But I'd strongly advise you put those beauties back in your locker. If they're seen here, they're not likely to leave here, Luther. We'll put them through their paces on the outdoor range, when nobody's around. And any other army surplus items you may be ownin', if ye like."

He's right, I know it. Dumb move, bringing strictly military submachine guns to the office. Vassily must have rattled me more than I'm admitting. "SAS bastard," I mutter, latching the case.

"Deluded you are, Luther," he says. "Just an old constable who once walked a beat in Belfast."

//

Later that afternoon, Dugal asks me to come into his office. He's looking abashed. No, he's looking scared.

"Well, Luther, I contacted the agencies we were discussing this morning," he says quietly. "I passed on your information to my contact people there, as you suggested. To my amazement, they *were* surprised. In fact, they had no idea he was back."

"No shit."

"But they were also skeptical that it was in fact Vassily on the phone. I mentioned the tape. They said it could have been any number of Brighton Beach Russians who phoned you. They suggested a false alarm, a nervous cop. Could it have been someone else, Luther?"

"With all due respect, LT," I say, "*Fuck yourself up the ass!* I *know* Vassily, and you know I know him!"

I throw the tape at him, but don't see whether it hits him or not because I'm out the door, out of the station and off in the TT very fast. With my duffle. I go downtown, use the cell to track Dog down, have a face-to-face. I misjudged him. He's got his security in place: three of the scariest looking homies I've ever seen, packing Uzis, sticking real close. Everybody in Kevlar.

I miss the cool scene. I only hear about it from IB, who's waiting outside my apartment when I get home early that evening.

Around four in the afternoon, a UPS box lands on Dugal's desk, IB tells me. "Next thing I know, I'm hearing this scream. Jesus, it was bone chilling, sounded like a woman being raped. I see Dugal come lurching out of his office, puke all over his shirt and suitcoat. Man, he was really green. Like lime green. Never seen skin that color before. Didn't know skin could turn that color. He runs to the men's room. So me and Tommy slide in, check out what's on his desk."

"And?"

"It's a head! A fucking human head, in a plastic bag. Styrofoam packing pellets are scattered all over the place, man. And this head, in a clear plastic bag. It's in pretty good shape, looks to me like that guy Nick you were waltzing with when we busted the stables."

I don't say a thing.

"Christ, Luther! Aren't you even a little bit shook by this? A little surprised at least, maybe that might be in order?"

"No."

"No?"

"I knew it'd happened. Vassily phoned me last night." Then I start laughing. IB looks at me like I've completely lost it. He looks, in fact, extremely disturbed. And very, very anxious. "Just never thought," I manage, "that old Vassily'd send the thing to Dugal. I'm sorry as hell I missed that one."

//

I decide I love malls. I don't even go inside my apartment after IB drives off. I get back in the TT. Five minutes, I'm in Home Depot, picking up this and that—small wire cutters with rubber handles, a box cutter, black electrical tape, duct tape, small hammer, brads, couple kinds of epoxy, bunch of long extension cords. Five minutes after that, in one of the big RadioShacks, the sort that still carries all kinds of electrical doo-dahs for the hobbyists, not just boom boxes and cellphones, I buy a pressure plate, soldering iron, the smallest gauge electric wire they stock, some resistors, a little circuit board, the biggest surge protector I can find, a couple of knife switches.

Go home, have a beer and a tab for dinner, then get very busy. Decent building, decent carpeting in the hallway. I pry up, very carefully, a patch just in front of my door, find it's thick enough, slice it thin with the box cutter. Glue the pressure plate to the flooring, attach two wires. Tuck the wires tight and close along the bottom of the door frame, run the rolls into my place. Carefully replace the carpet, see there's no telltale bulge from the pressure plate, tap a couple of brads into the pile so the carpet's secured, the brad heads covered by its fabric. Fasten the surge protector under the kitchen counter. Solder the wires to the surge protector's main plug, the one that goes into the wall fixture. Plug a lamp into the surge protector, switch it on. Open the door, walk past it three or four times. Every time my weight comes down on the hidden pressure plate, the light goes on. Goes off again as soon as I step off the plate. Jammin'. Anybody comes by my door, I'll know it.

Run extension cords from every lamp in the place to the surge protector. Even if I'm asleep in my bedroom, the lights are going on if anybody comes calling. Then I splice some wires to the surge protector, run 'em along the floor molding to knife switches. One by the bed, one by the bathroom, two in the living room. Try 'em—flip up any switch, every light in the place goes off. Shut any one, all the lights go on. Finally I take two bulbs out of the track lights in the living room, replace them with the brightest, most powerful halogens the system can handle. Aim them at the entrance door. Anybody comes through it, they come into pitch black, then get blinded by the halogens when I flick a knife switch.

It'll jolt them, confuse them for a few seconds. A few seconds is all I'll need to shoot them down.

Perimeter secured.

//

Dugal calls me into his office next morning. "Your friend from Brighton Beach made his point yesterday, Luther. I assume you've heard about it?"

"Yeah, and I checked the head this morning already. It's Nick, like Vassily said. Got no tongue. Like Vassily said."

"So, security. Anything you want. A tail on you, 24/7? Move to a safe house? If not, six-man squad of tacticals around your apartment every night? Or a plainclothes unit, positioned inside your building? What'll it be? Just tell me what you need."

"Nothing."

"Cut the crap, Luther. You've been targeted. Do you seriously think I'm going to let one of my men go unprotected in these circumstances? Think again. You will be protected."

"Listen, LT. If Vassily comes, or even if he doesn't handle it personally—which he's well able to do, by the way—and just sends some guys, they'll be very, very good. Ex–Spetsnaz, like him."

"All the more reason to have a strong force close to you."

"All the less. You put any people at all around my place, they'll be killed. I guarantee they will be killed, silently and efficiently. The best men you have, they're anywhere near me, you will—repeat, will—lose them."

"These guys are not superhuman, Luther, and we do have some good men."

"Not good enough. True, Vassily's guys are not superhuman, just supertrained. They will bleed and die like anybody else. But your best men won't see them, won't hear them. They'll just get very suddenly liquidated."

"Now wait a minute here, Luther . . ."

"You have got to trust me on this, LT."

Dugal's caving, I can see it in his face, but his frustration won't let it go.

"They'll all die, LT. Nobody on our team has to die if this goes down. Except maybe me, but I don't think so. If I'm wrong, it's just me. Not five or six others."

"What about FBI, DEA? I can get them."

"Fuck that." I laugh. "They'll probably shoot me. By 'mistake.' "

"So I'm supposed to simply sit here with my thumb stuck up my ass while you've got a big red target pinned on your chest?"

"I've taken some security measures at my place that will work fine, LT. Vassily probably knows this, because he knows me. He may decide not to risk trying a hit there."

And then I flash on something important. Unless Helen's connected, Vassily doesn't know I'm a cop. The fuck thinks I'm a drug dealer like him. This is a big advantage. I try to explain it to the LT.

"Vassily just believes me or one of my team ratted the deal out to you. That's why you got Nick's head, not me. So this is what I need," I say. "First, as far as the FBI and the DEA go, I do not exist. You don't know where the anonymous undercover cop with the Vassily connection is. All you know is that you gave him a leave of absence and he's vanished. This is crucial."

"Done."

"Second, I need to park my car in the underground lot here and leave it for a while. Can you get me an unmarked—not a Crown Vic, for God's sake—with out-of-state plates?"

Dugal ponders this for a moment, perplexed. "Got it!" he says.

"Two nights ago, uniforms out in Hereford pulled over a guy on a traffic violation, saw a bag of something the size of a hay bale in the back of the vehicle. Proved to be marijuana. Locked up the idiot, impounded the vehicle. How about a Grand Cherokee, brand new, dark green, with Pennsylvania plates?"

"Perfect."

"I'll have it down here in an hour," Dugal says.

"Not here, LT. Get 'em to leave it in the Dulaney Mall lot, key tucked behind the front plate. I'll pick it up when I need it, nobody knows anything about it. Can you fix it like that?"

"I'll make it happen. I'll tell the Hereford boss we've got intelligence on where that guy was delivering the smoke, that we're leaving the vehicle out as a decoy. It's a narc case now, and I am the County narc boss. They won't question it."

"So I'm gone," I say.

"Absolutely. But please, keep in touch with me as much as you can safely manage. I hate the idea of you running around by yourself out there, considering the degree of threat."

"Oh, you'll see me. In fact I'll be in and out of the squadroom from time to time."

Dugal looks surprised.

"No place to run, no place to hide, but I can slip and slide where I need to."

"Play it your way, Luther," Dugal nods, not understanding at all.

If he had any idea the way I'm going to play it, I'm thinking as I leave, he'd have me locked up.

27

Vassily comes very fast and very violent. The Spetsnaz way.

Only not for me. Not yet.

I'm cruising downtown a few nights after my Dugal deal, on my way to Annie's, when I catch the squeal over my police scanner. "Officers down, North Avenue and Greenmount."

Shit. Not "officer." Officers.

Swerve wildly across three lanes of the Jones Falls Expressway, ignoring a massive squeal of rubber as other cars brake hard and pissed drivers lean on their horns, and just manage to skid unhit up onto the North Avenue exit. Gun it east. It's less than half a mile. I know it's bad when I'm still blocks away. Too many strobing lights, too many meat wagons.

Badge my way past the cops still stretching yellow tape. Dog's sitting on the sidewalk, slumped back against the age-blackened tall stone wall of the huge cemetery that occupies the southeast block of Greenmount and North. His eyes are open, staring at nothing. I start to run.

Big jolt when he suddenly turns his head, blinks, nods. I'd thought he was greased, thought the guys moving around to tag and bag four other bodies would get to his next.

"Went down like you said, nigger," Dog tells me when I crouch beside him. "Outta nowhere, never seen it coming. Kevlar? Shit. My three guys? Never got their Uzis off Safe. Three in the face each before they could move a fuckin' finger."

"Goddamn. You okay, though?"

"How else I be talkin' with you, fool?"

"I see four down, not three. Civilian get in the way?"

"Nah. A Spets-shit. Three-man team of hitters. Holed my homies first. They done doin' that, I double-tap one of the fucks with hollow points. Dome shots. But that's fuckin' it, and pure luck, man. They that fast, man. Other two, they vanish. Over the wall and up through the cemetery. Like they ghosts or some shit. Never had time for a look, never had another shot."

Dog swivels his head side to side, like he isn't believing what he just saw. Shook bad. Never seen him anything but totally chill before.

"Why not me first, Luther?"

"'Cause you niggers all look alike to whitey, man. You always telling me that. The hitters have you made, you woulda been first."

"Was always frontin' on you, dude," Dog laughs. Weak. "Never really believed that old-time racist shit. Spent too much time in all-black 'hoods, I guess. Maybe I believe it now."

"Don't. Some whities ain't that dumb. You got two Russians know your face now. Hope you know theirs, 'cause this is the start, not the end."

"Yeah." Dog nods. "Just this afternoon I hear somethin' funny. Every one of the Russian fucks we busted in the stables? They nowhere, man. They disappeared."

"Except Nick," I say.

"Where that fuck at?"

"Well, his head landed on Dugal's desk via UPS. The rest of him, who knows?"

Dog laughs hard. "Body parts in three states, Nick and all his fucks. Must be what saved my ass just now. Any of them coulda made me."

"Yeah."

"Man, his own crew! That Vassily, he like to party *hard,* don't he? You down with that, Luther?"

"I got my party favors ready," I say. Dog searches my eyes for a long moment. Then he smiles. "I believe you do."

//

Not quite ready, I'm thinking after I leave Dog and head toward Federal Hill. Not quite.

Been trying to get inside Vassily's head. Shooter knows he's a target. Shooter knows he's got to keep moving, jig here, jag there. But he'll do it in his territory, where he knows the ground. So we search, we find, we draw him out, we hit Shooter there.

Typical. Crude and violent, no finesse, that Spetsnaz style. So I'll do just what Vassily expects, for just long enough to convince him he's right, long enough so he's sure I've gone purely defensive. Then I'll suddenly flip it, do what he'll never expect—move fast and violent but silent on him. An assault where he stays. Where he feels safe. In Brighton Beach.

Got all my dispositions clear in my mind. I've chilled Helen with a bullshit story about being on night shifts for the next few weeks. We do some nooners at my place, I keep her happy enough. It'll be a while before she clicks to anything strange going on. I'm hoping it'll be over before she does. If it is Helen's sketch, if she's connected and gives up anything to Vassily, it'll be disinformation only.

I've calculated the risk to Annie, decided it'll be close enough to zero, and over coffee in her kitchen that night tell her just enough to get her to agree to let me sleep over in one of the many bedrooms in her place if I suddenly come calling one night. Any room I want, she says—just as long as I don't get any ideas about slipping into her's. I grin back at her. She's only trying to stay light about something she senses isn't.

In the days that follow, I use the bus or the Grand Cherokee with PA plates. Never park the Cherokee too close to home. Leave it in a mall lot nearby. Check in with Dog every day, sometimes twice a day. He's feeling nothing, hearing nothing from his undercover in the gang crew or anyone else. No Russians anywhere, far as Dog knows.

My duffle with that dull black aluminum case—as well as two GI-issue fragmentation grenades—moves with me.

I finally reach JoeBoy. He's been off on some secret shit, but yeah, he can get what I ask him for, no problem. "Sounds like you're having some fun. Me, I'm bored shitless," he says. "Mind if I take my furlough, spend it with you?" I do mind. He gets it, unlike everybody else I've been dealing with. Disappointed, yeah. He agrees to package the stuff, send it wherever I tell him.

A week goes by. Seems like a month. Nothing. No tails I can detect. No phone calls from Brighton. Very quiet where Dog stays. Not a single gang hit, not one drive-by, but the street price of smack is soaring, he says. Sudden increase in folks signing up at methadone clinics.

Then a call at home. On the landline phone, not my cell. Pulse goes up the usual fifteen beats per minute. I'm cool. I let it ring once more while I switch on the tape recorder. Then I pick it up.

"So you are home, maggot!" Jesus, it's Gunny.

"Where else would I be?"

"Some friends of yours said out of town. Told your momma that when they dropped by this morning, wondered if she knew where her little boy might possibly be. Nice friends you got, Luther. They frightened your momma pretty bad."

"What'd you do?"

"Wasted the motherfuckers."

//

He had. I get the story from the Virginia state troopers who pick me up not ten miles off the Nice Bridge heading toward Tyding's Landing. Needed the speed, couldn't detect any tails, so I left the Cherokee in a mall lot and took my car. Gunny must have told the troopers to watch for a TT. Didn't warn them I'd be doing 110 on a 55-limit highway, though. It takes another three miles and lots of flashing lights for them to catch up and make the pull-over. I'm thinking a speeding stop as the window glides down, I already got my license, registration and badge out when the trooper's Maglite hits my eyes, blinding me.

"Y'all must be Ewing," I hear.

"Yeah, yeah, see the license, the badge? Mind getting your light outta my face, sir?"

"Sorry about that." The light goes off. "Well now, Mr. Ewing, if y'all don't mind, I'm gonna ride shotgun with you here in this race-car, and you're gonna follow my partner in the cruiser."

"I gotta get down to Tyding's Landing. It's important."

"Your daddy ain't there," the trooper says, opening the passenger door and squeezing himself in. "This thing German? Thought Germans were big folks. Why'd they go and put the kiddy seat up front?"

"Where's my father?" I ask, pulling out and tailgating the cruiser, which moves pretty smartly up to seventy-five and holds the speed, lights still flashing.

"Saint Mary's Hospital, but he's okay. Took a shot to the leg. You shoulda seen what he done to the folks who fired on him. They're not in no hospital, nosir. My chief'd like to ask y'all what you might know about this commotion."

"Where's my mother?" I'm dreading the answer.

"She's real fine. She's fine and safe. Your daddy'll tell ya. Yessir. Your daddy is not a man I'd want to get on the wrong side of."

"So what went down?"

"Shit, three Russkis did. Your daddy had a thirty-round clip in that M16 of his. We counted the holes. Every last one of the thirty ended up in one or another of those peckerheads. They look like possums that tried crossing the highway at night just about the time an eighteen-wheeler had the right of way."

About nine this morning, the trooper tells me, a black Lincoln

Town Car apparently turned off the highway and took the shell drive down to the house. Gunny, the trooper goes on, says he was over to this pond where some girl you brought down for a visit popped a granddaddy snapper he'd been after for two years. Says he reckoned that granddaddy wasn't living in that pond all alone, must have had him a mate, and the reason he'd always missed was because his eyes were just not what they used to be. So he'd had a 4× scope mounted on the 16. Went to the pond early, tossed his bait, waited around a while, no snapper takes it. Probably already asleep in the mud. So he's walking home with a full clip, he sees three white guys in suits in his yard, one of them reaching in the door, trying to grab your mamma. She's yelling blue murder. Well, they see Gunny coming, pull pistols, start shooting at him. Dumb fucks, he says, thinking they're going to hit him seventy-five yards out with pistols.

So, Gunny says, he just brings up the 16 to his shoulder, gets a real pretty picture through that nice new scope, drops the guy at the door with one in the head, puts a few more into the body on the way down. The other two peckerheads, they keep shooting, but they're moving fast for that Lincoln. So Gunny keeps the crosshairs traveling with them, empties his clip. Hardly notices he's taken one in the leg until he tries to walk to the house.

"Your mamma phones 911, we show up, and it looks like what happened's exactly what your daddy says happened," the trooper concludes. "The peckerheads all had New York driver's licenses, they all had semi-auto pistols, there was 9 millimeter brass right near 'em. And they were sure as hell shot to shit. What your daddy can't say, and my chief wants to ask you, is why?"

So it wasn't an assassination. Vassily wanted them dead, he'd have sent shooters with AKSUs. It was a snatch. Or suppossed to've been, if Gunny hadn't busted caps and stopped it cold. Vassily wants hostages? Wants to draw me out that way? Means one thing,

I think. The big fuck is worried. He doesn't feel confident his hitters can take me down even in Baltimore. Good. He's unsettled. Unsettled men make mistakes. He's just made a big one.

I spend five minutes drinking coffee with the state police captain in the hospital lobby. He's a tall, thin black man with a face as devoid of expression as any I've seen, but the white troopers call him "Cap" with lots of respect. I tell him as little as I can get away with—narc working undercover in Baltimore, recently involved in a major heroin bust, the dealers being Russian mobsters from New York. The Russians must have somehow ID'd me, done some digging about my family, come on down looking for me, or for information about me. I give him Dugal's name and numbers so he can confirm.

He declines with a wave of his hand.

"I've known Gunny a bunch of years now. He said y'all was Special Forces once, now a cop. I didn't doubt his account of this morning. Just wanted to hear from you what it was all about," Cap says. "Now I do believe I know all I need to. We don't see much like this, in these parts. Can't say I appreciate you bringin' this shit down here. Then again, ain't your fault. More likely a sign you done a hell of a good job. We'll look after Gunny real good, real close, 'til y'all let me know we don't need to anymore. Go see your daddy now."

I get up, ready to head for Gunny's room. The Cap takes my arm, moves up close. "I was you, I'd be wonderin' how in hell them Russians even knew I had a mamma and a pappa, let alone where they livin'. I was you, I'd be thinkin' pretty hard that maybe somebody on my side up there Baltimore way, he got hisself a big mouth. Big dangerous mouth. Kind of mouth needs to be shut. Permanent like? Y'all catch my drift."

"Sure do, Cap. Thanks."

Helen.

"Luther, you dickhead, you musta fucked up real bad, whatever it was you were doing. Leavin' assholes like the ones I greased still runnin' around," Gunny booms when I enter his room. "What kind of piss-poor squad you workin' with? Am I gonna have to come up there and straighten out a major clusterfuck?"

"Real, real sorry, Gunny. Jesus, I am sorry." I tell him more or less what I told the trooper captain. Aside from a single intravenous and a fat bandage on his thigh, he looks like absolutely nothing out of the ordinary happened that day. He looks like he had some fun, like when we popped that snapper. But his face turns grave when I repeat the last thing Cap said.

"Bend me over and pop my can! Now things coming clear. You best watch your back real close, Luther. You got a traitor near you. Find him. Terminate him."

"I'll be working on it."

"Shee-it! Workin' on it? We move swift, we move silent, we move deadly. You don't, you're KIA."

"Yessir."

"You're distracted, Luther. Get clear and cold real fast. Don't be carrying a load of worry about your momma. Cap sent her off with two troopers in a cruiser. She'll be staying with friends at Camp Lejeune."

"And you?"

"You got shit for brains? I'll be outta here in three, four days. I'll have claymoors and an M60 at the house in twenty-four hours. Any damned fools come around, I blow their shit away," Gunny says. "You know it, too.

He pauses.

"But you won't get cold and clear. You'll be thinking too much about your base camp, I do anything like that. So I'm going down to Lejeune as soon as they'll let me. If you give me the right answer to one question?"

I nod.

"A question I ask you once, maybe twice before. You still operating under orders, coming down the chain of command? Or is this some freelance, private war you got goin'?"

"Orders, everything by the book. Authorized mission."

"Then move out, soldier. Move swift, move silent, move deadly. Grease the motherfuckers. Your momma and me, we'll stay safe and sound at Lejeune 'til the mission's completed."

"Aye-aye, Gunny."

//

Two nights later, first Tuesday in November, I'm in my apartment, weapons out of their cases and loaded, now SOP. I'm chill, clear. I'm using my tabs in the prescribed dosage only, to prevent the seizures the drug's designed to prevent. I flushed all the Ativan and anything else down the toilet the same night I secured my apartment. Just sitting there in the dark. Clear and cold, combat ready.

That doesn't stop the rush and the jolt when every light in the place goes on. I grab an MP5, seize the handle of the wire that runs to the frag taped next to the door and snug it into my gun grip hand, hit a knife switch. The lights go out. I think I hear murmuring out in the hall, think I hear a little metal against metal, like a lock being picked.

Imagination. The doorbell rings. I stay quiet. Rings again. Then a loud rap. Then "Hey, Five-O, you there?"

Fucking Ice Box, at the top of his range. I drop the frag wire, but take the gun to the door, keeping well to the side of it.

"What?"

"Shit, Luther. Open up. Gotta talk to you." Definitely IB. But maybe he isn't alone, so I unlock the door quietly as I can, crouch down to the left for a clear field of fire, sight on the knob. Left finger on a knife switch. "C'mon in," I call.

I hit the switch when the door swings open. IB's hands go by reflex to his eyes, blinded by the spots. So do Annie's. There's nobody else.

"What the fuck was that all about?" IB says, stumbling in.

"And what the fuck is all this stuff?" Annie says, blinking hard but quickly picking up me and my piece, and the other weapons near me.

"Exactly what it looks like," I say.

"Christ, Luther, this must be what a bunker in a war zone looks like," Annie says.

"Not even close," I say. "Why'd you two come by?"

"Gotta have a drink first," Annie says, brushing by me to the fridge, yanking a bottle of Stoli from the freezer, taking a big slug straight from the bottle. She makes a face. "You just scared me so bad I almost wet my pants." She hands the bottle to IB, who knocks back a big hit.

"So *what!*" I shout.

"You want the bad or the good first, Luther?" IB says.

"Bad. How bad?"

"As it gets. That young ex-marine, the Mexican guy on your team at the meet with the Russians? Found him dead in his bed this morning. Three in the face. They can't figure out what hit him. Or how the hitter got in and did it and got out so clean."

"Oh Jesus fucking Christ," I say. How'd Vassily ID my guy? Video in the stable? How he'd track him, locate him? Nightmare image: Somehow, some way I named a name to Helen. Nah, couldn't be. I couldn't have done that, not even on an Ecstasy night. No way. I don't talk in my fuckin' sleep. Horrible flash: I do. Helen was all over me about Mikla once. Jesus fucking Christ.

But then IB unfucks it for me, big time. "It ain't much consolation, but we finally busted Buzz Cut's chick partner. Young undercover guy, in a club last night. The little bitch is, guess what, American-born Russian from Brighton Beach. And, Luther, you are not going to believe this."

Annie hands me a mug shot. I have to look twice, then look back again before I'm sure it isn't Helen. They could be twins, they're that close.

"Guess you gotta forgive me for mentioning that sketch resemblance," IB says. "Hell, when I saw her in the holding cell I started talking to her like she was Helen. But she just looked at me like she'd never met me before in her life. Which, it turns out, she never had. Just to double-check, I called Helen. Sure enough, she was in her dorm room."

"How'd you get that number?"

"Oh," Annie says, "I did that little thing I do with your computer. Quite a list there, actually. You rate 'em by stars, do you? Helen's a four. I happened to notice a certain 'AM' with five and a question mark. What's that mean, Luther?"

She's laughing then. But she squelches it quick when she sees the look on my face. "Luther, you never let on things were this serious. I'm going out of my mind with worry here. What are you planning? What can we do to help?"

"I can't tell you what I've planned, what I might have to do."

"C'mon Luther. You see who you're talking to here," IB says.

"Can't tell because if I do it, it'll be so illegal I'll spend the rest of my life in prison if I get caught. You want to be in the position of maybe having to testify under oath against me? Maybe losing your own careers?"

"I'll risk it, if it comes down to that," Annie says. "You need us, Five-O."

"Yeah. But I won't let you risk it. You can't know anything."

"Then how the fuck are we gonna help your sorry ass? I am not liking any of this one bit," IB fumes. "I am getting very definitely pissed. And put that fucking gun down, for Christ's sake. You're making me nervous."

I do. Then I go into the bedroom and come out with two small boxes, recent purchases. "There is a thing you can do. I don't think you'll be in any jeopardy if you do it. I wouldn't ask you to do anything illegal."

"Fuck that, Luther," Annie snaps. "Get to the point."

"Okay." I hand her the box marked A, give IB the one marked B. "Inside there's a brand-new worldwide cell. I won't give you the numbers. I'm the only one who's ever gonna know them. So if they ever ring, you can be sure it's me."

"I'm feeling I need to know a little bit more here, Luther," IB says.

"Simple. If I vanish for a while, one day a UPS package will land on your doorstep. All you have to do is keep it until you get a call from me on that cell, then send it on to where I tell you to send it. If the call doesn't come in on that cell but on your regular cell, means I'm not phoning because I want to, but because someone's forcing me to. Hang up immediately. Then ditch the packages where nobody'll ever find them, and ditch the phones too. Fast. Nothing else. Okay?"

"We can do that," Annie says. But she looks . . . don't know exactly. Maybe sad, like she's mourning.

"Thanks. Now get out of here quick. IB, make sure you aren't tailed. You get a sniff of a tail, even just an instinct, call me here immediately, let me know where you are. This is important, big man." I grab his shoulder. "Important."

IB nods, holds my eyes just a beat too long. "Later, Luther."

Annie just turns, head bowed, and leaves. IB follows.

28

It's time.

So just do it.

First thing next morning I FedEx my list to JoeBoy. Include the addresses the packages need to go to. Plus a "Valid Without Photo" Maryland driver's license in my name, all my credit cards and a note asking him to take that furlough right now to Key West. "Make it conspicuous, you fuck," I write. "Take my cards to the limit if you want. Make me a real fine paper trail that proves I was there."

Then I drive the Cherokee to Baltimore/Washington International Airport, park it in the long-term lot. I catch the shuttle bus to the terminal, humping gear like any other traveler. Only my gear includes a beat-up old guitar case—specially modified inside to cradle the Weatherby. I do not buy a ticket, board a plane. I walk through departures to arrivals, go to the Avis booth, and rent a midsize sedan using Buzz Cut's license, one of Buzz Cut's credit cards. "Your car's in space sixty-four, Mr. Raskolnik," the Avis girl says. Gives me a big smile.

I'm a dead man, traveling.

I drive to Brighton Beach, cruise the neighborhood in the late afternoon, dictating information on buildings, subway station locations, one-way street patterns into a tiny Olympus digital recorder. Then I drive to Newark Airport.

I do not board a plane. I turn in the Avis car, have a burger and a Coke in one of the airport bars, then rent a midsize sedan from Hertz, using another of Buzz Cut's cards. I check into a motel two exits south off the Jersey Turnpike. As I listen to what I've dictated, I use a soft pencil to overlay the info on a street map I'd bought. I sleep for eight hours. I do not dream.

I love malls. Next morning I drive to one a few miles from the motel. I find a hair place called Cutz, have my cropped head completely shaved. At a Gap I pick up a pair of black jeans, a pair of green cargo pants, a black hooded sweatshirt, a blue nylon windbreaker, an acrylic knit watch cap. In a store called Beau's I buy a charcoal suitcoat and matching pants, already hemmed. White poly dress shirt and a rep striped tie too. At Shoeworld, the cheapest wingtips they have. Lunch at McDonald's.

In the afternoon I cruise Brighton again, dictating more details. I park a few times, quickly measure some distances, some building heights with a small Bushnell rangefinder. I tell everything to the Olympus. The situation is looking fair, not great. Lots of ways in and out, the ocean's only two blocks from Brighton Boulevard. But the fucking subway line here's above ground, running high above the street on a rail system supported by massive steel I-beams, riveted, crissed and crossed and thick with maybe eighty-five years of periodic paint jobs. The fucker shakes when a train goes over. Only plus to it is the noise; it'd cover the sound of a shot. Then I drive to La Guardia, turn in the Hertz car, pick up a compact from National. I check into a Ramada Inn, have a steak with baked potato and sour cream in the place's restaurant, go back to my room, add the day's data to my map. Later, at the bathroom sink, I get all the curls out of this wig I'd bought using hair straightener from Duane Reade. Wet and messy. I cable-surf for a while in bed. I sleep for eight hours. I do not dream.

Next day, wearing the sweatshirt under the blue windbreaker, the long wig and the watch cap, I park the car and walk around Brighton Beach. Nobody looks twice. I search for a building, I watch and time the ebb and flow of foot traffic and street traffic. I have lunch in a little Russian place, more deli than restaurant, careful to speak only English. A Russian-speaking stranger might be enough for someone to drop a dime in this 'hood. I walk two blocks to the boardwalk, watch the gray Atlantic grow restless and grayer as the day declines, notice the only strollers are geriatric cases. Not a soul on the beach. Then, in the dark of early evening, I walk Brighton Boulevard right in front of the Palace twice, going six blocks past Vassily's club one way, then eight blocks past on the other side of the street.

I drive to JFK, turn in the National car, rent a sedan from Alamo. That's enough of this CIA–type shit. No way I've been tailed or trailed, no way anybody knows where the fuck I am. Probably didn't even need to take it so far, but I allowed for the chance Vassily's web might be wide beyond belief. Best to go too far than not far enough. I check into a motel. Sleep eight hours. No dreams.

Drive into Manhattan, park the car, take the subway to Brighton Beach next morning, wearing the suit, carrying a briefcase. No wig. I walk. Check out the building I'd settled on the day before. Five stories, a bakery occupying the ground floor. The other four floors are empty. The neighboring buildings are all four stories only. I circle. Firescape in the back, easy climb to the roof. I walk, spot at least one watcher near the Palace. A Fed for sure, most likely DEA. Fucking amateur night. If I made him so easy, Vassily made him and any others backing him up probably ten minutes after they started, whenever that was. Probably laughed his ass off over it. He knows they can't do a fucking thing to him. They got a team up in a building doing a video number, Vassily probably waves and smiles in their general direction each time he enters his club.

I walk more, quartering the area, stop in a store here and there, buy a few small things I'll just dump in the trash later. I note the bakery closes at six, same time it did the previous two evenings. The building stays dark. I hit the boardwalk. Nobody but geriatrics and an empty beach. I recheck my building at eight, at ten. Still dark. I go around behind, remove my shoes, start to scale the fire escape. Every few rungs I flick on a mini Maglite, looking for scrapes or smudges in the thick crust of grime and rust. Nothing. Nobody's climbed the escape in a very long time. I edge over the low parapet onto the roof. Move to the front, look down on Brighton Boulevard. Angle's not the best—those fucking elevated tracks are almost in the way, but there's a clear view of the Palace. All lit up now, people arriving in limos, others strolling. There's one of those classic New York water tanks on my roof. Wooden, with a copper roof, raised up on girders. I climb its ladder, check the hatch. Hasn't been opened in a long time, the seams are filled with dirt and debris.

I go down, crouch beneath the tank. I can see the Palace, see the sidewalk in front of it, though most of the street's blocked from view by the El. Good enough.

Go.

Subway back to Manhattan, drive out to Newark, sleep in a motel near the airport. Up very, very early next morning. I dress in thermal underwear, black jeans, black sweatshirt, the windbreaker. Everything else—the suit, shirt, underwear, wig, wingtips—I stuff in the little backpack I'd bought at that Gap. In my duffle, I carefully place the rangefinder, Zeiss compact binoculars, a single box of rifle ammunition, a space blanket, a water sack, three empty plastic soda bottles, three MREs, a sock filled with sand, the wig and cap. Pat down: HK in a shoulder holster, Walther tucked in the small of my back. Two extra magazines for each. The SIG's in its ankle holster. After I check out, I put on the wig and the cap, have coffee and an Egg McMuffin at a McDonald's. Toss the backpack into the dumpster in the rear as I drive off.

Park the car in Hoboken, catch the PATH train into Manhattan, the subway to Brighton. I'm carrying only the duffle and that guitar case. The bakery hasn't opened yet. I go up the fire escape, settle in on the roof under the rusty, riveted iron girders supporting the water tank. I take out the binoculars. Clear sight of the Palace's main entrance and the service entrance 10 meters to the left. I take out the

Bushnell. Range, 473 meters, with an error factor of plus or minus 6 meters.

I wait. I think. Cold, clear. The range is a stretch for the Weatherby, even if I use the quick-release scope mounts to change the 3×–9× variable for an 18× Leupold target scope. Had no time to get hold of a serious, tuned sniper rifle. The scope has no bullet-drop compensator, no illuminated reticle. Just a quarter–MOA target dot. Made for the bench, the rifle range. Not for wetwork.

I will make it work.

I put the sand-filled sock on a low rung of the iron ladder to the water tank. I open the guitar case, take out the Weatherby, rest the fore end on the sandbag, sight in on the Palace. I have a shot. Bad angle, but a shot, a very long shot. The parapet would be a more stable rest, but I can't use it, could be spotted there. Have to stay back here under the tank. I lay the Weatherby in the open case. I've taped the shiny stainless fluted barrel with black duct tape. The stock's dark gray synthetic, mostly Kevlar.

I settle in for the long wait. I think. When I get bored with myself I watch the street a while. Lots of broad Slav faces, even though most of them are Jews. That's who turned this place into Little Odessa. Jews the Soviets finally let emigrate, back when there still was a Soviet Union, not Russia and Ukraine and a bunch of those Stan countries. Should've called it Little Kiev.

Trains rumble past at no regular intervals I can figure. The whole fucking roof shakes when they do. Very weird feeling when something that seems so solid starts to move under you. Heard people who've been through earthquakes say that's even weirder; the whole world shifts. Felt this milder version a few times in Sarajevo, near misses by big howitzer shells.

To get my head ready, start to visualize, like in Sarajevo. Visualize the rifle butt snugged firmly into my shoulder, left palm under the forestock two inches forward of the magazine with fingers clawed up, right hand filled by the buttstock palmswell, trigger finger extended just far enough so the first pad is on the curved smooth metal, cheek welded to the stock comb at the exact height it needs to be for a straight alignment with the scope's ocular. Easy, easy. The muscle memory's still fresh. The mental memory's fogged in. Vague gray images of unheated rooms with windows blown away, the Barrett tripod nailed to the floor, Mikla's voice calling out ranges, possible targets, the scope reticle centered, the squeeze, the sudden huge blast.

Jesus! Just a subway going by fast.

When it gets good and dark, I drill with the Weatherby. Fuck. The target Leupold's useless even though the Palace front is garishly and brilliantly illuminated at night. The target dot's too small, too hard to see. I switch back to the 3×9 with its heavy duplex reticle.

I begin to think goatfuck. I should have moved more deliberately, come in properly equipped with the right rifle and the right scope—a Steyr SSG, a Remington 700 in .308. Even better, a Sako, like Mikla used. But that would've taken time, left a trail when I made the purchases. I want this done by a ghost no one saw, no one heard.

One shot. That's all I'll get. Then I'll vanish.

I wait. I piss in one of the empty soda bottles. I take an Immodium so I won't have to shit. I eat half an MRE, cold limas and ham. I sip from the water sack. I see Vassily leave his silver Mercedes and enter the club around eleven. I see him leave around three A.M. He's in and out too fast to make anything happen. I wrap up in the space blanket and sleep as long as I can.

Next day I'm cold, shivery. I do crunches, push-ups. I'd like to walk around, but I can't risk being seen. I do a lot of visualizing. Good jolt when Vassily's silver Merc pulls up around 10 P.M. Letdown when two guys I never saw before get out and go into the club. I piss in the bottle, eat the seond half of the MRE. Same two guys leave the Palace at midnight. I keep the Zeiss binoculars on the place 'til the 3 A.M. closing. Not an attractive crowd. Red-faced men with big bellies, women over the top with jewels and furs and too much makeup and overdone hair. No taste at all. I sleep until I can't sleep anymore.

Wait and watch the third day. Nothing. The mind games start. Time has nothing to do with the hands on the chronometer anymore. It's all in the light, the long slow arc of it, the shifting of the shadows. Deal with the cramps in the legs, cramps in the arms, as they come. Flex, relax. Deal with the wandering attention—snap it back, lock it on the mission.

It's always this way. Deal with it. You're trained to deal with it, Shooter. But it's hard anyway. It's always hard past a certain point. It never eases. It gets harder still.

Fight it. Beat it.

Use all the experience . . . fight to stay clear, stay concentrated. I begin to crack along my fault lines. Think of Mikla in a blown-out apartment, think of squeezing off the Barrett, think of the rush when I made a hit. Think of her little notebook, list of shots taken, hits made, a couple of pages stuck together by something stiff, dark brown.

Don't think. Breathe. Relax each muscle group one by one, starting with your toes.

Do this, Luther. Keep doing it.

The Merc pulls up close to midnight. Vassily's out fast and in through the service door. Zeiss glasses to my eyes. Shivery. The crowd leaves at three. The fucking Merc's still at the curb! A long, long time passes. I don't want to check my watch, find it's only twenty minutes. No, it's gotta be near dawn. My eyes strain, it gets hard to focus.

Then the Palace service door moves. Or does it?

Move fast anyway. Drop the glasses, pull the Weatherby, lay the fore end on the sandbag. Swing a little right. No, go left. Get the crosshairs on the door. Move faster.

The door opens. Light blue steel.

There's three, weaving a little, still drunk. Has to be a chest shot, this rifle at this range. Round's already chambered. Cocked. Hunting cartridge, Weatherby loaded with a Barnes X-Bullet. Only 130 grains, but leaves the muzzle at 3,600 feet per second. Penetrates, mushrooms, huge wound channel. Chest shot. No instant kill, but anywhere in the chest, he'll choke to death on his own blood in less than three minutes.

The guy in the middle, his big arms draped over the shoulders of the men flanking him. Fucking drunk, Vassily. I love that mad Russian. Center the reticle his sternum, move it six inches right: windage allowance. Breathe deep, exhale half.

Do it!

Boom.

I take my finger off the trigger. There's no shot. Fucking subway roars past, by the time I see twin red taillights Vassily's slipped right out of the crosshairs and into his car.

Too fucking dumb to live! Suck the fucking barrel and pull the trigger, maggot. And I hate it more because I know exactly why I've blown it. I chose the easy way, couldn't face making it personal. Not even after all the shit Vassily's done. Because once we fought side by side, became brothers. Wanted it real cool and businesslike, just a job, not revenge, not justice, not execution.

Fuck me. I went the pussy route on this. Vassily wouldn't have. Bad, bad choice.

Abort.

29

I toss the fucking useless Weatherby into the case, but I don't go. No fucking way.

Grab my cell, punch in Vassily's number while his car's still idling at the curb.

"Hello, brother," I say when he answers. "You just came out of a blue steel door at the Palace. You're wearing a gray suit with a red tie. I had you in my crosshairs. Could you feel it, my friend? Could you feel the death coming at you?"

"Big joker you are, little brother," Vassily laughs. "I wouldn't be feeling shit if this was true. I'd be too fucking dead."

"You are dead, my good friend. You just don't know it yet. Your Merc is pulling out now, you're heading south on the boulevard. There's a cross street about a hundred meters in front of you."

The Merc suddenly speeds up, fishtails through a hard right turn.

"Wow, I could hear the tires squeal on that turn, Vassily. But I can still see you. Watch out! Almost sideswiped that parked taxi. Vassily, some advice. Your driver is really shitty. Get a better one."

"You sound like happy man. You sound like you want to get happier. How do you plan to do that, little brother?" Vassily's voice is soft now, all the laughter gone. "You going to shoot me sometime? Or maybe you want only to talk to me?"

"And say what? Say take your hitters out of Baltimore if you want to live, Vassily my brother? Would you do it? Somehow I have trouble believing in this. Too late, I think, for this."

"Never too late between friends. Was only business. You understand business. Ups and downs. Always some way to smooth things out, make things right."

"Always? Maybe I'll consider, consult with my friends."

"Seems to me we are possibly even, little brother. I got three or four of yours, that Dog and your father get what, four of mine? Maybe is enough, yes?"

"Not even. You fucked with my family, Vassily. Brother never does that to brother."

"I make bad mistake with that. I admit this. I am sorry for it. No harm would have come to them, I swear this true."

I laugh. "True? You know the meaning of truth? Hard to believe, brother. But I'll consider. I'll consult. I'll be in touch. Count on it."

I pause. Vassily stays silent.

"Right now I'm going to pack up and climb down from this roof. Nice view from this roof, over the bakery. Maybe I'll come up here again sometime. Just for the view."

I click off, shoulder my gear and sprint for the fire escape. I figure I've got four to six minutes before Vassily can punch in a number, get someone sober on the line, bark some orders, and get some heavies over here from the Palace. Plenty of time to duct-tape two blocks of C4 under the corroded black iron grating of the fire escape's top landing, insert detonators, run a very thin black tripwire across the grating. Though I doubt, if they're Spetsnaz, they'll hit it. They'll spot it, disable it.

I do it anyway.

Then I pull on thick leather gloves and basically slide down the fire escape's ladders. I hit the concrete hard at the bottom and start running. I'm just getting into a subway station when a white flash from behind throws me a new shadow. Split-second later comes this sharp crack, instantly followed by a deep, rolling boom.

Overestimated the fucks. But I don't turn, I don't stop. I go.

//

From my room in a cheap hotel on the Upper West Side of Manhattan, I start the back-up plan—which, dammit, should have been my alpha assault instead of that stupid sniper goatfuck. I call Annie on the worldwide cell around midnight, when I'm pretty sure she'll be home alone. The phone clicks on after the second ring, but there's only the sound of breathing at her end.

"Did the package arrive?" I say.

"Yes."

"Please give it to IB tomorrow. Not at work. He'll tell you where."

"Yes."

"Thank you," I say. "Later."

"Wait!" Annie says. "Do you have to do this thing? You're going to murder him, aren't you?"

"Nothing to discuss."

"There is. You're a cop. You can't go through with this. Please don't go through with this." She's near tears, by the hitch in her voice.

"No choice, no option. No way to go but all the way."

"Oh God, oh God."

"I need that package. You'll do it?"

"Yes."

"See you." I switch off.

Then I call IB. He picks up on the first ring, blurts, "Where are you, man?" I hear babies wailing in the backgroud.

"In the fucking Bahamas, sipping daiquiries, dipshit. You get that package?"

"Yeah, it arrived."

"Tomorrow Annie's going to give you hers. Set it up so it's private, okay? Watch for tails."

"Can do. No problem."

"Day after tomorrow, can you catch a nine-thirty A.M. Metroliner out of Baltimore and get off in Philadelphia, with the packages in a duffle?"

"Yeah, sure."

"I'll find you there. I'll take the duffle, you take the next train back to Baltimore. Right?"

"Yeah, sure."

"You don't sound pleased. I'm hearing a definite lack of enthusiasm, big man."

"Hey, you were the best partner I ever had, so get fucked, all right? I'll be there. Just make sure you are too."

//

IB's there. We don't meet in the cavernous main hall of the station, with its hundred-foot-high ceiling and ornate arches and moldings. I catch him in the bowels below, on a half-lit platform, people hurrying for the stairs and escalators to get out of this claustrophobic place and up into the airy, bright hall.

IB carefully puts two black ballistic nylon packs down on the concrete at my feet, standing real close and looking hard at my eyes.

"Got a hinky feeling here, Five-O," he says. "Not liking what I think you're heading into."

"Just a little thing that's got to be done. No problems," I say, grinning. IB only scowls.

"That's what I figured. Means it's bad. Means you're going to be violating our oath. Oh, fuck the oath. What you got in mind just ain't right, man. It violates the whole reason we became cops."

"Maybe the reason you became a cop."

"So Five-O's above all that do right, do good shit, huh?" He's pissed now.

"No."

"Then what? What?"

"I'm not up to it, IB. Psychologically. Morally. You're a great cop. I never was, never will be. I'm a mechanic, man. Good at just one thing."

"Fuck that, Luther," IB says. "Shit, I can't decide to go with you and watch your back, or arrest your skinny ass right here. I just know I got probable cause—those fucking bags."

"You can't do either. You know that. You know what you got to do. Get on back to Baltimore. Get home to MJ and the twins. If you absolutely can't keep from brooding about any of this, think what my poppa always said about shit happening in Nam."

"What's that?"

"'Don't mean nothing. Walk on.' Just walk on, IB. I'll catch you later."

I take the bags, lope up the stairs into the hall, scoot down others to another platform, and in a little while catch a train to New York. Back at my hotel by midafternoon. I open up the bags, slit open the UPS packages, spread every item out on the chenille bedspread. Take a tally. It matches my list, not one damn thing missing. Even a little extra something I hadn't thought of, but JoeBoy was sharp enough to remember. In an orange plastic prescription vial, one crunchy—what we called the cyanide capsule we carried on missions, just in case we got captured and things got too bad to bear.

//

I'm cruising along Brighton Boulevard very late the next night, wearing the blue windbreaker with the hood of my sweatshirt up over my head. I'm real good to go, now. Clear and cold. I'll haunt the Palace night after night if I have to.

But I won't, 'cause I got unbelievable luck, I got magic Comanche medicine on my side. The silver Mercedes is parked in front of the blue steel door. Ten paces away, hands in the kangaroo pocket of the sweatshirt, I syringe five-minute epoxy onto a palm-size slab of titanium. I stop when I reach the Merc, lean against the right rear side panel, facing the Palace. Immediately I hear the driver's door open. I turn, as I do slipping the slab tight up inside the rear wheelwell with my right hand. The driver never catches the move, he can only see me from the waist up as he comes around the car. "Get the fuck away, slob," he growls.

"I'm not touching your pretty car, man," I say. Then, when he keeps coming as if he wants to play muscle boy, I switch to Russian. "You better be carrying something very good. Something better than the .45 that's about to double-tap you in the belly."

He hesitates for a moment. "You just go to the door there, you tell whoever's just inside that Shooter wants to talk to Vassily," I say, hard. "You smart enough to do that? Vassily, he's going to be very pissed if you don't. You might wind up like Nick. You remember Nick, don't you?"

That flicks his switch. He goes to the blue steel door, raps a coded rap, whispers a few words to whoever cracks it open. Then he moves back to the front of the car, facing me.

The door swings wide suddenly and Vassily moves toward me very fast, while the driver starts to reach inside his suitjacket. Not so fast I couldn't have dropped him, but I'm not even carrying a gun. I let Vassily get me in a bearhug, lift me off my feet.

"I can snap your neck like twig," he whispers in my ear.

"But you won't, because you don't want to be the star in the movie those DEA guys across the street are making with their digital camcorder."

"You are too smart for your own good, little brother. I snap your neck some other time for sure," he hisses in my ear, then breaks the hug but keeps his hands on my shoulders, huge grin on his face. "Big balls you got. No HK under your arm tonight. Seriously crazy. Must be hole in your head."

"Nah, I was born this way."

"So little brother, nice trick you play with fire escape. Four of my guys. Four."

"Sorry about that. I set it up in plain sight, just a little joke, you know? I figured your Spetsnaz boys would have a good laugh disabling it. Somebody trip on his dick or what?"

"Stupids walk right into it, they're in such big hurry to get to roof where they're going to find nobody anyway. Ah, my friend, why does it have to be this way? All these stupids. Think what we could do, you and me together. Why this way?"

"Because I'm a cop, Vassily."

"You're shitting me?" He scans my eyes, bursts into laughter. "You fuck. You did have me in crosshairs that night. But you don't pull trigger because you are fucking cop, and cops don't go around assassinating people. This I can't believe. Shooter a cop. My God, what's happening to world?"

"It turns once every twenty-four hours."

"That is fucking problem. Nothing stays same, always change, change, change. Makes me dizzy, this shit. I suppose your blackie friend, that Dog, he is cop too?"

"Yeah. Except he's not as scrupulous about the rules as I am. If it had been him on the roof, you would be dead."

"Long shot," Vassily says doubtfully. "But he is pretty good up close, the way he took down my guy in Baltimore that time. But hey, this is America, this why I love it. In Moscow those guys across street don't bother with any fucking video. Don't care they got nothing on me for any court. A big crowd of Moscow cops would just come into club and shoot me full of holes. I love America."

"Don't lose your head over it. Take some advice, brother. Stop hitting down there. Stop everything down there. You don't, the Dog, cop or not, will be coming only for you. You'll think you're back in Moscow. And a little warning. I'll be with him, and so will some very good friends of his from the Bronx, couple of them as good as me, maybe better. I know this because I know them from Iraq. And they aren't cops."

"Fuck that! Fuck you all!" Vassily's suddenly angry. "Nobody threatens me."

"Hey, am I threatening you, brother? Like I said, some advice only. Some truth. Between you and me, it can be finished. We call it even, like you said the other night. You stop, I stop. All of it stops."

Vassily laughs, gets me into that hug again. "This is good, little brother. I give my word. All of it stops. Fuck me, the balls on you. No gun! But you walk away from here now, you don't need one, you don't need to look back. I won't see you again, which makes me sad. But that's the way it has to be, yes? You go back to Baltimore now?"

"Tomorrow morning. Go carefully, brother," I say. He kisses the top of my head. I walk off.

//

Amazing, the tech JoeBoy sent me. I get into it. I get deeply into it. I hardly leave my hotel for the next couple of days. I order a lot of Chinese and Thai takeout.

Because I'm so busy lying in bed watching every fucking move Vassily makes on a mega-cool handheld next-gen Global Positioning System. The latest and best GI, fully operational but not even issued yet, except to spook units. I've programmed the entire New York street grid into it, and that slab of titanium under Vassily's wheelwell is the next-gen model emergency beacon air force pilots just started carrying, so search-and-rescue guys can locate them if they go down behind enemy lines. I can pinpoint the Merc to within less than a city block.

I keep bursting into laughter over it. The signal's bouncing off a very secret military satellite, and I just know a bunch of air force tech geeks are running around completely insane and screaming over the glitch in their system. Huge fucking glitch, emergency beacon on the move along the streets of New York when they know damn well there cannot possibly be a downed pilot in fucking Brooklyn or Queens or anywhere in the vicinity.

One hitch—the battery's only good for ten days, tops.

Within three, I've got a pattern of movement. Vassily must be feeling easier in his mind now, must think I have gone home, 'cause he's moving pretty regularly at regular times. I even get a fix on where the fuck lives. A house on a block near the beach in Far Rockaway. I drive out there next dawn in a rented Taurus, cruise around until the GPS is screaming I'm almost on top of the beacon. I park the car, let the GPS guide me in on foot.

X-ring. The Merc's in the driveway of a small but very nice-looking brick house, half a block from the beach. All the houses well maintained, driveways full of good cars like 700-series BMWs, some Cadillacs, a Lincoln or two, one Audi A8. No obvious security anywhere, not even around Vassily's house.

I come back around midnight, the GPS telling me the Merc's at the Palace, prowl around wearing next-gen night vision goggles, another toy from JoeBoy. I spot some little security cameras very discreetly placed just under the rain gutters before I'm in their scan range. I circle, looking for a gap in their coverage. There's a large oak tree up close to the rear of the house, looks like it blinds the cameras in one line back to a corner of the backyard. I could come up that line, then crawl the last few meters to a window. I peer at the window. There's a guy there, lit only by the glow of a small bank of video monitors. He's asleep in his chair. I move in, check what's on the monitors. I'm right about the oak's video shadow. Very carefully I move around the house, checking out door and window security. Standard wired alarms, easy enough to disable. I can be in that house without anybody knowing.

I go back to my hotel. It's after two A.M., but with twins that means IB's probably awake. I hit the worldwide cell.

"Yeah?" IB says. Wailing in the background.

"Almost done. Anything happening?"

Long silence.

"C'mon! Anything happening? Give."

"Luther, I don't want to be the one to . . ."

"Give!"

"Dog got shot yesterday."

Oh fuck. "Dead?"

"In a coma. They don't know if he's gonna make it."

"How?" I will away the rage that's tearing at me, fill the vacuum with determination.

"Two white guys. Dog's crew took 'em out. But one round from a three-round burst hit Dog in the cheek, just under the eye. Little bullet, like a .22."

"I know what kind of bullets."

"And Five-O, your apartment," IB says, hesitates again.

"What? It's just a fucking condo."

"They're calling it a gas explosion for the media. The walls are still standing and all, but somebody busted your windows with a couple fragmentation grenades. Everything inside is shredded. Looks like fifty guys with straight razors went berserk for a half-hour or so. You'd been in there when it happened, you'd be ground beef."

"Shit like that is why I *ain't* been there. Why I'm here. Later, big man."

Lie back on my bed, all the lights out. Chill and clear. Police sirens out on Broadway doppler past. I barely notice. I'm feeling lots of things. Surprise is most definitely not one of them.

30

Twenty hours.

That's Vassily's remaining lifespan. Or mine.

Twenty hours.

I sleep the first eight, go out to a diner for late breakfast, take a walk in Riverside Park. Pretty place, by New York standards. I pass a playground shaded by massive oaks that must be a hundred years old. It's full of white kids making a happy din, watched over by young black and Hispanic women. The kids are swarming all over monkey bars and slides and a bunch of big hippos half sunk in what looks like asphalt.

Late lunch—meat loaf, mashed potatos and baby green beans at a place called French Roast on Broadway. Walk the streets for a couple of hours, then go back to my hotel and take a ninety-minute nap. That's a full sleep cycle; we just go through several of them when we sleep all night.

I shower, pull on black jeans, a skin-tight black spandex gym shirt with long sleeves. Lace tight my Chuck Taylors, the white rubber sole edges blackened with a Sharpie. Check the GPS; the Merc's moving through Brooklyn. Check a little later, it's at the Palace. I'm skipping dinner.

I spread out gear, have a solid smile at my tools. Got the highest high tech, got some real antiques. At one end of the bed I place an MP5K with two 30-round clips taped together, two spares taped together too. Plus two frags, two white phosphorous grenades. If this turns into a goatfuck, big flash and bang-bang won't mean a thing.

At the other end of the bed I arrange what I hope to use—a garrote, high-tensile steel piano wire about thirty inches long attached to nonslip Zytel handles at either end; a black leather lead-loaded sap, the kind that's been around forever; a GI field surgery scalpel in a nylon sheath; a roll of mil-spec OD duct tape; a mil-spec Taser; a folding calfskin case that holds lockpicks, wire cutters, silver conductive tape, black plastic electrician's tape.

Finally, a piece that's the biggest grin—a hushpuppy, otherwise known as a High Standard semi-auto pistol with an integral silencer. First used by the OSS during World War II, still the quietest firearm there is, got its nickname because operatives liked to use it to kill guard dogs without anybody hearing a thing. Only a .22. Enough for a dog, but not a man. Unless you put the barrel about an inch or two from his ear or eye and snick off three or four rounds fast as you can. That's a guaranteed kill. I load one ten-round clip with Aguila subsonic sixty-grain lead solids, slide it home. No spare. If the job isn't done with ten, then it's a goatfuck and time for full-auto MP and grenade action.

I slip into a ballistic nylon ALICE harness, clip everything that can be hung exactly where ergonomics and planned order of use demand. All set. I sit in the room's one overstuffed chair, GPS on the little side table next to it, and breathe myself chill and clear.

Four to six hours. That's the lifespan now.

Around midnight I rise from the chair, put on my windbreaker, bag everything that isn't harnessed, carefully wipe down the room to get rid of any fingerprints, carefully scan to be sure I've left no trace of myself, and leave the hotel. I drive out to the Rockaways. I back my car in between two disabled ones at a closed, darkened gas station not six blocks from Vassily's. I check the GPS. Vassily's Merc is still in front of the Palace.

I wait. I breathe. I remember the wiggy Zen dude on an Alpha team. "Become one with the arrow." The arrow. It knows nothing of place or time. It justs moves, straight and true.

On the GPS, I see the Merc start to move. For a bad minute or two it seems to be heading into Manhattan. It stops. It moves again, this time toward Rockaway. Vassily must have dropped somebody off. ETA to his house is thirty-five minutes. I take half a tab of military-issue Dexedrine. No rush with that small a dose, but soon enough I feel my reflexes honed, sharp as the scalpel I'm carrying.

Fuck the black hood. Fuck camo grease. I take a tube of lipstick I'd bought in the city, deep bloodred, and draw one lightning bolt on my forehead, three bolts on each cheek.

At 3:47 A.M. the GPS signals the Merc is in Vassily's driveway. I wait thirty minutes, leave the car and start the stalk to his house, keeping to backyards as much as I can, moving in silent dashes from cover to cover. Soon I'm in that corner behind Vassily's. I stay in the big tree's video shadow, crawl the last few meters. Night vision. Same fuck's in the same chair, video screens casting a blue-green glow on his sleeping face. Insert the lockpicks in the first of two on the back door, delicately free one. Pick and free the second. Sweaty minute with tweezers, wire cutters and conductive tape bypassing the alarm system before I can quietly open that door.

I'm in.

And almost in sudden collision with a muscle boy heading toward the video room. So close I can smell his sour, alcohol-drenched breath.

Pure reaction. Zero thought. Like it isn't even me doing it. Like I'm outside myself, watching, but seeing only a blur because it's happening so fast. Muscles moving totally on autopilot, no conscious signals from the brain, no orders coming down to swing one Zytel handle of the garrote under his chin and around his neck, catch it, pull my hands across each other with all my strength. The piano wire, yanked taut, almost takes off his head, stopping only at the spine. He's dead weight, about to thud to the floor. I catch him, ease him down. Freeze in a crouch.

I'm back in myself, thinking.

Not a sound from the video room. Some minutes pass. Nothing. Then a muffled snore.

I rise, move, slip into the room, slowly slide the long barrel of the High Standard to within an inch of his ear. *Snick, snick, snick.* He just slumps a little lower in the chair.

Freeze again. Listen hard. Some minutes pass. I hear nothing. I crouch and take off my shoes. I slow-scan the house, room by room, hushpuppy at low ready position. Nobody else on the ground floor.

I go upstairs, wary of creaky steps. Three rooms, doors of two wide open. Check those first. Nobody. The door of the third's cracked a few inches. I touch the edge with the tips of my left fingers, push gently, easing it open.

Lightning blinds me, a bolt of pain rocks me, I hear the snap as powerful hands break my arm. The training—crush your natural instinct to pull away. Move fast and hard forward, throwing whoever's hurting you off-balance. Hesitate for a second, you're hurt worse, then dead.

I charge into the agony, slamming the door with my shoulder, the useless arm folding as my body collides with another, front to front. I jam the barrel of the hushpuppy into his crotch. *Snick, snick, snick.* The hands on my arm unclench, the body lurches back, an unearthly scream fills the room.

I switch on the anglehead flashlight attached to my harness. Vassily's down, both hands clutching his crotch, biting his lower lip so hard blood starts to flow. Still somehow managing a growly animal moan.

I'm wavering, the arm sending jolt after jolt to my brain. I manage to fumble a morphine styrette out of a pouch on my harness, jab the needle hard through my clothes into the bicep of the broken arm. Somehow I find the other half tab of Dex in the pouch, pop it in my mouth, swallow. Gotta dull that pain, but can't get morphine-woozy. Not yet. I holster the pistol, pull out the lead-loaded sap. I kick Vassily as hard as I can in the ribs. There's an involuntary roll away from the blow, though both his hands stay locked to his crotch, and as he rolls I see my target. I bring the sap down viciously just at the base of his skull. He goes as limp as a dead fish. He'll be out cold for a half hour at least.

Damage assessment. I quarter the space with my flashlight, see a bathroom past the far side of the bed. I go there, switch on the light. Place the roll of duct tape and the scalpel on the white Formica countertop by the sink. With two fingers of my right hand, I start at my shoulder and very gingerly probe down my left arm. About three inches below the elbow I hit a hot spot—lightning flash in my eyes, followed by a wave of nausea. I go into the pain, pressing harder. The top forearm bone is fractured, but there's no lump, no jagged end pressing out, trying to break through the skin. I slit my windbreaker and the tight shirt with the scalpel. There's a bad bruise growing around the hot spot, but the forearm's only slightly off true. Christ, it could have been so much worse, I think.

I look around for a possible splint. Nothing. I scan again. Nothing but a fucking toilet brush. Improvise, Luther.

I do. I put the head of the brush under my foot and snap off the plastic handle. It's maybe twelve inches long, flat enough, maybe an inch or two wide. It'll work. I start unpeeling duct tape from the roll until I've got a few inches free. I stick that bit just under my elbow, let the roll dangle while I place the white plastic handle along the top of my forearm so it covers the hot spot and runs straight down almost to my wrist. Fighting the pain, I raise my arm from the shoulder, elbow bent, and find I can just hold the handle in place by jamming the forearm into my wide-open mouth. It's awkward as hell, it hurts like hell, but I start wrapping the duct tape around the arm. After two turns the tape holds the handle in place, so I lower the arm and wrap neat and tight all the way to the wrist. I cut the tape roll loose with the scalpel, smooth down the last few inches.

Then I go check Vassily. He's in the fetal position, hands still in place. I tear off his pajama pants. Three little exit wounds low on his buttocks. Not much blood. Looks like the lead solids went through clean without hitting any major vessels. I roll him on his back, pull away his hands. Two little holes hard to see through the pubic hair, one more hole through the middle of his dick and testicle sack.

Nobody dies from that.

I want him to feel his death.

Using my shoulder and good arm, I bend one of Vassily's heavily muscled legs until the heel is touching the back of the thigh, and duct tape it in place tight and strong as I'm able. Do the same with the other leg. I tape his wrists to his ankles, his ankles together. I use a lot of tape, wrapping and wrapping until I'm sure there's no way in hell he can possibly move.

Then I lie down on his bed. I breathe. Get my pulse down, tighten and relax one muscle group after another. I don't check my watch. It's still dead black outside, not even the first faint ghost of day. I breathe, I go deep into the pain and dominate it. Get cold, get clear. The world stops turning. Or I enter another one.

No idea how much time passes before I hear the moans, then the snarls, then the curses. I sit up. "Fuck you, little brother!" I hear. I turn, see Vassily trussed on the floor, round face slightly hollowed at the cheeks, blood and drool oozing from a corner of his mouth. But his eyes. His eyes are sharp, hard, glinting like blue diamonds. I haven't been asleep, I know this for sure, but there's the quality of a dream about this.

That vanishes when I move to stand up and my left arm sends me the agony through every nerve it has. My face must go into some rictus, because Vassily laughs, then is seized by a fit of coughing. "I snap you like twig, little brother," he's able to snarl when the coughing stops. "I been shot worse than this. And still Vassily lives. I will live to spit on your grave, cocksucker."

Suddenly I feel no pain, just a great weariness. Not what I expected to feel.

Now I only want this to end.

I go to the bathroom, get the scalpel. I check the room for any other gear I may have shed. No need for a wipe-down. I've been wearing surgical gloves from the moment I started picking the back door locks. That seems like such a long time ago. It seems forever since the piano wire sliced a neck, the High Standard snicked in somebody's ear.

"You hear me, little brother? I will spit on your grave." Vassily's voice seems to have risen. "Like I spit on that bitch Mikla's. You know what, Shooter? She was worst fuck I ever had. Oh, how she cried for you after you got shot. But it's me she was fucking."

I look at Vassily. A face I knew so well, a face I'd seen bright with joy, flushed with anger, utterly blank and impassive when he killed in combat. I scarcely recognize it now. I wonder who I am looking at. I walk closer to him. His hard eyes flick toward my right hand. When they come back to mine, they've changed somehow. There's something new and strange in them. I look down at my hand. I see the scalpel. I kneel beside him.

"You sure you have balls for this, little brother? You very sure? Because I don't think so," Vassily says. "I think you will start to tremble now, I think your hand won't move, I think you will run, little brother. You don't have balls for this. You who I snap like twig."

Our eyes stayed locked. Mine must be blank, for his are searching. "Honor. Trust. Friendship. Better if I let you die in Sarajevo, instead of risking my life to get you to airport and out of there. Little piece of shit."

"Vassily, my friend," I hear myself almost crooning. "Trust?

Honor? You stop, I stop, we said. You gave your word, remember? You broke it."

I find his carotid artery with my right forefinger. He twists his neck violently. I slip around, pin his head between my knees. Search and find the spot again with one finger. I don't slash. I slip the gleaming point of the scalpel slowly, smoothly through his skin, just deep enough to nick the artery, open a small slit. A light spray of blood arches maybe a foot in the air.

I stand up fast, take a step back.

"Fuck you, you little shit," Vassily spits. Another fine, rising spray of blood, tiny drops falling onto his face.

"Watch closely, my friend. Feel it happening," I hear myself say. "With each heartbeat, your life drains away."

Another spray. Now I recognize that new thing in his eyes.

Terror.

I start to back away.

"A hundred, maybe a hundred and twenty more heartbeats, Vassily. That's your time."

"Never," he says. Another spray, arching higher now. Then the delicate drops, softly falling.

Red rain.

Out of the room now, padding down the stairs. Shoes back on. Check the video room. Pick up three cartridge cases. Check the corpse by the kitchen door. Grab the garrote. From above, thin and somehow watery, Vassily's voice: "Shooter! I shit on your damn soul. Shooter? Little brother?"

Shooter's gone.

Out the door into sea-fresh air, deep black shifting to dark gray as the first faint glow of false dawn lightens the far, far line where ocean meets sky.

About the Author

MICHAEL CROW is the pen name of a prizewinning, critically acclaimed novelist whose works have been translated and published in nine languages.